The Barefoot Bride

"Just where the hell have you been?" Saxon demanded. He slung her over his shoulder as he trekked back to the mansion, then suddenly stopped. "Well, aren't you going to fight me? Toss me to the ground? This docile obedience is completely out of character for you."

"Tell you what, outlander. I'll let you tote me around iffen you'll head fer the barn. Thur's lots o' hay in it."

"You're in serious trouble," he said, sliding his hands down her thighs as he placed her back on the ground. "I told you not to walk at night anymore. What if those men come back for you? What if they're lurking in the shadows? What if—"

"What if you jist hesh up and kiss the breath plumb outen me? What if—"

His mouth swallowed the rest of her words . . .

Other **AVON ROMANCES**

COME BE MY LOVE *by Patricia Watters*
MY LADY NOTORIOUS *by Jo Beverley*
MY REBELLIOUS HEART *by Samantha James*
SAGEBRUSH BRIDE *by Tanya Anne Crosby*
SUNSHINE AND SHADOW *by Kathleen Harrington*
SURRENDER MY HEART *by Lois Greiman*
WILD CONQUEST *by Hannah Howell*

Coming Soon

ALMOST A LADY *by Sonya Birmingham*
FORBIDDEN FLAME *by Selina MacPherson*

And Don't Miss These
ROMANTIC TREASURES
from Avon Books

COMANCHE WIND *by Genell Dellin*
HIS MAGIC TOUCH *by Stella Cameron*
THEN CAME YOU *by Lisa Kleypas*

Avon Books are available at special quantity discounts for bulk purchases for sales promotions, premiums, fund raising or educational use. Special books, or book excerpts, can also be created to fit specific needs.

For details write or telephone the office of the Director of Special Markets, Avon Books, Dept. FP, 1350 Avenue of the Americas, New York, NY 10019, 1-800-238-0658.

The Barefoot Bride

REBECCA PAISLEY

AVON BOOKS  NEW YORK

If you purchased this book without a cover, you should be aware that this book is stolen property. It was reported as "unsold and destroyed" to the publisher, and neither the author nor the publisher has received any payment for this "stripped book."

To Sergio
The man who showed me what
inner fire is, who helped me
light my own, and who lent me
some of his when mine went out.
See how brightly the golden bricks
are shining, my love.

THE BAREFOOT BRIDE is an original publication of Avon Books. This work has never before appeared in book form. This work is a novel. Any similarity to actual persons or events is purely coincidental.

AVON BOOKS
A division of
The Hearst Corporation
1350 Avenue of the Americas
New York, New York 10019

Copyright © 1990 by Rebecca Boado Rosas
Published by arrangement with the author
Library of Congress Catalog Card Number: 89-91863
ISBN: 0-380-76019-3

All rights reserved, which includes the right to reproduce this book or portions thereof in any form whatsoever except as provided by the U.S. Copyright Law. For information address Joyce Flaherty, Literary Agent, 816 Lynda Court, St. Louis, Missouri 63122.

Special Printing: June 1993
First Avon Books Printing: March 1990

AVON TRADEMARK REG. U.S. PAT. OFF. AND IN OTHER COUNTRIES, MARCA REGISTRADA, HECHO EN U.S.A.

Printed in the U.S.A.

RA 10 9 8 7 6 5 4 3 2

Chapter 1

S axon's life was like a fairy tale, complete with wicked witch. But, unlike a fairy tale, he saw no happy ending in sight.

He yearned to throw his snifter of brandy at the portrait of the witch, his grandmother, that hung on the opposite wall of the sumptuous drawing room. But such an outburst would only please the woman. Instead, he twirled the stem of his glass and smiled the lazy, mocking grin he knew infuriated her.

Araminta bristled at both his smile and expression in his sapphire eyes. Her twiglike fingers whitened around the knob of her ebony cane. "Well? What do you think about my decision, Saxon?"

Saxon fumed inwardly. If her news didn't involve his sister, Desdemona, he'd relish telling her exactly what he thought of it. After all, his favorite diversion in life, second only to enjoying a beautiful woman in his bed, was unseating Araminta from her golden throne. But the future of his delicate sister was at stake in Araminta's newest scheme, and so he let her question go unanswered. He did, however, obtain a small measure of satisfaction in knowing his silence would irritate her.

And she *was* annoyed, both by his silence and by the telltale red mark she suddenly noticed near his throat. "If you think your shirt collar covers that lip rouge on your neck, think again. Which woman—"

"Woman?" he asked and wiped at the remnants

1

of passion on his neck. "I got tired of women, Grandmother. Now I'm running around with vampires. It's much more exciting."

She sighed and stalked to the liquor cabinet, her black gown trailing behind her like a gloomy shadow. When she'd poured herself a generous amount of sherry, she held her glass up. "Here's to the end of your incessant womanizing. Here's to the end of your tarnishing the Blackwell name. Here's to the future Mrs. Saxon Blackwell."

Saxon ran his fingers through his raven hair and concentrated on holding back his fury. The muscles in his tall, lean frame swelled with the effort.

Araminta cackled with delight at the evidence of his anger. "Well, which lady will it be?"

"You mean I actually have a choice?"

She frowned. "I do not appreciate your sarcasm."

"None intended. Are you really giving me permission to choose my own bride?"

"As long as you choose one soon, yes."

He immediately decided it would take him at least forever to find the right bride, since no such woman existed. Yes, forever was soon enough for him. "I'm young and have plenty of time."

"Unfortunately for you, I do not have the same amount of time you do. You know my heart is weak. I could die any day. And if I do—"

"Your heart, Grandmother? It's always been my belief that you don't possess one."

Her brow lifted in exasperation. "If you are finished taunting me, may I—"

"Continue? Oh, by all means. Let's see . . . you were regaling—I mean explaining to me the details of your will, were you not?"

"You will not be making light of the situation if I die before your wedding. In that event, Desdemona *and* my fortune will go to my distant cousin in England. You know very well that pitiful sister of yours will never marry, so the responsibility of providing an heir to the Blackwell fortune is yours. It's time you face up to that obligation, and my new will forces you to do just that."

She made her way to the door, her long chin sticking out far ahead of her face. "I will leave you to deliberate in solitude. No doubt you wish to figure out how you will contest my will. But I warn you now, Saxon. It, like my decision, is ironclad."

He glared at her. Contesting the will was exactly what he'd been planning to do. His gaze fell to the onyx brooch at her throat. It looked like a Cyclops's eye. Sometimes he thought that ugly piece of jewelry was connected to Araminta's brain. It seemed to tell her everything she needed to know. Even now it was transmitting his thoughts to her: that was apparent in the way she smiled before she left the room.

He snuffed out the memories her malevolent sneer brought to him and walked to the window, snatching at the tassel of the heavy damask draperies.

"Araminta Blackwell," he whispered. "A true witch if there ever was one. I don't know how, and I don't know where, but I swear I will find a magic more powerful than yours."

Saxon stared at the crystal chandelier above the dining table without really seeing it. Several weeks had passed since Araminta had demanded he marry, and he hadn't thought of a single way to postpone it, much less get out of it.

Until now. Until Araminta herself had given him the means. But he couldn't let her see how excited he was about her idea. He knew her so well. If she saw his elation, she'd change her mind.

"Saxon! Did you hear what I said?" The bones in Araminta's hand fairly clanked together as she rang the breakfast bell.

He hoped the reflection of the chandelier disguised the twinkle of delight in his eyes. "Uh, yes, Grandmother," he mumbled. "You want me to go to North Carolina and investigate the possibility of buying land there.'' He picked up a knife and let it dangle between his fingers, allowing his action to further demonstrate his seeming indifference.

Araminta scowled. ''Pine trees, Saxon. How many times did you mention the pine forests in North Carolina after the war ended? You were utterly fascinated with them. Your stories of them came back to me last night. You do know what pine trees mean, do you not?''

''They meant shade when I was traveling through them with my regiment.''

Araminta sighed, the air rattling in her throat. ''Pine trees are green gold mines, my boy. They mean turpentine! The nation is in dire need of it now. You will go to North Carolina and make a detailed report for me. I want to know everything there is to know about turpentine production.''

Another thrill whipped through his body. He was actually going to escape Araminta for a while, and time in North Carolina meant a temporary respite from the problem of marriage too! ''Very well. I'll go,'' he said with feigned resentment.

Araminta smiled smugly at her bread. ''Why don't you look up your acquaintance down there? There's no sense in paying for lodging when you can stay with him for nothing.''

Saxon gave a slight nod. He'd already planned to find Heath Mansfield.

''I still do not understand why you consider a *Southerner* a friend,'' Araminta continued. ''As a Union soldier, it was your job to get rid of as many of those backward creatures as possible.''

''Whether you approve or not, Heath *is* my friend and, as such, I'm sure he'll be more than willing to share with me whatever knowledge of turpentine he has. At the very least, he can put me in contact with experts. So instead of wishing for the demise of that *backward creature*, I suggest you—''

''I care nothing for your suggestion, that man, or your friendship. However, perhaps it is good you didn't kill him after all. He will undoubtedly be useful to me."

Saxon laid his knife aside before it could find its way into her chest. "I'll see him and get myself invited to stay with him. Heaven forbid I spend any more money than is necessary."

Araminta smoothed back her wiry white hair. "You will leave as soon as I make the arrangements. And Saxon?"

"Yes?" he answered, watching the gleam of her brooch.

"You will marry as soon as you return."

The day of his departure arrived, but not soon enough to suit Saxon. Grabbing his saddlebag, he left his bedroom and proceeded quickly down the dark hallway that led to the staircase. But as he passed his sister's bedroom, his pace slowed. With a heavy sigh, he dropped his bag and looked into the room.

Desdemona sat near the window, sunshine flickering through her long ebony hair. As he watched her, the years fell away, and he saw her as a little girl. He could still hear the sweet sound of her voice, could still recall her bright, happy smile. But most of all, he remembered the warmth of her tiny hand when she used to touch his cheek.

But her voice had been silent for years. Her soft, full lips never smiled, never opened for anything but the meager amount of food she ate. And her slender hand was always cold. Saxon was sure only a miracle could remove her from her remote world and return her to earth.

Sighing again, he knelt beside her. "Desdemona, I'm leaving today on a journey to a state called North Carolina. I don't know how long I'll be gone, but when I come back I'll bring a gift for you. Something from North Carolina that will help you to understand where I've been."

Her amethyst gaze remained directed at some imaginary vision on the floor.

He took her cold hand and placed it on his warm cheek. "Remember when you used to touch me like this, Desdemona? Remember how it was your favorite thing to do when you wanted your own way? And remember how it always *got* you your way, no matter how badly I wanted to refuse you?"

The familiar sadness welled up within him when she did not respond. "You might not remember, Desdemona, but as long as I do, you will still be that same happy girl."

He twined his strong fingers through her fragile ones and pressed her hand to his mouth before he stood. After one last look at her lovely face, one last touch of her silky hair, and one last, long sigh, he turned and left.

He sailed South aboard one of the Blackwell steamboats. When the vessel reached the port of Wilmington, North Carolina, he mounted his horse, Hagen, and headed toward Moore County, where Heath lived.

The ride from the coast took three days, but now, as he rode through the majestic forest and breathed deeply of the cool, pine-scented air, his saddle-weary body relaxed. The place was as beautiful as he remembered it when he'd ridden through with General Kilpatrick during the war. Staring down at all the white sand, he wondered once again how it got there, miles away from the seashore. He had no answer, but he didn't mind. Part of the charm of this area was its mystery.

He stopped Hagen, and reached up to pull a pine cone from a low branch, grinning over the favor Araminta had unwittingly done him. Allergic to smiles, she'd break out in hives if she could see how happy he was at this moment.

Of course, there was no way she'd let a lucrative business like turpentine production slip through her fingers. Though he'd pretended ignorance the day she brought up the subject, he knew very well it could mean another fortune. He had no doubt Araminta would buy acres of land here. Hell, he wouldn't put it past her to try and buy the whole damn state. And she'd send him here to check on things often. He'd never leave the social whirl of Boston forever—he relished the fast-paced life he led there. But returning to North Carolina for short periods wouldn't be distasteful in the least. Especially when it meant leaving the wife he'd already decided to detest.

It wasn't hard to find Heath Mansfield. Everyone knew him, and Saxon was given directions to Carthage, the largest community in Moore County. He left Hagen in front of the brick courthouse located in the town's center and quickly found the carriage factory where Heath worked.

Their reunion left the townspeople to wonder about their sanity. They shouted, hugged, playfully knocked each other around, and then shouted, hugged, and playfully knocked each other around again. Their display of excitement went on for so long, Heath's boss finally got tired of waiting for his employee to return to work and gave him the rest of the day off. Heath showed Saxon around town, and later the two visited with Heath's parents.

It was the first time Saxon had ever seen Heath's home, and he was appalled at his friend's poverty. But though the Mansfields had very little, they shared generously with him. He resolved to find a way to repay their kindness.

After supper he and Heath rode through the pines until they arrived at the exact spot where they'd met a few years ago. The memory of the two of them standing in that pine forest, their guns pointed at each other, neither having the heart to shoot, and then both of them laughing at the absurdity of the situation, made him smile.

"Why didn't you shoot me that day, Sax?" Heath asked.

"Probably for the same reason you didn't shoot me. I thought maybe you were a better shot than I was and hoped if I didn't shoot, you wouldn't either."

Their laughter filled the cool, tangy woods. "You know," Heath began, wiping tears of merriment from his eyes, "I still don't know if you can shoot straight. All we did that day was talk about how much we hated the war."

"That, and keep you and your mother's silver spoon collection from being found by my regiment, that pillaging gang of ruffians."

Heath's smile faded and was replaced by a look of gratitude. "I never got the chance to thank you for hidin' me and Ma's treasures, Sax."

"It would have been much easier to hide only the spoons, but since you wouldn't relinquish the box, I had to hide you too," Saxon said and laughed again.

"If any other of General Kilpatrick's soldiers had found me, they'd have shot me without a thought. You were a traitor for those ten minutes it took you to cover me with all that brush. Why'd you do that? You barely knew me."

Saxon studied Heath's blond hair, brown eyes, and crooked grin. "You look like a good friend of mine in Boston—Max Jennings. You even smile like him. He fought, too, but rode with a different company. I'd sure as hell have wanted someone to help Max if he'd been in the same situation. I guess that ridiculous smirk of yours saved you, Heath." Saxon held out his hand, and the warm handshake that followed expressed all the unspoken feelings between them.

Heath pointed to a distant tree. "See that lone pine over there? It's got a low-hangin' branch with two pine cones on it. Squint and you'll see 'em.

Now, you try for the one on the left, and I'll try for the one on the right.''

Saxon squinted, nodded, and readied his rifle. When both men were ready, they aimed and fired.

Both pine cones exploded off the branch.

Both men doubled over with laughter. ''Damn, Heath!'' Saxon yelled. ''It's a good thing we didn't shoot that day, or we'd be *buried* here instead of *talking* here! Now tell me a little about turpentine.''

''You'll need to go on over to Jackson Springs,'' Heath said. ''And you might want to take a look at Blue's Crossin' too. Your grandmother's right about the turpentine industry. If she's able to purchase timberland, there's no tellin' how much money y'all can make.''

''You mean *Grandmother* can make. It'll be *her* money buying the land, *her* money starting the business,'' Saxon said bitterly.

Heath gave him a sideways glance. ''But won't you inherit it all one day?''

Saxon's jaw clenched. ''On one condition. I've got to marry first.''

''Got somethin' against women?'' Heath smiled crookedly.

''I like everything about women except marrying one. But Grandmother is adamant. Either I marry or I'll be disinherited.''

''Saxon, you're a Harvard graduate. Make your own fortune!''

''I'm proud of Blackwell Enterprises, Heath. It's a fine, strong company. Although it belongs to Grandmother, I've worked hard to make it what it is. Don't get me wrong, though. I've no doubt I could make a fine life for myself without Blackwell Enterprises. I tried once, but my new place of business burned to the ground, and the man who'd financed it for me left town the next day. I never found proof Grandmother was behind it all, but I know she was. After that, she informed me that should I ever attempt to leave Blackwell Enterprises again, she would send Desdemona to an insane asylum. And there's no way in hell I'll let something like that happen to my sister.''

Heath inhaled sharply. ''Is Desdemona . . . insane?''

''She doesn't speak, and she's a bit out of touch with reality. I don't call that insane, but Grandmother would have no trouble having her committed.''

''But as her adult brother, surely you have the right—''

''The courts have given Grandmother complete custody of Desdemona, and since I've no money of my own I'm not considered a suitable guardian. I have no rights at all.''

''But even if startin' your own business means Desdemona goin' to an asylum, she wouldn't have to stay there for long,'' Heath ventured. ''I know you'd make money quickly, Sax. With it, you'd win custody of Desdemona and be able to get her out of the institution.''

Saxon tangled his fingers through Hagen's mane, fury gripping his insides. ''You've never seen Desdemona. She's so pale it's as if she wallowed in a tub of flour. And she's no bigger than that scrawny pine sapling over there. I know she wouldn't last a day in an asylum, much less the time it would take me to make enough money to win custody of her. I could never risk it, Heath.''

''You know,'' Heath said thoughtfully, ''I had you figured out to be a lucky man, Sax. In a lot of ways you are, but livin' with that witch grandma of yours . . . If I were you I'd do anythin' to escape her. I'd stay here in North Carolina forever. I know there's Desdemona to worry about, but at least you're free from your grandma now. Take advantage of it and enjoy the time away from her.''

''Take advantage of the time away . . .'' Saxon's head snapped up, his mind working furiously. ''Heath, I'd say getting together a detailed report on the turpentine industry would take a long time. It can probably stretch into months, don't you think?"

Heath grinned. "*Many* months."

"If I were to send Grandmother a letter . . . tell her the research will take me months to do . . . If I were to tempt her with figures of all the money there is to be made here . . . If her greed were tickled like that, she wouldn't think of doing anything bad to Desdemona in my absence."

"It's a brilliant plan! And I know a place where she'd never be able to find you if she decided to look. She'd think the research was takin' you far and wide! It's a place where a man can enjoy all the beauty, peace, and freedom the world has to offer. Just the medicine you need, Sax."

Saxon reined in Hagen beside a pine and pulled at a piece of the bark. "Where is this utopia?"

"Western North Carolina. The Appalachia."

"The mountains?"

"I'm tellin' you, Sax, you haven't lived till you've seen the Blue Ridge. I'd tell you what it looks like, but there are no words to describe that kind of scenery."

"Where would I stay?"

Heath grinned and shook his head. "There are some inns along the way, but I recommend sleepin' right under the stars. Gets a little chilly at night, but at this time of year you aren't gonna freeze. You can make that report for the witch when you get back here. Or better yet, I'll start it for you. Do it, Sax. Go see those mountains."

Saxon smiled back, his eyes aglow. This was the perfect way to assist the Mansfields. "Tell you what, Heath. Why don't you do the entire report for me? I'll pay you well."

"The hell you will! I'll do it for nothin'."

Saxon raised an ebony eyebrow. "Sorry. If you don't take payment, I'll have to stay here and do the report myself. A damn shame, Heath. Those hills are probably just what I need."

Heath cocked his head and smirked. He was trapped, and he knew it. He held out his hand for Saxon to shake, and the deal was sealed.

As they rode back to Heath's house, Saxon was deep in thought. Postpone his return to Boston. A damn good idea. By doing it he was helping Heath and defying Araminta.

The Appalachian Mountains. Perhaps a little more uncivilized than he cared for, but anything was better than marriage.

The journey had taken over two weeks, but now, as Saxon lay back on the cool mountain ground, he was glad he'd followed Heath's advice. He had no idea which ridge he was on, and what's more, he thought with a lopsided grin, he didn't care.

Sun courted shadow here. There were miles and miles of unsurpassable beauty. Every azalea and rhododendron was ablaze with blossoms. The mountains seemed blue, but when Saxon blinked, they turned to green and then to gray and then to every imaginable color. The azure of the sky teased the emerald depths of the lush woods and, through it all, the area was splashed with the reds, yellows, whites and purples of the wildflowers—as if some mischievous angel had gotten hold of a paint palette and splattered her favorite hues.

As he stared out at the scenery, he tried to think of how to fill his time but couldn't come up with a thing to do. Soon his senses were so lulled by the mountain tranquillity, he closed his eyes. As he drifted to sleep, the last thing he heard was the lullaby of the mourning dove that watched him from a flowering dogwood.

An unfamiliar sound soon awakened him. He had to shake his head several times before he realized it was a growl.

A huge black bear stood a short distance away, its enormous paws swiping at empty space as if in anticipation of clawing at flesh. Saxon scrambled up from the soft bed of tender plants he hadn't realized were the bear's meal. He walked slowly toward Hagen, dread pumping through him when he saw his horse had come untied and was free to flee if he was so inclined. "Easy, boy," he whispered to the skittish steed. "We can outrun him or shoot him. Easy, easy."

At that moment, the bear lumbered forward. Hagen reared in fright and promptly galloped into the thicket, carrying Saxon's rifle with him. Left with only a knife, Saxon cursed and snatched the blade from his boot.

He whirled to see the monster coming straight at him, the layers of fat and muscle on its tremendous body rolling up, down, and sideways. He stood rooted, his entire body quivering with readiness.

But though the steel of his dagger soon disappeared into numerous places on the bear's body, the animal was merely maddened by the pain. It wrapped its thick arms around its opponent and squeezed.

Saxon's breath rushed from him. His ribs felt crushed; his blood stopped in his veins. The pressure in his head was so great, he felt it would surely burst. His arms, pinned down by his sides, lost all feeling. He could not wield his knife.

The mourning dove had fled, and the growl of the bear was the only sound he heard as he watched the slobbering monster's head descend. He saw the bear's mouth open but quickly looked away from the horrible teeth that would surely bring about his death.

As he turned away, he saw something red flash in the brush of rhododendron ahead, but before he had time to identify what it was, the bear's teeth sank into his shoulder, and the raw agony that streamed though his every nerve made him scream.

The echo of his shriek was accompanied by a blast of gunfire. With one last roar, the bear crashed to the ground, carrying Saxon with it.

Saxon managed to roll off the bloodied corpse, and just before his eyes closed, he saw other eyes, green as the verdant mountain forest, peering down at him. The face in which they were set was freckled and tawny, and the hair that surrounded the face was long, curly, and red.

As he lost consciousness, he could have sworn what he saw was a girl.

Betty Jane swiped at a cobweb that floated from the ceiling of the small log cabin and then poked Saxon's side, eliciting a low moan from her patient. "Well, he's the groanin'est man I ever laid eyes on. He ain't quit a-wailin' since Chickadee brung him."

"Iffen a bahr'd got holt o' you, you'd be a-whinin' too," her husband, George Franklin, said. He leaned back in his creaking hickory chair and began to whittle. "Wonder what he's a-doin' up here? Ain't never seed him afore."

"You don't never see nothin'. You ain't been no further'n over yonder in years," Betty Jane said, pointing toward the window. "And quit a-shovin' them shavin's all over the floor!"

George Franklin ceased whittling for a moment to push the point of his knife up into his beard and scratch his chin with it. "Reckon I go whar I have ter go. Don't see no reason fer gwine nowhars else."

The loud voices woke Saxon. He realized he was naked but couldn't understand why. He slowly opened his eyes, and through the haze of pain he saw meager furnishings around him. However, the bed in which he lay was soft, and the thick quilt wrapped around him lessened the chill that wracked his body.

He looked up at the old woman who stood next to the bed. "Who are you?" he whispered.

"Good, yore awake." She reached for a bottle from a table and held it to his lips. "Swaller it on down."

Saxon turned his head, the obnoxious smell of the potion warning him of its taste. "What is that?"

"Yarbs."

"Yarbs?"

"Ain't you got no yarbs whar yore from?"

He struggled to understand.

"Yarbs!" Betty Jane repeated. "What's in this here bottle is wolfbane root with a smidgeon o' snakeroot."

George Franklin flicked a wood shaving from his thigh. "Done tole you ter put likker in it, Betty Jane. Them yarbs ain't gwine do nary a bit o' good withouten no likker added."

Betty Jane stared down at Saxon for a moment before she dragged a jug from beneath the bed. She uncorked it and poured a generous amount of its contents into the small bottle.

Saxon watched her every move, certain she'd poison him. "Is it possible that *yarbs* are *herbs*?"

"Iffen *herbs* be wolfbane root and snakeroot, then you figgered right." She held the bottle to his lips again. "Go on and drink it."

"What will it do to me?" Damn! Where the hell was he, and who were these people?

"Nothin' you don't need done. It's fer yore fever. Now drink it."

"Ain't no use in a-forcin' him ter do what he ain't gwine do," George Franklin remarked. "That man's a-wantin' proof yore tonic ain't gwine kill him." He brushed more shavings off his trousers, stood, and ambled toward his wife and Saxon. Taking the bottle from Betty Jane, he tilted it to his mouth and drank deeply.

"It ain't fer you!" Betty Jane snatched the bottle away from him and pushed it into Saxon's hand.

"Go on and drink it," George Franklin advised. "She ain't gwine let up till you do. The woman's as stubborn as a blue-nosed mule."

Reassured by the fact the mountain man wasn't dead after drinking the potent liquid, Saxon downed the remainder of the herb potion. His stomach promptly revolted as the fiery brew hit it, and with clenched teeth he resisted the wave of nausea that flooded his insides.

George Franklin chortled loudly, his long beard bouncing on his concave chest. "Reckon you ain't never tasted yarbs and corn likker a-mixed together afore, have you, mister? It's them yarbs that make it bitter. The whiskey's smooth as water once yore used to it."

"Turn over and let me git a look-see at yore back agin," Betty Jane ordered. When Saxon obeyed, she picked up a few mushroomlike plants that burst open as she touched them to Saxon's skin, spreading brown powder over the claw wound. "Wrapped up them bites on yer shoulder but left this here scratch uncovered. It ain't real deep, but these here puffballs'll draw outen the pizen."

George Franklin watched the procedure with detached interest. "You orter leave him ter bleed, Betty Jane. Blood's the best coverin' thur is."

She ignored her husband. "About out o' puffballs, mister, but don't you worry none. We can use cobwebs or soot till I git out fer more puffballs."

Saxon grimaced into the pillow. If he survived his wounds, he had a sneaking suspicion the woman's doctoring would kill him. "Did I see a girl with red hair and freckles, or was that my imagination?"

"Chickadee's real," Betty Jane said. "And iffen it warn't fer her, we'd be a-knockin' together yore coffin."

"A mere *girl* killed that monster with one bullet?"

"Tuk aim and farred," George Franklin said.

"Heared tell you stuck that bahr some," Betty Jane said. "But you didn't never hit nary a good spot on him."

Her husband smirked at that. "Don't take it hard, mister. A outlander like yoresef don't know much about bahrs. Chickadee's knowed fer her bahr killin'. Why, I reckon even some o' us hill folk cain't hold no candle to Chickadee McBride when it comes ter bahrs.''

Saxon winced with both pain and disbelief. Was it really possible a *girl* had saved his life? Dammit, what if she'd missed and killed *him* instead?

''What's yore name, mister?'' Betty Jane asked. ''And whar you from?''

''Saxon Blackwell. Boston, Massachusetts.'' He held out his hand for both people to shake.

''We're George Franklin and Betty Jane Beasley,'' his host said. ''And since it 'pears you ain't no Fed'ral, yore welcome ter stay as long as you need to.''

Saxon smiled. ''I'm grateful for all you've done. The medicine, the bandage, and for bringing me to your home.''

''We didn't have nary a thang ter do with a-brangin' you up here, Saxon,'' Betty Jane said. ''Chickadee brung you.''

Saxon tried to remember what happened after the attack, but could recall nothing. ''I can't imagine how she managed to get me into her wagon, but I hope to have the opportunity to thank her soon.''

''Wagon?'' George Franklin grinned. ''She ain't got no wagon. She packed you on her back.''

''A *girl*? Carrying a man of my size?''

''Chickadee ain't no reg'lar girl,'' Betty Jane announced. ''She can outdo most menfolks around these here parts. Got the strength o' them bahrs she kills. Wouldn't never know it ter look at her, though. Some say it's her spirit that gives her strength. But she's a livin' legend, shore and sartin.''

Her husband nodded. ''She's a mite wild though. Cain't be brung to taw neither. Me and Betty Jane's tried ter larn her what manners we know, but that girl's as hardheaded as they come. It ain't that she's a bad-un though. Got the biggest dang heart you ever come acrost, but she's tough enough ter raise hell and then put a chunk under it.''

''Most all mountain girls is strong-spirited,'' Betty

Jane explained. "But most of 'em got the sense ter back down when they need ter. Chickadee don't got that kind o' sense. When she gits somethin' in her mind, ain't nobody or nothin' that can stop her."

Saxon was thoroughly intrigued. "Where is she now?"

"Well, she brung you, tole us what happened, and then lit out runnin'," George Franklin said. "Said somethin' about yore horse. Reckon she went after it."

Saxon started to inquire further about the outlandish mountain girl, but his words were cut off by the banging of the door as it was flung open.

In its frame, a white wolf at her heels, stood Chickadee McBride.

Chapter 2

Saxon had never seen a girl wander around bare-footed, but he had to admit even her dusty feet didn't detract from Chickadee's wholesome charm. She wore a snug homespun shirt that clung to her as beautifully as any satin bodice, and tight buckskin breeches from which hung several raccoon tails. Her hair was a glorious mixture of red, orange, and gold, falling to her shoulders in a smooth cascade, with a small twig sticking out of the left side. Her full lips were closed, but Saxon suspected she was suppressing a grin when he saw how her green eyes sparkled. And when he noticed all the freckles on her peachy face, his own smile came readily.

She propped her rifle up against the door and walked into the cabin with a lithe, easy gait, her arms swinging by her sides as if she hadn't a care in the world. When she stopped at the bed, she took hold of Saxon's quilt and yanked it off.

"That bahr git you anywhars else 'sides yore back and shoulder?" Her gaze swept over his nude body.

Saxon snatched the blanket back, confused as to whether the flush he felt creeping up his face stemmed from her casual inspection of him or his reaction to it.

Her lips tilted. "Ain't no need ter git red-faced with me, mister. You ain't got nothin' I ain't never seed afore." She slid her arms beneath him to lift him.

19

Saxon let go of his quilt and grabbed the bedpost. "Just what do you think you're doing?"

She straightened and looked at him as if he were a naughty child. "Aimin' ter take you ter my place. This here bed's the onliest one Betty Jane and George Franklin's got betwixt 'em, and you ain't gwine stay in it." Again, she bent and tried to haul him into her arms.

Saxon continued to cling to the bedpost, amazed at her strength. He felt thoroughly foolish holding on to the post like some shrinking virgin, but there was no way in hell he was going to let her carry him.

"I don't recall saying I *wanted* to stay with you, Miss McBride."

She rolled her eyes. " 'Pears ter me I'm gwine have ter take you outen here a-willin' or not." She took Saxon's wrist and squeezed until his fingers unfurled from around the post. Saxon reached up to yank her hand away, but a wave of pain rolled through his body, weakening his efforts.

Chickadee took both his hands captive and frowned down at him. "I jist want ter hep you, mister. But iffen you'd ruther not have my hep, I'll git shed o' you and leave you out in the woods ter tend ter yoresef. One thang fer shore though—you *ain't* a-stayin' here!"

Saxon pulled his hands out of her grasp. "It was never my intention to intrude on the Beasleys' hospitality, but I'm perfectly able to walk out of here by myself!"

"Then git up."

Saxon started to do just that when he remembered his nakedness. "Mrs. Beasley, would you mind getting my clothes?" She handed them to him, and he looked at his three observers expectantly. "Well? Do I have to dress with half the world watching me?"

George Franklin snickered. "You-uns hear what he said? Half the world, and us jist three people!"

"Stay and hep him inter his pants, George Franklin," Chickadee said. She muttered something and then laughed as she and Betty Jane left the cabin.

Saxon was indignant. What right did that half-man girl have to treat him this way? She was undoubtedly the crudest, most ill-mannered human being he'd ever met!

"Reckon you better git inter these breeches, son," George Franklin advised. "Chickadee'll come back and git you iffen you ain't out thar soon."

With much aid from George Franklin, Saxon dressed. He cursed the wave of weakness that engulfed him and resisted the temptation to sit back down on the bed. He was a man, and by God, no mountain chit was going to prove otherwise! He made his way unsteadily out of the cabin.

"Chickadee, let him stay, least till his fever's gone," Betty Jane said, watching Saxon totter on the porch step. "It ain't fittin' fer you-uns ter be a-stayin' in the same cabin no how. That Saxon Blackwell's a man, and yore a girl."

"He ain't gwine stay here, and that's it. He tries somethin' with me, I'll shoot him. He ain't that bad hurt, and you-uns don't need no outlander ter worry over. He's my responsibility, and I aim ter   "

"I am no one's responsibility, Miss McBride." Saxon careened off the rickety porch and staggered to Hagen. He opened one of his saddlebags, pulled out a few bills, and handed the money to Betty Jane. "I'm grateful for the care you gave me, Mrs. Beasley. I hope this will cover the cost of the medicine and shoulder bandage."

Her eyes caressed the money before she thrust it back at Saxon. "Them yarbs didn't cost me a thang, and I ain't acceptin' no payment fer that rag wrapped around yore shoulder. 'Sides that, them that's friends don't need no thanky."

"And I am, indeed, honored to have you both as friends," he said to her and her husband. Making a great show of ignoring Chickadee, he turned to Hagen and grabbed the saddle. He lifted his foot to the stirrup, but the pain in his shoulder prevented him from mounting.

Chickadee's dazzling white grin taunted him. "Want a leg up?"

He didn't deign to answer. Scanning his surroundings, he spied a tree stump, led Hagen to it, and stood on it to mount. Without so much as a nod to Chickadee, he clicked to Hagen and rode out of the yard.

He'd only ridden a short way down the path when he shuddered violently. A cold chill, like icy sleet, settled over him before he crashed to the ground.

He didn't have to open his eyes to know where he was. Chickadee's image burst into his pulsating head, and he knew without a doubt he was in her cabin and in her bed, naked again. He stifled his groan of embarrassment.

There was no help for it. He was as weak as hell and knew there was no way he could leave without passing out. Damn that bear! Damn these hills, and damn his cursed body for betraying him at such an inopportune time!

But most of all, damn Chickadee McBride!

"Ain't no use a-pretendin' yore asleep, Saxon Blackwell. I can see yore eyeballs a-twitchin', and I know yore awake."

He opened one eye. She was sitting on the floor atop a bearskin rug, her wolf beside her. He wondered which of the two was the more feral. "Why does everyone keep taking off my pants? My wounds are on my back and shoulder, not my . . . uh . . ."

"Yore ass?" Chickadee stood and crossed to the fireplace.

As she opened the lid of her pot, the most nauseating odor Saxon had ever smelled permeated the room. "What are you cooking? Your dirty socks?"

Chickadee stopped stirring and shook the wooden spoon at him. "I ain't a-takin' no more sass offen you, hear? This ain't socks, you worthless cuss. It's greens!''

"It smells awful."

Chickadee sniffed the air. "Smells like pokeweeds to me. And it don't matter how they smell no how. Yer gwine eat 'em."

Saxon punched his pillow. "I don't want any."

Chickadee stuck her spoon into the top of her breeches and went to the bed. Staring up at her, muleheadedness written all over his face, was the most aggravating man she'd ever met. Still, with his muscular body, coal-black hair, straight nose, high cheekbones, and sky-blue eyes, it wasn't too much of an effort to look at him.

She touched the cleft in his chin. "Why ain't you got no beard? I heared about this cure? Well, it says iffen you put cream on yore face and let a cat lick it off, you'll grow a lavish o' hair thar. Ain't you man enough ter grow hair withouten no cat ter hep you?"

Saxon managed to squelch a string of profanities. "The question, Miss McBride, is why don't *you* have a beard? As masculine as you are, surely you have to shave every morning to keep people from guessing your real sex. Perhaps you have a bit on your chest?"

She slapped her knee and laughed. "Why don't you and me make us a peace? I ain't much fer feudin', and thangs'd be a sight easier betwixt us iffen we could get along whilst yore a-mendin'." She held out her hand.

Warily, Saxon shook it. "How long do you think it'll be before my wounds heal?"

"Well, a-seein' as how yore a outlander and you ain't been a-takin' yore pain too good so fur, it'll prob'ly be—"

"The worst pain I've got right now is you!" Saxon glared at her, his pride hurting more than his injuries. "Good Lord, woman! How the hell would *you* act if a bear shredded *your* back to ribbons?"

"I got more sense'n ter leave my gun whar I cain't

reach it so's a bahr could git me! And yore back ain't no ribbons. It's got a scratch on it, but it ain't near as bad as yore a-sayin' it is. Yore the complainin'est man I ever—"

"You—"

"Jist last year, we was all a-huntin' this bahr, and ole T.J. Howe? Well, that bahr got him good. Lost his leg, T.J. did, but nary a time did I hear him say nothin' about no pain. He tuk it all like a man."

It was all Saxon could do not to reach up and strangle her. "I *am* a man, Miss McBride. But I'm made of blood, bone, guts, and nerves. I'm *not* made of steel like you mountain people are!"

Chickadee giggled. Her brilliant smile caught him off guard, and despite his tremendous irritation, he couldn't help returning her grin.

"We ain't made o' steel, Saxon Blackwell. We're the same as you. We jist don't bellyache as much." With that, she turned and went back to the hearth. She filled two bowls with the greens and carried them back to the bed.

Saxon grimaced at the meal she placed in his hand. "Isn't there anything else to eat?"

"Sow belly, but it ain't cooked. Want it raw?" She smiled at the look of revulsion on his face and went to sit back down on the rug.

Tentatively, Saxon tasted a bit of the food. It wasn't unpalatable, but the taste was rather strong for his liking. "If you changed the water several times while you cooked these greens, they probably wouldn't be so . . . so potent."

"No, don't reckon they would. But iffen I was ter do that, the pot likker wouldn't be no good."

"Pot liquor?"

"The juice. The cookin' water. Richens the blood y'know." She finished her meal, set her bowl aside, and began to ruffle through her wolf's fur. "Khan's prone to fleas. Ever' now and then I pick 'em offen him. Gits ticks too. You ever shooted ticks offen a wall?"

Saxon placed his bowl on the table by the bed. "No, I've never had the thrill."

"Well, you wait till thur nice and fat, and then you pick 'em offen the animule. Rub 'em in a little sap and they stick real good to the side o' a wall. Once thur up thar, you shoot 'em. Iffen you hit 'em, they splatter all over. Me and T.J. Howe used ter have contests up yonder at Misery's ole place, but we shooted up his walls so bad, he got riled. He didn't have no call ter git so riled, neither. He warn't even a-livin' at that place no more. Builded hissef a new cabin, but he still guards that ole one jist like he did when he lived in it. Ain't no more'n a broken-down shack, but ter hear him tell it, it's a castle."

Rather than being harsh to his ears, her mountain dialect was curiously soothing to Saxon. And her voice had a pleasing lilt to it, almost as if she were singing.

"Saxon? You hear what I said?" She fixed her mesmerizing green eyes on him.

Saxon was hard-pressed to escape their hypnotic spell. "What? Oh. Yes, I heard every word. Who's Misery?"

"Orneriest man ever lived. Ole Misery's jist about as a-grouchin' as you are. His real name's Caleb Brown, but we call him Misery on account o' no one's ever met up with him when he warn't a-totin' some misery or another."

"I thought mountain people didn't complain."

"Most of 'em don't. 'Course, thur's allus a bad apple. Misery's the bad-un around here."

"So where do you do your tick shooting now?" He rolled to his side so his view of her was better.

"Ain't done none since T.J. Howe lost his leg. Reckon I could do it by mysef, but it ain't fun withouten no lay."

"A lay? So you gamble?" Maybe she really *was* half man, he chuckled to himself.

"Not fer money. Ain't none o' us got too much o' that up here. Afore T.J. Howe lost his leg, the loser'd have ter chop the winner's wood. 'Course, now that he ain't got but one leg, I chop his wood fer him fer nothin'. Bring him and his sister, Liza, meat too.''

''That's a kind thing for you to do.''

''T.J.'d do the same fer me. Folks up here take keer o' one another. Ain't it the same whar yore from?''

''Being neighborly has no specific place in this world.''

She cocked her head sideways, her red hair falling over her breast. ''Then why'd you act so dangblasted hotheaded today when I was a-tryin' ter hep you?''

''I'm not used to women like you. I apologize.''

Satisfied with his answer, Chickadee nodded and went to the bed. ''It's a-gittin' late. Move over.''

Saxon's eyebrow rose rakishly. Things were moving right along, it seemed. Was this how he was to repay her? Well, she *was* a pretty bit of female, he mused. And they *were* alone in a secluded cabin. And it *had* been weeks since he'd bedded a woman.

He started to move over for her. But as he did, a sharp pain shot through his shoulder. If he could barely slide over in the bed without his wound aching, how could he perform in it? he wondered.

Chickadee sighed impatiently. ''I said move—''

''I heard you!''

''Then git over so's I can git in too!''

His shoulder throbbed painfully. What if he tried making love to her and couldn't do it? Weighing the risks, he decided a wound to his pride would be infinitely worse than the one to his shoulder. ''I thought you were going to sleep on the rug,'' he finally said.

Chickadee turned and looked at the bearskin. ''That's a skin, and I ain't a-sleepin' on it when I got this bed right here.''

Saxon bunched up the quilt around him and proceeded to get out of the bed. Chickadee pushed him back. "Whar you gwine?"

"The bearskin looks comfortable enough to me. This is your bed, and you've every right to it."

Chickadee wrinkled her nose. "We can share the bed."

As soon as I'm able, he promised her silently and stood, his head reeling. Chickadee allowed him to go, a mischievous grin on her face as she slipped into bed. Propping herself up on her elbow, she watched Saxon shuffle to the bearskin.

As Saxon neared it, Khan's head went up. When he came closer, the wolf eyed him warily, and when his toes touched the edge of the rug, the animal bared his teeth. Saxon jumped back immediately. As he did, he stepped on the quilt, and the top of it was yanked out of his hands.

The sight of his bare backside brought a peal of laughter from Chickadee. When Saxon bent to retrieve the blanket, Khan snapped at his hand, and Chickadee could barely control herself. She laughed so hard, the bed shook.

Saxon never took his eyes off Khan. He wanted nothing more than to turn around and beat what little sense she possessed out of Chickadee, but he didn't dare. The wolf was snarling, and nude or not, Saxon wouldn't have moved a muscle if the Queen of England herself had been behind him.

Speaking carefully, he asked, "You knew he was going to do that, didn't you?"

"Yep."

"Why didn't you warn me?"

"Some thangs are better larnt by yoreset. Now you know that thar skin belongs to Khan. He don't mind you a-settin' on it durin' the day, but he don't share it at night."

Saxon let out a slow breath. "Well, now that you've belatedly informed me of that fact and had your laugh for the day, would you mind helping me out of this predicament?"

"Git yoresef outen it. Yore a man, ain't you?"

Her challenge narrowed his eyes. Hesitantly he bent for the quilt, and once again Khan growled. "Chickadee, come over here and help me before I've got his teeth marks on me as well as those of the bear."

"Say please. Don't you got no manners?"

He gritted his teeth. "Please."

Chickadee snapped her fingers, and Khan laid his head back down and closed his eyes. Saxon reached to the floor and jerked up the quilt. He whirled on Chickadee and started toward her, but another low growl from Khan warned him that what he had in mind would be a grave mistake. So angry he could barely see straight, he searched the room for any other place he could possibly sleep. There was none. The bed, with Chickadee, was his only choice.

"You afeared I'll rape you? Is that why you don't want ter sleep with me?"

His jaw dropped. "That's the most ridiculous thing I've ever—"

"Don't think I could do it, do you?"

"I've no doubt at all you could, were the circumstances right, but there are other factors to be considered."

"Y'mean yore wounds?"

He swallowed his impatience. He'd never imagined he'd one day be standing naked in some mountain cabin with a brute of a girl talking about her raping him. And the addle-brained little thing didn't even realize why it was impossible! For someone who was obviously well-acquainted with the sight of male anatomy, she sure didn't understand much about how it worked.

"Since you're taking great pleasure in trying to embarrass me, Miss McBride, allow me the same pleasure. Could it be that under that experienced exterior of yours there lurks a virgin?"

She smiled at him, not at all flustered. "I ain't never laid with a man afore. T.J. Howe kissed me once, but I didn't like it much so I never let him do it agin. Buck Hawkins tried ter touch my tit last year whilst we was a-pickin' blackberries, but I hauled off and let him have it. He ain't never bothered me agin."

"Then why did you bring up the subject of rape? If you don't know what lovemaking is all about, how do you think it possible to violate me?"

This was the most ludicrous conversation he'd ever had with anyone in his whole life. But as absurd as it was, he was determined to see it through and back Chickadee into a corner out of which she couldn't escape. Surely with the Harvard education he had, he could beat this little mountain twit at her own game.

And the best way to do it would be to call her bluff.

"Well?" he pressed.

She watched the mellow reflection of firelight slither through the ice-blue of his eyes, and a funny little feeling jumped around inside her at the sight. "I seed animules a-doin' it," she replied flippantly. "Don't look ter me like thur's much ter it."

He raised his eyebrow sardonically. "Oh, really? Would you care to try it then?"

She laid back down and stared at the ceiling.

Saxon sported a triumphant grin. Sure he'd bested her, he walked to the bed, but just before he got into it, she answered his question.

"I'm gwine on eighteen. Ain't old, but I reckon it's old enough. Shore, I'll try it with you."

Saxon's knee slid off the bed. Without a word, he turned and went to the farthest corner of the room and spent a long, uncomfortable night there.

The aroma of simmering meat woke him. His fever was gone, his back felt fine, and his shoulder didn't hurt as much as he expected it would. What sort of mysterious medicine was in Betty Jane's puffballs?

Her back to him, Chickadee didn't realize he was awake, and he was content to watch her move about. She was humming some happy tune, her red curls bouncing on her slight shoulders. Her arms were as slender as the branches of a young tree—Saxon was sure his hands could span her waist—and her bottom was small and firm. That amazing strength she possessed was apparently in her legs, he decided. Though she was doing nothing but ambling from corner to corner, he could see the ropes of muscle in her thighs dance beneath her breeches.

Chickadee heaped meat onto a plate and carried it to a small hickory table that already held a platter of eggs and bread. This done, she wiped her hands on the sides of her breeches and turned toward Saxon.

"How long you been a-gawkin' at me?" She looked away from his penetrating, robin's-egg–blue gaze, finding it strangely disturbing.

"Awhile," he answered lazily.

His voice, like a fresh mountain breeze, cooled her despite the warmth of the cabin. Unaccustomed to the shivery feelings, she shrugged them off. "Well, come on and git yore mouth greased up. Once these vittles is cold, that's the way you'll eat 'em. I ain't gwine keep 'em hotted fer you."

Saxon dressed quickly, no easy task since he held on to the quilt at the same time. Then he joined Chickadee at the table and helped himself to a generous portion of the meal. Cool, delicious water accompanied it, and Saxon couldn't remember ever enjoying a breakfast as much. As they ate, he tried to draw Chickadee into conversation, but she only muttered short answers and never once looked up from her plate.

"Mealtime's fer eatin', outlander," she finally said and sopped up meat juice with a piece of cornbread. "Thar's a place fer talkin', and the table ain't it."

"But conversation can make a meal more pleasurable. Food should be enjoyed at a leisurely pace. Savored.''

''You eat the way you want, and leave me ter eat the way I want. I enjoy my meals jist fine.''

''Well, at any rate, thank you for the breakfast. I don't think I've ever had meat as tender as that was.''

''Bahr meat allus eats good iffen you cook it right.''

Saxon glanced at his empty plate, the meat he'd eaten suddenly heavy in his stomach. ''Why didn't you tell me it was bear? I thought it was—well I don't know what I thought it was, but I had no idea it was bear!''

She picked at her teeth with her nail. ''Didn't think it'd differ. Ain't bahr meat good enough ter a outlander?''

''Why do you keep calling me that?''

''It's what you are, ain't it?'' she answered smoothly.

''Yes, but the way you say it makes it sound like it's an undesirable thing to be.''

Chickadee leaned back in her chair and studied him. Again, her insides seemed to coil. ''What's it like, a-bein' a outlander? You live in a big, fancy city?''

''I live in Boston,'' he replied, scrutinizing her just as blatantly. ''And I don't think there's any way to define what an outlander is. It's all a matter of what you're used to.''

''You been around the world? You ever seed a real Chinaman?'' She leaned forward expectantly.

Saxon watched her breasts strain against the closing of her shirt. ''I've seen Chinese people. Does China interest you?''

''What about Mexicans? You seed them too?''

''Yes, I've seen Mexicans too.''

''You ever shooted a elephant?''

Saxon grinned. ''Why would I want to do that?''

''Fer them teeth. I seed a paintin' o' one one time,

and I ain't never fergot them long white teeth that stick outen thur mouths. Wonder how many bullets it'd take ter brang one of 'em down?''

"Is that all you ever think about? Killing things?''

Chickadee pondered his question, her hand absently rubbing Khan's head. "I ain't never kilt nothin' that didn't insist on it. I kill ter eat or ter keep from a-bein' et mysef. I like them elephants' teeth, but I wouldn't really shoot one jist fer that. I ain't much fer people who hunt fer the sport of it.''

Saxon watched Khan lay his huge head on Chickadee's dainty lap. "I wasn't aware white wolves lived here.''

"Khan's from Canada. A while back thur was this trapper who come up here. Said he'd been up in Canada and shooted a wolf thar. Felt bad about it when he seed her babies come a-runnin' out ter her. One run away, but Khan stayed by his mama. When they come here, he give him ter me. Said he couldn't take keer o' him no more.''

"How did you come up with his name?''

"Didn't. The trapper did. I woulda named him Snow on account o' he blends right in with the snow.''

"Khan suits him better. It's a much more noble-sounding name than Snow.'' Saxon continued to watch her tanned fingers slip in and out of the thick fur on Khan's neck and couldn't help wondering how those same fingers would feel playing through his own hair.

"His middle name's Snow,'' she decided quite suddenly, determined to make her preference clear to Saxon. "Khan Snow McBride. Onliest family I got.''

"What happened to your parents?''

Chickadee's features clouded. "Mama died four years ago. Tuk real sick, and not even all them yarbs Betty Jane used could keep the breath from a-slackin' in her throat. Never did even find out what ailed her.''

Saxon reached for her hand and squeezed it gently. "I'm sorry. It must have been hard for you."

Her hand began to perspire in his. "I managed. Betty Jane and George Franklin looked after me till I growed."

"You lived with them?"

"Lived right here. I was only thirteen, but I knowed how ter take keer o' mysef. Betty Jane did thangs like a-makin' my clothes and soap, but I fed mysef."

"What about your father?"

Her expression darkened. "His name's Barton Winslow, but I never knowed him. He was from up North. Maybe New York, but I ain't shore. Anyhow, he wandered up here a-lookin' fer gold in the streams, and mama? Well, she tuk a heart-burnin' to him. Warn't no preacher-parson around, but up here a man's word's his bond, and Barton Winslow tole mama he was gwine marry her. But when she was a-childin' with me? Well, he jist up and tuk off, a-takin' ever'thang mama had. Even her little bit o' gold."

She cleared the table, her face still troubled. "I never knowed what mama was like afore I was born, but Betty Jane says she was the happiest woman in these here parts. But after Barton Winslow left her, she was low in the mind. She was a good enough mama, but she didn't smile much that I can recall. One day I'm gwine find Barton Winslow and make him suffer the way he made mama suffer."

"Murder is against the law, Chickadee."

"Didn't never say I'd kill the man. 'Course, never said I wouldn't, neither. Y'see, I got a mind ter git out and see this country one day, Saxon. Ain't never gwine leave these hills ferever, but thur's a passel o' thangs I don't know nothin' about. And who knows? Maybe whilst I'm a-travelin', I'll come acrost ole Barton Winslow. The world's big, but thur's only so many places a man can hide."

Saxon folded his arms across his chest. Funny, he

almost pitied this Barton Winslow. Like she said—there were only so many places a man could hide.

And woe unto the man who really angered Chickadee McBride.

Saxon spent the day alone in the cabin, Chickadee having gone out to do God only knew what. He'd wanted to go with her, but she was adamant that he stay and rest, and she stationed Khan at the door to make sure that's exactly what he did.

She left him a flask of the same potion Betty Jane had given him. When she returned he was asleep, the empty bottle still in his hand. "Cain't hold yore likker, Saxon Blackwell." She laughed to herself, and after starting supper she went back outside, Khan trotting behind her.

Saxon woke just in time to see her and the guard wolf leave. Having been imprisoned in the cabin all day, he seized the opportunity to escape. Not knowing where else to go, he followed Chickadee.

She stopped at a bubbling creek. Like a lover's hands, the mountain wind caressed her skin as she shed her clothes. Inhaling deeply of the earthy perfume of her woods, she tested the water, smiling when it bit at her toes.

Saxon crouched behind some brush and grappled for a thick stem when Chickadee's bareness was revealed to him. She wasn't the first nude woman he'd ever seen, but she was undoubtedly the most perfectly shaped one. There wasn't an extra ounce of flesh on her; her skin covered her form like a tight satin sheath.

As she bathed, Saxon tore his mind from her loveliness and thought about how well she fit in with her environment. This particular place, like Chickadee, was as yet untouched by encroaching civilization. With her mass of wild red hair, smattering of tawny freckles, emerald eyes, and untamed personality, she blended into this uncultivated paradise as well as any native animal.

She soon emerged from the stream and began to dress. Saxon hurried back to the cabin and was feigning sleep as she walked through the door. Her shirt was damp, her breasts wonderfully outlined as Saxon watched through slitted eyelids. He let out a sleepy moan. "You're back."

"'Pears so."

"What's for dinner?"

"What you got a taste fer?"

He folded his arms beneath his head. "Lobster."

Her brow furrowed. "Ain't never heared of it, and what I ain't never heared of, I don't eat. We're a-havin' chicken and dumplin's."

Saxon ate heartily and wondered if it was Chickadee's cooking or the fresh mountain air that gave him such an appetite. "What did you do all day?" he asked.

"Chopped some wood fer Betty Jane and George Franklin, then tuk Khan up to whar we both like ter go. We jist set thar fer a spell afore we come back down and went ter check on ole Widder Tucker. She's ailin', y'know."

"But you were gone all day. Is that all you did?"

"Is that all? It's a right fur piece up to whar me and Khan like ter be. And wood choppin' ain't somethin' nobody can do in jist a few minutes. You ever chopped wood?"

A simple question, innocently asked, but it made him feel ashamed. "No, I never have."

"What do you do?"

He leaned back and thought of his fine Boston and New York offices. He was proud of the successes he'd made for Blackwell Enterprises but bitter that Araminta forced the work on him. He knew the satisfaction he gained from his accomplishments would be much sweeter if he were staying with the company of his own free will and not because Araminta chained him to it.

Still, his way of life *would* appear grand to Chickadee. And for some reason, he wanted to impress her. "I dabble in various ventures. My grandmother owns several businesses, and I help her run them."

She detected a sour note in his voice. Something was bothering this man. If she riled him, perhaps she'd find out what it was. "You don't really do nothin', do you?"

He scowled fiercely. "I just told you I—"

"What kinds o' businesses does yore granny have?"

Certain he was about to stagger her, Saxon smugly made her wait a few moments before he answered. "She has a fleet of steamboats, an iron factory, a—"

"But you don't never go out and work on them boats. And you ain't never been in that fact'ry neither. Never dirtied yore hands with the real work that makes them businesses work fer you." She watched his face redden and prepared to go for the kill. "It's them workers you hire who make the money. Thur hands that bleed and blister—"

"But I *run* those damn businesses! Do you realize how much paperwork is—"

"A-workin' with a pile o' papers ain't no real job." Her soft lips quivered with a restrained grin.

Saxon's ire rose. What the hell did *she* know about the business world? "Those *piles of paper* are very imp—"

"You go off ter play in the mornin's. Them businesses ain't nothin' but games people is allus a-tryin' ter win. The winner is whoever has the mostest money in the end."

"Now see here, miss—"

"You ain't never done a lick o' hard work in yore whole life, Saxon Blackwell. Ain't never muscled up nothin' heavier'n that fancy saddle you ride on."

"I'll have you know that—"

"You fight in the War Amongst Us?"

Saxon ran his fingers through his hair. Dammit! Why couldn't he seem to beat her at this match of wits? "Yes. I fought in the Civil War. Is *that* sort of work acceptable to you?"

Again, she grinned at his discomposure. "I tuk keer o' one o' them Yankees. He was bad hurt, and me and Betty Jane cured him.'Course, I did the same thang fer a Confederate. I didn't take no sides. Heared tell lots o' people up here did though. Some sided with the South, and others jined up with the North. And some families was divided. The Mc-Gills? Well, one o' them boys weared blue, and the other weared gray. Sad story, that one. They both come home a-wantin' ter visit thur mama, and when they seed each other, they drawed thur shootin'-arns and farred. The youngest died, and the oldest laid down on his brother and cried over what he done."

Saxon's anger dissipated. Sheer waste. That's what the war had been. "Did you have much trouble up here?"

" 'Cept fer them two soldiers I tole you about, this place warn't bothered a'tall."

"You *are* rather alone up here. Why don't you live closer to a town?"

"Don't need much from no town. And ever' time I go ter git bullets, salt, or sugar, I allus git made fun of. I don't let it bother me too much, but I git ill over it sometimes."

"You get sick?"

"Sick?"

"You said you get ill."

"Sick means sick and ill means agger-pervoked. Them folks make me ill on account o' thur so fritter-minded."

Saxon hid his grin by rubbing the two-day growth of stubble on his face. He'd traveled through several mountain towns on his way up here and spoken with many of the people in them. But Chickadee was of a different breed altogether. Sure, she was a mountain person, just as they were, but in comparison she was half wild.

Well, she couldn't help it. She lived alone in near

isolation, and losing her mother the way she had . . . She really did quite well considering no one had ever taught her the proper way to behave. From what he'd observed, Betty Jane and George Franklin had little control over her. Yes, Chickadee McBride was certainly an enigma.

But she was a delightful one, albeit a bit saucy.

She watched how his eyes sparkled when he was deep in thought and decided she could get used to looking into eyes like his. Strange. Eyes were eyes, the way she'd seen it. But no one else's eyes had ever made her feel this way. "I seed you a-watchin' me when I tuk my bath."

He wasn't sure he'd heard right. "What?"

"Saxon, when yore a-feelin' a mite stronger, I'm gwine larn you how ter creep around these here woods jist as quiet-like as a Indian. You don't stand no chance a-tryin' ter hide from nothin' as much racket as you make. Yore lucky I knowed it was you or else I'd a let Khan tar you up."

He didn't know whether to laugh or be embarrassed.

"You gwine sleep in the corner agin?" She took a drink of her water and swished it around her mouth.

Again, he resisted the temptation to laugh at her. She was so ill-mannered, but it was entertaining to watch her. "Tell me something, young lady. Would you really have let me make love to you last night?"

"Nope."

He grinned broadly. "Then why did you say—"

"Knowed iffen I called yore bluff, you'd back down."

Chapter 3

Saxon tried to keep count of the days as they passed, but as they became weeks, the mountain tranquillity eased his concern about time. And because he'd advised Araminta the turpentine research would take him months, he remained confident her greed would prevent her from doing Desdemona any harm.

Though he still tired more easily than usual, his wounds healed rapidly. But he didn't know whether it was his nature to heal quickly or if the magic mountain medicines had brought about his swift recovery.

Chickadee, never having been this close to a man before, didn't quite know how to take Saxon. His city ways often confused her, and she wondered about that melancholy, haunted look she saw in his eyes occasionally. The sight of him mesmerized her in a way she didn't understand. Many times she caught herself staring at him, quickly looking away when he gave her a knowing smile.

Because Saxon's strength was returning, they began taking long strolls along the winding paths. On one such stroll, Chickadee pointed to the sun-crowned mountain in the distance. "When I was a little girl, I used ter thank them sunbeams over thar was God a-comin' down to earth," she said and sat on the ridge. Picking up a stick, she wrote in the dirt. "That's my name, Saxon. That trapper who give me Khan larnt me ter write it."

Saxon sat and saw her childish scrawl and misspelled name. "You've never gone to school?"

"I reckon thur's a few schools around here, but thur too fur ter git ter ever'day. I'm too old now anyhow."

"You're never too old to learn. If you could go to school, what would you want to study?"

"I'd ask the teacher how ter spell my real name."

"Chickadee isn't your real name?"

"You ever knowed a person named Chickadee fer real? Naw, Chickadee's only a name my mama used ter call me. She said that the day I was born, thar was this little chickadee outside the winder jist a-sangin' its heart out. From then on, Mama called me Chickadee."

He smiled and reached for her twig. Their fingers touched, and they both let go of the stick as if it were on fire. Saxon had no idea what Chickadee was thinking, but he pondered the reaction he'd had to the touch of her finger. Such a simple, innocent touch, and yet it warmed him all over.

He looked back down at the twig, trying to remember what it was he had been planning to do with it. "What's your real name?"

His deep, melodic voice slithered into her ears and waltzed through her mind, its music causing those unfamiliar feelings to sing through her again. "Keely," she said, unaware she was whispering.

Her thickly fringed eyes held him captive. He tried and failed to think of even one porcelain-fine Bostonian woman who could compare to this freckled, enchanting girl beside him.

"Ain't you gwine write my real name?"

He forced his eyes from her face and concentrated on the task at hand. "Keely is a beautiful name. Wouldn't you rather me call you that?"

"Suit yoresef. I'll answer ter either one." Careful not to touch his fingers again, she took the stick back from him and painstakingly copied what he'd written.

"What do you do for money, Keely?"

For a few moments she watched two blue jays frolic in the birch tree that shaded her. "Never need much money, but when I do, I sell sang."

"Sang? Is that some sort of animal skin?"

She lowered her head and giggled. "Lord o' mercy, Saxon. Sang ain't no animule, it's a plant! Smells good, the leaves grow in bunches o' five, and it's got little red berries. Got ter be real keerful ter get the roots."

"What's it used for?"

"Medicine. Heared tell they ship it over to China. Them China folks must want it somethin' fierce. I git a good price fer it. Come late summer I'll take you a-huntin' fer sang. I know whar it grows real good, and I'll take you thar iffen you promise not ter tell nobody whar my spot is."

He smiled with sudden comprehension. Ginseng. That's what *sang* was.

Law, the man had a handsome smile, Chickadee mused. A lazy grin that was sort of mocking. It made her smile back at him. "And when tree leaves commence a-turnin' yaller, I go a-galaxin'. Galax has purty heart-shaped leaves and grows good under rock cliffs. I pack it in wet moss till I can git it ter market."

"Do you know what galax is used for?"

"Do you?"

Obviously she didn't know. "It's used for Christmas decorations."

With a toss of her head, she threw her hair off her shoulders. "Reckon iffen people got money, they'll spend it on jist about anythang."

"Don't you ever wish you had more money?"

"Once, Mama and me went to Asheville? Well, I seed the God-burnin'est, shiniest, purtiest carriage you ever seed. I decided I wanted ter be rich one day so's I could ride in a fancified carriage like the one I seed."

"And now?"

"Now I'm growed, and carriages don't mean a dang thang to me."

"But money will buy more than carriages, Keely. Have you ever wondered what it would be like to wear a satin gown and soft slippers?"

"I got a gown. Belonged to my mama. She made it. Growed the flax hersef and spinned out the thread in the yard with the sun a-shinin' down on her whilst she worked. I thought she was the purtiest mama-woman in the world when she got that dress done and put it on."

He leaned forward and whispered, "Would you wear it for me one day?"

For the first time in her life, she felt shy. A strong wind seemed to be blowing through her insides, and much to her dismay, she knew she was blushing. "What fer? Iffen I go a-trippin' through these here thickety woods with a dress on, I'd fall flat on my face fer shore." She finished speaking abruptly and bent her head, her hair falling to the sides of her face. When Saxon remained silent, she was glad for the time to gather her thoughts.

There was no use denying it anymore. She liked this man beside her, and that was that. He was the opposite of everything she understood, but her feelings for him would not be stilled. Yes, he was handsome. And since she'd studied his body while he'd helped her with some of the chores during the past weeks, she knew he had every bit as much muscle as mountain men did.

But aside from looks, he had fine manners. He treated her like a lady, pulling out her table chair for her and assisting her off the porch and over rocky areas when they walked. Only once in her life had a man complimented her: T.J. Howe had said her teeth were real white. But Saxon? Saxon said her smile was brighter than the mountain sun. She could get quite used to hearing flattery like that. Suddenly, she found herself dreading the day Saxon would return to Boston.

Boston. Was life easier in a city? Probably so. Saxon certainly didn't know how to take care of himself. He'd almost been killed by a bear, and he hadn't even known what sang was! Poor Saxon. He was totally defenseless.

At that thought, her head snapped up and she glanced at him out of the corners of her eyes. He didn't *have* to be defenseless, she mused. She could teach him everything she knew. When she was finished, he'd be able to survive in the pits of hell if he ever got down that way. But more than that, she thought with a mental grin, the lessons would take a lavish of time. And having Saxon around was right nice.

"I figger you'll be a-stayin' here as long as it takes fer you ter git all yore strength back, Saxon, so whilst yore in these here mountains, thur's one thang you got ter know about 'em. They don't give up thur treasures fer nothin'. You and me's in a cove. You said yoresef thur ain't no towns close, so you have ter larn ter git along withouten 'em."

How her eyes sparkled, he thought. "Are you saying you don't think I can take care of myself?"

She grinned into a cupped hand and then pointed to the distant blue-green ranges. "Them hills is hard, patient, and lastin'. They don't cave in fer nobody. That's the way you got ter be too."

He smiled. What could she teach him, Saxon Blackwell, that he didn't already know? "I must have very grave problems. Pray tell, what are they?"

She wondered how to explain survival to him. "Well, a-gittin' along up here's a lot more'n jist knowin' how ter shoot straight. It has ter do with yore way o' thankin' too."

She wet her lips with a pink tongue very much the color of the wildflower bed beside her. "Y'see, yore mind's softish. You got too much o' some thangs and not enough o' other thangs. You ain't balanced so thur ain't no peace in you. And yore money ain't never gwine give it to you. Money might even be a-makin' you worser."

How refreshingly naive she was, he mused. "So you're saying having money is wrong."

"Naw, it ain't wrong. But it can make you fergit a passel o' thangs. Money's cold. Cold cain't make warm. And a warmer life's what yore a-honin' fer."

"Honing?"

"What yer a-pinin' away fer."

He leaned closer to her. "Why do you think you know so much about me? We've only known each other for a short—"

"A person don't have ter know another person fer years ter know about him. All's you need is a pair o' eyes in yore heart and you'll know all you need ter know."

"And what have you decided about me . . . besides my being soft in the mind?" He swallowed his laughter.

"Well, you got a good heart, but iffen you was ter relax a mite more, it'd be better. Y'see, Saxon, yore jittery. You worry, and you bigger and bigger them worries till yore so dang fidgety you don't know what ter do. I see you a-tryin' ter fergit what's a-plaguin' you, but ever' now and then yore as dour as a ole rain crow. And lessen you git shed o' them devils inside you, you ain't gwine last long up here.

"Yore a good man inside, Saxon Blackwell," she continued, reaching out to touch his cheek. "Yore jist a mite jangled. Ain't nothin' that cain't be cured though. All's you need is a little heartease."

Peace swept through Saxon at her touch. Like a gentle rain, it flowed within him. And it drenched him with an odd desire to tell her things about himself. He'd never found talking about himself an easy thing to do, but now . . . well, it didn't seem so hard. Not with her.

He took her hand and kissed it softly. "Money *does* mean a lot to me, and I suppose it always will. But I—I didn't always have it. I don't remember it well, but I once lived in poverty. My mother died giving birth to my sister, Desdemona, and Father died of cholera soon afterward. Desdemona and I stayed with neighbors until Grandmother came from

England for us. She'd intended to take us back with her, but when she saw the fortune to be made in the maritime trade in Boston, she decided to take up residence there. It was only then I ever knew wealth."

And only then that I knew hatred and fear, he added mentally.

His voice was edged with deep hurt, Chickadee noted. The sorrowful sound was almost inaudible to her ears, but it fairly shouted in her heart. "Iffen yore family was so poor, why didn't yore granny share her money?"

Saxon shook his head. Araminta had never shared anything but the sting of her cane. He swallowed, wanting to change the subject, but that bizarre need to talk to her remained. "Father was born and raised in England. The Blackwell name is an old and respected one over there, and when Father married a common workman's daughter, Grandmother disinherited him. My grandfather had died years before, leaving all his money to her. I'm sure he never believed she'd do such a thing to her only child, but that's what she did. So Father and Mother left England and went to Boston. Probably to get away from Grandmother."

Chickadee noticed the pain in his sapphire eyes and understood he was telling her more than he wanted to. Something was very wrong with the man who was rapidly becoming special to her.

"Grandmother is—she's—" He broke off. He'd never shared his deepest emotions with anyone and had no idea why he felt the driving need to spill them before Chickadee at this moment. His confusion irritated him. "Never mind," he said, standing and pulling her to her feet. "Show me some of those things you say I need to learn."

She wisely refrained from asking anything more. Another time, perhaps, but not now. Instead, she kept up a stream of chatter as she explained what each plant was and the various ways to use it.

He listened absently, but his heart wasn't in what she was saying. She'd struck a chord somewhere

deep inside him, and once again made him feel that
she was, in some way, better than he.

She had nothing, but she had everything.

And Saxon still wasn't sure what it was she had.

A-settin' by the glow o' the flames. That's what she
called what they were doing this evening, and Saxon
liked the way that sounded. Her cabin was small,
but it had a charm all its own—much like that of its
owner. He sat back in his white, oak-seated chair
and crossed his legs.

In the one room there were only two hickory
chairs, a small hickory table, a smaller rhododendron root table, the bed, and her mother's spinning
wheel. But there were plenty of shelves. And on
those half-log shelves, Chickadee stored all sorts of
treasures.

She had a peacock feather in which she took great
pride, explaining that she had traded a whole bearskin for it. There were wooden bowls she'd hol-
lowed out herself, shiny rocks, birds' nests and tiny
pine cones. Empty whiskey flasks served nicely as
vases and were always filled with wildflowers.

But her most prized possession was the old
wooden stock of a rifle, the rest of the gun long
gone. It was propped up on the mantel—the place
of honor in Chickadee's home. She said it was from
an uncle's rifle, who she believed had fought on
King's Mountain during the Revolutionary War.

"Thur was this British feller called Ferguson who
worked fer another British feller called Cornwallis,"
she explained. "Well, this Ferguson carried on that
iffen the mountain people didn't give in, he was
gwine strang 'em all up and burn down the whole
dang mountain. Them mountain men warn't much
fer what he said a'tall, so they tuk up thur weapons
and licked them redcoats at King's Mountain.

"The way I heared it tole, they didn't git along
too good with some king, and he warn't a-treatin'
them real good neither. So they crossed the ocean-

sea and went ter Pennsylvania. From thar, they moved on down, a-pickin' up other people till they finally got here. Been here ever since and reckon allus will be.''

Her special way of telling things made history much more interesting. He leaned back until his chair rested against the log wall. Chickadee sat by the fire, knife and wood in hand. "What are you making?" he asked.

Without looking up, she replied, "Nothin'. Sometimes you whittle jist fer the sake o' whittlin'. You can git a lot o' thankin' done like this."

Saxon smiled. He felt so warm, so cozy in this peaceful cabin. "And what do you think about, Keely?"

A faraway look came to her beautiful eyes. "Reckon I try ter thank on purty thangs. Don't make no sense ter thank o' thangs that'll make me upset."

Somehow, Saxon knew that would be her reply. He grinned again and marveled at how easy it was to be happy with this carefree mountain girl. He'd almost forgotten what laughter felt like. And poor Desdemona hadn't known it in years.

Chickadee saw that sorrow floating in his eyes again. "You want ter give this a try, outlander?" She held out the piece of wood and knife.

He accepted them, and she took another wooden object from one of her shelves. She sat back down, held it on her lap, and with a piece of bark, began to pluck the strings stretched across it. The music was so hauntingly beautiful, Saxon was mesmerized.

"George Franklin made this dulcimore, but I larnt mysef how ter play it by recollectin' the tunes Mama used ter hum."

He smiled at her pronounciation of *dulcimer* and watched how gracefully her slender fingers moved on her instrument. As he listened, he imagined her in his arms as they waltzed across a ballroom floor. He saw her in a silk gown of jade green with emeralds twinkling at her ears and throat. He saw—

"Saxon, ain't you a-listenin' ter me?"

Her soft voice wafted through his dream, bringing him back to reality.

"I said you need ter be a-gittin' ter bed. You ain't all the way normal yet, and you need ter sleep."

"What about you?"

His eyes stroked her as gently as she caressed her dulcimer. She never knew a person could *feel* a look. She got up and slipped into bed, turning her back to him. When he got in beside her, her skin rippled strangely. She lapsed into silence.

"What are you thinking about, Keely?"

After a moment she turned and looked at him. "When yore a-sparkin' up thar in that Boston city, what kinds o' thangs do you tell them girls?"

He slid his hand through her hair. "Well, if you were the girl I was courting, I'd tell you your hair is like satin." His thumb edged toward her eye, and he brushed her lashes with it. "And I'd tell you your eyes are the kind a man could gaze into forever, your lips are ripe peaches, your skin is the finest velvet. I'd say your voice rivals the most beautiful music, and the freckles on your face are like a dusting of golden stars. Your enthusiasm makes me smile and never want to stop smiling, and the jingle of your silvery laughter makes it seem like Christmas every day."

"And . . . and would you mean all them thangs?"

"I do mean them, Keely," he said softly.

"So yore a-tellin' 'em to me fer real? You ain't jist—"

"I'm telling them to you for real."

She was quiet, and so was he. The only sound that could be heard in the small cabin was the rustling of the wind outside, and their own breathing. Pale moonlight swept through the two tiny windows and crept into the many crevices of the walls, and shadows performed on the ceiling like happy, dancing people. Saxon and Chickadee watched them, each deep in thought.

And when sleep finally overtook Chickadee,

Saxon pulled her into his arms and thought how right it felt to have her there.

His days took on the timeless serenity of the mountains themselves, as Chickadee had told him they should. But when he *did* fall into one of his silent, troubled moods, she cured him by handing him an ax.

His first attempts at chopping wood were a far cry from Chickadee's smooth expertise. She made it her business to sit on a stump and alternate between instructing him and laughing at him. His pride suffered, but not as much as his blistered hands.

Saxon had never been a weak man, but with all the strenuous chores he was doing now, his body became leaner and harder, and he often caught Chickadee's admiring gaze, which did much for his flagging male pride.

She soon began to teach him the art of survival. She usually told him things he already knew, but she took such great delight in "a-larnin' " him, he often pretended ignorance for her. He enjoyed indulging her and looked forward to the reward of her smile when he "done good."

But one thing he didn't know about was bear tracking, and the respect he had for his mountain teacher grew steadily when she took him along on a bear hunt.

"Most bahrs around here is about four to five hunnerd pounds," she informed him, her eyes darting through the rhododendron thicket. "Some git even bigger. After she's et enough, the female'll go on inter her den in late fall or early winter. The male don't go inter the den. He'll keep on a-scroungin' fer food, but he'll usually crawl down up under inter somethin' sooner or later."

Down, up, under, into, Saxon repeated silently. Four prepositions in a row. And the way she said it, the sentence actually made sense! "Do you think we'll find a bear today?" He listened to every sound that swept through the forest and tried to discern what each of them was.

Chickadee walked to a large tree and picked up a handful of something from the ground. When Saxon joined her she showed him the bits of leaves, soil, and nuts in her hand. "This stuff's called mast. These are hick'ry nuts, and bahrs go plumb wild over 'em."

"So there's a bear around here?" Saxon peered into each nearby bush, certain the beast would soon attack.

"One *was* here, but it's gone, and it ain't a-comin' back."

"How do you know that?"

"Look how the mast's all tore up. See how it looks like somebody raked it? A bahr done it. It tuk its paw and went through all this mess a-huntin' fer the nuts."

"But how do you know it's gone and that it isn't coming back?"

"Look what yore steppin' in," she said, a merry twinkle in her eyes.

"Damn!" He stood quickly and wiped his soiled boot on the wildflowers.

"Bahr's don't do that in thur feedin' grounds. They won't foul up the place whar they eat. That mess you stepped in is a shore sign the bahr that was here moved on."

"Some things are better learned by myself, right?" He threw her a crooked grin.

They moved quickly through the dense brush. Saxon examined everything they passed, hoping to pick up signs of a bear. But Chickadee's trained eyes frequently rolled when he showed her something he was certain was evidence of a bear. He soon gave up trying to impress her. This was her territory, her domain, and he let her lead the way.

"Y'got ter use yore ears too, Saxon. See how thick that laurel is? Well, you jist cain't believe how fast a bahr can git through it. You can hear it a-goin' at it, but you cain't see it.'Course, most times Khan can flush one outen 'thar.'Cept fer when he don't got no hankerin' ter do it. He ain't like no reg'lar dog, y'know.''

Saxon glanced at the white wolf. Khan returned the glance with blue-eyed disdain before turning his attention back to Chickadee.

''I don't think Khan likes me, Keely. Every time I try to pat him, he walks away, and he never comes when I call him. He eyes me as if he'd like to rip me to shreds, and though you say he doesn't mind sharing his bearskin during the day, he won't let me near it.''

She bent and kissed the top of Khan's head. ''Never knowed him ter be jealous afore, but I reckon that's what he is. It's usually jist me and him, and he prob'ly ain't a-takin' too kindly ter havin' you around. He'll git used ter you. Ever'thang takes time, Saxon. I done tole you that afore, but you keep a-rushin' thangs.''

''Still, it would be nice if he and I could get along.''

She took a moment to think about the problem. ''Tell you somethin' about wolves, outlander. In thur minds, they thank they deserve respect. And they do, the way I see it. I been with Khan fer gwine on four years, and I've noticed a lavish o' thangs about him. A-seein' as how yore a lot taller'n he is, he's prob'ly a-thankin' that you believe yore better'n him. Git down on yore knees and make shore yore head's lower'n his. That way, he'll be bigger'n you, and he might see you in a different way.''

He looked down, watched the wolf yawn, and thought of Little Red Riding Hood. *My what big teeth you have, Grandmother*, he mused, staring at the inside of Khan's mouth.

''Git on down thar, Saxon.''

''He'll probably bite my nose off.''

''Yore nose is long. Wouldn't hurt yore looks nary a bit ter git a smidgeon of it nipped off.''

"Are you saying my nose is ugly?"

"Does it differ? What you got is what you got."

"At least I've *got* a nose. With that tiny thing *you've* got, it's a wonder you can breathe."

"I can breathe jist fine. Now, are you gwine git down thar on the ground with Khan, or are we gwine stand here all day a-talkin' about noses?"

He thought maybe talking about noses was a hell of a lot safer than coming nose to nose with a wolf. Taking a deep breath, he bent to the ground directly in front of Khan. He made sure his head was lower than that of the wolf, and when it was, he raised his eyes to meet Khan's curious gaze.

They stared at each other for several minutes before Khan yawned again and went to relieve himself on a nearby tree.

"Well, reckon that's what he thanks about you, Saxon," Chickadee said.

Still on his hands and knees, he laughed out loud.

As they continued the trek through the woods, Chickadee began walking a bit slower. "It's jist a feelin'. Don't go a-gittin' all excited. I ain't seed or heared nothin' yet."

But Saxon *was* excited. He was beginning to understand the thrill hunters experienced tracking wild animals. Risky, to be sure, but when man was pitted against nature, the atmosphere itself took on an air of stimulating expectation.

"Look here, Saxon," Chickadee said in a low voice while she pointed to a rotten stump. "Bahr tracks. This here stump's so soft with rot, the bahr sank right inter it when it got up on it. And look up thar," she said softly, gesturing at a low-hanging branch. "See how them leaves is turned wrong side out? The bahr was a-grabbin' onter that branch when it was up on the stump."

She walked ahead, her keen hunter's eyes noting each thing in her surroundings. Saxon followed closely, his own eyes wide with anticipation.

"It ain't too fur away."

"How do you know? Did you hear it?"

She pointed to some moss on the ground. "Thar's one o' its tracks. See how the moss is all crushed? Well, iffen the bahr was long gone, that moss woulda had time ter puff back up agin. But it's still smashed real good."

"Where's the bear though?"

"Yore a-rushin' thangs agin."

He suppressed a chuckle.

They soon came to a gigantic oak tree, and she froze. Absorbed in watching everything around him, Saxon ran right into her.

"Dang it, Saxon!" she whispered loudly. "Are you plumb bereft? Watch whar yore gwine! You ain't never gwine be nothin' but a outlander lessen you pay attention to what yore a-doin'!"

He swallowed his laughter.

But she saw his tight grin. "Somethin' a-ticklin' you real good, ain't it? Well, a-seein' as how you thank all this is real funny, go show that bahr over thar how big you can smile. Maybe you can even git it ter smile back."

The smirk on his face faded immediately. He looked all around but didn't see anything.

Chickadee saw how tightly he held his rifle, and it was her turn to grin. "In the tree."

Sure enough, there in the branches of the oak tree a short distance away was a big black bear. "Aren't we going to shoot it?" Saxon asked. "It knows we're here."

"As much racket as you been a-makin', it'd have ter be deaf not ter know we're here."

The bear moved, and Saxon cocked his rifle.

"Why you gwine shoot it?"

He lowered his rifle. "Wasn't that the reason for this hunting expedition?"

"Naw, we got plenty o' bahr meat at home. I jist wanted ter show you how ter track one."

"But won't it attack us?"

"Nope. Least not right now."

"How do you know that for certain? We could turn around, and it might jump out of that tree, and it might—"

"When a bahr's up in a tree, watch its head. Iffen it don't look at you, it ain't a-comin' down. But iffen it swangs its head around and looks like it's a-countin' how many hairs you got a-hangin' outen yore nose, then you know it's gwine come down after you."

Saxon noticed the bear wasn't paying them the slightest bit of attention. Damn! His first opportunity to take a shot at one of those vicious beasts, and this one had to be unaggressive!

"I know you was a-itchin' ter take a shot at that ole bahr, Saxon," Chickadee said as they returned to the ivy-hedged path. "But she might have babies somewhar. Respect. Ever' plant, stream, rock, and animule here deserves respect. You take what you got ter have, but iffen you take more'n that, one day you ain't gwine have nothin'."

Saxon stopped walking, smiled, and ruffled her hair. When he started to take his hand away, the expression in her eyes told him she liked it and hoped he wouldn't stop. Gently, he slipped his fingers through her tangled mane and kept them there, waiting to see what she would do.

His touch sent a ribbon of heat curling through her—as if he were made of fire. Unbidden, the memory of the one kiss T.J. Howe once gave her came to mind. It had been quick and wet, and her and T.J.'s teeth had clinked together. Would it be that way with Saxon? Probably not. Outlanders did everything differently than mountain folks.

"You ever wonder what it'd be like ter kiss me, Saxon Blackwell?" Quickly she bent her head. She knew she was too blunt. Betty Jane told her that often. But, well, sometimes being bold was the only way to get what you wanted in this world.

Saxon tilted her chin up. "I've wondered, Keely."

A reply eluded her. Dumbstruck, she could only

look at him, her mind whirling with unspoken thoughts, her voice refusing to put sound to them.

But he didn't need to hear them: he could see them. He might not know much about mountain life, but he knew about women, and as he gazed into Chickadee's ever-changing eyes, he realized no matter where or how women lived, most of them had something in common.

Passion.

Some were shy about it, others were quite open. Chickadee was open in many ways, sometimes painfully so. But now, right now, she was timid. This mountain ridge might belong to her, but the invisible aura surrounding them now was *his* dominion, and he knew it well.

He dropped his rifle and slowly pulled her toward him. He saw her swallow and smiled down at her. Tremulously, she smiled back, her slight grin vanishing when she saw his lips descending.

She knew a moment of panic, but some age-old instinct forced her to keep still. Saxon's arms went around her, and once again his touch burned her. His hard chest pressed against her breasts; her nipples hardened. Somewhere, deep within her, a sweet ache began, and of their own accord her arms stole around his waist, her fingers still wrapped around her rifle.

Saxon lowered his mouth to hers. Her inexperience was obvious in the way she kept her lips tightly pursed. He set about correcting that matter immediately. Slowly, gently, his tongue teased her lips open. When they parted, his kiss deepened slightly, and he savored the taste of her. She trembled against him at his unexpected action.

This was nothing like T.J. Howe's kiss. This kiss somehow removed all the bones from her body and left her with nothing but flimsy skin. Indeed, it was an effort to stay standing, and she wondered whether she would fall without Saxon holding her so securely.

Saxon took his time. This was her first real kiss, and he could well remember the feelings that accompanied the first encounter with desire. But as he continued to kiss her, he became a little wobbly-kneed himself. Strange. He liked kissing well enough and most assuredly enjoyed what could follow it, but he'd never reacted this way before. Wanting a stronger dose of the magical essence that could cause such an unusual sensation in him, he deepened the kiss again and enjoyed the warm rush of emotion for a long time before he reluctantly ended it.

But though the kiss was over, the thrill he'd experienced from it remained. He hadn't felt this way over a kiss in years! Maybe it was Chickadee's enthusiasm for life that had affected him, he mused. Her zest was certainly contagious.

He smiled wistfully when he thought about how Desdemona might respond to the cheeky girl in his arms. And his grin split his entire face when he thought of what Araminta's reaction would be.

He stared down into Chickadee's glazed eyes, his own eyes narrowed in sudden excitement. Araminta Blackwell. She undoubtedly had a long list of *suitable-for-marriage* ladies, all refined Boston beauties. Women so completely opposite from Chickadee, that the comparison was absurd.

Absurd? Outmaneuvering Araminta was absurd?

With rising exhilaration, he realized that Araminta had made a grave mistake in her latest scheme. She'd stated nothing in her new will about *whom* he had to marry and had given him leave to choose his own bride.

Chickadee with Araminta. Chickadee with Desdemona.

Chickadee McBride Blackwell.

Saxon's laugh of victory rang out over the smoky blue hills.

Chapter 4

Chickadee pushed him away with all the might she possessed. Saxon, taken off guard, fell to the ground and felt her rifle barrel digging into his chest.

"I know you've kissed girls who kiss back a sight better'n I do, but you ain't got no call ter laugh at me. Say yore sorry, or I'm gwine shoot that smile plumb offen yore face."

Certain she was bluffing, he grinned and reached up to move her gun. A bullet whizzed by his ear.

"Don't thank I'll do it, do you? Say yore sorry."

"I wasn't laughing at you."

"Yore a dang liar. You was—"

"I was laughing at the circumstances. I've never kissed a woman with a wild bear so near by. The thought struck my sense of humor." He pushed her rifle away and got to his feet.

"Well . . . I'm sorry I got so riled. I didn't hurt you none when I pushed you down, did I?"

His eyes flashed blue fire. "Dammit, Keely, I'm a man! A fall to the ground ain't—*isn't* going to injure me!" He stepped so close to her she was forced to bend her head way back to see his face looming above her. "I realize you are the way you are because you've had little contact with other people, but there's one thing about the sexes you need to understand. Men are stronger than women. You're capable in many respects, but *I* am a man, and *you*

57

are a woman. There's a big difference. One you'd do well to remember!''

''I ain't seed you do nothin' I cain't do 'cept write! And you said yoresef I can larn how ter write too. As fur as I can see, thur ain't no difference in a man and a woman but what's betwixt thur legs!''

She flounced away then. Saxon picked up his rifle and stormed after her. His eyes centered on her back, he didn't notice how wildly the laurel thicket was moving. It wasn't until a bear cub meandered out of the brush that he realized the danger.

Though the cub was behind her, Chickadee felt fear replace the marrow in her bones. She whirled to face the little animal, her mind swarming with prayers the bear wouldn't whine. She motioned for Saxon to circle around the cub. ''Don't even look at it,'' she whispered. ''Git around it quick but stay fur away from it.''

But the path was narrow, hedged with the thick ivy. Though he did his best to give the cub a wide berth, it wasn't wide enough to suit the small beast. The cub opened its mouth and called for its mother.

''Lord o' mercy!'' Chickadee ran to Saxon and grabbed his hand. But they ran only a short distance before Saxon stepped into a tangle of vines. He tried to yank his hand out of Chickadee's, but her hold on his wrist was unbreakable. Their fall sent Chickadee's rifle sliding into the thicket beside them. She tried to reach for it, but Saxon lay atop her, preventing her from moving.

''Git offen me!''

The worst sound he ever heard froze him in mid-action. The mother bear came thrashing out of the brush, black eyes shining with fury, huge mouth open wide. Khan bared his teeth and lunged at it, but with one vicious swipe, the bear threw the wolf into the laurel.

Every muscle in his body taut, Saxon knelt, put the stock of his rifle to his shoulder, took aim, and fired. The bear screamed but continued to run toward them. Again he cocked his weapon, sure he'd only wounded the bear, but before he had time to pull the trigger, the monster swayed and then crashed to the ground, its enormous head mere inches from Chickadee's feet.

He stared at it briefly before he remembered Khan. "Khan!" Much to his relief, the wolf came slinking out of the thicket, apparently unharmed.

Chickadee hugged her pet when he came and licked her face. "Whar'd you larn ter shoot like that, Saxon? You got that bahr directly in the heart, and that ain't easy. 'Specially when the bahr's a-runnin'."

"While you may find this hard to believe, you aren't the only person in the world who can handle a gun," he said smugly.

"Don't recollect a-sayin' I was. Jist didn't know a outlander could shoot like that."

With a heavy sigh, he stood and pulled her to her feet. "Are you hurt?"

She started to tell him in no uncertain terms that a little fall to the ground wasn't something that would hurt her when she remembered she'd asked him the same question a short while ago when *he'd* fallen. Suddenly she understood what he'd been trying to tell her.

It was pride that made men different from women. Her own was hurting, and now she realized what Saxon had been going through these past weeks with her.

"Reckon I'm a mite bruised," she lied, rubbing her bottom. Instinct told her that was the right thing to say.

Saxon nearly burst with self-satisfaction. But when he saw the merriment dancing in Chickadee's eyes, his anger returned with a vengeance. "Why don't you reach out and pat me on the head, Keely? That action would certainly complement your patronizing thoughts!"

His abrupt fury confused her. "Dang it, Saxon!

When I do thangs you thank only menfolks can do, it riles you. And when I try and make you feel more like a man, yore still riled! Jist how the hell do you want me ter act? I ain't never tried ter be nobody but who I am, but I'm a-tryin' ter git along with you, and—"

"Just stop patronizing me!"

"I ain't never heared that word in my life, but iffen it riles you when I do it, I'm gwine do it ever' second, ever' minute, ever' day!" She glared at him, her eyes traveling rapidly over his face. "What is *patronizin'*? Reckon I need ter know what it is afore I can do it ter you."

His anger was doused by a sudden stream of amusement, and his laughter echoed as deep as the mountain ravines. When he got control of himself again he saw Chickadee staring at him as if he'd lost his mind. But he felt perfectly sane.

Suddenly, he knew he was going to make the wisp of a girl who stood before him his bride.

Covered with blood from head to toe, Saxon literally tore the shirt from his back and kicked off his boots so frantically they flew into the nearby bushes. His breeches soon followed, and he took a headlong dive into the clean stream. The soap smelled strong, and ordinarily he might have wondered if it would eat through his skin, but at this moment the only thing he could concentrate on was working it into a lather as swiftly as possible.

Chickadee sauntered to the edge of the stream. "Did you lose yore supper?"

He threw her a nasty look and soaped up his hair.

"Reckon you ain't never seen bahr innards afore, have you, outlander? Turn yore stomach, did it?"

Saxon scooped up water and threw it at her. She deftly avoided the shower and laughed at him. "When you have ter shoot somethin', the leastest thang you can do fer it is make use of it. We couldn't leave that bahr thar ter rot, Saxon. Had ter skin it and make it ready ter eat. It's gwine meat us fer a month.''

"I'll never eat bear meat again in my life."

"You'll eat it. Bahr meat don't differ from any other kind o' meat, the way I see it. Yore jist not used ter a-havin' ter skin—''

"Nor will I help you skin anything again, Keely. If you enjoy being up to your elbows in blood and guts, by all means indulge yourself. But I'm not doing that again!'' He scrubbed his arms until they reddened.

"Thought you was a man.'' She backed up and sat on a good-sized rock, waiting for him to rise to her challenge. She was well aware of how her statement would make him feel, but she no longer cared about his pride. He'd made her mad that afternoon, and he wasn't going to get away with it. She still wasn't exactly sure what *patronize* was, but she suspected it had something to do with upsetting his pride.

Saxon glowered at her. "I'm in no mood to argue about my masculinity. If my dislike for skinning a *bahr* makes me less manly in your eyes, so be it. Think exactly what makes you happy.''

She propped her rifle upright and leaned on the stock. "You still got blood on yore cheek.''

Saxon washed his face and promptly got soap in his eyes. "Oh hell! What's in this soap anyway?''

"I ain't much fer soap makin'.''

"I don't give a damn about what you're much for! I asked you what was in this soap!''

"Reckon Betty Jane uses wood ashes and animule fat jist like ever'one else.''

Wonderful. He was cleaning himself with ashes. Belatedly he remembered he still had a bar of bay rum scented soap in his saddlebag. Now he was going to smell like the inside of a fireplace. What the hell else was going to happen to him today? "Do you have a good reason for coming out here to watch me bathe?'' he snarled. "Perhaps you think I might drown?''

"You embarrassed?"

He squeezed the soap so hard it flew out of his hand. As he watched it descend, he knew if he failed to catch it, Chickadee would laugh at him. She was taking great delight in making fun of him, and he knew she was now doing it on purpose.

The soap, as if guided by heaven, landed directly in his palms. He threw her a smug look but was maddened anew when he saw her condescending smirk.

"You ashamed o' yore body, Saxon? Is that why yore allus a-runnin' fer cover when you ain't got no clothes on?"

"I do *not* run for cover!"

"Yes you do."

"No I—" Dammit to hell! Why was he arguing with her? Who cared what she thought anyway? Still, it was just a little too much to bear. "You're not married, and you've had little intimate contact with men, Keely. So how is it you are so well-acquainted with the sight of a nude male?"

She picked up a handful of small pebbles, and one by one threw them his way. "Me and T.J. Howe used ter go a-swimmin' buck-naked. Our mamas never knowed."

"Have you done that recently?"

"Nope. Don't seem right now that I'm growed."

Saxon's eyebrow raised. "What's the matter? Are you ashamed of your body?"

"Nope."

"Then get in here with me."

"Done washed already."

"Who said you had to bathe again?" Saxon, on his knees, started to get to his feet. As he did, he noticed Chickadee looked away. "Are you afraid I'll rape you?"

"Seems we done had this conversation afore."

Saxon settled back into the water. "Yes we have. But I was wounded then, remember? My injuries are healed now."

Chickadee quivered. He was doing it to her again. Making her feel that strange way. Like . . . like she was pining away for something only he had the power to give her.

"Come in with me." He stood, his body completely revealed to her. She jumped from her rock and ran back to the cabin, Saxon's laughter ringing in her ears. "What happened to all your bravado?" he called after her.

As he finished bathing, he thought of his marriage plans again. How was he going to convince Chickadee to become his bride? From what she said about her mother, he realized she believed in that ridiculous fantasy called love. But Saxon had no such beliefs, nor would he pretend he did: Chickadee would see right through him. But dammit, there had to be a way! A way to make her want to be with him.

The feel of her lips on his came to mind. She'd enjoyed that kiss. And her body had told him she wanted more.

He'd seduce her. Saxon knew he was famed for his abilities to entice even the most proper of Boston women into his bed. And women, blue-blooded or mountain-blooded, were all the same.

The way he saw it.

"You look beautiful, Keely."

Chickadee whirled in the middle of the cabin, her mother's skirts wrapping around her legs. "It swallers me."

The dress was too big, but the indigo blue of the homespun cloth was lovely on her, and instead of hiding her shapely form, the gown emphasized her slenderness. Saxon knew every maiden in Boston would be put to shame beside her.

"It's large, but you're still pretty in it."

She stopped spinning. "Y'mean it?"

Saxon sat by the fire. He withdrew a cheroot from the pocket of his shirt and lit it, a blue haze of smoke surrounding him. "Why don't you believe my compliments? Do you think you're ugly?"

"I ain't had many other womenfolks around me ter compare mysef with. But one time I seed this girl with hair so yaller it looked like it was made o' sun. You like girls with yaller hair?" She sat at his feet.

He picked up a lock of her hair. "As a matter of fact, blonds were the only women who attracted me. But I find I'm beginning to prefer redheads."

His warm fingers played in her hair and heated her body. "I like black hair," she said. She snapped for Khan and, as if it were the most important thing in the world to do, she examined her pet's fur, keeping her head low lest Saxon see her flush.

"Ah, so you like my hair. What else do you like?"

She raised her gaze. "I like the smooth way you talk."

She liked the way he talked? He'd thought she was going to tell him how handsome he was! He chuckled at his own conceit. "Let's go to bed." He slid out of his boots and shirt and reached for the fastening of his breeches.

The widening of her eyes stilled his actions. *Go slowly, Sax,* he told himself. *Gain her confidence first. Frighten her and you'll never succeed.*

He left the pants on. "We don't have to sleep together anymore, Keely. I'll make a pallet on the floor."

"Naw. Ain't no need fer that. I reckon iffen you was gwine try somethin' with me, you'd already o' tried it. 'Sides, yore too much of a gentleman ter do that."

Gentleman? Guilt engulfed him. His plan was proof he was no gentleman. "Then shall we?" he asked, sweeping his arm toward the bed.

When they were both in it, he took her hand and brushed it across his mouth. "You know, Keely, I've known scores of women in my lifetime, but never one like you."

She wanted to pull her hand away before she was

burned alive by the fire inside her, but that same fire
welded her hand to his. She found she had neither
the strength nor the inclination to stop his feathery
kisses. "I—I ain't never knowed a man like you neither."

His trail of kisses meandered down to her lower
arm and wrist. "I suppose that gives us something
in common. I wonder what else we have in common?"

Chickadee's eyes fluttered shut. "I . . . don't
know."

"Do you like to dance?"

"Yes," she managed to choke out. "One time me
and T.J. Howe danced to George Franklin's fiddle
music."

Saxon smiled. "And how did T.J. hold you then?"

"By my hands."

"That's not the way I dance."

"How do you do it?"

Again he smiled, glad the dimness of the room
prevented her from seeing his grin. "Well, I hold a
woman in my arms . . . like this." He slid one arm
beneath her and the other over her. "I hold her close
. . . like this." He pulled her toward him until their
bodies touched. "And if I really enjoy being with
the lady, I bend my face to her ear and whisper into
it." Lips to her ear, he murmured, "Like this."

Chickadee trembled from head to toe. Her insides
went from freezing to burning. Ice and fire, both
within her, both too intense. But she wanted to understand.

"Isn't this better than just holding hands?" Saxon
whispered. "Don't hear a fiddle, Keely. Listen to a
symphony. Imagine soft, slow music. Feel how it
wafts into your ears, sweeps through your mind,
and makes your body feel like floating."

His lips met the warm satin of her neck and jour-
neyed to the silken hollow of her throat before they
wandered to her mouth. Her breath, as sweet as the

mountain air, blew over him just before he kissed her.

Her lips were not pursed this time. Her mouth was soft and yielding, and Saxon savored the taste within it. Like a bee in a beautiful blossom, he gently plundered the exquisite nectar he found.

And like a flower invaded by a foraging bee, Chickadee swayed with the weight of the emotions Saxon brought to her. The thought of resisting him never entered her mind; only giving him what he sought mattered. The petals of her pristine passion unfurled languidly.

Saxon did not accept her gift. She was not ready for more than a kiss, and he would give her no more. But remembering how easily she took offense, he ended the encounter as smoothly as possible. "So sweet," he whispered, his lips still touching hers. "Would that I could kiss you until dawn creeps into our private haven."

"What?"

"I would like nothing better than to kiss you until morning. All night, my lips on yours, my arms around you. I can think of no pleasure more desirable."

If his touch inflamed her, his sentiments set her ablaze. Never had she heard such sweet-sounding words, and oh, how she yearned to hear more.

He did not disappoint her. "There are no forests in all the land that rival the verdant green of your eyes, my little mountain girl. In them I see gems far brighter than the most exquisite emeralds. I watch your spirit dance and see the happiness of your soul frolic within the crystalline depths of those magic orbs, and I wish for you to always remain happy. May you forever be the way you are, Keely McBride. Special."

He had no difficulty whatsoever thinking of what to say. Though he was extravagantly seducing the girl who lay quietly in his arms, he meant everything he told her. And he wanted to tell her more.

"While I traveled up to your mountain, I saw a deer. I'd never seen anything so perfectly harmonious with nature, until I met you. Your smoothness of form never fails to enchant me. The suppleness of your body is not unlike that of the young deer. When you move, I hear no sound, but see only nimble poise. Though you've had no training in the arts of elegance, each of your actions is executed with grace."

She struggled to understand him, but he was using so many words she'd never heard before. Nevertheless, the sound of his voice assured her he was still complimenting her. And the way she saw it, one good turn deserved another.

"You ain't so awkward yoresef, Saxon. I got ter admit, I was right proud when you larnt how ter traipse through the woods real quiet-like. You done real good, y'know. And when you brung down that bahr this afternoon, I was powerful surprised. You shoot near about as good as me."

"Coming from you, that's quite a compliment. I appreciate your respect."

"And you kiss a sight better'n T.J. Howe. Y'know? I wouldn't mind a-kissin' you all night long neither."

"I imagine we'd both fall asleep before we could accomplish that feat."

"We could try it though."

Once again, he gathered her into his arms. "Yes, Keely. We certainly could at that."

When Saxon awoke, she was gone. He thought nothing of her absence until he heard a growl coming from the yard. He flew from the bed, grabbed his rifle, and ran outside.

There sat Chickadee, Khan, and a bear cub beside her. "What's that beast doing here?" he asked.

She withdrew some blackberries from the basket at her feet. The cub gobbled them greedily. "This here little bahr's a orphan. It was his mama you kilt yesterday. She woulda tuk keer o' him, so I reckon it's our duty ter do the same. Jist till it's a mite bigger."

He eyed the bear warily. "It won't be staying in the cabin with us, will it?"

She giggled. "Law, yore somethin' else, Saxon. Who ever heared of a bahr a-livin' in a cabin?"

He'd never heard of a wolf living in a cabin either, but Chickadee was obviously unable to understand the similarity. "But what if you tame it so completely it never wants to leave?"

"I ain't gwine do that. Ever'thang's got its place, and it's got ter stay thar. What's wild has ter stay wild. Iffen this cub don't want ter leave when it's time, I'll have ter be mean ter it. Hurt its feelin's by a-flangin' sticks and a-screamin' at it. I won't like a-doin' that, but sometimes it's the onliest way. It's got ter stay wild."

"Yet you have Khan. A wild wolf."

"He's free ter go. Jist don't want ter, is all. I tried ter set him free once, but he come back. He was already half tamed when that trapper brung him, though."

"He rarely leaves your side, does he?"

"Hardly never. Whar I go, he goes."

A Canadian wolf in Boston, Saxon mused. Well, Araminta would have a house pet. The thought made him smile.

"What are you a-grinnin' at?"

"Uh . . . I'm smiling about last night. Who fell asleep first?"

Chickadee hid her blush in the cub's neck. "You did." Saxon had slept in her arms, she recalled. And while he'd slept, she'd rained kisses all over his face and told him how handsome she thought he was. She'd spent nearly the whole night trying to understand what it was she felt for the outlander in her bed.

When morning came, she still had no answers.

"How'd you like ter go ter me and Khan's special

place? Takes a while ter git up thar, but you ain't never seed a purtier place, Saxon. We could take us some lunch iffen you want. Ain't got nothin' better ter do. Sound good ter you?''

He nodded. ''Let's ride. Mounted, it wouldn't take us as long to get there.''

Chickadee stood and brushed off her breeches. ''No, don't reckon it would. But I ain't gwine ride no horse.''

Saxon frowned. ''Why not?''

''I—I don't like the way they smell. They stank.''

''Stink? You can split open a bear's entrails yet shy away from the scent of horseflesh?'' He stepped off the porch and went to meet her in the yard. When he reached her he took her shoulders. ''Come now, Keely. The truth is you're afraid of horses, aren't you?''

She snatched his hands away. ''Ain't afeared o' nothin'! 'Specially no stupid horse!''

''Hagen is gentle as a lamb.''

''Hagen?''

''Copenhagen, my horse. All you have to do is sit in front of me. I promise I won't let you fall off.''

''Done tole you I ain't gwine ride no horse!''

Smugly, Saxon folded his arms across his chest. ''So there's a streak of cowardice in you after all. I knew if I looked for it long enough, I'd find it.''

''Coward?'' she yelled, her hands on her hips. ''I brung that dang horse up here, didn't I? I ain't no coward!''

With a sweep of his head, Saxon pointed to Copenhagen. ''Prove it then.''

She looked at Hagen, who was munching contentedly on a patch of fresh grass. ''Said we'd take lunch. Reckon I better git that together first.''

''Making excuses?'' Saxon asked as she disappeared into the cabin.

''Shet up!''

* * *

''No, Keely,'' he said when she went to the right side of Hagen. ''You always mount from the left side.''

She stepped back, certain she'd already irritated Hagen with her mistake. ''Didn't know horses knowed thur right from thur left.''

''They don't, but—'' Saxon bent his head and snickered. ''Just come over to this side.''

She did as requested and stared uneasily at the stirrup. ''Well, ain't you gwine give me a leg up?''

''Get up yourself.'' He handed her the reins.

Hagen, sensing Chickadee's inexperience and nervousness, promptly took advantage of the situation and began to paw the ground and chomp at the bit.

''He's a-tryin' ter kick me!'' Chickadee squealed, jumping away from Hagen. She threw the reins back at Saxon.

''He's not trying to kick you. He's merely anxious to be on his way. It's been a while since he's been ridden, and he's restless.''

''Why don't we jist go afoot?''

''Fraidycat.''

Her green eyes were afire with indignation. ''I ain't no fraidycat!''

''Then get on that horse!''

''That's easy fer you ter say. You been a-ridin' since you was little. I ain't never been on a horse in my life!''

''And I'd never been on a bear hunt in mine. Nor had I shot or skinned one until yesterday. But I did those things, Keely. I may have been awkward doing them, but I did them.'' Once again, he held out the reins.

With trembling fingers, she took them. ''All right, Hagen. You and me's gwine ride. I ain't much fer ridin', but yore uppity master here's got a lesson ter larn about Chickadee McBride.''

Her face set in grim lines of determination, she reached up and took fast hold of Hagen's flowing mane, tugging on it to make sure it wouldn't come out when she hauled herself up. Satisfied it wouldn't, she pulled her foot up to the stirrup and mounted.

She wasn't as graceful as she usually was, but Saxon was pleased with her attempt. And he started to tell her so when she yelped once and promptly fell off the other side.

He couldn't control himself. He knew he shouldn't laugh, but Chickadee McBride bested . . . well; it was something he never thought he'd see.

"Iffen I could git up, I'd shoot you, Saxon. And when I'd done that, I'd shoot that stupid animule next!"

He bent and looked under Hagen's belly, Chickadee still on the ground on the other side. "Get up and get back on," he told her merrily.

"No."

"Get up."

"I said no!"

Saxon walked around Hagen and yanked her to her feet. "You're going to ride this horse, and you're going to do it right now."

"Really? Who's gwine make me?"

Saxon smiled a lazy, mocking grin. Without a word, he went behind her, slipped his arms beneath hers, and began to carry her around Hagen.

He'd only taken a few steps when she squirmed to the ground, curled her arms over his shoulders, and threw him over her back. When he was laid out flat, she twisted one of his arms behind him. "I said I ain't gwine ride that animule, and I ain't gwine ride it."

He struggled, but couldn't move without causing extreme pain to his arm. "Dammit, Keely! Don't you want to learn new things? You weren't born knowing how to shoot. And you didn't come into this world knowing how to throw grown men to the ground either. You had to practice those things. It's the same thing with learning to ride! Now, if you don't want me to lose my ever-growing respect for you, get on that horse and ride him!''

She saw his eyes were sparkling with anger. For many moments she stared into them, her own eyes glittering defiantly as she silently dared him to break the hostile silence.

"Well?" he finally asked. "Are you brave or aren't you? Where's that stalwart spirit that so intrigues me?"

She mumbled something Saxon assumed was a curse and staggered to her feet. Hagen turned his head to look at her, long blades of grass hanging from his mouth. "Thank that was real funny what you did to me, don't you, you sorry excuse fer a ridin' critter!"

"He didn't do that to you. You fell off all by yourself. When you get in the saddle, find your balance. Don't lean so far over the other side."

"Why don't it got some kind o' handle on it? 'Pears to me it'd be a sight easier ter git on and stay on iffen thur was somethin' ter hang on ter."

"There are saddles that have large pommels, but this one is not that kind."

"I don't know what a pommel is, but y'know, iffen a feller was ter invent a saddle with a handle on it, I bet—"

"Stop stalling and get on."

She snatched the reins from him, stuck her tongue out, and turned toward Hagen. She mounted as she had before and when seated, she took a handful of Hagen's mane and squeezed hard. "All right, Saxon. I'm on. Now nice and easy-like, you git on too."

"No."

A yell rose in her throat, but she squelched it, knowing a sudden shout would startle Hagen. Between clenched teeth, she hissed, "Iffen you don't git on, I'm a-gittin' off. And when I do, I'm a-gittin' my shootin'-arn and—"

"Ride him. Take him for a short, slow walk

around the yard. I swear nothing will happen to you. Just press in with your knees, and he'll go."

"Not withouten you."

"I hate to do this to you, Miss McBride, but you've given me no choice." Smartly, he slapped Hagen's rump. The horse jumped slightly and then ambled into the yard, still chewing his mouthful of grass.

Chickadee closed her eyes and laid low over his neck. "Lord o' mercy, Saxon, please hep me! Come and git him afore he lits out a-runnin' with me on him!"

Nonchalantly, Saxon took a seat on the porch step.

"Saxon, you worthless cuss! Dang you, he's a-settin' in ter git all fidgety!"

"If he were any more relaxed, he'd be dead. Sit up straight and get the feel of his gait."

She continued to cling to Hagen's neck.

"If you don't do as I say, I'll come slap him again. And then you'll really know what it's like when he's fidgety."

She sat bolt upright.

Saxon stifled his laughter. "Now, take one rein in each hand. It should go through your pointing finger and your middle finger, the rest of it lying inside your palm. Use your thumb to keep a good grip on it."

She tried to do as he instructed but soon gave up and held the reins in balled fists. "He ain't gwine mind iffen I hold these here strangs like this, is he? I cain't do it the other way."

"Very well, we'll practice that later. Now, when you want him to go to the right, pull gently on the right rein."

She pulled it, her arm straight out before her and moving sideways to the right.

"No, Keely. Keep your elbow close to your body. You've got too much slack in the reins. Tighten them up."

Every curse she knew filled her mouth, but not a one escaped. She was going to ride this dumb horse and show Saxon she was no coward. As he said, she tightened up the reins, kept her arm close to her torso, and pulled the strap of leather.

Hagen turned to the right.

"Don't reckon no coward could ride like this, Saxon." Tentatively she pulled on the left rein, and Hagen responded to her command.

Again, admiration filled Saxon. He doubted there was anything in the world that beautiful mountain girl couldn't do. She could be nervous about things, but she conquered that uneasiness and faced the task at hand as her people before her did. Her ancestors had been confronted with many hardships in carving out a life in these mountains, but they'd endured it all with undaunted mettle. Yes, the blood of a greathearted people flowed through Chickadee's veins.

Boston didn't stand a chance.

Chapter 5

The trip to Chickadee's special place took two hours, even on horseback. But when they arrived their efforts were amply rewarded. Chickadee's hideaway was truly paradise. As Saxon gazed out at the rich, turquoise-green beauty of the Blue Ridge, he suspected he could touch the sky, it was so close. The cool air filled him with an unfamiliar euphoria as if it were laden with some magical property.

Chickadee saw his pleasure. "Ain't it purty?"

"I never knew such beauty existed. Why don't you live up here instead of down in your little cove?"

She sighed. "We're a-trespassin'. The man who owns this spot's got his ass on his shoulders. Lareny Lester's his name. He lives in Lenoir. Techous is what he is."

"Techous?"

"He gits riled easy and quick."

Saxon went to sit on a flat rock. "What does he do with this land?"

"Nothin' as fur as I noticed." She sat beside him. "Reckon he jist likes a-ownin' it. But he don't even let folks up here. I'm a-tellin' you, Saxon, he's so tight with ever'thang he's got, when he grins his pecker skins back."

Saxon threw his head back and laughed, wonder-

75

ing if Chickadee would describe Araminta as eloquently.

"One time me and Khan come up here, and ole Lareny was already here? Well, he seed us and near about falled offen the mountain a-trying' ter chase us away. And I mean ter tell you, he was a-blastin' away somethin' fierce with that ole shootin'-arn o' his. Tole us iffen he ever seed us up here agin, he was gwine have us throwed in jail."

"Yet you and Khan come up here anyway."

"Cain't stay away. I love this place, Saxon. I feel good when I come here. Reckon iffen I *did* have any money, I'd use it ter try and buy this place from Lareny. Not that he'd sell it, but I'd try. And iffen it was mine, I'd build mysef a cabin and live here till the day I died. Ever'body's got dreams, y'know. That's mine."

When they finished their picnic, Saxon lay back and folded his arms under his head, unaware he was scowling.

"You got that troubled look on yore face agin. I brung you up here ter git some heartease."

Saxon almost laughed. He'd been thinking about Araminta. One thought of her erased anything remotely related to heartease. "Sorry. I guess I'm just lost in thought."

She mistook the emotion in his voice for homesickness. "You must be a-missin' Desdemona. But cain't she git along withouten you? She's got yore granny thar, don't she?"

"Yes," he snapped. *But Grandmother hates her grandchildren,* he explained silently. Familiar, bitter feelings erupted inside him as the years fell away and he was a little boy again. His heart pounded with the pain that would never go away.

He forced a smile, took one of Chickadee's curls, and brushed it across his nose. It smelled of fresh air, of woods and mountains, so very unlike those potent, cloying perfumes the Boston maidens wore.

Its soothing scent imperceptibly calmed his hammering heart.

But Chickadee saw the way the stormy midnight blue of his eyes faded to soft, peaceful azure. She wondered about that odd fear and pain she sensed in him. Puzzle pieces floated around in her mind, a few of them finally connecting.

Saxon always changed when he spoke of his grandmother. His memories of that woman hurt him. What in the world had happened to him? "What's Desdemona like?" she asked, hoping information about his sister would reveal more.

"She's lovely but . . . totally silent. No one knows what to do with her, so—well," he said guiltily, "she spends most of her time alone. I believe she prefers it that way because she never looks for anyone. She never really does anything but sit and stare into empty space."

"Why don't she talk?"

He sighed heavily. "No one knows. The doctors can't find anything wrong with her."

"Thank it's in her mind then?"

"More than likely."

Compassion for the girl she'd never met filled Chickadee. Desdemona didn't talk; Saxon was tormented. Sweet Lord in heaven, what had happened to them?

"Maybe Desdemona's a-pinin' away fer heartease. And since she don't talk, she cain't ask fer the comp'ny and affection she needs. Thur ain't no medicine like love, Saxon."

He scoffed silently at her fantasy about love. Love had nothing to do with anything. It would be Chickadee's outrageous enthusiasm that might possibly get through to Desdemona. "I wish she knew you," he said slyly. "I bet *you'd* be able to make her smile."

"She don't smile neither?"

"Never."

"Law, I ain't never knowed nobody who didn't never smile.'Cept ole Misery and Lareny Lester."

He cupped her cheek in his hand. ''Perhaps when you're doing all the traveling you want to do, you'll come to Boston and meet Desdemona.''

His hand was so warm. Warmer than sunshine. ''Ever up that way, yore house is the first place I'll stop. But Boston ain't real close, is it?''

He turned over onto his belly and kissed the tip of her nose. ''It's far away, Keely. And right now, I can't imagine being so far away from you.''

His eyes, as they gazed down at her, were bluer than any blue thing she'd ever seen. His hair, wavy and soft, was as black as mountain coal. And his lips—oh, what things they could make her feel with their sweet words and kisses. She reached for him, and when his lips met hers, no thrill she'd ever had could compare with her wild surge of happiness. Kissing Saxon was a good thing. Nothing that caused this kind of pleasure could be wrong.

And it was the sort of bliss she knew she'd miss sorely when he was gone. Sudden sadness replaced her delight. ''Saxon, I don't want you ter go.''

''My life is in Boston, little one.''

His plan was working, he realized. She was getting used to having him with her. It was time to start making sure she couldn't live without him.

Again, he pressed his mouth to hers and smiled when she wrapped her arms around him. Ever so slowly, his hand crept down her shoulder and edged her breast. It was firm yet soft in his palm. Gently, he kneaded it.

''Saxon—''

''Shhh.'' A deeper kiss quieted her.

She began to take his hand away, but when he circled his palm upon her breast, that yearning made her middle sink again. Faintly, she heard the rustling of the trees as the breeze blew through them, and from somewhere a bobwhite was calling.

But nothing, no sound was more beautiful than the song Saxon's body sang to hers.

Her hand, instead of moving his away, tightened

on his fingers. And when his kiss deepened further, her low moan filled his mouth. She didn't resist when he unbuttoned her shirt and cupped her bare breast.

Reverently, Saxon held the silken globe. When the dusky crest hardened beneath his hand, he moved his lips to it, his actions eliciting another moan from Chickadee. Slowly, his tongue flickered over the rigid peak, and when Chickadee began to ease her body closer to his, he took her into his arms and rolled onto his back.

Her hair was like a shower of autumn leaves falling all around him. Gently, she blushed, her tawny skin becoming an apricot rose hue. Her eyes, like twin patches of the richest grass amid a field of warm earth, smiled down at him, the shine they held lighting his own.

While she lay atop him, he removed her shirt completely. Her shoulders felt and looked like rich cream, yet no expensive oils had ever been smoothed into them. No luxury had ever been Chickadee's, yet her very simplicity spoke of sumptuous elegance.

He pressed his face into the warm valley between her breasts, his hands curled around their outer sides. "Keely, you are the most beautiful woman I have ever known. And no matter where I go, I'll never find another girl as lovely."

He thought about how many times he'd said those same things to other women. He'd never meant them before, but he did now.

Chickadee warmed with pleasure. That this outlander—this impossibly handsome man—would say such flattering things and mean them, was something she'd never dreamed would happen.

She squirmed downward and rested her chin on his chest. "You say the nicest thangs, Saxon. You must have strangs o' girls back in that Boston city. I bet they line up a-wantin' you ter say them thangs to 'em.''

"I've no one special waiting for me in Boston, and after knowing you, I can't think of a single girl there with whom I'd like to be doing this."

"You like a-kissin' me?"

"I do." He could have sworn he heard her purr.

"Y'know. I used ter thank this was wrong. Mama never tole me nothin' about menfolks, but . . . Saxon, this ain't wrong. Whilst you kissed me a minute ago, I was a-thankin' on how right it was. It didn't hurt nobody a'tall."

Slowly, as he'd done with her, she unfastened the buttons of his shirt. When his bare chest was revealed, she bent and took one of his nipples into her mouth, her tongue imitating his earlier actions.

Saxon closed his eyes. Desire, hot and demanding, stabbed into him. How he wanted her! How the hell had this happened? Wasn't *he* the one who was supposed to be in control of this game of seduction? It was *his* plan, yet Chickadee, at this moment, was holding all the cards.

And it wasn't only that, but guilt was beginning to twist through him too. He'd never had a second thought about what he did to women, but now . . . "Keely, wait."

Her eyes met his, but her lips stayed on his nipple.

He sat up and pulled her into his lap. "Do you know what's happening between us? What this is leading up to?"

She pulled at the slight matting of hair on his chest. "It don't have ter go no further than what we let it go."

"But Keely—"

"How fur do you want it ter go?"

He frowned. That was supposed to have been *his* question. And when he asked it, she was supposed to tell him she wanted to make love. He'd have done as she requested and made her want more. She'd have married him and gone on to Boston. The scheme had been simple, and it should have been easy to accomplish.

So why was he so hesitant to see it through?

His hands went to her cheeks. "Why do you even have to ask me that? Don't you *know* the answer?"

She nodded.

"Keely," he began, and swallowed whatever was lodged in his throat. "I . . . you . . . What do *you* want?"

She took his hands and held them tenderly in her lap. "Saxon, I don't really know what I want. All's I can tell you is when you look at me in that special way, when you smile at me or touch or kiss me, I git a powerful hankerin' fer somethin' I don't understand."

She pressed his hand into her belly. "It sets in right here. It's a warm feelin', like thur was a spark in thar, but then it gits bigger and hotter, and soon it's like a far a-blazin' all through me. I ain't rightly shore what it is, but I got a feelin' you do."

"I do know what it is. But I—" *Some womanizer you are, Sax,* he told himself. *You've got her right where you want her, and you can't make yourself take her.*

"I trust you, Saxon. Jist like you confidenced in me when I tuk you a-huntin' fer that bahr. You knowed I warn't gwine let nothin' bad happen, and I know the same thang about you right now. Iffen you know what it is I'm a-honin' fer, I'll trust you whilst you give it to me. Well, Saxon? Are you gwine do what both you and me want you ter do?"

"It's not as simple as that, little one. I don't want to hurt you, and—"

"It's gwine hurt?"

He couldn't look at her. He bent his head and watched her lace her fingers through his. "Yes, your first time will hurt, but that's not what I was talking about."

"Iffen it hurts, why do people do it?"

"It doesn't hurt the man. Only the woman."

She pondered that. "Well, that ain't fair a'tall. Menfolks a-gittin' thur jollies, and women—"

"It's only the first time, Keely. After that, it doesn't hurt anymore. You know so much, yet you know so little. How can I explain the way of things to you?" He laid her down in his arms, much as he would hold a baby. "You don't really know anything about lovemaking, do you?"

"Tole you I seed animules—"

"It's not the same thing. Animals do it to procreate, and emotions aren't involved. With people, feelings are—"

"I know those feelin's. I'm a-havin' 'em right now."

Again, he turned his eyes away from her and looked up to watch a cloud sail by. Ordinarily, he was little better than one of those animals. Emotion never entered into his lovemaking.

And it didn't now either, dammit! His whole future was at stake, and nothing else mattered. Without Chickadee, there would be no outwitting Araminta, and Desdemona would never learn to smile. And since he had no intention of marrying anyone other than Chickadee, his inheritance was in jeopardy too. Everything depended on making her his wife.

His eyes narrowed in resolution as his hand swept to the fastening of her breeches. This had to be done; he'd do it quickly and think no more about it. He still avoided her eyes as he went about his task, something inside him not wanting to see the innocent trust he knew was in them, and when the buttons were undone, he slipped his hand inside.

She fell back over his arm, her hair cascading to the ground. As his hand dipped lower, the fire she'd spoken of began to consume her. Instinctively, she arched her hips while she clung to his neck, and when his fingers sought and found her most secret place, the age-old beat of passion caused her to move rhythmically against his warm palm.

Saxon ignored the nagging voice of his conscience and laid her down on the mountain floor. With one smooth action, he slid her breeches over her hips and down her legs. He then removed his own clothing and, careful to elude her trusting gaze, he rolled atop her.

He didn't want to see her body, couldn't look at her face, and prayed she wouldn't speak. He wanted no reminders of who this was lying beneath him, guileless, unsullied. He prepared to do what he knew he had to do. He spread her legs with his own, the saber of his manhood soon finding the opening of the velvet sheath he would claim.

Chickadee tensed, and when she did, she felt him do the same. "Saxon," she said softly, "make it nice ter me. I know it's gwine hurt, but whilst yer a-doin' it, could you tell me more o' them thangs I like ter hear? Maybe iffen I was a-listenin' to 'em, this wouldn't hurt as much."

He groaned. Dammit, why couldn't she be quiet for once in her life? And why did her voice have to be soft as summer rain?

"Saxon?"

He entered her slightly. Not far enough to cause her the pain she was worried about, but far enough for her to understand what he was going to do. Taking a deep breath, he pressed his lips to her ear. "Keely, relax. Open to me and remember how beautiful, how very special I think you are. Let your feelings go, and enjoy them."

She nodded and then trembled, her breathing irregular. Saxon's heart skipped a few beats. She was afraid, yet she had all the faith in the world in him.

He slipped to the ground and stared at the sky.

"Saxon? Is thur somethin' wrong? Warn't I a-doin' it right? I don't know much about sweetheartin', but I'll do whatever you tell—"

"I've got a headache."

* * *

Chickadee filled the cup and set the flask back down on the bedside table. "Drank it. It's fer yore headache."

Saxon took the cup and drained it. He wanted the whiskey more than whatever else was mixed in with it. Dammit to hell! What else *was* in it? His whole body shuddered as he swallowed.

"Yaller root's bitter, but thur ain't nothin' like it fer aches. Cherry bark tastes a sight better, but I'm plumb outen that. I'll make you a cold pack o' catnip leaves ter set on yore head too. You can stay on the bed and rest."

"Couldn't I just have plain whiskey?"

"It's the yarbs that chase away the headache. The whiskey's only part o' the tonic."

He ran his hand through his hair. "Just give me a cup of pure whiskey. Better yet, give me the whole jug."

"You a drankin' man?" She handed him the liquor jug.

He uncorked it and took a long swallow. It burned all the way down, but he didn't care. "I am now." He took another taste, wiped his mouth with the back of his hand, and looked up at her. "This kind of whiskey is illegal. Did you make it?"

"Naw, I ain't got time fer thangs like that. George Franklin's got him a likker farm. It's hid real good though. Them fed'ral people's been up here lots o' times a-lookin' fer George Franklin's stills, but they ain't never found 'em. You ain't gwine tell on him, are you?"

"No. The way I feel right now, I may just go help him make more." He was beginning to feel numb.

"Thur ain't no bad likker, Saxon. Some's good, some's better. But you got ter be real keerful with that though. It sneaks up on you. One minute yore a-feelin' good, and the next minute yore laid out on the floor."

Unconsciousness. That sounded just fine to him.

"Real strange how that headache come on so fast.

Lay and rest or it's gwine git worser.'' She pushed him into the feather mattress. ''I'll lay down with you.''

''No!'' He jerked out of bed and swayed. Tucking the jug of whiskey beneath his arm, he stepped outside. After sitting awhile on the porch step, he drank more of the corn liquor. It was easier to swallow the potent fluid now.

''Go back in the cabin, Keely,'' he ordered when she joined him.

''But—''

''Do as I say!''

She sat on the other end of the porch step. ''You don't want ter be with me no more, huh? You think I'm a bad-un, don't you? What we almost done today . . . It *was* wrong, warn't it, Saxon?''

He didn't answer. Instead, he lifted the jug to his mouth, and once again drank deeply.

''I'm sorry,'' she murmured. ''I shouldn'ta let thangs go as fur as they did. But thur warn't no way I could hep it. I didn't have no control over—''

''I don't want to talk about it anymore.'' She was in no way to blame for what had happened that afternoon. *He'd* been in control of every feeling she'd felt.

Chickadee watched him carefully. ''You didn't have no dang-blasted headache today, did you?''

''No, but I suspect I'll have one in the morning.'' He staggered into the yard. ''That is if this whiskey doesn't kill me before then.''

She watched him lurch down the path and felt her eyes sting. Angrily, she swiped at her tears and snapped for her wolf. ''He's contrary tonight, Khan, and it'll ill him more iffen I go with him. He'll be gone fer good soon, boy, but he's still here now, so stay with him.''

Saxon didn't know what was worse. The dirt in his mouth, or Khan's breath blowing in his face. Khan? Dirt? Daylight? Where the hell was he? Damn, how his head pounded! He wondered how he could get to the stream he heard behind him without moving.

"Khan, do me a favor." The wolf gave no indication he'd even heard the request. Nevertheless, Saxon continued. "Get hold of the collar of my shirt. You can do it, boy. Drag me to that water, and I promise I'll pay you back."

Khan's eyes closed to mere slits.

Despite the way he felt, Saxon managed to grin. If his friends could see him now—Lord, how they'd love this. Saxon Blackwell, face in the dirt, bargaining with a wolf. And all because of some freckled slip of a girl.

Groaning, he got to his hands and knees and crawled toward the stream. Stones bruised his knees, but no pain on earth could feel as bad as the pounding in his head.

Except maybe a rattlesnake bite.

The serpent lay curled up only inches away from his hand, its tail clattering. Saxon's eyes widened, but he remained absolutely still. Khan, however, rose and, head lowered, crept toward the agitated reptile.

"Khan," he whispered, "go get Keely."

If Khan understood, he didn't obey. He continued to slink toward the snake, his huge teeth bared. When he was a scant foot away, the rattler struck out at Saxon.

But Khan was faster. Just as the serpent stretched out its body, the wolf lunged and grabbed it behind its head. With sharp, vicious movements he shook the snake, the rattler's body swinging so fast it was nothing but a grayish-brown blur.

Saxon scrambled to his feet and took a few steps backward. As he did, he heard more soft clicking. Turning around, he saw another rattlesnake, this one bigger than the first. It too was curled up, ready to strike, and again he froze.

But an explosion of gunfire made him jump. His

eyes never leaving the snake, he watched it writhe and die.

"Reckon iffen thur's trouble ter be found, you'll find it, Saxon Blackwell." Chickadee lowered her rifle and ambled toward him. "Enjoy yore night outside?"

Saxon glanced at Khan and saw that the first snake was little more than bloody pulp. On shaky legs, he finally made his way to the stream, thankful it was so cold. "Save the sarcasm, Keely."

"Somebody's a-fixin' ter git married."

Saxon tried to bring her into proper focus. Had he mentioned marriage to her last night?

"Them snakes is a omen, outlander. When you see two snakes at once it's a sign that somebody's a-fixin' ter step offen the carpet." She waded in after him and put a flask in his hand. "Got this from Betty Jane this mornin'."

"More moonshine?" He turned chartreuse.

"Whiskey's the best cure thur is fer what's ailin' you, but no, thur ain't no likker in that. That's—"

"Never mind. Don't tell me." He drank it all. It turned his mouth inside out, as he had known it would.

"Come on back to the cabin, Saxon. Lunch is ready, and I reckon you could use somethin' in yore stomach."

"What happened to breakfast?"

"Et that hours ago. I come out here ter git you, but you wouldn't move nary a muscle. I tole you ter be keerful with that likker. It's so strong you can near about taste George Franklin's feet in it. He hoed the corn, y'know."

Saxon grimaced. "Don't tell me anything else about that rotgut. The mere mention of it makes me sick." As proof of his words the world began to spin, and the last thing he saw were Chickadee's arms as they reached out to catch him.

* * *

"If you say one word about what happened to me, I'll cheerfully wring your neck, Keely." Saxon had just awakened. He realized he'd passed out again, but even worse, he knew without a doubt she'd carried him from the stream to her bed. Plus, he was naked as the day he was born.

"Warn't gwine say nothin' about nothin'." She sat on the bearskin rug, shredding oak sticks into thin ribbons. "Ain't gwine do nothin' but set here a-broom-makin'. Ole broom weared out. Hate that it weared out too. A new broom sweeps clean, but the ole one knows whar the dirt is."

Lulled by her soft voice, he closed his eyes again. "What did you make for lunch?"

"That's breakfast a-simmerin'."

"But you said—"

"That was yesterday's lunch. You slept all day yesterday and clear through the night too. Now it's breakfast agin."

He rolled his eyes. Moonshine. Mountain poison. Well, Chickadee had warned him, and he hadn't listened. He got out of bed and noticed she didn't look away from his nude form. Boldly, her eyes made a thorough sweep down his body.

Chickadee knew she was staring, but the sight of him tantalized her. While he'd slept, she'd watched him, memorizing every line and shadow of his sculpted features, finally admitting to herself she wanted him in a way she'd never want any other man.

Saxon made her feel special. His touch, his words, and his sweet, mocking smile had awakened emotions in her she hadn't known existed. He made her feel like a woman, and that was something she'd never cared a whit about. But there was more to being a woman than taking pleasure in a man's flattery and courtesies.

There was making love.

And yesterday she had her first real taste of what *that* aspect of womanhood was like. Had it and wanted more. Saxon would be leaving soon, but before he did, she was determined he make her a woman. A complete woman in every way. And she'd live on the memories of their lovemaking for the rest of her life.

Surely there was a way to make those memories happen.

That in mind, she continued to inspect his sinewy body. "Reckon yore a-needin' ter visit the outhouse, huh?"

He grinned boyishly and felt her eyes on him as he walked toward the door.

"Gwine out thar buck-naked, Saxon?"

"Who's going to see me?" Once outside, he stretched languorously and took in a couple of deep breaths. After his trip to the outhouse, he started back toward the cabin.

Chickadee had eyed him with undisguised longing a few minutes ago. He'd seen that smoldering look many times before and knew bedding her would present no problem at all.

But just as he had yesterday, he hesitated. *You're getting soft, Sax*, he berated himself. *Her emotions are like strings in your fingers, and you've only to pull them. She doesn't mean a damn thing to you. Do it, Sax. You're a master at this. Bend her, take her, make her yours.*

But what of her feelings? Could he take advantage of a girl as trusting and innocent as she? Would he be able to go through with it this time?

"Mighty fine mornin', ain't it?" someone suddenly asked.

He whirled. There on a stump sat George Franklin. "Heared tell you got yore first good taste o' corn likker, Saxon. I been a-farmin' whiskey in these here hills fer many a year, but I ain't never knowed a feller who tuk near about two days ter come outen what it done ter him."

He didn't know whether to run into the cabin and grab his breeches or act as if he owned the world and had every right to wander around naked in it.

George Franklin smiled a toothless grin, looked down at the tanned hide in his wrinkled hands, and picked up a block of smooth, carved wood. "A-makin' Chickadee some shoes," he explained, wrapping the soft hide around the wood. "This here's a last." He held up the block of wood that resembled the shape of a foot. Saxon shuffled in the dirt and quite casually clasped his hands together and let them fall to his groin.

"Chickadee could take 'em or leave 'em though," George Franklin went on. "Says shoes ain't nothin' but agger-pervokin' foot cages. But the thang is, she cain't never mem'ry ter put her right foot in the right shoe and her left foot in the left shoe. I done tole that girl the shoes'll form to the shape of her foot, but she cain't never mem'ry. Sometimes women's jist like that, I reckon. Couldn't git along withouten ole Betty Jane or Chickadee neither, but comes times when I wonder iffen women shouldn't stay in two places. On thur feet in the kitchen or on thur backs in the featherbed."

Saxon nodded helplessly.

George Franklin smiled and swatted a bee away. "Womenfolks need a firm hand, the way I see it, son. I let ole Betty Jane git away with some thangs, but thur comes a time when a man's got ter show them contrary females who's boss. Some menfolks ain't agin a-slappin' 'em ever' now and then, y'know. I ain't never slapped one, but comes a time when they need ter be larnt whar thur place is, one way or another.

"Anyhow, like I was a-sayin'," he continued, "it gits cold enough up here ter freeze the stank offen shit, and Chickadee's gwine wear these here shoes."

"Uh . . . would you please excuse me, Mr. Beasley?" He backed up toward the porch step and reached it before he realized he had. He knew immediately he was going to fall, but not for the world would he move his hands from their spot to save himself from tumbling. He fell to his backside first and then, much to his red-faced dismay, slipped off the porch step altogether, his hands still tightly clutching his manhood.

George Franklin leaned on his knees and scratched his nose. "Saxon, tell you what, son. I ain't gwine say nothin' about you a-runnin' around here a-showin' to God yore ass and ever'thang else. We don't do much o' that up here, but maybe you-uns do in that Boston city. Iffen that's how you git yore jollies, have at it, and with my blessin'. But that thar porch step? Rickety's what it is and near about as old as these here hills. Now, iffen I was you, I'd look whar I was gwine. Lessen you want Chickadee ter dig splinters outen yore—"

"Good day, Mr. Beasley." He staggered to his feet. "A real pleasure seeing you again."

With that, he ran into the cabin, aching to wrap his fingers around Chickadee's neck. He slammed the door closed and bolted it firmly. Whirling, he faced her fully, his wrath plain on his stormy features. "You knew he was out there, didn't you?"

She looked up from her broom. "Yep."

"Why the hell didn't you tell me then? How do you think I felt standing there bare naked in front of him?"

"Reckon you was as embarrassed as all git out."

Oh, how cool she is, Saxon thought angrily. Did she even know what embarrassment was? He strode toward her with two long steps and yanked her up, thankful her damn wolf was outside and not here to object to what was getting ready to happen.

Like George Franklin said—sometimes women needed to be put in their places.

"Since the day I met you, you've done your level best to embarrass me. Sometimes you don't mean to do it, but other times—I've seen that gleam in your damn green eyes. I've seen how your lips curl up when something awkward happens to me, and I've had enough. Do you hear me, woman?"

"Git yore—"

"Quiet!" he thundered, squeezing her shoulders tightly. "It's my turn now, and I'm going to make you blush, Keely McBride. I'm going to do things you never thought it possible to do to someone. And you—after you get over your embarrassment," he said, jerking her closer to him, "are going to beg for more."

She didn't care a whit for his feelings, and he'd been a fool to care for hers. She needed to be taught a lesson, and he was just the man to teach it to her. Finally, this was his chance to prove to her what a man really was. He'd show her in a way that would leave no doubt in her mind.

He swept her into his arms and, none too gently, deposited her on the bed.

Chapter 6

⟶○◯◯○⟵

She skirred to the side. His strong hand stayed her. She aimed her head at his belly and threw herself forward. He caught her and flung her back to the bed.

"I don't care if you *are* half man, Keely. What matters right now is I am *all* man. And soon," he said, reaching for the top of her breeches, "you will know exactly what that means."

Never before overpowered and not about to be now either, she began to struggle in earnest and promptly kicked out at him. When her feet met his middle, she reached for his shoulders to throw him over the bed and onto the floor.

But Saxon grabbed her ankles, his fingers wrapping around them like steel chains. "I know you'd like to show me all your mountain-fighting moves, Miss McBride, but I'm in no mood to see them at this time."

His sharp blue gaze nailed her to the feather tick. In his anger, his face seemed carved, as if it were sculpted from the strong but beautiful rock of a mountain, she mused. And those pieces-of-sky eyes of his. It was as if they were alive, with fingers and hands of their own. They had but to look at her and she responded.

Why was she fighting this man?

"Yore lips is so hard lookin', I'm a-wonderin' iffen

they turned to stone. Come down here and let me feel 'em.''

He watched her through slitted eyelids. She was doing it again. Turning all this around and taking control herself. There was no way in hell Saxon was going to let her do it this time.

"You're going to feel them all right. On every part of your body." He fell upon her, his hand rapidly unfastening her shirt. Without hesitation, he removed her breeches, and only when she was naked did he roll off her.

She closed her eyes. He'd yet to touch her, but her skin was quivering for the feel of him. He hadn't kissed her, but already her insides were shaking like a leaf in a strong autumn wind.

Saxon caressed her with his eyes before he laid his hand on her. Never had he seen such perfection. Her skin, her shape, her scent—she was exquisite. He hadn't planned on wooing her but, unbidden, sweet words came to his lips.

"God, Keely, you're a treasure that defies description. I feel like a starving man who's never had food and is only now beginning to taste it."

He touched his lips to her belly. His mouth began a trail of passion, starting at the tips of her fingers and lightly journeying up her arms, to the sweet slope of her throat, and down across her chest. He lingered at her breasts, his wet, warm touch making Chickadee writhe.

"You like this, little one?" As his lips continued down the silken path of her body, his hands slid up her thighs and into the velvet nest of her womanhood. There they teased and tormented her. They dipped low, tarried briefly, and finally dove deep within her.

Chickadee gasped, the fire of her desire pinkening her cheeks. "Flustered so soon?" Saxon asked, his fingers continuing their tender torture. "Why, we've barely begun. Before we're finished, your face will be as red as your hair."

Desperately, she searched for words to fling back at him. But her voice had fled at the onslaught of the emotions that had taken her captive. And no power on earth could have made her resist what he was doing to her. Right or wrong, she prayed he wouldn't stop.

His palm circled the mound of her femininity, his fingers still moving inside her. "Do you like that? How does it feel to know I've sought and found that which is most precious to you? Soon you'll know what it is to be a woman. And may you blush, Keely McBride; may all the timidity that hides in this perfect body of yours come to surface."

"Saxon." She arched into his hand—the source of the mysterious, rising want swirling through her. "Please . . ."

"Mountain girl," he whispered, his lips inching toward where his hand already was, "tell me what you want me to do." His mouth nestled into the soft triangle between her legs, his intimate kisses continuing downward.

"Law, Saxon! Yore a-kissin' me thar!" She brought her knees up, imprisoning his head between her thighs.

"Yes, I'm kissing you here. Kissing you, tasting you, just as I told you I would. So are you holding me captive to stop me, or so I won't get away?" He pushed her thighs apart and smiled at what he saw.

She was blushing furiously, her breasts rising and falling like two milk-white mountains riding out an earthquake. Her eyes were closed, but Saxon knew they were ablaze with fiery, emerald-green desire. And before he made her his, he wanted to see that verdant surrender.

"Open your eyes, Keely."

They fluttered once. "I cain't. I cain't do nothin' but lay here and wonder what yore gwine do next."

"Open them."

She did. And when she had, she saw his need for her. Saw the huge difference there really was between men and women. Never had she seen it look like *that* before. Embarrassed no end, she covered her face with her hands.

Saxon took her breasts into his palms. "You have five seconds to get out of this bed. Go, and I won't stop you. Do you understand I'm giving you a choice?"

"Yes."

Saxon counted to five, and Chickadee didn't move a muscle. Never would he have forced her to do anything she didn't want to do—and never had he been so gladdened by any woman's willingness.

Slowly, he removed her hands from her face and kissed each of her other features before he arrived at her mouth. As he captured her lips between his, he settled his body over hers.

"Keely, I want to make love to you. Your presence in this bed means you want the same thing. I've no headache, and I'm not going to stop this time."

She nibbled at his chin. "You didn't have no headache afore neither. And I ain't gwine try ter stop you. I'm a-burning' fer you somethin' powerful."

All right, Sax, he told himself. *This is it. Soon you'll have tied her to you just as surely as if you used ropes.*

Tied to him. A free thing bound forever. He closed his eyes and buried his face in the pillow.

"Saxon?" Chickadee hugged him tightly. "Ain't no need fer you ter feel bad. I'm growed, and I make my own decisions. Iffen I didn't want this, thur wouldn't be no way on earth you could keep me in this bed."

Her body was so soft beneath his, the arch of her womanhood burning into his moist belly. He groaned.

"Saxon, please. Please make love ter me."

Damn! He'd have to be made of iron to resist that sweet plea!

"Keely . . ." As he had before, he slid into her

slightly. "Remember what I said. The pain will last only a moment before you feel the sweetest pleasure known to man."

"Man?"

"And woman." He bent to kiss her, and when he did his mouth caught and smothered the raspy gasp of pain that rose from her as he thrust deeply into her. His lips clinging to hers, he became very still.

Chickadee shuddered beneath him. She wanted to throw him off, but as he lay unmoving upon her, the sharp ache within her ebbed away and was replaced by that same wild longing he never failed to make her feel.

Only this time, she knew he'd appease it.

"Keely—"

"It don't hurt no more, Saxon. Make me a woman now."

With slow, gentle strokes, he did just that. He sensed her rising need for him, but his own need for her was something he'd never felt for any woman, and despite his earlier decision to be quick about this, he wanted to give the girl who lay beneath him all the bliss he was capable of giving her.

"Move, Keely," he whispered. "Move with me."

At first she didn't understand what he meant, but when an elusive hint of some strange feeling began to grow in her belly, she raised her hips and circled them against Saxon's. She met each of his thrusts and felt him fill her so completely, she thought the emotions spinning inside her would surely make her burst.

"How beautiful you are," Saxon moaned. "How soft and wonderful is the deep, deep secret of Keely McBride."

As was her way, Chickadee threw herself into lovemaking with wild abandon. She wrapped her long legs around Saxon's back, imprisoning him in the embrace of her newborn passion. "Saxon, I'm gwine die," she cried, panting. "Stop. No, don't stop. Hurry up. Somethin' bad's a-happenin'."

He smiled knowingly. "I promise nothing bad is happening."

To prove his words, he quickened his pace, driving deeply within her. Chickadee writhed beneath him, mindless of the explosion steadily building. She clung to him, her nails raking his back, her lips forming his name in a silent plea for release. Her whole body craved that which was so close yet still so far away.

And suddenly it was upon her. Searing her, turning her into red-hot embers that flamed higher and higher, fanned by the gale winds of Saxon's sweeping passion. It was a mountain ablaze, this thing she climbed, but she scaled it with Saxon. She melted fast to him as he took her to the summit of the rhapsody he'd promised her. And there he kept her, tottering at the brink until he joined her.

Chickadee felt his powerful release, and his deep, throbbing sent her hurling back into a second rendezvous with the mysterious feeling called ecstasy. Again, the fire began, both burning and soothing her. She shook, rocking from side to side, her arms clinging to Saxon's neck as she reached for the peak of passion yet another time.

Saxon's body glistened, his muscles straining with exertion as he pushed her toward that flaming crest. And when she shuddered beneath him again, he knew he had fostered her bliss once more.

Wordlessly, wondrously, they descended together from that burning hill of desire, the flames of their passion slowly subsiding to a warm, tender heat. They gazed into each other's eyes for an eternity before Saxon finally slipped to the bed beside her.

But the quiet was abruptly broken when Chickadee sat up and saw the bedclothes. "Saxon! Oh, Lord o' mercy, Saxon, I'm hurt! I'm a-bleedin' from inside!"

His eyes flew to the red stain, and he quickly reached for her, enfolding her in the reassuring warmth of his arms. "You're not hurt, little one. That's the proof of your virginity."

"You mean that's normal?"

"It's normal and in no way dangerous to you."

Her fingers quivered over him, her emotions still swirling wildly within her. "Saxon, you . . . don't think I'm a bad-un now, do you?"

"Don't you think it's a little late to be worrying about that?" he teased, his smile spreading into the moist arch of her neck.

"But—"

"Keely, nothing as sweet . . . as absolutely wonderful as you are could be bad. But I've a solution to your worries." He sat up and pulled her into his lap. "As you know, I've got to return to Boston. But I want you to go with me. As my wife." Sure she'd jump at the opportunity, his face shone with confidence.

"Are you a-sayin' you want ter marry me?"

"Is the thought so appalling?"

Chickadee's gaze fell to his chest. "I cain't marry you, Saxon. It ain't that I don't like you, but . . ."

When her voice trailed off, he lifted her chin. "But what? Don't you want to marry me?"

"No."

"Keely, I don't understand. I thought we meant something to each other. I thought what just happened—"

"Would make it differ? Saxon, I like a-makin' love with you, but I ain't gwine marry you jist ter keep on a-doin' it. Marriage is more'n that, the way I see it. You got ter have love too. And y'know what I'm a-thankin'?"

"I can't begin to guess." Dammit! This was the first time in his life he'd proposed to a woman, and the little twit had turned him down! *Turned him down!* How could she, after what they'd just felt together?

"Well, as good as what we jist done was, I thank it'd be better iffen we loved one another. Seems to me love'd bigger it—give it more meanin'. I like you a powerful lot, but I don't thank I love you. You don't love me neither, so I ain't gwine marry you. Do you understand?''

He understood all right. Understood he'd underestimated her wisdom. He'd been a fool to think she'd fall for the trap he'd set. Unlike all the other women he'd left with bleeding hearts, this one could live without him. He could leave right this minute, and Chickadee would be no worse off because of it. Her life would go on just as it always had.

And his would never be the same again.

Once again, he put off his return to New England. Matrimony with some vapors-prone woman awaited him there. He knew he couldn't leave until he'd exhausted every possible way to make Chickadee his bride.

Nights found them imprisoned in that special cell of desire known only to lovers, and when morning came, they were often still incarcerated within it. And the joy they found in each other's arms wasn't confined to the cabin. When the sparks between them began to smolder, they succumbed to the fire wherever they happened to be, the mountains smiling down upon them.

It was an idyllic interlude, but as summer passed to autumn, Saxon became restless. Boston was calling him back. Desdemona's welfare and his future were threatened with each day that slipped by. He doubled his efforts to win Chickadee.

He tried to tempt her with descriptions of the gorgeous jewelry and gowns he would give her. He explained how certain foods would literally melt in her mouth if she'd only come with him to sample them. He compared his own carriage to the one she said she'd seen in Asheville when she was young. He teased and cajoled, but she still refused to be his bride.

The more he tried to entice her, the more she clung

to her ideas about love. She yearned for him constantly, but was hesitant to believe those feelings were true love. She knew he would leave, and though the thought made her ache, without love, she saw no chance of a happy marriage.

The day she and Saxon dreaded came all too soon. Dawn chased away night as always, but when those first timid rays of sunlight filtered into the cabin, they both knew what the day would bring. Neither of them spoke during breakfast, each silently wondering what the other was thinking, each afraid to ask.

"You et good, Saxon. Yore belly's tight enough ter crack a egg on. I reckon yore a-wantin' ter work some of it off." Chickadee cleared the table, the tin plates clanging in her shaking hands. "Let's go a-fishin'. We'll have a bait o' fresh fish fer supper, I'll fry cornbread—"

"I won't be here for supper." He put on his boots and stuffed his extra clothes into his saddlebag.

She caressed the raccoon tail at the waistband of her breeches, its softness nothing compared to the silk of Saxon's hair. Her eyes roamed his body from head to foot several times before she swallowed nervously and spoke. "You . . . Saxon . . . I never did take you a-huntin' fer sang."

He saw the sadness in her eyes and quickly looked away from them. "I hate to miss that."

"A-galaxin' neither. I really wanted ter show you my galax spot." She crossed to stand close to him.

The warmth of her body made him ache with the strangest emotion he'd ever felt. "At Christmas I'll buy an arrangement with galax in it and wonder if you were the one who picked it." By the end of his sentence his voice had become a whisper.

She reached for his hand and held it to her cheek. "You ain't never gwine come back here, are you? Once you git to that Boston city, yore gwine stay thar ferever."

His fingers twined her hair. Molten tresses he'd

always yearn to hold, to smell, to caress. "If Grand-mother buys that land in Moore County, I'll be back."

"But you'll be so busy with all that turpentine makin', you ain't never gwine have time ter git up here. You—"

"Keely, you could come with me. I've been beg-ging you to marry me for weeks. If you really want to be with me, why—"

"Done tole you why, and I ain't gwine change my mind."

"Then that's that." Saxon snapped his bag shut, reached for his hat, and went outside.

Chickadee followed close behind him. "Try ter git ter a town quick. I larnt you a lavish o' thangs up here, but you outlanders is better off whar thur's civilized thangs around you." She tried to smile but failed miserably.

Saxon pressed his forehead against Hagen's side, and he too tried to grin, to no avail. Straightening, he turned to her and pressed a thick wad of bills into her hand. "Take this money and use it for whatever you need. Winter's not far away, and there must be many things you could use to get ready for the cold."

She stuffed it back into his bag. "Don't want it."

"But—"

"No, Saxon. Not nary a penny."

He stared down at her, trying to capture her im-age, then realized he'd never forget what she looked like. Every time he saw emeralds, he'd remember her eyes. Ivory satin would remind him of her skin. That gingerbread Araminta's chefs made would bring to mind Chickadee's many freckles. Every time he looked at the crumbs on his plate, he'd think of them. And whenever he saw something that was sort of red, sort of orange, and sort of gold, her wild mane of hair would tumble into his thoughts.

And to remember her essence, he need only be close to nature. Soft, warm breezes and ferocious, freezing winds. Thunder, lightning, and sunshine, rain, and even snow. How they changed, the seasons. Just like Chickadee's thoughts and moods.

He kissed her then, and hoped his kiss conveyed his thoughts. He willed her to understand that he didn't love her, but she was special in a way he knew he'd never really be able to explain. She made him mad, she embarrassed him, and she made him think of things he'd never thought of before.

But most of all, she made him laugh.

"Take care, little mountain girl," he whispered to her. "I wish you nothing but happiness—the same joy you've given me these months I've been with you." He released her then and mounted quickly. "I'll miss you, Keely McBride, and I won't ever forget you."

She nodded and reached up to touch the lips he'd just kissed. Her fingers brushed them briefly before they swept away from her mouth, throwing one final kiss to him. With that, she snapped for Khan, and the two of them ran into the rhododendron thicket.

The copper swing of Chickadee's hair was the last Saxon saw of her.

His heart felt like a boulder in his chest. He traveled relentlessly onward, yet even when the Appalachia was behind him, he could still see the girl who lived there. Her image refused to leave him; her sweet voice remained in his mind. He ignored his feelings as best he could, but when he was two days out of the Blue Ridge, he did the one thing he'd restrained himself from doing since leaving it.

He stopped Hagen. Slowly, hesitantly, he twisted around in the saddle.

He sat stiffly as he looked into the distance. He could only see the peaks of the majestic ranges he'd left, but how he stared at them. His concentration was so intense, time ceased to exist for him, and the dark of night found him still astride his horse, still gaping at the obscure mountains.

And by the time the moon finally caught his eye, he knew what he would do.

The Appalachia. As he raced back toward it, he felt he was answering its call. And when the beauty of those lush hills finally surrounded him again, that thing called heartease poured over him.

Chickadee McBride.

She was like these mountains that sheltered her. She could be soft and yielding, but when it came to protecting herself, her spirit rose to her defense. And there was no getting around that tough shield that safeguarded her. It was as flinty as these rocky hills.

But as Saxon urged Hagen up the pebbled path, he smiled at his foolproof plan. Chickadee was different, she was special, but she lacked one thing to make her truly happy; one thing she would find impossible to resist.

Revenge on Barton Winslow.

The man could be dead or on the other side of the world, but Saxon had the power to find out.

So intense was his concentration on his infallible scheme, he never saw how close Hagen was to the edge of a rock-peppered gully, never heard the horse snort in alarm, and never felt him stumble.

Never realized the danger he was in until he was flying headlong into the deep ravine.

Chapter 7

Fire.
Damn that ravine and damn the three hours it had taken him to climb out of it! Dread flooding his veins, Saxon stared at the black pillar of smoke rising above the treetops. He drove Hagen onward unmercifully, but when the horse began to tire and falter, Saxon leaped from his back and ran the rest of the way up the steep, rocky cliff. He charged up an endless path, horrendous fear twisting through him. The smoke was thicker now; its acrid smell burned his nostrils as he neared the area where Chickadee lived.

Nothing could have prepared him for the sight that met his eyes. The cabin was burning furiously, but not even the fires of hell could have kept him from rushing inside in search of Chickadee. Flames licked at his coat, his sleeve began to burn, but all he knew was the panic that seared him at the sight of Chickadee lying in the far corner of the room, bound and gagged.

The fire formed an almost solid sheet of flames around her. He burst through it, almost falling when he tripped over a man's body. Ignoring the corpse, he slung Chickadee over his shoulder and made a mad dash for the door. Just as he was leaving the inferno, he heard Khan whining to him from the other corner.

"Khan! Damn! Wait there, boy!" he yelled. He

carried Chickadee well away from the blazing cabin, then laid her on a soft bed of flowers, nearly bursting with relief when she opened her eyes. "Keely, I've got to go get Khan!"

As he entered the cabin a second time, a flaming wall crashed to the floor in front of him. Burning wood flew everywhere, one piece landing on his boot. He saw it was the stock of the rifle Keely's ancestor had at the battle on King's Mountain. Without thinking, he picked it up and saw it was undamaged. He slipped it into his coat and started for Khan.

The floor around the wolf was burning into the ground beneath it now. Indeed, Khan was lifting his paws to keep them from the heat. There was no way Saxon could reach him. "Khan, jump! I'll catch you, boy! Jump!"

Khan circled once, his tail between his hind legs before he crouched and leaped through the fire into Saxon's waiting arms. He staggered backward through the door, fell off the porch, and tumbled head over heels into the yard just in time to see the entire cabin collapse. Khan sprang from his arms and headed straight for Chickadee.

The fury in her eyes was hotter than the fire. Saxon tore the gag from her mouth. "Keely—"

"It's about dang time you got here, you God-burn worthless—"

"About time? What the hell are you—"

"What did you do? Have a dang picnic in that ditch-gully I seed you fall inter?"

His muddled mind tried to understand how she knew about the ravine. He'd still been miles away then!

"When them bushwhackers got holt o' me, I jist knowed you was gwine come a-bustin' through the door, a-shootin' ever' one o' 'em. Afore they come, I'd been a-watchin' you fer near about three hours, but you didn't git here till the last dang minute! Some hero you are!"

"Bushwackers! What—"

"Untie me, Saxon! We got ter git that far out afore it reaches the woods!"

Two hours later the blaze was extinguished. The only thing left of the cabin was a hissing sound and some lingering smoke. Exhausted, Saxon and Chickadee lay on the ground, and she explained what had happened.

"Three wanderers come up here. I kilt one of 'em afore the other two tied me up. They found the likker jug and got so snockered, they started a-knockin' each other around. One of 'em crashed inter the fireplace, and embers was spilt out all over. I knowed thur was gwine be a far, but thur warn't nothin' I could do. Anyhow, I reckon them varmints was gwine rape me, but Khan came back from wharever the hell he was, and chased 'em off. I suspicion he got holt of 'em from the looks o' all that blood on him. Atter that, I reckon I passed out from all the smoke."

Saxon glanced at the huge wolf, did indeed see a scarlet stain around Khan's mouth, and was certain the other two men were dead. "Why didn't George Franklin—"

"Him and Betty Jane went ter town ter git salt. They—"

"Never mind that—are you sure you aren't hurt?"

"I'm only riled at you fer a-takin' yore own sweet time ter git up here! Now I ain't got nothin'! Ever'thang I had is burnt up! It ain't that I cain't build another cabin . . . but I come up in that one." She shook her head to throw off her self-pity. "Well, Saxon? What the hell was you a-doin' in that ravine? How come it tuk you so dang long ter git up here?"

He didn't know whether to sympathize with her or slap her. Finally, his anger won out. "How the hell was I supposed to know you were in danger? I didn't even see the smoke until I'd almost reached your cove! I—"

"Didn't you notice all the animules was in franzies? Ever'thang out here was shorely a-runnin' from the far!''

Now that he thought of it, he *had* seen a lot of fleeing animals. But he hadn't paid much attention. ''Well, I . . . Well, excuse me, Miss Know-Everything-About-Nature McBride! Excuse me for taking so damn long to come to your damn rescue! Excuse me for ignoring all those damn animals running around all over the damn place, and excuse me for taking three damn hours to get out of the damn ravine my damn horse threw me into, dammit!''

His wrath made her smile and, before long, she was laughing so hard she could barely breathe. ''Oh, Saxon, I'm so glad you come back! You jist cain't know how much I missed you! Yer gwine stay, ain't you? You ain't gwine go back to that Boston city?''

''Keely—''

'' 'Course, we'll have ter build another cabin. You ever builded a cabin afore? Well, it ain't hard, but it—''

''Keely, I'm not staying here, but neither are you. You're going to marry me, and we're going to—''

''Yore the hardheadedest man I ever knowed, Saxon! What's it gwine take ter make you understand, I ain't—''

''Hear me out.'' He stood and gazed down at her. ''I need you, and you need me.''

''Well of all the—'' She bolted to her feet. ''I chew my bakker jist once, Saxon Blackwell, so you better listen real good. I'm so poor now I cain't buy hay fer a nightmare, but I still got my pride. And iffen you thank I'm gwine marry you jist on account o' I lost ever'thang I had, yore—''

''Keely, let me finish explaining.''

''Keep my name outen yore mouth.''

''But—''

''Yore the biggityest man a-walkin' this here earth. I don't need you fer nothin'. I been by mysef fer nigh on five years now, and I been jist fine. I—''

''You need me, and I need you, and that's final!

And if you'll shut that caustic mouth of yours, I'll tell you why!"

"Spit on the apple and then git outen my way!"

"I'm going to ruin Barton Winslow. I'll hire detectives to find him, and when they do, I'll destroy him."

She took a step backward. "Yore gwine kill him?"

"If he's as greedy as you described him, losing everything he has would hurt him far worse than death. In fact, death would probably be preferable to a man like that."

"But what iffen he don't got nothin'?"

"He'll lose what little he has. I promise to make him suffer. I'll do whatever it takes to give you the revenge you've wanted all these years. And when he's ruined, no matter where he is, we'll pay him a little visit so you can tell him exactly who was behind his destruction. I'll let you have all the credit."

She smiled spitefully. "And after I tell him, I'm gwine fill his ass with buckshot. I'll—"

"You have to marry me first. Marry me and go back to Boston with me. Those are the conditions."

Her face fell. "But Saxon, I jist cain't."

"Don't you want revenge on Winslow?"

She kicked at a stick. "Do you love me, Saxon? Is that why yore a-tryin' ter make this lay with me?"

His heart thrashed wildly within the constricting cage of his chest. *I can't love you, Keely,* he told her silently, but said aloud, "You're very special to me."

"But you don't love me and I still don't thank I love you. What sorter marriage would we have? Withouten love—"

"We need each other. I already told you that. I'll destroy Winslow for you, and by marrying me you'll be helping me realize my dreams too."

"Saxon, you ain't a-makin' no sense. Put the milk down whar the goats can git at it."

He took a deep breath and prepared to be honest. "I've got to marry. If Grandmother dies before I have a wife, Desdemona and my inheritance will both go to a cousin in England. You're the bride I want to take home.''

She watched him carefully while she absorbed that information. The festering pain that came from speaking of his grandmother crawled across his face. Why didn't he just leave that woman once and for all? ''Saxon, take Desdemona and run. If you hide her good, nobody cain't never send her to England.''

''Do you think that hasn't crossed my mind? I assure you it has. Dozens of times! But how would I support—''

''Work hard jist like the rest of us, I reckon.''

Saxon paced the mountain floor. ''I'm not afraid of hard work. I can't remember a time when I *haven't* worked hard. But if I stole Desdemona away, I'd have to start my own business, and it would be pretty damn hard to do that with the entire world crawling with Grandmother's detectives. One of her bloodhounds would find—''

''Then don't start no business.'' She kicked the stick again. ''Live offen the land like I do. Works fer me. It'll work fer you too iffen—''

''Keely, you've never seen Desdemona. She's as fragile as fine crystal. She'd never survive a life of hardship.''

''Then leave her whar she is till—''

''Until I have enough money to care for her? Do you know what Grandmother would do if I attempted that? Send Desdemona directly to a mental institution! And no court in the land would deny her right to do so. She has complete custody over Desdemona. Keely, can't you see? There's no way around the stipulations in Grandmother's will! I can't just kidnap Desdemona and expect to live happily ever after. I haven't the means to take care of her. Only money—''

''Money! Allus money!'' She kicked the stick clear across the yard. ''You don't hardly never thank on anythang but money! Yore whole life, all yore decisions—ever'thang in yore whole world goes around a-bein' rich! You cain't never relax. Cain't never stop fer a dang minute ter see how blue the sky is. Money! Allus—''

"Only money can give Desdemona the life she needs to stay *alive!*" He went to her and looked into her eyes, willing her to understand. "Keely, I have to have my inheritance. Please say you'll marry me."

She saw the hope, the plea in his azure eyes, and realized then he had his sister's best interests at heart. But she also suspected the thought of living in poverty was an uncomfortable one. He just didn't understand the fortune was blinding him to the more important things in life. For as long as Saxon believed money and well-being were the same, he would never find the one thing he needed to be happy. The thing called heartease.

But though she understood all those things, she was also wise enough to realize such a drastic change had to come from within. She couldn't bring it about. Only he could.

"Keely, think about this carefully," Saxon pressed. "It's not only Barton, but you'll see more of this country, like you told me you wanted to do one day. And Desdemona . . . wouldn't you like the challenge of making her smile, talk? You said all she needs is neverending attention. Wouldn't you like to see if that belief turned out to be true?"

Her stubbornness began to waver under the weight of all his arguments. "Well . . ." she began, still sorting through her thoughts, "I ain't a-sayin' yes yet, but . . . Well, iffen I was ter marry you, who'd take keer o' the Beasleys, T.J., and Widder Tucker? They depend on me ter take keer of 'em."

He took her into his arms. "The money you abhor will take care of them all. Once I'm married, I'll receive a hefty sum of money each month from Grandmother until the estate passes to me when she dies. I'll hire someone to see that your people never lack for a thing. Surely there's someone you know who'd be willing to take care of all your friends? Someone you'd trust."

"Well, thur's Johnny Webber. He lives down yonder in the next holler. And he's all sorts of a feller. Cain't track bahrs as good as I can, but he ain't a got a drop o' streaked blood in his veins. Big and stout too. Why, I reckon he could pack a log to hell and back afore breakfast."

"And living up here, he could probably use some money," Saxon speculated slyly.

Money again. She sighed. Still, who was she to deny financial aid to her people? Just because *she* didn't need it or want it didn't mean her neighbors felt the same way. "Well, heared tell Johnny's sweet on Liza Howe, T.J.'s sister. Yeah, I reckon he could use some money iffen he's a-plannin' on a-takin' him a bride. Prob'ly make thangs a sight easier fer 'em."

"Much, much easier," he agreed quickly.

She withdrew from his embrace and went to sit by Khan. "I jist don't know, Saxon. I cain't stand the thought of a-leavin' these here hills ferever. I don't know nothin' about Boston. What iffen I don't like it thar?"

Saxon's mind whirled with possible ways to get around this problem. "All right," he said hesitantly. "You can return to your mountains whenever you want. Just marry me, let me present you to Grandmother, get to know Desdemona, and then you can come back here. Or, if you'd prefer, you can wait until the Winslow business is over."

"You'd let me leave you and never go back ter you?"

He swallowed convulsively. Why was that thought so appalling? "Our lives would go on as always," he said, his voice wavering. "All I need is your name on a marriage certificate, and then—well, then you'll be free to do whatever you want. I'll have met the conditions in Grandmother's will, Desdemona might show some response to you, and you'll get revenge on your father. What's to think about? We'll both win, for we've nothing to lose."

He pulled her to her feet. "As my wife, you'll have everything you need. If—when you return to the Blue Ridge, it'll be with the protection of my money. You say you don't need it, and you don't have to use it if you don't want to. But if anything ever happens to you or your friends, the Blackwell money will be there for you always. You'll never have another worry, nor will your people here."

Chickadee laid her head against his chest. Life was hard up in these mountains, she admitted to herself, and despite everything she did for her neighbor-people, they still lacked many things she had no way of giving them. It would be mighty selfish of her to deny them those things just because she resisted the idea of marriage without love.

Besides that, it wouldn't be a *real* marriage. Saxon said she could leave Boston whenever she wanted to go. In a few short months, she'd be right back here. She'd have avenged her mother, cheered up a sad girl, and done some traveling. Saxon was right. What was there to think about?

"All right, outlander. You done got yoresef a bride. But I ain't a-stayin' in that thar Boston city long, hear?"

Once again, a bizarre feeling of loss slithered through him. He could barely manage a nod of agreement.

When the Beasleys returned, they found Saxon and Chickadee in their cabin. After hearing about the fire, Betty Jane insisted Chickadee stay in bed for a whole day. But on the second day, no amount of pleading could keep her there any longer. "Lord o' mercy, you-uns! I ain't sick, and I ain't gwine stay in bed! And pull in yore horns, Saxon, or I'll cloud up and rain all over you."

"But—"

"Got wood ter chop. I'm gwine fell ever' tree—"

"I already spoke to Johnny Webber," Saxon broke in. "George Franklin took me down there yesterday morning. Johnny will see to everything."

" 'Swhat he said all right, Chickadee." George Franklin moved his chaw of tobacco to the other cheek. "I was thar. And Saxon here give Johnny a pile o' money, the bigness you ain't never seed in all yore days. Right gen'rous of him. 'Peared to me it was more'n enough money fer what ole Johnny'll be a-doin'."

"And look here, Chickadee." Betty Jane pulled out a thick roll of bills from her apron pocket. "He done give us some too. I warn't gwine take it from him, but I thought I could use it ter buy some boughten cloth ter make curtains fer the new cabin George Franklin's gwine make you whilst yer gone. I was even a-thankin' o'—"

"Hesh up, woman." George Franklin shook his head. "Yore the talkin'est woman in these here hills. I reckon you could talk the legs offen a stove, and that ain't no lie."

"You—"

"I said hesh! Dang it, Betty Jane, the last time I seed a mouth the bigness o' yores, it had a hook in it."

Chickadee smiled. Lord, how she'd miss these two. She quickly bent her head and successfully controlled the sadness that surged within her. "Well, Saxon, we may as well be on our way."

Betty Jane gave her two packages. "This-un's yarbs fer iffen you ever git a-feelin' low. And this other-un's breeches and shirts. And the shoes George Franklin made fer you too. We know you'll be a-wearin' boughten clothes up thar whar yore gwine, but sometimes you might git a hankerin' ter wear what yore used ter."

"And here's yore rifle," George Franklin said and handed it to her. "Found it throwed out beside yore cabin. Didn't even git scorched."

Saxon took Chickadee's hand, and the little group

went outside. Chickadee hugged her two elderly friends and mounted with no aid from Saxon. Grinning, he mounted behind her, and nodding goodbye to the Beasleys, he urged Hagen down the mountain gap, Khan trotting close behind.

Chickadee squirmed around in the saddle to wave. Never in her life had she felt so afraid or dispirited, but she forced herself to smile. Her bright grin was the last thing Betty Jane and George Franklin saw as their special girl disappeared from sight and headed for the faraway—and unsuspecting—city of Boston.

Chapter 8

As they traveled toward Moore County, where Saxon had decided they would marry, they stopped to send Araminta a telegram requesting that she send one of the Blackwell steamboats back to the port of Wilmington. He made no mention of his new bride, only notifying his grandmother he was ready to return to Boston.

No inns along the way would allow Khan entry. Saxon tried to convince Chickadee the wolf would be fine outside, but she refused to stay at a place where her pet wasn't welcome. And so, though the snap of autumn was in the air, they slept under the sable quilt of night, the Carolina stars twinkling down at them.

Once in Moore County, they headed straight for the Mansfield home. Heath was delighted with Chickadee. The two became immediate friends, their closeness causing Saxon's eyebrow to rise frequently. He convinced himself it wasn't jealousy he felt, only surprise. He was learning many things about his fiancée, and her special ability with people was one of them.

At Tyson and McNeill Mercantile, Saxon purchased Chickadee's first "boughten" gown. Since it was to be her wedding dress, he tried to persuade her to buy a white one. But Chickadee spied a tomato-red frock and would have no other.

And so, when the day came, Saxon escorted his

red-clad mountain girl to Bethesda Presbyterian
Church at the head of Rockfish Creek, a rustic setting that suited her nicely. The Mansfield family and
a few of Heath's friends were the only guests attending the small wedding, other curious spectators
shying away from the white wolf who lay sleeping
in the churchyard.

After the reception at the Mansfields' home, Heath
and his parents offered the newlyweds their bed-
rooms. But Chickadee wouldn't hear of it. The
Mansfields argued, but her stubbornness won out,
and Saxon soon found himself waving good-night
to the family as he and his bride headed out for another night in the woods.

"Warn't it purty, Saxon?" Chickadee snuggled
down into the bearskin with him. "The weddin',
the cake—Miz Mansfield spended all mornin' on that
fancified cake."

Saxon smiled. The cake had been void of all the
usual wedding decorations, the icing white and
plain. He reached for Chickadee and held her close.
"Keely, why didn't you accept Heath's offer to let
us use his bedroom? I'd never have taken his parents' room, but Heath could have slept—"

"That's a small house, and you make a lot o'
racket when yore a-makin' love. Most times you jist
moan, but ever' now and then, when it's a-gittin'
real good, you holler. I was jist a-savin' you from
embarrassment, outlander. Mr. and Miz Mansfield
prob'ly wouldn'ta said nothin', but Heath woulda
loved a-teasin' you about it termorrer."

Saxon chuckled. "Yes, I imagine he would at
that."

Chickadee ran her hand over his broad chest and
down his flat belly, and slid her fingers into the soft
matting of hair at the apex of his thighs. Slowly, her
hand curled around his rigid masculinity.

Saxon moaned.

"See what I mean, Saxon? We ain't even done
nothin' yet, and yore already a-groanin'."

His laughter was muffled in her thick hair. "Am I really that loud?"

"Iffen I didn't know better, sometimes I'd thank somethin' bad-awful was a-happenin' ter you. The way you carry on, it's like you was a-bein' tortured or somethin'."

"Oh, and you don't make a sound?" He pulled a piece of pine straw from her hair and tickled her cheek with it.

She grinned impishly. "I don't go inter franzies like you do. I reckon I might holler when it's good enough ter holler over. But till it is, you ain't gwine hear me carry on over it."

"Just how much better do you think it could be?" Saxon jerked the bearskin up over his shoulder. "You're the wildest woman I've ever had in my bed, yet you—"

"You been with other women? How many? Who—"

"Jealous?"

"What of? What you done afore we met up ain't none o' my business. I was jist a-wonderin'."

"Why do you want to know?"

For one short moment she was silent, but her grin was tremendous. "Well, I'm gwine find them women when we git to Boston so's I can ask 'em what all they did in the bed with you. I'm purty new at all this Saxon, and I was a-figgerin' maybe them other ladies could tell me—"

Saxon laughed uproariously. "If you ever approached one of those prim, pristine . . . uh, *virgins* with what you've got in mind—" He laughed again. "Good God, Keely! You wouldn't really do that, would you?"

Her lips moved slowly across his. "Naw. I got more sense'n that. But thur really *are* thangs I wonder about."

"Such as?" he asked, amused by her boldness.

"I could show 'em ter you better."

"Why don't you just tell me what they are, and I'll tell you what I know about them?"

She shook her head and wiggled under the bearskin. "Some thangs are better larnt by yoresef."

He felt her lips nipping at his belly. "Learn, Keely," he said softly, his fingers tangled in her hair. "Learn."

"A-aimin' to." She found his navel and thrust her tongue into it. Saxon's body jerked spasmodically at her actions, and her lips spread into a smile upon his skin. "You smell so good. That bay rum stuff's powerful fancy, ain't it, Saxon?"

"Bay rum," he mumbled absently, feeling her kisses meandering closer and closer to the base of his manhood. Even now, her cheek was brushing against it.

Like fast-disappearing smoke, his many past lovers floated through his mind. Those icy maidens had probably never even *heard* of what Chickadee was doing right now. And if they had, they'd certainly never entertain the notion of doing it.

That was his last thought as Chickadee did exactly what he'd hoped she would. Her lips, like a tight circle of warm velvet, sought, found, and loved him. She now repaid with gentle, sensual homage that which had given her such joy so many times.

He groaned. He'd never felt such exquisite bliss. "Keely, oh sweet Keely," he gasped as her soft, heated mouth continued its tender torment.

She was glad she'd decided to try making love to him in this way. He'd often done this same thing to her, and the way she saw it, she owed him the same pleasure. She wasn't sure if she was doing it right, but with Saxon carrying on so loudly, she suspected she wasn't doing too badly.

Though the air around him was cold, Saxon's body burned as if with fever, his every nerve aroused. Moan after moan escaped him as her tongue and her kisses caressed him in a way no one else ever had.

She shivered with delight at his joy. Pleasing Saxon gave her a satisfaction that had no equal. After a few more long moments, she got to her knees and straddled him, careful to keep the bearskin over them both.

Saxon opened his eyes, and with the help of the bright moonlight, saw mischief in her sparkling gaze. *"Now* what are you going to teach yourself?"

"I done good, huh?" She leaned over him and kissed the tip of his nose. "I'm a fast larner, Saxon."

His arms went around her, and he started to roll her back to the ground, afire with his need for her. But she forced him still. "I ain't done a-larnin' yet, outlander."

"But—"

She pinched his lips closed and inched her torso downward until his virile staff slid into her. Saxon's eyes widened, and with every ounce of willpower he possessed, he tried to be silent. But when Chickadee sat up and began to rotate her hips, a quivering yell escaped him.

"Go on and holler, Saxon. Ain't nobody around ter hear you."

He reached for her waist, lifting and lowering her. But Chickadee would have none of it and took his hands away. "Y'know," she said, still circling slowly, "yore allus on top. And that ain't fair a'tall, the way I see it."

"Not fair," he murmured shakily.

"Yore allus in control o' our lovemakin', and I thought this a-bein' our weddin' night and all, it was time ter try new thangs." She tightened her knees around him, all the while continuing to hold him in the silken, ever-moving cavern of her femininity. "I had a hankerin' ter know what it was like a-bein' on top. Hope you don't mind none."

"I don't mind," Saxon muttered, his teeth clenched.

She leaned back against his bent knees, her hips still rotating, ascending, descending. "Y'know, I could git used ter a-bein' on top like this. I got control o' ever' feelin' I'm a-feelin'. I got control over yores too, huh?''

"Con-control," he stammered, his body quaking.

"Yep, I can go fast like this," she chimed, circling rapidly, "or I can do it real slow-like." The cadence of her lovemaking dwindled down until Saxon grabbed her waist once more, again trying to move her.

"Fast," he grunted. "Fast, Keely."

She removed his hands and laughed, the silvery tinkle of her laughter dancing through the thick, cool woods. "Reckon the time fer talkin' is over now, outlander," she told him merrily as she lowered herself down onto his chest. "I'm gwine make serious love ter you now."

She rested her face in the crook of his shoulder and concentrated on the feelings building within her. Her movements were slow, but as her desire heightened, her rhythm increased, and she was soon gyrating her hips to the beat of her and Saxon's mounting pleasure.

Saxon knew his end was near, but he struggled to contain it an almost impossible task since Chickadee was in command. His past lovers had been more passive, and he'd had no idea what it was like with the woman on top. But he did now.

It was hell. Sheer, wonderful hell.

With strength that bordered on desperation, he held back, every fiber of his body burning and melting with the need for release. And when he felt Chickadee tense, he prayed she was every bit as ready for the sensual explosion as he was. He reached around her and cupped her bottom firmly, guiding, coercing her into that sweet paradise he could barely wait to reach.

"Oh, Saxon." She moaned softly and shuddered.

He shouted his own bliss but never heard himself yelling. Throbbing wildly within her, he spilled his seed, his muscles quivering with the pent-up need, finally assuaged.

"It's over," he heaved. "Thank God."

Wilmington buzzed with all the usual activities of a seaport. Chickadee's nose wrinkled at the scent of the salty, fishy air, but she was enthralled by all the sailors loading and unloading ships' cargoes. She stared at the clippers, schooners, and steamboats, wondering how such large, heavy vessels could possibly stay afloat.

"Which one's yore granny's?" she asked Saxon.

He scanned the water, soon spying the *Sea Siren*, Araminta's most opulent steamboat. She usually reserved it for her own travels or for the magnificent parties she gave aboard it. Sending the *Sea Siren* was probably her way of reminding him of the Blackwell fortune, Saxon mused.

As if he could ever forget anything concerning his grandmother. Quickly, he squelched the little-boy fears, the bitter torment he could not seem to lay to rest.

"Keely, you're in for a real treat. She sent the *Sea Siren*, and you're going to sail to Boston in style."

But in Chickadee's eyes, stylish in no way described the baroque elegance of the steamboat. Standing in the great central compartment, she stared up at the molded ceiling, her gaze riveted to the crystal chandelier. Beneath her feet was rich carpet, and all around her were paintings in gilded frames hanging on rosewood-paneled walls. Mirrored pillars, their tops and bottoms decorated with golden sea creatures, supported two balconies of staterooms. The very air she breathed had the odor of wealth.

"Do you have a preference of rooms, Mr. Blackwell?" The steward stood stiffly eyeing the white beast who was sniffing his pant leg.

"Grandmother's."

The steward's eyes bulged as Khan's snout inched

up into his crotch. He tried unobtrusively to push Khan away with his knee. "Uh, will the dog be staying with you, or shall I take him—"

"He goes whar I go." Chickadee snapped her fingers and Khan ceased his intimate investigation of the red-faced steward. "And Khan ain't no dog. He's a wolf."

The steward swallowed audibly. "Please excuse my ignorance, Mrs. Blackwell." He bowed and turned to Saxon. "I will escort you to your stateroom now, sir."

When they reached Araminta's personal quarters, Chickadee gasped. She stood on the threshold, her lower jaw hanging open. Saxon walked around her, removed his coat and hat, and hung them both on a brass hatstand. "Keely, I'm going to go check on Hagen, but I'll be back shortly." When she didn't answer, he turned and looked at her. "Aren't you going to come in?"

"What?"

He smiled and pulled her into the room. Khan followed and jumped to put his paws on Saxon's chest. Ever since the fire the wolf had shown him respect, obedience, loyalty, and most of all, affection. "Yes, Khan," Saxon said as Khan drenched him with wet wolf kisses, "I like you too." He gave the wolf a brief ear rub, ruffled Chickadee's hair, and left, the steward following him.

She never even heard him shut the door, so great was her amazement at her surroundings. The entire room, decorated in varying shades of blue and pink, was sumptuous. All the furnishings were elaborate, but the monstrous bed held her attention the longest. The coverlet was of shiny rose satin. From each of the bottom corners, fine lace flowed to the floor like frothy bubbles. The bedposts, carved with painstaking detail, nearly reached the ceiling. Why one old woman needed a bed of that size was beyond Chickadee. She couldn't for the life of her understand how Araminta could use so many pillows. There were at least ten, in all sizes and shapes.

"Lord o' mercy, Khan. Either the woman's the bigness of a house or she don't sleep alone."

Khan wagged his tail, loped to the bed, and leaped gracefully onto it. He walked in small circles before he settled down in the lush satin, crossing his front paws in satisfaction as he closed his eyes.

Chickadee shrugged her shoulders and proceeded to make a fire in the marble fireplace. When the blaze was dancing merrily, she sat on the floor and untied the knotted ends of a bulging piece of cloth, dumping its contents onto the immaculate blue carpet.

Saxon walked in to find her up to her knees in pine straw. "What are you doing with that mess?"

She didn't look up but continued to twist, bend, and braid the pine needles. "You ain't got much o' a mem'ry, Saxon. Afore we left the hills, you said you was gwine stop somewhar and git yore sister a present."

"What does that have to do with all this pine straw?"

"Well, you never got Desdemona nothin', so when we got here to Wilmin'ton, I gathered up these twankles whilst you was a-talkin' to the captain o' this here ship-boat."

"Twinkles?"

"Well, outlanders call it pine straw."

"You're going to give Desdemona a pile of pine straw? Oh, Keely, she'll love it. I can just imagine the fun she'll have with it," he said sarcastically.

"Y'know Saxon, a idee would bust yore head wide open. I ain't gwine give her no pile o' twankles. What do you thank I am? Mizzled?"

He smiled and kissed the top of her head.

"A-makin' her a basket's what I'm a-doin'. You said yore granny's got big, fancy gardens, and I figgered come greenup time Desdemona might like ter have a basket fer when she goes out ter pick all them posies."

Saxon's smile faded. Desdemona had never picked flowers in her life. She didn't care about things like that. She didn't care about anything.

But his smile returned in a flash when he remembered that Desdemona had yet to meet Chickadee. "Could the basket wait for a while? I thought you might like to go topside and watch as we leave."

Chickadee stood, brushed off her breeches, and snapped for Khan. The wolf paid her no mind. "Khan, you ornery—"

"Let him sleep, Keely. He's been traveling for weeks."

"Yore granny ain't gwine mind him a-sleepin' on that fancified bed?"

"Of course not!" Saxon smirked devilishly. "I'm sure Grandmother wouldn't mind a bit sharing her bed with the new Blackwell pet."

The *Sea Siren* glided safely through the waters of the moody Cape Fear River, her competent captain steering clear of the treacherous shoals that were the cause of many shipwrecks. And when the luxurious steamboat slipped out of the mouth of the river, Chickadee shivered with awe at her first sight of the ocean-sea. As if to impress her, the white-capped waves battered the sides of the boat, spraying her so thoroughly that she was soon drenched from red head to bare feet.

Saxon tried to take her back to the room, insisting she needed to get out of her wet clothes, but she refused. Though the sea enchanted her and the boat amazed her, her heart was pounding so furiously, she thought it would surely fly out of her chest and sink into the water at any moment.

The coastline of her home state was slowly disappearing.

Saxon saw the sadness in her eyes and swallowed a strange feeling of dread to tell her, "You'll be back, Keely."

She buried her face in his coat. "Saxon, will you do somethin' fer me?"

The melancholy glimmer in her eyes made him ache for her. "Anything."

"Well, when you and me are a-lovin' up on each other, I fergit about all other thangs. It's like nothin' matters but what we're a-doin'."

"Enough said, Mrs. Blackwell." He swept her into his arms and carried her to their stateroom. There they both stared at the plush bed and smiled at the thought of the passion that would soon be given free rein in it.

Of course, they had to get Khan off first.

"Lordy," Chickadee whispered, her breath visible in the cold air of the harbor. She pulled Saxon's coat tightly about her and watched the *Sea Siren* pass the other ships that bobbed like corks in the New England waters.

The journey, most of which she had spent in Saxon's arms, was over now. The familiar, soothing beauty of the Appalachia was far behind her, and just ahead, noisy and crowded, was Boston.

As the *Sea Siren* approached the wharf, she gripped the railing and stared at the dockside, a commercial district of striking brick and granite warehouses, and wide streets. Everywhere she looked, she saw people hurrying. Many were running, but even those who were walking were quick about it. She scanned the area thoroughly for signs of anything that would make the people rush about so, but she saw no fire or any other sort of danger.

"Welcome to Boston." Saxon put his arm around her and gently caressed her cold cheek. "What do you think of it?"

"Well, it ain't the Blue Ridge," she murmured, stroking the raccoon tails at the waistband of her breeches. "Law, Saxon, look at that woman. She's got a umbreller over her head, and it ain't even a-rainin'."

Saxon saw the woman in question and smiled. "That's a parasol. It's used to keep the sun off her face."

"Y'mean she don't want any sunlight ter lit on her?"

"Not a ray."

"But—I ain't never heared o' nothin' so silly. Why don't she jist stay in the house?"

His answer was cut off by the *Sea Siren*'s whistle. At the sudden noise, Khan began to howl. Even after the whistling ceased, he continued, eliciting stares from the people gathered around the landing.

Preparations for departure were made quickly, and Chickadee soon found herself in front of Saxon's personal coach. Drawn by four gray thoroughbreds, the black barouche was gilt-trimmed; the Blackwell crest was emblazoned in gold on the door. Two footmen, dressed in elaborate livery, were positioned at the back. The postilions wore the finest buckskin breeches she'd ever seen. Their high-top boots gleamed, as did their black silk coats and the gold braid that adorned their caps.

While one of the footmen tied Hagen to the back of the carriage, Saxon assisted her inside. The interior was as luxurious as the outside, the walls and cushioned seats covered with gold satin damask.

"Wolf!"

The sudden shout interrupted her examination of the coach. "Saxon, whar's Khan?" She jumped to the ground and noticed a crowd of people not too far away. Between the spaces of their legs and skirts, she saw a flash of white. When she saw a dockworker cock his pistol and butt his way through the throng, she turned back to the carriage and pulled out her rifle.

Saxon grabbed it. "Just what do you think you're—"

"Khan's over thar, and I swear iffen one hair on him is hurt, I'm gwine blow somebody's fool head off!'' She snatched her gun from his grasp and ran toward the horde of people, Saxon at her heels.

When she arrived at the scene, she saw Khan was cornered between two buildings. ''Dang it! Move!'' she screamed, jostling people out of her way. Not one person paid her a bit of attention, everyone anxiously waiting to see what would happen between the armed dockman and the snarling wolf. Chickadee, with practiced ease, shot three consecutive shots into the air.

''Dammit, Keely!'' Saxon yanked the gun away from her.

The crowd broke apart immediately, all eyes switching from the feral beast to the redheaded rustic. Chickadee ignored them all and ran to Khan, but just before she reached him, a deep voice stopped her.

''Step away from him, miss,'' the dockhand said, his pistol leveled at Khan.

''Step away?'' Her hand flew to her thigh, and from a long leather sheath she withdrew a sharp hunting knife. Saxon read her mind, but the knife was slicing through the air before he could take it away from her.

Precisely as she intended, the tip of the blade sank into the toe of one of the dockman's boots, the hilt quivering. When the man looked down, Chickadee ran to Khan and threw her arms around him.

''Look . . . look what she did!'' the worker exclaimed. ''These are the only boots I own!''

''And this here's the onliest pet I own, mister!'' Chickadee glared at the man and the shocked audience. ''Khan warn't a-hurtin' nobody. He was jist a-sniffin' around, and all you-uns crowded around him so's he couldn't go nowhars! Dang shameful's what it is!''

''All right, Keely,'' Saxon said. ''No harm was done.''

''No harm?'' the dockhand bellowed, gesturing

toward his boot. "I expect to be paid for this damage."

Saxon sighed. "Tell me how much they cost, and I'll—"

Cutting him off, Chickadee grabbed her rifle from him and aimed it at the workman. "You ain't a-gittin' nothin' fer them boots, you God-burn varmint." She snapped her fingers. "Khan you ain't had yore supper yet, have you?"

The wolf's tongue slipped out of the side of his mouth, his saliva dripping to the pavement, his glacial blue gaze centered on his would-be killer.

"Keely, stop this nonsense," Saxon said, attempting to wrest the rifle from her.

She kept a tight hold on the gun. "Nonsense? This here cuss was gwine shoot Khan! That ain't no nonsense. Git him, Khan."

The wolf bared his teeth and with his head hung low, slunk toward the dockhand. The workman raised his pistol once more, but Chickadee shot the gun out of his hand.

Several women screamed, the men gaped. Saxon clenched his jaw. "Keely, are you quite finished?"

"No, I ain't. Ain't gwine be finished till this here buzzard says he's sorry ter Khan. Go on, mister. Say yore sorry, or I'll let him tar you up."

Saxon tried again to take her rifle from her, but she still refused to relinquish it. "Keely, this is ridiculous. Whoever heard of apologizing to a wolf?"

"I got my tail up and stinger out, Saxon, so hesh up. I ain't a-studyin' you no how."

"But—"

"What is the meaning of this?" The crowd parted for the policeman as he approached Chickadee and Saxon. "Young lady, what are you doing with that rifle?"

Saxon sighed. "Officer, this is all a terrible misunderstanding. She was only trying to protect her—"

"She threw this knife at me!" the dockman cried.

He pulled the blade from his boot. "I only wanted to keep this beast from attacking someone, when this female heathen—"

"Heathen?" Chickadee shouted. She crossed and snatched her knife back. "Listen here, mister. Khan warn't gwine hurt nobody, and iffen you don't say yore sorry fer near about a-killin' him, I'm gwine take this here blade and cut yore ass too thick ter fish with and too thin ter fry!"

Saxon blanched, recognizing the genuine menace in her voice. "Keely—"

"Miss, you are obviously not from here and apparently don't understand the seriousness of your actions," the policeman interjected. "Lower your rifle immediately, or I'll be forced to arrest you for threatening this man."

Chickadee whirled on him, her eyes spitting green fire, her finger toying with the trigger of her gun. "Yore a-lookin' at me like I was a bottle o' stale piss, Mr. Sheriff, and I don't take kindly ter nobody inspectin' me that way. All's I want is fer this here varmint ter say he's sorry ter Khan, and then I'll be on my way."

Saxon stepped between the policeman and Chickadee, his hands spread out in a pleading gesture. "Officer, I'll gladly pay for the man's boots so we can be done with this matter. Keely meant no harm, and you're correct in assuming she's not from here. I realize wolves aren't allowed to roam freely here in Boston, and—"

"They most assuredly are not!" the policeman agreed vehemently. "What if this beast had attacked someone?"

"Wouldn'ta been no more'n these here people deserved!" Chickadee shouted. "They surrounded Khan and he don't like a-bein' penned in!" She turned back to the dockman. "You gwine say yore sorry, mister, or—"

"I'm sorry!" The workman swabbed his forehead with a handkerchief. "Just give me the money for my boots, and I'll leave you and your damn wolf alone forever!''

"Money?'' Chickadee shot back, pushing the barrel of her rifle into the man's chest. "I'm gwine thresh the straw jist one more time fer you, mister. You ain't gwine git one penny fer them sorry boots on account o' you started this whole thang!'' With each word she uttered, she thrust the rifle into him harder, pushing him backward.

"Keely!'' Saxon reached her in two strides, his money pouch already open in his hands. He took out a wad of bills and threw them at the man. Taking Chickadee by the shoulders, he pulled her away, his tight grip defying resistance.

"Dang you, Saxon! Why'd you pay that worthless rascal?''

"Keely,'' he said into her ear, "stop this at once.''

The hushed command, told her he was dead serious. And the look in his sharp, azure gaze made her own eyes widen. She couldn't understand why he was so angry. After all, all she'd been trying to do was right a wrong. But apparently, fool-headed as he was, he didn't see that.

"Please excuse the disturbance, officer,'' Saxon said. "I'll make sure such an occurrence never happens again.''

"See that you do. And if I ever see that vicious animal loose again, I'll shoot him myself. I've no idea why you have a wolf, and I've no wish to hear your reasons. Just take him and this . . . this *yokel* out of the city and to a place where neither of them can do any further harm!''

Chickadee bristled at the name he'd called her but said nothing as Saxon's grip on her shoulders suddenly increased in strength.

"Officer,'' he said sternly, "this woman is my wife. She is not a *yokel*, she's an Appalachian mountain girl. There is a big difference between the two. Good day.''

Chickadee wrinkled her nose at the officer and let

Saxon lead her away from the crowd. One woman
in the group gathered her skirts away from her as if
the mountain girl would contaminate them. Chickadee glared at the woman but refrained from com-
ment. Khan, however, displayed his dislike by lifting
his leg and spraying her fine gown with his special
scent as he passed her.

Saxon turned at her hysterical blubbering and saw
the suspicious yellow stain on her ivory dress. With
a tremendous sigh, he pulled out his money pouch
yet another time and handed some money to her
escort.

"Damn," he muttered as he ushered wolf and
wife back to the carriage. "If I don't get the two of
you home, the whole Blackwell fortune will be spent
in one afternoon!"

Chickadee simmered in silence as they traveled to
the estate, located in the lush countryside outside
the city limits. When he tried to soothe her, she
threw her shoes at him. He soon gave up and turned
his thoughts to what happened at the wharf.

His jaw tightened with the memory. "Damn," he
muttered again. He was usually cautious in all his
endeavors, anticipating possible problems and finding solutions for them before they even arose. His
years with Blackwell Enterprises had taught him
that.

"Damn," he muttered for the third time as he
continued to ponder the situation. The excitement
he'd felt about outsmarting Araminta and finding
possible help for Desdemona had overwhelmed him
to such a degree that he hadn't fully comprehended
that he planned to move a mountain into the middle
of a city. For though his barefoot bride was now
Keely Blackwell, she was first and foremost Chickadee McBride.

That thought weighed heavily on his mind when
the carriage turned at last into the long, elm-lined
drive to the Blackwell mansion.

Chapter 9

The silent plea in Saxon's sapphire eyes roused Chickadee's anger. "Saxon, you didn't have no call ter order me—"

"I'm sorry I was curt, but I wanted to prevent your arrest. You didn't want to go to jail, did you?"

She shrugged her shoulders. "I'd jist break out."

"Keely, this is Boston," he said gently. "There are rules here, and there is a certain—"

"They ain't my rules, and I ain't gwine larn'em. I cain't treason my values jist on account o' thur different'n the ones you-uns have. I done tole you ever'thang deserves respect, and that wolf killer back thar owed Khan a apology. I ain't no city lady, but I got my beliefs about the right way o' livin' and ain't no rule that's gwine change 'em."

She was right, and he knew it. She was who she was, and he had no right to chastise her. Besides, she had a point about standing up for her values, and he respected her for defending them. "I apologize," he said, his fingers whispering across her palm.

Satisfied, she settled into the soft cushions and watched him surreptitiously. He was antsy, she noted with a mental frown. Gone was all the heartease he'd only just begun to attain in the Blue Ridge: his eyes held a look she'd seen many times in hurt or defensive animals; he sat rigidly, as if relaxing would crack his body; and his slight smile was forced, as if he'd pulled it from his pocket and attached it to his face.

Following his line of vision, she saw the house and remembered this place held bad memories for him. Even as he watched it come nearer, a dreadful sadness was creeping across his finely sculpted face. The tension that shrouded him was almost tangible.

When the carriage came to a halt, one of the footmen opened the door, holding out his hand to assist Chickadee. She looked at his open palm. "Iffen it's money yore a-wantin', you best know I'm as poor as gully dirt, Mr. Carriage Man. Saxon's the one who was raised on a floored pen around here."

The footman grinned. "I only thought to aid you in alighting from the carriage, miss."

"Aid? You hear that, outlander? Respect's what this here feller's a-givin' me." She placed her slender, tanned hand in the footman's white glove and allowed him to help her from the coach. Khan bounded out after her, and with a shake of his head, Saxon too stepped out.

While he gave instructions to the footmen regarding Hagen's care, Chickadee stood gaping at the huge, white structure before her. The granite mansion stood on an eminence way above the level of the driveway. She counted eight Corinthian columns, and decided that number was probably needed to hold up the three-story monstrosity. The glistening windows that dotted the alabaster facade were covered with lacy wrought-iron grilles, and each story had its own balcony that extended the length of the house.

As she stared in disbelief, the awesome, whitewashed door slowly opened. A distinguished-looking man stood on the threshold, his hands, too, encased in snowy white gloves. "Mr. Blackwell." The name rolled off his tongue as if saying it left a bad taste in his mouth. "Welcome home, sir."

As Chickadee listened to his voice, the picture of a jagged rock bouncing down an equally jagged hillside came to mind. He was looking down that beak on his face as if it pained him sorely to see Saxon again. His black dot eyes were narrowed in contempt, and his thin, colorless lips were pinched so as not to utter any more gracious salutations than were necessary.

Saxon's head snapped toward the man. "Thatcher, how is Desdemona? She's here, isn't she?"

"Miss Desdemona," the man said, and took a long, slow breath designed to irritate him, "is as she always is. I believe her to be in her bedroom."

Saxon nodded and pointed to the baggage. Thatcher sniffed once before he proceeded down the marble steps. As he walked past Chickadee, she reached out and took hold of his arm. She might not be in love with Saxon, she mused, but she sure wasn't going to let anyone insult him! "Yore about as friendly as a bahr with a sore ass, feller. Maybe Saxon didn't notice it, or maybe he don't keer none, but I seed the way you looked at him."

Thatcher stared at her hard before he jerked his arm away from her and brushed the sleeve of his spotless coat. "If it's work you want, I must insist you use the servants' entrance. You may wait for me there, but it is highly doubtful that a woman of your . . . uh, *quality* will find employment here."

"Thatcher!" Saxon roared. "That woman is—"

"Yore a strut fart, mister," Chickadee said coolly, her simmering green eyes never leaving Thatcher's insulting black ones. "It contraried me the way you looked at my husband. You don't like him none, do you?"

"Your hus—" Thatcher looked at Saxon and then back at Chickadee. "You're *married* to Mr. Blackwell?"

"Reckon that's the onliest way he could be my husband."

When Saxon didn't deny what Chickadee said, Thatcher bowed his head. "My apologies to you both.'' With that, he straightened and went down the remaining steps. Grabbing the bags, he took them inside the house, pausing at the door to allow Chickadee and Saxon to enter.

Saxon took Chickadee's arm and led her inside. ''Take the bags to my room, Thatcher, and see to it that a bath is made ready for my wife. Also, tell that little maid, Candice, that I will be up to see Desdemona shortly.''

Thatcher nodded and began to close the door. But before it was shut, Khan wiggled his way through the narrow opening, yelping when Thatcher tried to kick him back outside. Saxon pushed the door wide open for the indignant wolf. ''Khan will be allowed to roam as he pleases. If I ever hear of you mistreating him, you will answer to me.''

''As you say, sir.'' Thatcher marched down the spacious, arch-divided entrance hall and scaled the spiral staircase.

Chickadee watched him go. ''He walks so straight, it's like he's got a arrow rammed up his spine.'' She giggled and looked around her. ''Saxon, I ain't never seed nothin' like this here house in all my days.''

''You like it?''

''Didn't never say that.''

''Don't you?''

''It's a mite big, ain't it? And what fer do you-uns need so many chars?'' she asked, pointing to the sets of ladder-backed Chippendale chairs lining the hall. ''And what are all them decorations up on the ceilin' fer? What do you-uns do? Lay on the floor and stare up at 'em fer fun?''

Ignoring his chuckle, she looked at the wall. ''Paper on the dang walls. Iffen that don't beat all.''

He regarded her with amusement. ''It's called wallpaper.''

''What genius came up with that name?'' She crossed the floor to a gleaming Queen Anne dropleaf table and picked up the delicate vase that sat on it, nearly dropping it when a screech suddenly shot through the foyer.

"Put that down immediately!"

In the archway of one of the doors opening into the foyer stood Araminta Blackwell, her pale blue eyes sparkling with disgust and anger. Her hands, their skin like parchment, were folded around the silver knob of her ebony cane, and her onyx brooch glittered as brightly as her eyes.

For one brief moment Saxon looked away from it, struggling with remembered horror.

"Saxon, I command you to get this person out of my house. I will not tolerate your fortune-hunting doxies here."

Chickadee a fortune hunter? The ridiculous accusation eased his tension, and a shiver of excitement coursed through his frame. The moment had arrived. Smiling a lazy, mocking smile, he led Chickadee to his grandmother.

Araminta gasped when Khan sat down by her feet. The wolf looked up at her and began to pant, long streamers of his spittle sluicing to the fine kid slippers that peeked out from beneath her black gown. Her gasp dwindled to a silent scream at the sight of his huge, wicked teeth. She backed away, her arm searching wildly for the door frame.

"Ain't no need ter faint or nothin', Araminty," Chickadee assured the horror-stricken lady. "Khan wouldn't never hurt no one lessen they asked fer it."

Struggling to regain her icy composure, Araminta straightened, but was promptly infuriated by Saxon's taunting grin.

"Careful, Grandmother. If you do anything at all Khan could interpret as a threat, I assure you, you will regret your actions. Now, shall we converse over tea?" He tucked Chickadee's hand in the crook of his elbow, led her into the drawing room, and assisted her into a lemon-yellow satin chair. "And you,

Khan. Over there," he said, pointing to the thick Oriental rug in front of the fire.

The wolf wagged his tail and ambled to the warm hearth. Once there, he lay down, rolled on his back, and with his feet up in the air, turned his head toward the doorway to watch Araminta enter.

She stepped in slowly, her precise movements designed to demonstrate her command of the mansion and everyone in it. She held her head high and pointed her cane regally at Chickadee. "You will remove yourself from this house immediately. And take that beast with you." she ordered, glancing at Khan.

Silence settled over the room. Araminta waited for her demands to be met, Chickadee sat openmouthed at the woman's rudeness, and Saxon, smiling broadly, tried to decide if *he* wanted to break the news to his grandmother or if he wanted to watch Chickadee do it.

Finally Chickadee arose and crossed gracefully to stand before the outraged woman. The wrinkles radiating from Araminta's nose in cobweb fashion made Chickadee think of a spider. Araminta the Spider Woman. Skinny enough to wash in a gun barrel and so ugly she'd probably gag a maggot.

She successfully controlled the bubble of laughter that tickled the back of her throat. What was it about this silly stick-woman that made Saxon so edgy?

And yore a-tryin' ter make me feather-legged too, she told Araminta silently. "Got a case o' the uneases, Araminty? Come on over here and set a spell whilst I tell you all the gwines-on's." She took Araminta's arm.

"How dare you put your hands on me!" She raised her cane above Chickadee's head.

Khan became a white blur as he bounded toward his mistress. In one smooth motion, he leaped high into the air, caught the ebony cane between his teeth, and wrested it away from the terrified Araminta. When he landed, his ears were laid back flat, a low growl coming from his throat.

Chickadee sighed. "Araminty, I done tole you not ter rile him. You cain't bang me over the head withouten Khan—"

"Saxon!" Araminta jerked her arm from Chickadee's grasp and started for her grandson. But before she'd made much progress, Chickadee grabbed her arm again, this time holding it with such force that the sleeve of Araminta's dress was torn from the bodice.

"Thatcher!" Araminta sputtered, clasping her scraggy hand over the rip. "Saxon!"

"Sit down, Grandmother," he said coolly. "Surely you're not forgetting your duties as hostess? The dress can be repaired later. Pour the tea." He sat in the chair beside Chickadee's, crossed his legs, and drummed his fingers on his knee.

Chickadee looked at the huge silver tea set. "I'll pour it, Araminty," she said, firmly leading the woman to the settee and pushing her down onto it. "You jist set thar, and I'll give you yore tea."

Araminta stared ahead blankly. "Saxon, if this is your attempt at humor, I assure you it is a feeble one."

He heard the distress in her voice. Someone else might have interpreted it as defeat, but Saxon knew she was merely gathering her wits about her again.

"Lord o' mercy. These here dishes are shore purty, Araminty," Chickadee said as she poured tea into a cup and onto the Aubusson carpet.

"Dear God!" Araminta flew out of the settee, showing more energy than she had in years, and snatched up a napkin.

But Chickadee grabbed it out of her hand. "I made the mess, and I'll clean it up. You got any vinegar? Ain't nothin' like vinegar ter git stains outen thangs, y'know. 'Course, this here stain ain't real bad. More'n likely, nobody'll even notice it." With her foot, she rubbed the tea deeply into the rug. "See?

Cain't hardly see it no more.'' She held the cup of tea out to Araminta, the dark brew sloshing over the rim and into the saucer.

Her hands trembling, Araminta took the cup but set it down. ''Saxon, I demand you tell me what this is all about. This . . . *rustic* has been here all of fifteen minutes, and already there is dog spittle on my shoes, there is dog hair on my Chinese rug, my cane is ruined, my sleeve is torn, and there is tea on the carpet! I do not know who this person—''

''This *person* has every right to be here.'' Saxon crossed to Chickadee's side. ''I have met the stipulations in your will. This beautiful girl is my wife, Keely Blackwell.''

Araminta grabbed at her brooch and swayed back into the settee. ''Reckon yore my granny now too,'' Chickadee said. ''You want I should call you Granny or Araminty? Yore a sight older'n I am, so I reckon it's yore right ter tell me what you want me ter call you.'' She bent and patted Araminta's trembling hand. ''How old are you anyway? About a hunnerd?''

Araminta's gaze hardened at Saxon's expression. ''The marriage certificate,'' she snapped at him. ''Produce it immediately.''

''Oh, we're married all right,'' Chickadee said. ''Stepped offen the carpet in a real church with a real preacher-parson in front o' about fifteen folks. I had on the God-burnin'est purty dress you ever laid eyes on. Would a-weared it to this here city, but I spilt gravy on it. After that, I stepped on the hem whilst I was a-dancin' and ripped up the skirt real bad. Miz Mansfield tried to fix it fer me, but she couldn't do nothin' with it and finally throwed it away. We had the weddin' party at her house and was all a-laughin', a-wearin' the bells, and—''

''I cannot begin to express how little I care.'' Araminta held out her skeletal hand. ''Saxon, the document in question.''

He smiled, withdrew a cheroot from his pocket,

and lit it, knowing the smell of the smoke irritated her. He deliberately blew it her way before he reached inside his coat and pulled out a sheet of paper. "Here's the pine forest report you wanted, too," he said, tossing a packet to the settee.

Araminta ignored the report and took the document. Chickadee sat down beside her and pointed to a name on the certificate. "See that thar name? That's me. Keely McBride. But you can call me Chickadee. Ain't nobody calls me Keely but Saxon, and I been a-thankin' he's the onliest one I'll let call me that. That way, it'll be special."

Araminta ignored her and continued to inspect the document, her eyes narrowing as she scanned it and verified its legality. The uncivilized girl who sat beside her was Mrs. Saxon Blackwell. The certificate fluttered to the floor. "I will have this mockery of a marriage annulled, Saxon."

"On what grounds?" He walked to the fireplace and flicked ashes into it. "Keely and I are both of marriageable age, there were witnesses at the wedding, you know the certificate is legal, and," he said, pausing to grin rakishly, "I assure you the marriage has most definitely been consummated."

Araminta raised her hand. "Spare me the sordid details." She rose, clutching her skirts tightly, her white fingers a frightening contrast to the midnight hue of her gown. "You have disappointed me, and for that you will be sorry. If you are entertaining the thought that you have bested me, you are woefully mistaken."

"Really? And what, pray tell, will you do?"

"The will. I'll change it if you do not divorce this—"

Saxon laughed. "Change it again, and your reputation will be ruined, Grandmother. There are some who already think the first ultimatum you gave me was cruel, and if you alter the will to cause—heaven forbid!—a *divorce*, what will people think of your scandalous action?"

Speechless with impotent anger, Araminta could only glare.

Saxon turned away from the hatred in her eyes and forced down his haunting memories again. "I realize the bulk of the fortune will not be mine until your death, but you are required to provide me with a monthly sum of money now that I am married. I'll expect the funds due me as soon as possible. And lest you forget, Grandmother, let me remind you again of the damage your . . . uh, *good name* will suffer should you tamper with the will. I'll not hesitate for an instant to make your vindictive actions known to all of Boston."

Araminta's wrath exuded from every pore. The Boston Brahmins—the elite society of the city—would undoubtedly look down on her if she dared *force* Saxon to divorce his wife. Just as he'd said, an act of that kind would cause a horrible scandal. And if she disinherited him, as she had done with his father, that, too, would tear her reputation to threads, for Saxon had, indeed, met the will's stipulations to the very letter. Light-headed with rage, she turned to leave.

"Araminty?"

The look Araminta gave the mountain girl could have turned the sun into a snowball. "My name is not Araminty. It is Araminta. Mrs. Blackwell to the likes of you."

Chickadee wrinkled her freckled nose. "You and me's kinfolks, and I ain't gwine call you Miz Blackwell. It's either Araminty or Granny. What's yore druthers?"

Araminta scowled at her and then bristled at the sound of Saxon's smug laughter. Surely there was some way to make this mountain person leave! Her eyes narrowed wickedly.

Desdemona. The asylum! She would have her granddaughter committed and refuse to allow her release until the heathen was out of Saxon's life. Society wouldn't blame her for sending Desdemona to the institution for "treatment." Everyone would understand and sympathize. And she would vehemently deny any and all accusations Saxon might throw at her. No one would believe him anyway: all of Boston knew Desdemona was insane.

She would make the arrangements secretly and without delay. The solution found, a smile replaced her frown as she looked at Chickadee. "It does not matter what you call me. I have no intention of being around you anyway."

Chickadee sighed and pulled the raccoon tails from the waistband of her breeches, stroking them lovingly before she pressed them into Araminta's hand. "Had these here coon tails fer gwine on ten years, Araminty, but I'm gwine give 'em to you. Don't reckon you and me's ever gwine wash hands together, but thur still ain't no reason why we cain't at least be civil. These here perfectly matched tails can be the commencin' of peace betwixt us."

Araminta dropped the tails as if they'd set her hand on fire. She whirled to leave the room, slowing as she passed Khan, who was chewing her ebony cane into splinters.

"Araminty?"

Araminta stopped but did not turn around.

"Did it rile you when I asked iffen you was a hunnerd years old? Iffen it did, I'm sorry. You really don't look a day over ninety."

A visible shudder shook Araminta's body as she disappeared through the door. Saxon's deep laughter echoed throughout the mansion.

Saxon's bedroom of dark green and gold reminded Chickadee of her mountains in autumn. She thought it the most beautiful room she'd ever seen until she beheld Desdemona's a few hours later. Desdemona's room, decorated in peach and teal, was the Blue Ridge in springtime. Chickadee professed it to be as lovely as the silent girl who rarely left it.

"Your waistcoat is being pressed as we speak, Mr. Blackwell," Candice, the young maid, nervously told Saxon as she laced a pink ribbon through Desdemona's hair. "And Miss Desdemona is ready. But sir, if I may be so bold . . . are you sure it's your wish to take her downstairs for dinner? Mrs. Blackwell instructed me to lay out only one place setting. And she has never allowed Miss Desdemona—"

"I will take full responsibility for bringing my sister to the dining room, Candice." When the maid curtsied and left to get his coat, Saxon knelt by his sister and placed her hand on his cheek. "Desdemona, I'm home."

Desdemona continued to stare at a miniature painting of her mother and father on her bedside table.

Saxon felt that familiar sadness rise within him. But it faded instantly when he remembered who was standing beside him. "Desdemona, there's someone here I want you to meet. This is your new sister-in-law, Keely."

Chickadee held out the pine-straw basket she'd made. When Desdemona made no move to take it, she sat down beside the quiet girl. "Made this fer you, Desdemona. It's fer a-totin' posies."

"Keely is from North Carolina," Saxon explained. "I told you I'd bring you something that would help you understand where I went, and there's no better way to describe the beauty and wonder of North Carolina than to show you its most remarkable native. I met Keely in the mountains when she saved me from a bear."

Chickadee laughed and smoothed Desdemona's black curls. "Saxon warn't real smart. He left his shootin'-arn on Hagen's back, and the critter lit out with it. When I first met yore brother, he couldn't a-growed pole beans in a pile o' horse—"

"Uh, Keely has been looking forward to meeting you, Desdemona," Saxon broke in quickly. He made a mental note to ask Chickadee to refrain from using strong language and just as quickly decided it would do no good.

"And yore ever' bit as purty as Saxon said you was, Desi."

Desdemona turned her head to stare at nothingness.

"Stay with her for a moment while I see what's keeping Candice with my coat, Keely," Saxon said. "I'm anxious to confront Grandmother once and for all. I've done everything she demanded, and there's not a blessed thing she can do. I can't remember the last time I dined with Desdemona downstairs, and despite what Grandmother has to say, the meal we share tonight will be the first of many more."

When he was gone Chickadee knelt and reached up to hold Desdemona's satin-encased arms. "Desi, darlin', you don't talk. Saxon said you don't even smile, and that ain't right. It's Araminty, ain't it?"

Desdemona's eyes widened.

"That ole spider woman prob'ly skeert the voice plumb outen you when she come ter this here city. I know she's yore granny and all, but she's mean enough ter pour water on a poor ole widder woman's kindlin'. Now Desi? I know you cain't talk, but I suspicion thur ain't nothin' wrong with yore ears. You listen ter me real good, sweet thang, and we'll see iffen you don't smile when I'm finished explainin' the way o' thangs ter you."

She patted the girl's hands and stood. "I ain't got it settled in my mind real good yet, but somehow I'm gwine larn ole Araminty some manners. This afternoon she was a-lookin' at me like I warn't worth dried spit. I'm a-tellin' you, she was nigh in a franzy that Saxon married me. I done already figgered it out that she was a-wantin' him ter marry a Boston girl. I had a mind ter slap her down fer a-treatin' me the way she done, but my mama-woman raised me better'n that."

Chickadee began to laugh. "You got ter stretch out a snake real good afore you can measure it, darlin', and that's what I'm a-aimin' ter do. Once I got that spider woman figgered out, her and me's gwine pass some words. She's right used ter folks a-fallin' over back'ards fer her, but she ain't gwine play that thunder with me. And she's a-baitin' trouble by a-treatin' you the way she does, Desi. It's shameful her not a-lettin' you eat with her. And Lord only knows what else she does ter you.''

She pulled Desdemona from the bed. ''Saxon says he's gwine give her what fer ternight at supper. But I reckon he's been a-tryin' ter handle that woman fer years. 'Pears to me he ain't done too good so fur. He thanks he's done winned the battle, but he ain't, Desi. Spider Woman'll bite back, shore and sartin. 'Sides that, he ain't allus gwine be around here no how. He's got them fancy offices ter go ter.''

She brought Desdemona into her embrace. ''But I'll be here, Desi. I ain't gwine be here fer long, but I ain't gwine let ole Araminty hurt you whilst I'm here. I'm gwine stay with you. You and me's gwine be like sisters, and I swear I'll take up fer you. You done got yoresef a guardian angel, sweet thang. But this angel's got horns and a pitchfork along with her wangs.''

Saxon returned then, and though there was no smile on Desdemona's lips, he could have sworn there were smiles in her eyes.

Chapter 10

"Desdemona, go to your room." The crisp order delivered, Araminta seated herself at the head of the table.

Desdemona turned toward the door, stiffening when Saxon caught the sash of her gown. "Come back here. You're a member of this family, and you'll eat with us from now on."

Araminta watched with rising vexation. "Desdemona, you will do as *I* told you. Your brother has no say."

"Why don't he?" Chickadee returned Araminta's glare with equal defiance. "He's the spear-side o' the family."

"Saxon, if it is your sister's solitude that worries you, send your trollop upstairs to dine with her," Araminta suggested coldly. "As simple as they both are, I imagine they will get along famously."

Chickadee's laughter drowned out Saxon's muttered curse. She snapped for Khan and walked to the table. She reached for a soft roll and fed it to the hungry wolf. "Me and Desi's got somethin' in common all right, Araminty. And that's the bad-mouthin' we take offen you. But you'd best be keerful lessen you want them ill words flanged back at you."

Saxon, who had been about to join his mountain girl in her challenge, closed his mouth abruptly when Desdemona let go of his hand and joined Chickadee

147

at the table. She too reached for a roll, intending to feed it to Khan as Chickadee had done.

Araminta slapped her granddaughter's hand. Desdemona dropped the bread back into the silver basket and turned to flee. Again, Saxon caught her. Khan watched the scene briefly, then lifted his paws to the table and gobbled up every roll left.

Araminta quivered with anger. "Thatcher, get that animal out of this house!"

Which one? Thatcher wondered. He sniffed and went to the wary wolf.

"I wouldn't do that if I were you, Thatcher," Saxon said, pulling Desdemona back to the table. "Khan enjoyed that bread, but what he normally eats is raw meat."

Araminta stood. "I will not tolerate this blatant disregard for propriety. Go for the authorities, Thatcher."

"The authorities?" Saxon bent his head and grinned. "Now, Grandmother, calling in the authorities because of your own granddaughter-in-law would cause an uproar of the grandest kind. What would Mrs. Preston say?"

"Who's Miz Preston?" Chickadee asked, wondering why the mere mention of the woman's name silenced Araminta.

Saxon took a moment to seat Chickadee and Desdemona, making a great show of seeing to their comfort before he sat down in his own chair. "Tell Keely about Mrs. Preston, Grandmother."

"You have made your point," Araminta snapped.

Saxon acquiesced with a nod of his head, and then motioned for the serving girl to set three more places at the table. "What's this thang a-doin' down here?" Chickadee asked and held up the tablecloth to look at the small stool she had knocked over. "This whar you-uns hide furniture you don't want no more?"

"The stools are placed under the table for the ladies' comfort, little one. You rest your feet on them."

Law, these rich folks is somethin' else, Chickadee mused. "The way you-uns talk, this Miz Preston sounds like she's a queen. 'Pears to me—"

"I, for one, do not care how anything appears to you," Araminta interrupted.

"Grandmother, when Keely is introduced to society, she will certainly meet Mrs. Preston. Surely you don't want your new granddaughter-in-law to speak ill of you."

Araminta wearily slithered back into her chair.

"Mrs. Preston is the most highly respected woman in Boston society," Saxon explained. "Our local matriarch, wouldn't you agree, Grandmother?"

Araminta realized he was taunting her and enjoying it immensely. He didn't care a whit about Eugenia Preston or the woman's opinion, but he knew very well that Araminta cared deeply. She pursed her lips in irritation.

"Yes, well, as I was saying," Saxon continued merrily, "Mrs. Preston's fourth cousin is married to some English earl—"

"It's her *third* cousin who is married to a *fifth* cousin of the royal family," Araminta corrected him haughtily.

"How kind of you to set me straight, Grandmother," Saxon said and grinned. "Anyway, Keely, because of Mrs. Preston's . . . uh, *ties* with royalty, she is Boston's grande dame. Of course, her enormous fortune doesn't hurt her respectability either. You'll meet her soon, little one. I do think Keely should meet some other women, Grandmother. Having friends will help her adjust to Boston and also fill her time when I'm not here. I'll depend on you to help me with that."

Araminta choked on her wine. "You—unthinkable! If you believe I am going to assist you in any way with—"

"Oh, but you will," Saxon said, attacking his oysters. "You will escort Keely to various ladies' activities, because if you do not, I will take her to them myself."

"You wouldn't dare!" Araminta stood again.

"Why wouldn't I? I've always wondered what you women do at all those get-togethers. I might enjoy attending them, now that I think of it. That way I could get all the latest gossip and not have to wait for the wind to carry it to the male socials. We men never know what's happening in the circles of the fair sex, and—"

"You can be sure there will be gossip!" Araminta screeched. "It will be about *you!*"

"And when have I ever given a damn about what people say about me?"

"Saxon, I ain't gwine eat these thangs." Chickadee was paying no attention to the heated argument taking place in front of her. She was studying her oysters with confusion and disgust. "They don't look like they been cooked, and I don't eat no raw meat."

At Saxon's nod, a serving girl removed Chickadee's plate of oysters and replaced it with a bowl of creamy soup. "Aren't you going to sit down and join us for dinner, Grandmother?" He hid his grin in a bite of brown bread.

Araminta watched Chickadee pick up a dessert spoon and slurp up the soup. Her gaze then went to Desdemona, who, after looking at Chickadee, picked up *her* dessert spoon and began to swill down her soup in the same loud manner. "See what you have brought upon us all, Saxon. Think about it, because I assure you your punishment for the disrespect you have shown me will—"

"I suggest, Grandmother, that if you find our company repulsive, you go eat in your room as you previously suggested we do. We have no intention of leaving the dining room, and will be taking all our meals here."

"But . . . but look how they are eating!" Araminta returned, aghast as she pointed to Chickadee and Desdemona.

Chickadee, who had finished her soup, was exasperated with her knife and fork. She put them aside and ate her roast mutton with her hands. "Saxon, temorrer I'm gwine sharpen these here knives fer you. Thur so dull you could ride'em to mill and back withouten no blanket. Desi here give up on hers too, didn't you, darlin'?"

Desdemona remained silent, intent on finishing her meat. Her mouth and fingers were greasy, and there was a large smear on the front of her pink gown. But Saxon gave her an encouraging smile. "Yes, Grandmother," he said softly, "see what I have brought upon us all."

"They are eating with their hands!"

Chickadee looked up from her plate. "Iffen my knife warn't so dang dull, I wouldn't use my hands, Araminty. I got manners same as all you-uns. But 'sides that, fangers was around long afore forks. Maybe the good Lord above *meaned* fer us ter use our hands."

"The good Lord? What do you know about Him? In my dictionary, a heathen is a person who does not acknowledge the teachings of God or the Bible."

Saxon's ire was immediate. He stood, threw his napkin to the table, and took a step toward Araminta. His extreme anger erased all thought of trying to remain genteel in his dealings with her.

"Keely was right in saying I am the man of this household, Grandmother! I have done everything you commanded, and in doing so have stripped you of your previous power over me. You may simmer in your wrath, or you may accept the changes that will undoubtedly take place in your life. What you choose to do is entirely up to you, but I—"

"You will pay for your insolence." Araminta turned to look at Chickadee. "And as for you, you are a most repugnant person. Your manners are as atrocious as your grammar, appearance, and—"

"Here's to you, Araminty," Chickadee said and lifted her wineglass, noticing that Desdemona imitated the action. "Yore snuff's a mite strong, but I got ter hand it ter you. You don't give up easy, and I reckon you and me's gwine have us a time on account o' I don't give up easy neither!"

Fuming, Araminta swept from the dining room, the odor of her perfume lingering over the table like a cloud of cloyingly sweet roses. Saxon blew a sarcastic kiss at her back and sat down again. "Shall we finish our meal, ladies?"

Chickadee awoke with a start, disoriented until she remembered where she was. The bedroom was dim and chilled, the fire having gone out. Glancing at the heavy, scary canopy above her, she reached to Saxon's side of the bed, wanting to feel the warmth of his strong arms around her while she went back to sleep, but her hands encountered only cold, empty space. Then she remembered he hadn't come to bed with her. She found the warm robe Candice had brought to her and left the bedroom.

At the upper landing of the staircase, she walked into a table. "Dang it," she muttered, "What fer do these Blackwells got ter have all these God-burn tables and chars a-settin' around in ever' corner?" she asked Khan. "A person could git kilt jist a-tryin' ter git around!" She rubbed her bruised knee and grabbed the banister.

"You reckon thur's anythang dangerous a-settin' on these here steps, Khan? Iffen thur is, I ain't a-takin' no chances." Swinging her leg over the slick railing, she slid all the way down.

She swiftly reached the bottom, dismounted, and wandered around the ground level of the mansion until she saw light coming from beneath a closed door. She opened it and saw Saxon sitting in an overstuffed chair in front of the fireplace. He hadn't heard her enter, and he hadn't seen her yet, either.

As always, her breath caught in her throat when she studied his features.

He still wore his evening clothes, but the elegance of his attire in no way diminished the aura of potent masculinity that accompanied him as faithfully as his shadow. He'd removed his dinner jacket and waistcoat. Those, she noted with a smile, were thrown in a heap on the floor. His cambric shirt was open, revealing the muscled expanse of his broad chest, the whisper of hair covering his skin like soft slivers of midnight.

His hair was mussed, the golden light of the fire flickering through its raven waves like stars shooting across the dark night sky. His eyes, half shielded by his thickly lashed lids, stared directly into the flames, as if that eerie blaze was telling him something of great importance.

She noticed a bottle by the leg of his chair. He'd been drinking, she realized, and when she saw shattered glass in front of the lyre-shaped fire screen, she knew anger was the reason behind his bout with brandy. Even now, his jaw was clenched, indisputable evidence of his inner turbulence. He must have had words with Spider Woman.

"Are you going to spy on me all night, or are you going to join me, Keely?"

She nearly jumped out of her robe at the sudden sound of his voice. "Saxon, I—"

"Come in and shut the door."

She sat on a velvet empire sofa and waited for him to speak, but he only picked up the bottle and drank, his gaze never leaving the fire. "Saxon, why ain't you in bed? I can tell yore a mite upset, but likker ain't—"

"You know nothing about me, Mrs. Blackwell," he slurred. "Despite what you say about those heart eyes, you will never know who or what I am."

Lord o' mercy, he shore was ill ternight. "I know yore mad about somethin' and I suspicion—"

"The word is *suspect.*" His eyes finally settled on her. "You don't *suspicion.* You *suspect.*"

She bristled. "Don't them words mean the same thang?"

"No they do not." He gulped more brandy. "You don't really hate Barton Winslow. You don't know what genuine hatred is. You may want revenge on him for what he did to your mother, but you can't truthfully say you hate the man."

"What does that have ter do with—"

"*I* know what hatred is, though." He rose and crossed to stand in front of her. "I've lived with it for years. Every hour, minute, second, hatred closing in, coming nearer until finally it owned me." He spun and weaved to the fireplace. There, he put his arm on the mantel and leaned his head on it.

Chickadee sat in confused silence. Saxon obviously wasn't receptive to her opinions tonight, but she knew he'd never have begun this conversation if he hadn't needed to talk.

"Hatred," he mumbled, his face still buried in the vee of his bent arm. "A profound hostility, Keely. Loathing."

"Yep, I reckon hatred's both them thangs, Saxon, but y'know," she said, pausing when he turned to face her, "hatred ain't somethin' that can git ter you lessen you let it. Iffen somebody hates you . . . well, that don't set real good on nobody, but it ain't got ter break yore life ter pieces."

"What do you know about hatred?" Saxon tried to put his elbow back on the mantel, but it slipped off. "Has anyone ever hated you?"

She met his hostile stare with a look glimmering with understanding. "Yore granny cain't stand me. And I don't much believe Thatcher's got a hankerin' ter be my friend neither. But I ain't gwine let it bother me none."

The smile he gave her didn't reach his eyes. Swaying, he drank more brandy, but even as he swallowed, his cold gaze never left her. "Of course you don't care how Grandmother or Thatcher feel about you! Soon you'll be returning to those ridge mountains or whatever the hell they're called, and you'll never have to see Araminta Blackwell or Thatcher again. Keely McBride Blackwell—not a care in the world does she have!''

He toasted her with the bottle and then staggered to a tremendous shelf of books. As he walked past them, he slid his thumbnail across their leather-bound spines. The noise made him think of a drum roll—the kind played before an execution.

Chickadee sank back into the soft pillows, knowing Saxon was by no means finished with his verbal attack. Normally, she wouldn't have let him go a step further before setting him back on his heels. But she instinctively understood he was using her as a scapegoat for something that had nothing to do with her, so she waited for him to continue.

"Look at you sitting there," he growled from behind her, his hand vanishing into her hair. "No worries, no problems, eh, Mrs. Blackwell?''

"I got thangs ter misery over jist like ever'one else," she told him smoothly. "Life ain't no—''

"Save the lecture, Keely!'' He stalked to the other side of the room, stopping in front of a wall niche that was filled with a collection of handpainted thimbles and exquisite figurines. With uncoordinated fingers, he reached for one. "Look at this ugly lady. Whoever made her forgot to give her breasts. A titless lady!'' He laughed and then tossed the figurine into the hearth, where it shattered.

Chickadee smiled broadly. *That's it, Saxon. Git mad. Flang thangs and holler. Ain't nobody here but me and Khan ter watch you wrang it out, and we ain't gwine hold it agin' you,* she cheered him on.

"Did you think that was funny, Mrs. Blackwell? Perhaps you'd like to see it again.'' Saxon took another statue and hurled it into the fireplace, continuing until he broke every thimble and figurine. "Was that humorous enough for you?''

She giggled and shook her head. "Cain't you flang nothin' bigger?"

He smiled back before he lifted the brandy and finished it off. "Anything to make the lady happy." Viciously, he flung the bottle at the hearth, laughing at the sound of the loud crash.

She stood and clapped. Looking around the room, she spied a collection of fragile plates. Why these Blackwells needed supper plates in the book room was beyond her, but she'd put them to good use. She hurried to the case, opened the glass doors, and removed several of the costly plates. "Catch," she said, hurling one at Saxon.

He snatched it from the air, looked down at its gilded design, and smiled. Araminta had been collecting this rare Chinese porcelain for years. He stood on his toes, held the plate high over his head, and cast it to the hearth. Spinning, he caught the next one she threw to him, hurling that one also. Each time one shattered, he and his mountain girl laughed before smashing the next one.

When all the plates were broken, Chickadee calmly closed the case doors. "You done yet, Saxon?"

"Done?" His eyebrow raised mischievously. "Why, the night's still young!" He lurched to the liquor table and took another bottle from it. "Care to join me, little one?"

"Don't mind iffen I do." She went to him and took a long drink from the bottle before noticing a marble bust across the room. "Law, Saxon," she said upon reaching it. "This here man's so ugly, I bet his mama-woman borried another baby ter take ter the church-house!"

Saxon promptly choked on the liquor in his mouth. "That's Grandmother!" he sputtered gaily.

Chickadee joined him in his mirth. "This here's Araminty? Lord o' mercy! I tuk her fer a man!"

Saxon turned and laughed into the curtains, tugging on them so hard they fell from the elaborate cornice and veiled him from Chickadee's view. As he weaved around the room, trying to get the draperies off, she collapsed, laughing, to the floor, holding her belly.

Saxon, too, was chuckling from beneath his silken coverings, and when he ran into the sofa and tumbled over it, falling to the other side, his snickers became great whooping sounds. "Keely," he managed to call between chortles, "come get these curtains off me!"

She crawled over to him and yanked the draperies off. He lay sprawled spread-eagle on the floor, a silly smirk still tugging at his lips. "I tried to get them off myself," he slurred. "But I couldn't."

She giggled and pulled herself onto him, her breasts cushioning her against the hardened muscles of his chest. "You cain't talk real good ternight neither. I cain't hardly understand nothin' yore a-sayin'."

His amused gaze sobered when he saw her lush breasts spilling from her robe. "Well, can you understand this, little one?" he whispered.

His kiss was so gentle, she was surprised at its tenderness. His lips moved slowly, lightly upon her own, and her mouth began to tingle. Wanting more than a tingle, she deepened the kiss herself, her tongue seeking and finding all the warm velvet valleys of his mouth. The tingle that threaded through her changed into a burning rope that tied her to the stake of passion.

"Love me, Saxon," she purred, her fingers rippling up and down his side.

He lifted her head and tried to bring her into focus. "I can't, Keely," he said throatily. "I can't love anyone, because . . . I don't know how."

She wrinkled her speckled nose in confusion. "What do you mean, 'you don't know how?'"

He removed her robe, his hands savoring the satin skin of her back and shoulders. "I mean just that." Lifting his head, he pressed kisses to the shadowed hollow of her throat. "I don't know how to love anyone."

His head fell back to the thick carpet. She caught his gaze and held it fast, her eyes seeking Saxon's very soul. There, she saw a chilling misery. Saxon hadn't meant he didn't know how to make love, she suddenly realized, he'd meant exactly what he'd said. The man lying beneath her, so vulnerable, with such sorrow etched across his fine features, really believed love was something that had to be learned.

She sat up and pulled his head and shoulders onto her lap, her fingers whispering through his black curls. "Saxon, you and me's gwine git down ter whar the water hits the wheel. Yore swarved up."

"Swarved up?" He brought her hand to his mouth and ran his tongue down the length of one of her fingers.

"Yore confused. Mizzled. 'Pears to me that iffen brains was dynamite, you wouldn't have enough ter blow yore nose. Love ain't what you thank it is, Saxon. It don't got ter be *larnt*, you hear what I'm a-tellin' you?"

"Keely, Keely, Keely, Keely."

"Whaty, whaty, whaty, whaty?"

He chuckled and reached up for her again. She caught his hand and held it to her bosom for the longest time while she tried to sort through what little she could understand. "Saxon, ain't nobody ever really loved you real good, huh? I mean, yore Mama-woman and yore daddy, they died when you was jist a young-un, and Desi . . . well, she cain't never tell you nothin', and Araminty—" When his fingers tightened around her hand, her eyes closed.

In her mind she saw Saxon as a little boy. A frightened youngster whom fate had placed in Araminta Blackwell's wicked claws. She imagined how he must have been, so young, so scared, so vulnerable.

The hatred he'd spoken of earlier had begun the day Spider Woman came from England. But why had Araminta hated her own grandchildren, and if she detested them so, why had she even bothered with them in the first place?

"Saxon?" She looked down at him and saw he was asleep. "It's a God-burn miracle you turned out as good as you did," she told him quietly, her warm hand cupping his cool cheek. Lost in thought, she let her gaze wander around the room, taking in all the luxurious furnishings.

"This is jist the out-doin'est thang, Saxon. You was raised with ever'thang 'cept love, and I come up with love a-bein' near about the onliest thang I had. Mama? Well, she was a sad woman, like I done tole you afore. But she loved me. And I had Betty Jane and George Franklin too."

"Cold, Keely," he mumbled sleepily, moving closer. "So cold."

She reached for her robe and draped it over his shoulders. "Yore cold whar this here robe cain't warm you none." She sighed. "But I reckon thur might still be a spark o' somethin' kin ter what you used ter be afore Spider Woman come inter yore life. That skeert little boy's still in thar, and I can hear him a-callin' out fer what he didn't never git. He's in thar somewhars, and what we're gwine commence a-doin' is dry his little tears.

"Heartease," she murmured down to him. "It's what yore a-pinin' fer—what nobody can git by withouten. Done tole you that afore, but you don't never listen on account o' you thank you know it all. But you don't know nothin' 'bout nothin' 'cept money. But I ain't a-faultin' you none. I reckon since money's the onliest thang you've ever had, you thank it's what's gwine give you what yore a-honin' fer. What you need is *love*, Saxon. Like I done tole Desi, I ain't gwine be here fer long, but I reckon I'll be here long enough ter show you what love—"

She broke off. How could she make Saxon understand what love was if she didn't love him? Sure, she felt *something* for him, but she was reasonably certain it wasn't love.

"Well ain't this jist a fine fix we're in. You a-needin' love near about as much as you need air, and me . . . Saxon, what iffen I commenced really a-lovin' you and you didn't never love me back?"

"Love me, Keely," he pleaded, still fast asleep. He shifted in her arms and nuzzled his face into her bare middle, sighing contentedly. Chickadee held him tightly for a few moments, rocking him as if he were a baby. And like a mother, she suddenly felt a powerful urge to take care of the man who sought her comforting warmness.

"You ain't a-makin' this any easier, Saxon Blackwell, but I reckon the one who's worse offen betwixt us is you. Iffen it's love you need, I'll try and give it ter you. Ain't gwine give you ever' bit o' my heart, but, well . . . I reckon I can give you a smidgeon of it."

After all, she told herself firmly, she wasn't risking all that much. She could love him just a little bit—enough to make him see what love was all about. The way she saw it, a little love went a long way.

Careful not to awaken him, she wiggled out from beneath him and put her robe back on. As she did, she spied the marble bust of Araminta. The old woman seemed to be taunting her and Saxon. Without hesitation, she marched to the hideous bust and lifted it from its stand. She lugged it to the fireplace, and with all her strength, threw it to the hearth. It didn't shatter as the china had, but it did crack into two pieces.

"You cain't hate me any more'n I hate you, Spider Woman," she told the broken bust. "But love's stronger'n hate, the way I heared it tole, and it's love that's gwine vict'ry over you."

She sniffed in the way she'd seen Thatcher do so many times and went back to Saxon. She slipped her hands beneath him and, careful to keep her back straight, used the extraordinarily strong muscles in her legs to lift him. Once she was standing, she bent her knees and straightened quickly, slinging him over her shoulder.

"I know you cain't stand it when I tote you around, Saxon, but thur jist ain't no hep fer it tonight," she told him as she left the library. " 'Sides that, you ain't gwine mem'ry nothin' about this no how."

As she walked to the steps, she thought of the loneliness and cruelty Saxon had suffered for so many years. Slowly, one step at a time, she climbed the winding staircase, the pain in her trembling legs nothing compared to the ache in her heart.

Chapter 11

Chickadee's first thought the next morning was that Araminta would soon summon Saxon to the library. The woman would want a full explanation for all the destruction.

"But that ain't what yore gwine git, Spider Woman," Chickadee mumbled and got out of bed. She rummaged through her small bag of belongings and was soon dressed. After blowing a kiss to Saxon, who was still dead to the world, she snapped for Khan and made her way downstairs.

"Git on out thar and do yore business, Khan," she told the wolf as she opened the front door. "And you ain't got ter piddle around a-smellin' ever' God-burn bush out thar neither. I'm in a sweepin' trot, and I don't got time ter wait that long."

When the wolf returned, they went to the library door. "Git ready Khan. Ain't no doubt in my mind Araminty's got sand in her gizzard." She took a deep breath and swung the door open wide, her face breaking into smiles when she saw Araminta standing before the broken marble bust. "Mornin', Araminty!" she called, closing the door and sashaying into the room. "Purty dress you got on, but ain't you got nothin' else 'sides black? Black ain't ugly, but—"

"Where is Saxon?" Araminta inhaled sharply in an effort to control her anger.

Chickadee took a moment to swipe at a red curl

162

that was tickling her eye. "Well, he's got him a case o' the mulligrubs. Ain't nothin' ter git all broke up over though. A-sawin' gourds is what he's—"

"Go and get him immediately." Araminta turned and stooped to examine the broken glass and china on the hearth.

Chickadee stuck her tongue out at the woman's back and then winked at Khan. "Uh, Araminty? I know habits is thangs that's hard ter quit. I been a-tryin' ter stop a-sayin' *God-burn* fer years. It ain't nice ter say, but—"

"I cannot possibly be less interested in your repulsive expletives. It is Saxon with whom I want to talk, not you."

Chickadee bit her lip to keep back her laughter. Araminta was so imperious it was hilarious. "Yeah, well, I don't know what *expletives* is, but yore bossiness is a habit yore gwine have ter let loose. Did y'know a bossy woman and a crowin' hen allus come ter a bad end?"

Araminta reached for the mantel, her wrath so great she was at the point of collapsing with it. "If you do not leave this room, I will ring for Thatcher to come and remove you bodily. You have five seconds."

Chickadee only smiled. "Law, Araminty, you can fitify yoresef into the uneases faster'n I ever seed anybody ever do it afore. It ain't good fer yore health to git so riled. And ageable like you are, you'd best be double keerful, lessen you got a hankerin' ter say good mornin' to Saint Peter at them pearly gates. You'll last through a few more clean shirts, but yore a-gittin' on in years, y'know."

"How dare—"

"I ain't afeared o' Thatcher no how. I come in here ter speak at you, and that's what I'm gwine do. Go on and rang fer that sniffin' cuss iffen it'll keep you from a-gittin' all grum and chuff, but I ain't a-leavin' till you and me's backed and forthed!"

Araminta quaked with ire, but seeing Chickadee's

determination, she nodded haughtily. Chickadee, aware she'd just been given permission to have her say, smiled again at Araminta's royal attitude. "Put yoresef level in a char."

"I prefer to stand," came Araminta's icy reply.

Chickadee walked closer to her, so close she could see the powder-filled pores on Araminta's pallid face. "You *prefer* ter do a sight o' thangs, but thur's some you ain't gwine do no more. Leastwise with me."

Araminta backed up as much as she could, the mantel behind her preventing her from making much progress. When she was pressed up against it, she began to move sideways.

But Chickadee's arms shot out on either side of Araminta's scrawny neck, imprisoning her. "I want ter know why you hate Saxon, and yore gwine tell me."

Araminta lifted her chin. "I'll tell you nothing. The Blackwell affairs are none of your concern."

"Yore disrememberin' I'm a Blackwell now too, Granny. Saxon's my husband, and I got ever' right ter know why—"

"You have no rights in this house. You and Saxon are fools if you believe you can antagonize me and—"

"Shet up." Chickadee moved her face closer to Araminta's. "Saxon ain't no fool. I can take whatever sass you flang at me, but you scandalize Saxon's name one more time, and I'll hang yore hide on a fence, Spider Woman. When he's around, he can take keer o' you with no hep from me, but when he ain't around, you best not lay no slurs on him.

"I didn't come here ter flang no rocks at nobody, Araminty, but you been a-hurtin' fer this ever since you commenced a-bedevilin' Saxon when you come here ter Boston. He didn't tell you nothin' then on account o' he was little and afeared o' you. And you made shore he *was* skeert, huh? I got it all figgered out real good. Spent near all night a-thankin' about it, and thur's somethin' about Saxon that really ills you. Now what is it?''

Araminta's look of horror gave way to one of malicious calculation. ''If you will free me from this position, I would like to ask you a few questions myself.''

Chickadee yielded to the request, and Araminta settled herself into the sofa. ''What means did you use to coerce Saxon into marrying you? You aren't, God forbid, with child, are you?'' Her sharp, pale blue eyes raked Chickadee's slender form.

Chickadee was unable to resist plaguing the worried woman. ''I'm in the rise o' my bloom, and Saxon? Well, he's wilder'n a peach-orchard boar. And we done our weavin' at the same loom many a time, so I reckon my apron could commence a-ridin' high here afore too long.''

Araminta shuddered and made an oath she would never acknowledge the heathen grandchild's existence. ''If you think Saxon cares for you, you are—''

''Well, o' course he keers fer me,'' Chickadee snapped, her heart thumping oddly as she said the words. ''Why else would he a-married me?''

Araminta cackled. ''Saxon is a cold man whose only devotion is to money. Oh, I realize he believes he cares for Desdemona, but I suspect his pitiful display of affection for that feebleminded chit—''

''Araminty, I been a-layin' off ter slap the hell outen you, but I ain't gwine hold off no more iffen you say one more word about Desi.'' Chickadee stalked wrathfully to the sofa, and Araminta shrank back into the velvet cushions.

''Very well, we will leave Desdemona out of this,'' Araminta agreed shakily. ''But as I was saying, Saxon—''

''Warn't real shore how ter love nobody till he met up with me. I love him, woman, and he loves me!''

Araminta, sensing she was treading a very fine

line, wisely refrained from shouting back. "Sit down so we may converse in a civil manner."

"I *prefer* ter stand," Chickadee said, mimicking Araminta's haughtiness. "'Sides that, what I got ter say ain't gwine take long. I know you hate Saxon, and I done seed what that hatred's done ter him. But I'm a-tellin' you, Araminty, yore time's come. You can make yore threats, call fer Thatcher, send fer them Boston sheriffs, and throw a mess o' fits. But you ain't Queen Araminty no more!"

"You—"

"Hesh up! I ain't finished a-cleanin' yore plow yet." Chickadee reached out and took hold of Araminta's pointed chin. "I ain't never knowed a person as fractious as you. Why, I reckon even ole Misery or Lareny Lester back home couldn't hold no candle ter you, but that's neither here nor thar. Saxon's done ever'thang you tole him ter do. You said fer him ter marry, and that's what he done. You ain't got no leg ter stand on, Spider Woman."

Araminta stood, waited for Chickadee to move, and then proceeded to the far corner of the room. "Are you quite finished? Because if you are, I—"

"No I ain't finished. You still ain't tole me what I come in here ter find out, lady. Saxon ain't had no affection since his mama and daddy jumped the buckeye log, and a-seein' as how I love him as much as I do, I—"

"Grayson." Araminta spat out the name of her son before she turned her back to Chickadee and stared out the window. To herself she whispered, "Ah, Grayson. Your rebellious blood runs in your son's veins."

Chickadee, her ears trained to pick up even the slightest sounds in thick mountain forests, heard Araminta's muttered statement. She backed up until she met with the chair behind her and sat down. As she studied Araminta's back, her mind raced.

Grayson Blackwell had given up a fortune for the girl he loved, and in doing so, he had defied and left his mother. When he and his wife died, wasn't it possible that Araminta saw little Saxon as another Grayson? Chickadee's insides lurched as she sorted through the fragments of the puzzle.

In all probability, Saxon had been made to suffer for his father's sins, and Araminta, determined to keep him from committing those same sins, had raised him only with cruel threats. Maybe she'd even successfully forced Saxon to count on wealth for any and all satisfactions life had to offer. As young as he was at the time, he'd been soft clay in her hands, and she'd molded him into exactly what she wanted him to be.

A puppet whose strings she held.

Loathing filled Chickadee. Saxon was right. She hadn't understood what genuine hatred really was, before now. Not until she'd seen it with her own eyes and felt it invade the very depths of her soul. A shiver clawed down her spine.

"Araminty, yore so low, you'd have ter reach up ter touch hell," she charged, her voice dangerously soft. "Jist now whilst I was a-settin here a-thankin' on what all you done? Well, them feelin's o' hatred you got is so dang strong, I could feel 'em inside me. I ain't never felt nothin' so drearisome in all my days. It was like a power o' rain a-pourin' down on me, and it was cold. Colder and bluer'n a possum's balls in a skift o' snow."

Araminta's leer reminded her of the way a single hair curls when it's burned. And burning was exactly what Araminta deserved. Right at the stake like the true witch she was.

Araminta swept toward the door. She would write to the asylum this very afternoon. There was no time to waste in getting rid of the mountain creature. Her brooch glittering to the tempo of her regal stride, she reached the door and started to open it.

But suddenly, Chickadee was there, staying her hand. "I love Saxon, Spider Woman. And a-tryin' ter keep love away's about as useless as a bug a-arguin' with a chicken. I'll admit hatred runs a close second, and ter you Blackwells, money's in the race too. But love? It's powerful strong, and thur ain't nothin' in this here world that can lick it.

"Yore smart, Araminty," she continued. "I ain't a-takin' no credit from you. Yore slicker'n snot on a doorknob, but yore kind o' thankin' won't never git you nothin' but heartache, and that's a dang shame. But the way I see it, you deserve ever' bit o' hurtin' you git!"

At that moment the door opened. "Is something amiss?" Thatcher sniffed.

Bolstered by her servant's presence, Araminta smiled smugly. "Escort this *person* out of here, Thatcher, and then fetch Saxon from bed and to my study."

Thatcher glanced around, and when he didn't see Khan anywhere, he reached for Chickadee's shoulders, his black eyes aglow with pleasure at what he was about to do. Chickadee allowed him to place his hands on her before bending at the waist, pushing her head into his belly, and throwing him over her back. Khan loped out from behind the sofa, his blue eyes bright with feral challenge.

"Ain't nobody gwine pester Saxon, Araminty. And iffen you dare go up thar, yer gwine meet up with me and Khan at the door. You sip yore likker from a glass, and I take mine from the jug, but y'know what? You'd have better luck a-tryin' ter cut up a big hog with a little knife than you'll have a-tryin' ter lick me."

She smiled down at Thatcher, threw another sassy grin at the openmouthed Araminta, and flounced away, her red curls waving farewell over her shoulders.

When Saxon woke up and couldn't remember the night's activities, Chickadee took great delight in relating them. She'd looked forward to seeing his expression when she told the story, sure his grandmother's anger would bring him great satisfaction.

"I can't believe we did it," he muttered, grimacing into his pillow. "Do you realize how *expensive* those things we broke were? Why didn't you stop me?"

The lights in her eyes dimmed. "Money ain't more important'n feelin's! You was a-hurtin' last night, and it done you good ter shatter Araminty's thangs. You didn't never tell me what all she said ter you last night, but—"

"Nothing she hasn't told me time and again. She's disappointed in me and claims I'm a replica of my father."

"So what's the matter with a-bein' like yore daddy?" she asked, bringing his breakfast tray. "He give up a fortune fer yore mama-woman, and a man who does that? Well, he ain't nobody's fool, Saxon! He—"

"Keely, please stop shouting. Even a whisper would sound like a cannon to me this morning."

She mumbled a curse and went to the dresser for the bag of Betty Jane's herbs. After she'd mixed some with water, Saxon swallowed the bitter potion down, experience telling him the vile concoction would indeed make him feel better.

"Saxon, them thangs you broke—"

"I won't discuss it any further. What's done is done."

But she was by no means finished. "I know you don't mem'ry nothin' about last night, but you was happier'n a dog in a slaughterhouse a-tossin' them thangs around. Ever' time one broke, you was a-thankin' on Araminty. And now yore as worried as a frog with a busted jumper on a busy road. Worried over money! Cain't you never thank on nothin' else? Ain't thur nothin' else—"

"No! There isn't! Is that what you wanted to hear, Keely?" He snatched his plate from the tray, viciously bit into a flaky tart, and then picked up his fork.

"Yore wrong," she said hotly. "Thur's a sight o' thangs more important'n money. You ever give a thought ter the possibility that I might be a-childin'? Ain't a baby—"

"Are you pregnant?" His forkful of food stopped right before it reached his mouth.

"I warn't last month, but it's too soon ter tell about this month. Like I tole Araminty, you and me's been a-saltin' our beans right reg'lar, and a baby's somethin' we're gwine have ter thank on."

He returned his plate to the tray and got out of bed. He went to his desk, shuffled through some papers without really looking at them, and then turned back to her. "If you have a child, I'll see to everything. I'll keep him here with me, and—"

"But he'll be *my* baby too, and he ain't gwine be raised around Araminty! I ain't about ter let what happened ter you happen ter my young-un!"

"What are you talking about?" Saxon stormed toward her. "What happened to me?"

Though his irritation was obvious, she faced him defiantly. "My young-un ain't gwine be brung up a-thankin' he's got ter have money ter be happy! He's gwine come up with all the love I can give him. He might not have much more'n that, but that'll be enough, the way I see it."

"Are you saying I wouldn't . . . care for my own child?"

"Keerin' and lovin' differ, Saxon. If we have us a young-un, are you gwine *love* him or jist keer enough that he has ever'thang yore dang-blasted money can buy him?"

He ignored the challenge in her emerald eyes. He was in no mood to delve into the fairy-tale subject of love with her again. "There's a perfect solution to this problem," he announced quietly. "No more lovemaking, no baby."

As his answer sank in, her eyes made a thorough

journey down his bare length, the sight making her smile in appreciation. Saxon's suggestion would never work. She knew she didn't even want to try it. "That idee's about as useless as tits on a boar hog."

She slipped her arms around his waist, and his anger fled as quickly as his solution to their problem. Staying mad at Chickadee was impossible. "Keely," he moaned into her hair when she pressed against his desire for her.

"The onliest way you and me can stop a-makin' love is iffen we're separated, Saxon," she explained, her lips nipping at his shoulder. "I'm as hot as a June bride in a featherbed fer you, outlander, and—"

His laughter cut her off. "Then what do you suggest?" He slid his hands beneath her shirt and found her breasts, rolling their hardening peaks between his fingers.

She looked up at him, the luminous adoration in her eyes causing his own to widen. There was no mischief, laughter, or teasing in her gaze.

Just the whisper-soft sheen of devotion.

Never having seen it before, his first instinct was to move away from her, from the uncomfortable, bewildering emotions her tender look brought. But, as though he'd suddenly sprouted roots that bound him to the floor, he couldn't move a muscle.

She sensed his uneasiness and leaned into him. 'Y'know, Saxon, I been warm and happy in right many places afore. Ain't nothin' like a-settin' on a ridge with the sun a-pourin' down on you, and a featherbed's near about the most comfortable thang thur is. But here in yore arms? Well, I reckon they beat both ridges and featherbeds. I cain't even thank of another place whar I'd ruther be."

"Uh, Keely, I'm going to take you to the city today," he said a bit too hastily. "We'll visit a seamstress so you may be measured for new clothes. After that, I'll take you on a tour of Boston, and maybe tomorrow I'll take you to Cambridge and show you Harvard, where I went to school.''

The abrupt change of subject disappointed her. Well, years of hatred couldn't be erased in one day. "But ain't you got ter go ter yore office?''

"I've been gone for months. A few more days aren't going to make any difference. You need to become familiar with Boston.''

She followed him to the tub and handed him a bar of soap. "Saxon, I don't need no clothes. I brung lots o'—''

"You may wear your breeches around the house, but they won't be acceptable at socials. There'll be teas and—''

"Why do I got ter dress up ter drank tea?'' she asked, kneeling to lather his back.

Her fingers warmed him as the heated water never could. "It's not only teatime. The ladies go to poetry readings, gather to paint or sew, to discuss balls—''

"I cain't listen ter somebody read iffen I got on breeches? I ain't shore I *want* ter go ter any o' them git-togethers.''

"Keely, I once asked you to put your mother's dress on, and you were lovely in it. I want the pleasure of buying you more pretty things. You're a beautiful woman, little one, and you should dress beautifully.''

"But—''

"When I was in the Blue Ridge, I did my best to conform to your way of life,'' he reminded her with a twinkle in his eye. "Surely you'll do me the same favor.''

Chickadee was captivated by the mesmerizing blue of his devilish gaze. *Actually, I'd do anythang fer you, Saxon.*

"Well?'' he pressed, reaching for her.

"Saxon!'' she shouted when he pulled her into the tub with him. "I still got my clothes on!''

"So you do,'' he said, his fingers already unfastening the buttons on her shirt. "We'll have to do something about that, won't we?'' He tossed her shirt to the floor, and her breeches soon followed.

''Law, Saxon, we ain't never done this in the tub afore,'' she murmured, her lips at his ear, her legs wrapped around his waist.

''No, but that doesn't mean it can't be done.'' He lifted her and then slowly lowered her, impaling her so deeply, sensuously, she let out a moan.

''Why, Keely Blackwell! Was that a *holler* I heard?''

'' 'Pears so,'' she admitted. ''See iffen you can make me let out another one.''

He smiled. ''With pleasure, mountain girl.''

Chapter 12

Saxon ignored Araminta's summons, and he and Chickadee were soon in the carriage heading toward the city. Not having had much rest during the night, Chickadee drifted to sleep almost immediately. He maneuvered her so she rested against his shoulder, and he caught the fresh scent of her hair. Unable to resist picking up a soft lock, he brushed it across his lips and watched the scenery outside, the riotous splash of autumn catching his attention.

"Sort of red, sort of orange, sort of gold," he whispered, still twining Chickadee's hair between his fingers. "Just like this wild mane of yours."

"What? Are we thar?"

Her voice was as soft as mountain drizzle, that silent haze he'd so often watched blanket her precious hills on cool Appalachian mornings. *Hell!* he chided himself, cooing her back to sleep. *I'm getting sentimental!*

Absently stroking Chickadee's cheek, he pondered that new emotion. He'd never taken a second's worth of time to examine the colors of autumn, nor had he cared a whit about wet fog covering uncivilized hills.

He was becoming maudlin, and all because of the vivacious vixen in his arms. Who the hell cared if leaves were green, red, or purple?

Squeezing his eyes closed, he shut out both the

landscape and his soppy thoughts. He was acting as if Chickadee had stolen his heart.

He laughed quietly at that ridiculous notion.

No one could steal a heart that didn't exist.

"You have an eye for color, Mr. Blackwell," the seamstress said, looking over the dozens of bolts of fabric Saxon had selected for Chickadee's gowns. Everything complemented Chickadee's coloring to perfection.

"If I do, I most likely attained it from my years of doing business with you, Mrs. Tidd," he replied with a wink, and added a length of teal crepe to the heap.

Mrs. Tidd blushed. "Your business with me has been a joy, but I never believed you'd bring a *wife* to me. She's a lovely girl who really has no need for the corsets."

Saxon smiled, recalling the fit Chickadee had thrown over the corsets. Nor had she wanted parasols or bonnets. He walked over to the display of furs and laces, where Mrs. Tidd lengthened his list of purchases with capes, pelisses, mantles, and jackets. He also added fans, reticules, gloves, and muffs to the list, delighting the seamstress with his large order. She started to suggest he buy an assortment of nightwear but then blushed again. The virile Saxon Blackwell and his beautiful wife would only find nightgowns hindersome. Still flushed, she promised to have the order completed and delivered as soon as possible.

The next stop was the shoemaker's. There he bought his mountain girl kid, leather, and satin slippers as well as boots that laced up her instep. Though Chickadee was hesitant to give up her breeches and brogans, she was fascinated by all the new things that would soon be delivered to her. Her rustic upbringing hadn't squelched her inborn and typically feminine love of beautiful things.

But when Saxon took her to Cromwell's jewelry

store, she protested loudly. The sight of the glittering gems was enticing, but her strong sense of fairness refused to allow her to let Saxon spend any more money on her.

"I don't need any o' them jewries in that thar winder, Saxon. I let you buy them other thangs on account o' you said I cain't wear breeches to them socials that I ain't even decided I'll go ter yet. But I ain't got no need fer—"

"Keely, jewelry completes an outfit. But most importantly, little one," he said, pulling her into his embrace, "I've yet to give you a wedding ring. Surely you don't want Grandmother to think I don't . . . uh, *love* you enough to give you a ring, do you?"

She mulled this over. If only he meant what he said, she thought sadly. "Will this here store buy the jewries back? I won't never wear it in the hills."

His chest constricted at her question, an odd emptiness replacing the pleasure he'd had buying her a wardrobe. "I'm sure it will," he said softly. "But if it won't, we can always sell the jewelry privately."

When they left the store, the jeweler was much richer, and on Chickadee's left hand there sparkled a gold band encrusted with emeralds. The rest of the jewelry Saxon had purchased would be delivered the next day. Chickadee was overwhelmed, freely admitting the various pieces of jewelry he'd bought were the prettiest things she'd ever seen. But they made her sad too. They symbolized Saxon's wealth.

The thing he seemed to need most in the world.

Though there were street railways, Chickadee preferred to walk and thoroughly enjoyed the stroll through the Common, a large park full of stately elms. Saxon took her to Frog Pond, an old watering place where cows and sheep had once quenched their thirst, and told her he would take her ice-skating there when the water froze.

They spent the next four days sight-seeing. Chickadee saw Parker House, the oldest hotel in Boston, the handsome, medievallike King's Chapel, and the

Tremont Temple. Saxon pointed out Old Granary Burying Ground and told her who Paul Revere, John Hancock, Samuel Adams and Robert Treat Paine were, explaining their bodies were laid to rest there.

They ventured past the Old North Church, where Paul Revere's signal lanterns had been hung. The State House, where the Boston Massacre had taken place, was next on the agenda, and there Saxon showed Chickadee the balcony from which the Declaration of Independence had been read. She saw the Old Corner Bookstore and learned that leading writers such as Dickens, Thackeray, Hawthorne, Longfellow, Thoreau and Whittier once congregated there.

Chickadee studied it all with great interest, but her fascination with New England increased the day Saxon took her into Cambridge and showed her Harvard. They walked through the Yard, and when they reached Hollis Hall, Saxon told her the story behind all the cracks in the pavement around the old building.

"In 1776, after the Continental Army left Cambridge, the college students were able to return from Concord, where they'd fled," he explained. "When they arrived back here, they found iron cannonballs lying around the Yard. The students who lived here at Hollis Hall were obviously inventive souls and thought of a clever way to put the balls to good use during that very cold winter. They placed the balls into fireplaces and left them there until they were red-hot. Then, in braziers, they carried them into the chambers, where the heated balls would give off heat, thus warming the chilly rooms."

He stooped and pointed to the broken pavement. "When spring came, and the students had no more use for the balls, they threw them from their windows. When the balls landed, they made these cracks you see here."

Chickadee reached out and ran her finger over one large fissure in the stone. "Whar's them balls now?

I'd shore like ter have one fer my collection o' thangs. Y'know I got ter start a whole new one since my ole one burnt up."

He smiled and gently tugged at her red curls. Most people he knew collected priceless objects of great beauty. But Chickadee looked beyond outward appearances and saw the simple significance others rarely noticed. Her idea of a treasure, whether it be broken or ugly, was a thing that in some way held unique meaning for her.

"Keely, I've no idea where the balls are now. That tale I told you happened nearly a hundred years ago."

"Well, I reckon I can find other thangs. Ain't nothin' gwine replace that gun stock I showed you though. I tuck real good keer of it. Now it ain't nothin' but ashes."

"A real shame it was destroyed," Saxon said sadly, inwardly smiling because the stock she so prized was safely hidden away in his personal things at home.

It was well after nightfall before they returned to Boston from Cambridge, and Chickadee's stomach was rumbling. "Saxon, I'm so hungry, I could eat a bull and it be a-bellerin'. Cain't we stop somewhars and eat?"

"I'm sure our chefs will have dinner waiting for us. It wouldn't do at all for us not to eat it."

"But I ain't never et in a restaurant afore, Saxon," she said longingly. "I'll eat jist a little bit, and then when we git home I'll finish off whatever them chefs made fer us."

"You'll get fat eating like that."

She turned her grass-green eyes on him, the soft shine of the streetlamps reflected in them. "Please? Purty please with molasses on top?"

The sweet plea on her freckled face would have melted a glacier. He signaled for the carriage to stop in front of a quaint cafe. It was in no way elegant, but to the mountain girl, it was fancy indeed.

When they'd finished their meal of fresh fish, Saxon began to study the dessert menu, but a familiar face a short distance away stole his attention.

Dammit, it was Wesley Melville, a notorious womanizer! Though Saxon himself had a reputation with the ladies, he'd never set his sights on the ones who wore wedding bands. Wesley did not possess such scruples, and there was no way in hell Saxon was going to let his old rival turn on the charm for Chickadee. The thought irritated him greatly, and his irritation turned into full-blown fury when he remembered how very well Chickadee's clothes fit her. She might as well have been poured into both her breeches and her shirt! Dammit, why hadn't he thought to buy at least one ready-made frock for her?

Quickly, he signaled for the check, but the waiter was occupied. Chickadee saw Saxon's impatience and followed his line of vision to the waiter. When the man failed to come, she stood, put two fingers to her lips, and blew a deafening whistle.

Rattled to the marrow of his bones, Saxon yanked her back into her chair, his eyes narrowed. "That isn't the way to get anyone's attention, Keely."

She jerked her hand away from him. "I was only a-tryin' ter hep. That thar waiter man's so busy, he didn't never see you a-wavin' ter him. And what with all the loud gwines-on in here, he didn't never hear you a-callin' him neither."

"He would have come as soon as he—"

"Saxon!" Wesley removed his leather gloves, slapped them across his hand a few times, and then draped them over his lower arm.

Beneath the table, Saxon's fists clenched. "Wesley, it's been a long time." He forced himself to be polite. "Nice to see you again." He stood and held out his hand, which his foe touched lightly.

"Too long," Wesley returned, his gaze settling on Chickadee. "Last I heard, you were seeing Cynthia Hamilton, and now I find you out with another enchanting lady."

His smile was a snarl. "Whatever relationship I had with Cynthia ended when I married Keely."

Wesley raised a mahogany eyebrow. "Married?" He looked back at Chickadee, taking in her homespun shirt, her buckskin breeches, and the raccoon tails at her waist. "This girl is your *wife?*"

Wesley's condescending voice maddened him. "I said she was, didn't I?"

Chickadee stood and reached for Wesley's hand, shaking it firmly and rapidly. "God-proud ter meet you, Mr. Wesley. Been a-hankerin' ter know Saxon's friends."

Wesley's mouth dropped open briefly, before his smiling lips found their way to the top of Chickadee's hand. "Call me Wesley, Mrs. Blackwell."

His kiss left her hand wet and her stomach upset. There was something about Wesley she didn't like. Still, if he was Saxon's friend, she guessed that made him hers too. "And you call me Chickadee. Draw up a char, Wesley. What with the air a-stirrin' cool out thar, I reckon you come in here ter warm yoresef." She sat and looked up at Saxon, certain her friendliness with his friend made him happy.

But Saxon's face was anything but pleased. "Wesley, forgive our rudeness, but we were leaving when you came in. I've a lot of work to do tonight." He assisted Chickadee to her feet.

Wesley took a moment to study Chickadee's perfectly outlined form, her masculine attire revealing much more of her than a gown ever would have. He'd enjoyed trying to steal Saxon's women from him in the past, and the thought of seducing his *wife* gave him immeasurable satisfaction.

Saxon saw the look in Wesley's eyes and knew it well. "We'll see you soon, Wesley," he lied, having no intention whatsoever of allowing Wesley near Chickadee again.

"Nothing would give me greater pleasure," he answered suggestively; his eyes still feasting on

Chickadee. "I'd like to get to know this lovely bride of yours."

A shiver of warning swept through her at his blatant stare. This man was *not* Saxon's friend, she suddenly realized. No true friend would look at a man's wife in the way Wesley was looking at her. And the man was being so dang-blasted obvious about it too! Like he didn't care at all that his actions might upset Saxon!

"Y'know any painters, Wesley?" she asked sweetly.

"Why, yes. I know many of them. Does art interest you?" His gaze was still devouring her.

"Don't keer nary a jag about it. But tell you what, Wesley. You git one o' them painters, and I'll let him paint me fer you. Hell, I'll even pose bucknaked fer him. You can hang the paintin' on yore wall, and that way you can keep on a-starin' at me even when I ain't around."

Saxon gasped. "Keely!"

"Hold yore tater, Saxon. Wesley here's been a-peelin' my clothes off ever since he got here. 'Pears to me a paintin' would last a sight longer'n a short stare ever' now and then. You thank so too, Wesley?" She took a few steps toward him.

Wesley backed away. "I . . . uh," he stammered, his eyes begging Saxon to rescue him. "I didn't mean to stare at you. You misunderstood my look. It wasn't directed at you in any improper way whatsoever."

"I laid eyes on you fer the first time not more'n five minutes ago, you varmint, but it tuk you less time'n that ter show yore true colors."

As she continued to advance upon Wesley, Saxon realized he'd never seen the man flustered. Wesley was cool and collected at all times. But now, faced with this cheeky little spitfire, probably the first woman ever to rebuff him, all his bravado had vanished. Saxon grinned broadly despite his dismay over Chickadee's behavior.

"I wouldn't trust you behind a broom straw, Wesley," Chickadee flared. "And I ain't a-lookin' ter meet up with you agin!"

Aware everyone in the cafe was listening with rapt interest, Wesley's face reddened furiously. "B-Boston is a big city. We'll probably never meet again."

She continued to stalk him, Saxon right behind her. "Maybe not, but iffen we do, you'd best mem'ry I don't go to too many places withouten my shootin'-arn and my wolf. So lessen yore a-wantin' ter know what it's like a-gittin' tarred up by a wolf or what lead feels like buried in yore—"

She never finished her threat. Wesley reached the door and bolted out of it, his gloves fluttering to the ground in his haste to escape. Normally, Chickadee would have gloated, but not this time.

She could feel Saxon's gaze boring into her back.

Without turning to face him, she squared her shoulders and walked out of the restaurant to the barouche, leaving him to pay for the meal.

"Don't say nothin', Saxon," she told him when he joined her inside the carriage. "I suspicion . . . I *suspect* yore riled, but I ain't gwine apologize fer nothin'."

"I wasn't going to ask you to."

She peered at him from beneath her lowered lashes. He didn't *look* angry. In fact, he was smiling that lazy, mocking grin she so loved.

"Wesley's had that coming for a long time."

"But you was a-fixin' ter stop me."

"True," he admitted, reaching across the space between them to pull her over to his side. "And I still don't condone your behavior, but when I saw how upset Wesley was I couldn't help smiling. But Keely, you musn't make a habit of tearing into people like that. It's simply not done."

Her reply was a shrug of her shoulders, leaving him to wonder if she was agreeing with him or scoffing at him. He started to discuss the matter further but decided it would take more than one night to make her understand.

She directed her attention at the sights once more, soon noticing a dark, littered alley. "That's the torn-downedest place I ever laid my eyes on."

"The North End," Saxon said, his hold on her tightening. "It was once a nice residential area, but as the years passed, various mercantile industries began to take up more space. Eventually, many transient workers and sailors moved there, and the section became less desirable. Then when the potato famine hit Ireland, droves of Irishmen came to Boston, settling there in the North End. It's no more than a sordid slum now."

"Irish folks is bad?"

"You can't say a whole group of people is bad, Keely. I've nothing against the Irish, but many of them are bitter and hostile. They came here hoping for a better life, but most of them have failed at making much money. Large families live in one-room dwellings, and most are as poor here as they were in Ireland. I imagine that would make any man resentful."

Chickadee nodded thoughtfully as she watched a drunkard stagger down the sidewalk. "And thur prob'ly a-missin' thur homeland too, Saxon. They got here and had ter git used ter a whole different life. It's dang hard ter do that."

He admired her intuitive wisdom but experienced a sharp pang when he realized she missed her own homeland. "Just the same, the North End is a dangerous place. But come, we've no need to discuss that. What are you going to do tomorrow while I'm at my office?"

"Got it all figgered out. I'm gwine take Desi fer a long walk, and her and me's gwine see what sorter mischief we can git inter."

He chuckled and kissed her impish mouth. When they were but a short distance from home, they passed a large, beautiful mansion, much like the

Blackwell estate. "That's Ruford Sinclair's place,"
Saxon said. "He's Boston's answer to your Lareny
Lester."

"Stingy buzzard, huh?"

"He has the most valuable art collection around,
but he refuses to let anyone look at it." Saxon
pointed to two upstairs windows in the mansion.
"That room is always lit at night. It's where he has
his paintings, and he sits in there for hours staring
at his art."

"Why don't he want nobody ter see it?"

"I guess it gives him malicious pleasure to know
all those masterpieces are for his eyes only. He tells
people all about them, but when he's asked to share
them he laughs and refuses."

Chickadee stared at Ruford's lighted windows until they disappeared from view. A rumpus over
paintings of landscapes, people, fruit, and maybe
animals. Weren't *real* people, animals, fruits and
scenery a sight prettier to see?

Strange people, these Boston folk.

Chickadee pulled Desdemona along, forcing the
mute girl to quicken her pace. For over a week they'd
taken long walks together, and during those brisk
treks she refused to let Desdemona balk. She de-
voted constant, neverending attention to Desdemona, and her efforts were finally beginning to show
results.

"Come on, Desi, you can walk faster'n that. I'm
aimin' ter figger out jist how big this Blackwell estate
is, and we ain't gwine git nowhars iffen you don't
git a move on!" She sniffed at the air as they headed
toward the wooded area behind the mansion. "Winter ain't too fur away. Ain't gwine be long afore this
here place'll be white with snow. You ever been
a-sleddin'? You-uns even got sleds?"

Desdemona didn't answer, but she perked up at
the mention of sledding.

Chickadee stopped and adjusted Desdemona's

cloak. "Don't reckon nobody never takes you a-sleddin', do they, sweet thang? Well, don't you worry none. I'll take you. Hell, I'll even make you the God-burnin'est best sled you ever laid eyes on. All's we need is a good tree and some sharp tools. Reckon you could hep me find them thangs?"

To Chickadee's great delight, Desdemona nodded vigorously and pointed to the forest. And then Chickadee's delight turned into a burst of laughter.

Desdemona was smiling. Spreading from ear to ear, it was her first smile in years.

"Well looky thar!" Chickadee exclaimed. "A smile! I jist knowed you could do it!" She hugged Desdemona tightly.

From the drawing room window of the mansion, Eugenia Preston watched the two girls scamper into the woods. "My, my. I'm sorry I didn't arrive before your new granddaughter-in-law went for her walk, Araminta. I would like to meet the girl who makes Desdemona smile."

Araminta clutched her onyx brooch. "Smile?"

Eugenia turned from the window. "Smile. Desdemona just smiled over something Saxon's new wife said to her."

Araminta attempted to look pleased but failed.

"You must be overjoyed your granddaughter is showing such signs of improvement," Eugenia said slyly. "A smile isn't much, but it is surely the beginning. Desdemona is not insane at all, is she?" She regarded Araminta carefully.

"Insane?" Araminta's color heightened. "Why, whoever said she was?"

Eugenia raised a slate-gray brow. "How pleased you must be with Saxon's bride. She seems to be a most unusual girl from what little I've seen of her, but in only a short while, she's succeeded in doing what no one else has been able to do. She's broken through Desdemona's reserve, and for that, I'm sure you must be overwhelmingly grateful."

"Grateful," Araminta muttered. The preparations

for Desdemona's departure to the asylum had been completed, and the brainless chit was to have left in the morning! But now Eugenia Preston herself had noticed the subtle changes Chickadee had wrought in Desdemona—one ridiculous smile . . . Now there was no way on earth Araminta could send her to the asylum.

How was she going to force Saxon to get rid of Chickadee now? Araminta seethed inwardly, her blood pelting through her scrawny veins. A curse on that redheaded heathen! A curse that would banish the mountain girl from the face of the earth!

A curse that would not be long coming, if she had her way . . .

Chapter 13

As Saxon stepped down the staircase, he dwelled on the memory of the shy smile Desdemona had given him earlier that morning. She'd smiled every day for the past week. Those timid grins were thrilling things to see, and they were also proof Araminta could no longer threaten him with the asylum. With that worry gone, there was little with which she could torment him.

And because she'd lost the means she had to *force* him to stay with Blackwell Enterprises, he'd decided to stay with the company of which he was so proud. It was just as he suspected it would be. Remaining with Blackwell Enterprises because *he* chose to do so made all the difference. Life was looking up. Everything was almost perfect.

Almost. There was still that shivery, somewhat exhilarating emotion he experienced whenever he thought of Chickadee. It bothered him no end that she could make him feel that way without his consent.

He pondered the years during which Araminta had control over him, power over everything except his emotions. His private feelings and the fact they were his alone had been his sole comfort as he'd grown to manhood.

And now, just when he'd wrested so much back from Araminta, Chickadee had somehow taken command of the only things that were truly his: his emotions. Dammit! Would his life ever be entirely his own?

Chickadee. He slowed as he thought of her. He could still feel the warmth of her kiss as she bid him goodbye just minutes ago. He could even still smell the spicy scent of the sassafrass tea she brewed in the fireplace of their bedroom.

He was going to miss her. No matter how angry it made him to admit that, it was nevertheless true. He was going to miss her, because soon she'd be gone.

His detectives had located Barton Winslow in New York. Saxon hadn't begun the man's ruination yet, but he knew exactly how he'd do it. He had yet to tell Chickadee the news, but knew it wasn't fair to keep it from her.

He reached the bottom of the staircase and gripped the railing tightly. After he told her about her father, how long would it be before she left? Would she stay to see the man's downfall, or would she leave immediately, trusting Saxon to keep his end of the bargain?

Irritated anew over his strange attachment to her, he muttered a curse and stalked to the front door. With a quick glance at the upper landing of the staircase, he silently wished Chickadee good luck.

She was attending the ladies' sewing circle today. It was a good place for her to start joining society. It would be just a quiet, simple affair, and he couldn't imagine she'd be able to cause any chaos there. After all, she wouldn't be taking Khan, and she'd leave her rifle at home. What could happen?

"Saxon, I refuse to take that girl to the sewing meeting," Araminta snapped as she rushed into the foyer.

"Sorry, Grandmother. If you don't take Keely everyone will want to know why she's not there. And if you lie and make up some excuse, I will reveal your dishonesty at the first opportunity. I want her to make some friends. Can't you understand that?"

Araminta rubbed her arms to warm herself against the chill her cold anger brought her. "I will not take her."

"She's been invited. I ran into Mrs. Rush yesterday in town. You know how fast news spreads. Apparently every female in Boston has heard of my marriage, and all are anxious to meet Keely. And since I cannot be with her today, I'm counting on you to make sure things go well for her."

Araminta's eyelids fluttered like the transparent wings of a fly.

Saxon tapped his hat against his thigh, thoroughly enjoying Araminta's dismay. "You see, Grandmother, Keely and I were with Wesley Melville several weeks ago. When I saw Mrs. Rush yesterday, she informed me she'd heard about my marriage from Mrs. Douglas. Mrs. Douglas learned about it from Mrs. Eliot, who got it straight from Mrs. Bancroft, who got wind of it directly from Mrs. Melville. Mrs. Rush promised to do her utmost to see that Keely is introduced to all the proper people. Hence, the invitation for her to join the ladies' sewing circle. Which, if I'm not mistaken, meets at one o'clock today at the Rush estate. And you, *dear* Grandmother, will take her. Now, with your leave, I go to my office."

She caught him by his sleeve. "You know perfectly well they want to meet her because of the rumors that are undoubtedly flying about. They cannot resist—"

"Grandmother, what a terrible way to speak of your own friends! And as for the rumors, do as I do—ignore them." He reached out and patted her shoulder before heading out the door.

"But she has nothing to wear!"

Saxon turned slowly, his eyebrow raised. "Her clothes arrived yesterday. She'll be dressed beautifully. So you see? You've nothing at all to worry about."

* * *

"I heard she actually took a few shots at Wesley Melville," Sarah Bancroft proclaimed, nodding in assurance that her words were the truth not mere gossip.

"Told him she'd strip naked for him too," Evelyn Douglas whispered, her cheeks reddening. "You know, I always knew Saxon wasn't right for my Emily. Granted, he's a handsome scamp and will be as rich as Croesus one day, but to have him as a son-in-law! Well, the proof of his true character is that girl he married. Gracious me! I'm so glad I always took care to keep Emily well out of his way."

Hester Eliot smirked. "Evelyn dear, you'd have stripped poor Emily naked if you thought it might have made Saxon take a second glance at her, and you know it. It's common knowledge you've wanted that match ever since Emily sprouted breasts."

Evelyn gasped. "Why Hester Eliot! I never—"

"I wonder what Saxon would see in her?" Millicent Ashbury interrupted. "From what I've heard about her, she's the crudest person ever to set foot in our fair city. Why, even her name is outlandish. Imagine being named Chicken!"

"Excuse me, but I don't think her name is Chicken," Bunny Hamilton said quietly, reaching up to push a brown curl off her plump cheek. "I believe I heard it to be Chickadee."

The cluster of women turned to look at the overweight girl. "Bunny, what difference does it make, for heaven's sake?" Eleanor Peabody spat. "Chickadee is as ridiculous as Chicken."

"But no one can possibly judge her without even meeting her," Bunny pointed out timidly. "Surely the things you have heard about her are nothing more than overblown gossip. I'm sure she's a lovely, genteel girl."

The discussion was interrupted by a commotion in the hallway.

"No you cain't have my cape, you thievin' buzzard! Don't they pay you enough here so's you can buy yore own capes?"

"But I only thought to hang it up for you," the butler rushed to explain to the mountain girl who'd just arrived.

"Oh." Chickadee unfastened the front of the silken garment and handed it to him.

"And may I take that for you also?" he asked, gesturing toward the leather satchel she held.

"No, I'm gwine need it."

The butler frowned. "But it's a saddlebag."

"Onliest thang I could find ter put my sewin' in."

Eyes wide, the women watched the scene at the doorway. Araminta entered and shuffled to a vacant chair, leaving Chickadee under the archway of the door.

"Araminta," Millicent said, still staring at the person in the doorway, "is *that* her?"

Araminta yanked her needlepoint out of her bag and threw Chickadee a scathing look. "Yes, and before she even sets foot into this room, allow me to apologize for whatever she says or does. I can promise you all that before this assembly is over, each of you will understand how horribly humiliated I am by Saxon's marriage."

"Does she always talk like that?" Eleanor asked.

"It gets worse with every word she utters," Araminta snapped. "I did not want to bring her here, but Saxon—"

"Well, isn't anyone going to invite her into the room?" Bunny asked.

"Yes, Thelma," Sarah said. *"You're* the hostess."

Thelma Rush fiddled with her ruby ring. "But . . . Perhaps I made a mistake in inviting her. I only thought to do Saxon a favor by—"

"You're a very poor liar, Thelma." Hester chided. "You heard the rumors about her, and you couldn't wait to see if they were true. You're always the one who has all the latest gossip. The rest of us—"

"Hester, that's not true!" Thelma gasped. "I—"

"It is so true, Thelma," Evelyn exclaimed. "The proof is that you invited her!"

Thelma flushed scarlet. "But I had no idea she would be . . . like that!"

"What is she like?" Bunny heaved out of her chair. "How can we know until we acquaint ourselves with her?"

"Oh Bunny, do sit down," Millicent commanded. "Heaven knows none of us can see around you."

Bunny hung her head for an instant before she turned and waddled across the large room toward the doorway where Chickadee still stood. Chickadee watched her coming and thought she'd never seen a fatter person. Bunny fairly shook the floor as she advanced. But Chickadee looked beyond the rolls of fat on the girl's face and saw Bunny's smile. It was an honest-to-goodness real smile, the only one given her since she'd arrived.

"Hello," Bunny greeted her. "My name is Bunny Hamilton. It's such a pleasure to meet the girl who finally caught that handsome Saxon Blackwell. My sincerest congratulations on your marriage, Chickadee."

Chickadee shook Bunny's hand firmly. "Bunny? Uh, Bunny ain't no nickname fer somethin' else, is it? I mean, yore real name ain't Rabbit, is it?"

For a moment, Bunny looked confused. "Rabbit?" she repeated and then laughed. "Oh no! My real name is Hortense, but I hate that name. When my parents died and I came here to live with my relatives, my aunt nicknamed me Bunny. That's what I've come to prefer to be called."

"Well, God-proud ter meet you Bunny. I was a-wonderin' if thur was anybody here who was gwine welcome me in. Ole Araminty jist left me a-standin' here, and I didn't know what I was s'posed ter do. She's pained over a-brangin' me terday, y'know. 'Course, I don't keer nary a jag she's so ill. The iller she is, the tickleder I git."

Bunny held her hand over her mouth and giggled.

"Yes, well, come with me, and I'll make all the introductions. You'll have to forgive Mrs. Rush for not doing it. She's . . . uh, she's not herself today."

Chickadee took a moment to smooth down her salmon-colored silk dress, and then followed Bunny. She smiled at each woman to whom she was introduced, but not one lady returned her gesture of friendliness. Shrugging her shoulders, she sat down beside Bunny and opened the old leather bag. Every pair of eyes in the room was on her. Oblivious to the rude stares, she took many frayed squares of cloth from the satchel, making a pile of them on her lap.

"I ain't much fer sewin', but Saxon says you-uns do a lavish of it here in Boston. And what with the warm welcome you-uns give me, the leastest I can do is try and do thangs the way you-uns do 'em."

Not one woman deigned to answer, and because they were staring so intently at Chickadee, not one woman had noticed Eugenia Preston's quiet arrival.

She had nearly stepped into the room to demand an explanation for such rudeness when she realized who Chickadee was. With a finger to her lips, she asked for silence from the butler and then stood behind the door to peek through the crack. She knew spying was rude, but if the delightful tales she'd heard about the mountain girl and Wesley Melville were true—and she believed they were—she suspected the overbearing matrons in the room were about to suffer a similar fate. It was entertainment she simply couldn't resist waiting to see.

"Whatever it is you're making will certainly be vivid and pleasing to the eye," Bunny said, picking up one of Chickadee's bright squares of cloth. "You've such pretty colors here."

"Me and Saxon went through ever' closet in the house a-huntin' out ole clothes and other kinds o' cloth. Spended near all night a-rippin' 'em inter these here squares."

"She is most likely making a gown, knowing her

taste," Araminta remarked coldly, her smile as icy as her voice.

The other ladies twittered with laughter.

Bunny glared at each of them. "If she is indeed making a dress, it will be a beautiful one. With her coloring, the hues of her fabrics will be quite pretty on her."

"Nice o' you ter say, Bunny, but it ain't gwine be no dress. It's gwine be—"

"I'm sure none of us care," Araminta broke in. She tried to concentrate on her needlepoint, but her fingers shook as she thought of the things that would be said about her in the days to come. Even now, each lady in the room was absorbing everything that went on and would soon shout it out to all of Boston. Her fine, untarnished name would be stained irreparably.

Oh, how she relished the thought of punishing Saxon for doing this to her.

"Yes, well . . . who has news to share with us?" Bunny asked, realizing a change of subject was vitally needed.

With effort, the women tore their eyes from Chickadee and settled back in their chairs. After all, there would be plenty of time to gossip about the rustic later on.

"There is a certain Mary Lindlock I'd like to discuss," Hester said. "She's new to Boston, and while she's a pleasant enough woman, I'm sure we'd all like to know more about her before we accept her into our circle."

"Far be it from me to pass judgment," Sarah said, and threw Chickadee a well-aimed sneer, "but I must say I'm not at all certain Mary could ever be one of us. Why, do you know I actually heard her arguing over the price of a necklace the other day in Cromwell's jewelry store?"

"You don't mean it!" Eleanor responded. "Well, that is all the proof we need, ladies. Bickering over jewelry is simply not acceptable. It's—"

"Maybe that Cromwell feller was a-tryin' ter cheat her," Chickadee ventured. "I met him when Saxon tuk me thar, and I ain't a-tellin' no lie when I say he was a mite shifty-eyed. I tole Saxon—"

"No one asked for your opinion," Araminta snapped. "Samuel Cromwell is a respected businessman, and we have all patronized his store for years. You'd do well to keep quiet when it comes to matters you know nothing about."

"I'm sure Chickadee meant no disrespect, Mrs. Blackwell." Bunny tried to soothe the angry woman. "She—"

"And as for you, Bunny Hamilton," Araminta hissed, "your opinion is of no value either. I will speak to your Aunt Sue and Uncle Van and inform them of the impertinence you have shown your elders here today. Your cousin, Cynthia, told me herself she is exasperated with you, and from your actions today, I can certainly understand her feelings."

Bunny bent her head and noticed the warts on her hand were showing. She pulled her sleeve down over them and then stared blankly at her sewing. Exasperation had nothing to do with the fact that Cynthia hated her. It was her obesity that kept Cynthia from liking her. Cynthia had even said she'd rather die than be seen anywhere with her, and true to her word, she only accompanied Bunny to social gatherings when she was forced.

Bunny squeezed her eyes shut in an effort to control her tears. But one solitary drop rolled down her round cheek, splashing onto the cloth she held.

Chickadee watched the tear until it was absorbed into the fabric, her insides lurching with both pity and anger. Finally, her eyes the only part of her that moved, Chickadee looked up at Araminta, barely noticing that every woman in the room was leaning forward expectantly.

Araminta's hostile look withered into one of apprehension.

Chickadee stood.

Araminta's fingers trembled on the arm of her chair.

Chickadee took a step forward.

Araminta's needlepoint fell to the floor.

"Refreshments," the butler announced as he wheeled a large cart into the room. "Shall I serve, Mrs. Rush?"

"No. That will be all, Wells," Thelma replied, annoyed at the interruption. "Ladies, we shall dispense with formalities and serve ourselves."

Bunny was the first in line. She piled her small plate high with buttered bread and then reached for the spoon in the large honey pot, drowning the food with the sweet syrup. She dropped four sugar lumps into her tea and selected a fruit tart before she plodded back to her seat.

Chickadee watched her closely, and then, with a heavy sigh, she went back to her chair and began to stitch her tattered squares together.

"Chickadee," Bunny whispered, and pulled her sleeve down over her warts again, "what were you going to do to Mrs. Blackwell before the butler came?" While waiting for the answer, Bunny made quick work of her tart.

Chickadee noticed Bunny barely chewed her food. "Don't rightly know fer shore, but it warn't gwine be somethin' she'da liked much. I couldn't jist set here and let her rip inter you. It ain't right ter let friends git hurt."

Bunny's eyes sparkled with undisguised emotion. "Thank you. No one has ever done that for me before. I mean, I've never had any real friends."

Chickadee smiled. "Bunny, you—"

Her words were cut off by the butler's frantic shouting. "I heard something at the door, and when I opened it, the beast just ran in! I couldn't catch him!"

Thelma paled as Khan bolted toward her. "Oh dear God, he's going to eat me!"

The hysterical women ran into each other as they attempted to remove themselves from Khan's path. Their plates of honeyed bread flew into the air, dropped into elaborate hairdos, slid down faces, and smeared down elegant skirts. But they paid no mind to the spilled food and scurried about the room to get away from the vicious animal who'd come to attack them.

Khan paid no attention to the panicked women and ran straight to Chickadee. She tried to grab him, but Khan decided it was time to play and took hold of the saddlebag. He scampered into the middle of the room, shaking the satchel from side to side. Chickadee hurried to him. "Khan, give me that bag, you ornery thang!"

But Khan escaped her again and ran around the room, still swinging the bag vigorously.

And then the chaos he'd caused intensified.

Feathers, thousands of them, came floating out of the opening of the saddlebag, feathers Chickadee had intended to use in the quilt she was making. Like thick snow, they blew up and then down, drifting every which way as the terrified women ran through them.

"Ladies, he will not harm you!" Araminta shouted. She rushed to Chickadee and took hold of her arm. "Get him out of here immediately, you horrible little fool. How dare you allow him to create such havoc!"

Chickadee did not remove Araminta's hand from her arm. She simply stood there and waited for what she knew would happen in seconds.

And happen it did. Khan, whose game with the bag was not as important as his mistress's safety, sped toward Araminta, his momentum and strength knocking her away from Chickadee. Araminta, taken by surprise by the wolf's speedy actions, was unable to catch her balance and fell to the floor, her skirts billowing over her head to expose her fine underwear to anyone who cared to see it.

Chickadee snapped her fingers, and Khan obediently sat by her heels. With his paw, he swiped a feather off his wet nose and then looked up at his mistress. "Khan, you shouldn't orter a-follered me here, boy. 'Pears to me we're in the deepest kind o' trouble."

The women, who had ceased their frenzied running, stood in shock, rivulets of honey dripping from each of them.

And to the sticky fluid stuck Chickadee's quilt feathers.

Silence, tight and hostile, weighted down the very air. The expressions on the outraged women's faces fairly shouted what words could never have expressed. Finally, Araminta staggered to her feet. "I am mortified to the very marrow of my bones, ladies, that this has happened."

"You have done the unforgivable, Araminta!" Millicent barked as she removed a feather from her eyelashes. "To allow this heathen granddaughter-in-law to bring her . . . her savage beast to our—"

"I knew nothing of it!" Araminta returned. "I—"

"But you knew what kind of person Saxon had married," Sarah charged, picking feathers off her neck. "You should have warned us all!"

"I agree wholeheartedly," Eleanor broke in. She wiped honey from her cheek. "It is unfortunate for you that this hill person is a part of the Blackwell family now, but *we* should not be made to suffer as well!"

Thelma's hand trembled over the mess of feathers that stuck to the bodice of her fine gown. "Eleanor is absolutely right. I accept full responsibility for inviting Saxon's wife, but I will not be blamed for what has happened here today. As Sarah pointed out, it was your duty to warn us about her, Araminta. You failed to do so."

"No one is to be blamed for any of this," Bunny said, padding her way to Chickadee. "Chickadee's dog followed her here, and she had no way of knowing. Mrs. Blackwell was only doing what Saxon requested—''

''I do not need you to come to my defense, Bunny,'' Araminta bit out. Sedately, she gathered her sewing and her new cane, and turned toward the group of women once more. ''I have no control over this crude girl. I *refuse* to accept blame for what she and her animal have done.'' With that, she marched out of the room, failing to see Eugenia who was still hidden behind the door.

''It pains me somethin' awful ter agree with Araminty,'' Chickadee said when the woman was gone, ''but ain't nary a bit o' this her fault. I ain't agin' a-gittin' plumb franzied over thangs that are real bad, but you-uns is the yarnin'est bunch o' fritter-minded womenfolks I ever knowed. I promised Saxon I was gwine do my God-burnin'est best ter be as couth as I know how, but you-uns didn't never give me no chance a'tall. When I first set foot in here, I warn't offered no greetin' or no char. If it warn't fer Bunny here, I reckon I might still be a-standin' over yonder in that door. And you-uns even laid inter her fer a-bein' thoughty to me.''

She collected what was left of her sewing. ''When I was growin' up in the Blue Ridge, I allus wondered what it'd be like ter be fine-haired like you-uns, but I ain't gwine wonder no more. Yore heads is swolt up with highfalutin' idees that yore better'n anybody else, and a-tryin' ter git along with you's about as easy as a-tryin' ter stretch a gnat's ass over a washtub.''

Thelma frowned. ''Inform Saxon he will receive the bill for the damage your beast has caused to my furnishings.''

''And he will also pay for our ruined gowns,'' Evelyn and Hester chorused.

''You'll git yore money. But what you-uns is a-hurtin' fer the mostest is somethin' all the money in the world cain't never buy. And that's a warm heart.

Yore all so dang biggety that when you strut around, it's like you was a-balancin' yore family trees on yore noses.

"And even though it 'pears yore all a mite riled, thur ain't nary a doubt in my mind that yore all gwine light outen here as fast as yer pegs can carry you ter spread the word about me and Khan. Yore gwine say you was shocked speechless, only ain't none o' you gwine be speechless when you commence a-gossipin'. You'll be a-slangin' dirt faster'n a gravedigger in a few hours, and it's all I can do not ter meller each and ever' one o' you-uns right here and now in this day and time!"

"I have no idea what *meller* means," Millicent spat, "but if it is some kind of threat—"

"Oh, it's a threat all right," she flared. "It means punch. Beat. Thrash. Bang. Whip, and any other hittin' word that strikes yore fancy."

"I think we have heard quite enough," Eleanor chimed in. "You—"

"Shet up, lady. I got one more thang ter say afore I leave, and I'm gwine say it."

Thelma nodded at Wells, and the butler took a step toward Chickadee. Khan growled. Chickadee continued smoothly. "Iffen I hear one bad thang said about Saxon over any o' this, I'll come after ever' one o' you-uns like all wrath. Shame his name, and I'll disremember my manners and—"

The loud gasp that came from each of the women in the room cut Chickadee's warning short. She turned to see another woman standing behind her. With a heavily jeweled hand, the elderly lady gently nudged Chickadee aside and looked into the room, her gleaming gray eyes taking in each detail. Under her sharp scrutiny, the bedraggled matrons reddened and shivered.

"It would appear my tardiness has caused me to miss something more than mere time spent with all of you," Eugenia stated, her voice quivering with restrained laughter.

The women, all at once, tried to explain what had happened. They were silenced immediately by the same jeweled hand.

At the woman's haughty gesture, Chickadee rolled her eyes to the ceiling. Another Boston queen. "Go on in thar," she said, pushing the woman further into the room. "Set yoresef down and let them cats tell you what all went on. Listen real keerful-like so's you can git it all straight, lady. But like I done tole all them already? Well, when you go ter spread all the gwines-on, iffen you slur Saxon's name jist once, you can be God-burn sartin I'll throw a hissy-fit the likes of which you ain't never seed!"

Eugenia regarded her with a warm smile. "You are Chickadee Blackwell. Please sit down. I would like to talk to you."

Chickadee laughed. "Lady, the feelin's a-flyin' around this here room is hot enough ter roast the devil." She pointed to the other women. "Look at 'em all. Thur anger's a-makin' 'em shake harder'n a dog a-passin' peach seeds. I'd have ter be plumb bereft ter stay here a second longer."

She left quickly, Khan trotting behind her. Bunny, after an apologetic look at the group of women, followed them out.

"Eugenia!" all the women cried in unison.

"Ladies, please! I haven't had my tea yet." Biting back a smile, she made her way to a desk, sank into the chair in front of it, and accepted the tea Thelma handed to her.

The women drew up their chairs, and one by one explained in great detail what havoc Chickadee had caused. Nothing was left out in their explicit account, and with each women who had her turn at telling it, the story grew more fantastic.

"So you see, Eugenia," Millicent said, plucking another feather off her face, "the Blackwell family *must* be ostracized. That Chickadee heathen for obvious reasons, Saxon for ever wedding her, and Araminta—"

"Millicent is right," Sarah agreed, failing in her attempts to remove the honey from her skirts. "We simply cannot allow them to ever—"

"It was horrible," Eleanor added. "That dog—"

"Of course, you were only with her a few moments, Eugenia," Thelma said. "You cannot possibly know how utterly crude she is."

"Cares nothing at all for decorum," Hester panted. "Nothing at all for—"

"Oh, Eugenia, thank God you were late today," Evelyn gushed, and started off another spree of gossip.

As the ladies continued slandering the Blackwell name, Eugenia's thoughts turned to Chickadee. The girl was marvelous, she thought to herself. Outrageously spirited and wonderfully open. She was the exact medicine Boston needed to rid itself of the malady called boredom—an affliction from which Eugenia had suffered for years.

"Eugenia?" Millicent said. "Did you hear what—"

"I've heard enough." She reached into her bag and withdrew paper and writing utensils. "I believe we were going to discuss the grand ball today."

"We were going to draw up a guest list, weren't we?" Hester asked.

"Remarkable memory you have, Hester," Eugenia returned sarcastically. "No doubt it often serves you well. Now, about the guest list: I've exciting news. Lord Gilford Cavendish, duke of Amherst, will be coming from England to visit our fair city during the time our ball will be held, and his presence will certainly make it all the more grand."

"The duke of Amherst!" Eleanor gasped. "Imagine!"

"We'll take great pains with details," Millicent said. "Heaven forbid anything go wrong with the duke there!"

"Every single thing must be arranged with the utmost concern," Sarah agreed. "Especially the guest list!"

The ladies began chattering and giggling again. Eugenia watched them all with her sharp eyes. Finally, she bent her head, looked at the blank piece of paper on the desk, and began the list.

With fluid and beautiful strokes, one hand hiding what she was writing, the first name she wrote was Chickadee Blackwell.

Chapter 14

Saxon got out of bed and closed the bedroom windows; the breeze that blew through them was so strong it swept his black curls off his forehead. Chickadee waited until he'd returned to bed and then got up and let the wind back in. Turning toward her husband, she folded her arms across her naked breasts.

"I jist cain't abide them women, Saxon! Next to thur heads, the biggest bones in thur bodies is thur jaws! I mean ter tell you—"

"You don't have to tell me," Saxon interrupted with a chuckle. "Those women have been *jawin'* about it all over town. But Keely, what happened at the sewing meeting wasn't your fault. Forget about it. There will be other socials, and—"

"Other socials? Saxon, you beat all. Yore so slow-minded tonight, you'd pick up a snake and hit a stick! I'm a-tryin' ter tell you I ain't gwine ter no more of them dang-blasted git-togethers!"

"No one forced you to attend the sewing meeting. It was your own idea to go. But you did meet Bunny, and you said you liked her. If you hadn't joined the sewing circle, you wouldn't have met her. And Bunny can introduce you to younger women. Ladies closer to your own age."

She sighed. She was the only friend Bunny had, so how could Bunny introduce her to other women? And more than that, she thought, if the younger

204

women didn't accept Bunny as their friend, that made them just as fritter-minded as the old ones.

"Keely, please shut the windows."

She lifted both an auburn eyebrow and her chin. "No. I cain't stand it when thur's no air in here. It ain't healthy ter be withouten air. And I warn't a-talkin' about no winders. I want ter tell you what them biddies—"

"To hell with them. The only reason I suggested you become acquainted with society is because I don't want you to be lonesome. But if you'd rather not attend any affairs for a while, that's fine. You might feel differently later on, and then you may do whatever you wish."

She saw an unspoken plea in his eyes and knew he was hoping she would make another attempt with society. Her first impulse was to tell him she hated the very thought. But he'd brought up the subject of her having friends many times recently. It somehow seemed very important to him. But didn't he understand she didn't *need* them? She had Khan, Desdemona, that sweet maid Candice, and now Bunny. Why look for more friends when she already had four wonderful ones?

Saxon saw the battle going on in her mind by watching her bright eyes. "I'll never force you to do something you don't like, little one. You've no need to worry about that."

Her gaze returned to him, and she saw the hope in his eyes again. *Lord o' mercy*, she thought. When he looked at her like that, she couldn't think of anything in the world she wouldn't try to do for him. "Well . . ."

Her voice trailed off, and he knew she was considering his suggestion. He did indeed hope she would give society another chance: besides wanting her to make friends, he thought that getting her together with other women was the best way to show her how things were done in Boston. After all, he rationalized, surely if she were exposed to gentlewomen long enough, she would begin to imitate some of their feminine mannerisms. It seemed like such a gentle way for her to learn.

But, as he'd promised, he wouldn't force her. Instead, he would give her news he suspected would delight her. "Keely, close the windows, and I'll tell you something about your father."

Her breath quickened. "Y'know whar he is?"

"The windows, if you please."

She shut them so forcefully the room shuddered, and then she ran to him, leaping and flying toward the bed when she was still several feet away.

Saxon caught her as she sailed over him. Women had hurried to his bed before, but no one had ever flown into it. There was no woman on earth like Chickadee.

God, he was going to miss her.

"Saxon," she gasped, twisting in his embrace, "whar is he? Did you take all his money? Is he a beggar now?"

Her hauntingly beautiful eyes pulled him into their emerald depths. He tried to find his way to the surface of those bottomless pools, but only sank deeper. Drowning. He was drowning in them with no hope of salvation.

"Saxon, I'm gwine take a snit iffen you don't tell me about Barton!"

The information he had about her father was already at the back of his throat. All he had to do was get it to his lips and put sound to it. *He's in New York,* he explained silently. *A little over eighteen years ago, he sold your mother's gold nuggets, invested the money, and made a fortune on Wall Street.*

"Saxon?"

He'd wrestled with the decision to tell her the news all day, guilt at wanting to keep it from her gnawing at him like a termite at a piece of rotting wood. And now he felt himself wavering again. If he told her the truth, how long would it be before she left? That question sickened him with dread.

"I think he might be in . . . the New York area," came his feeble answer.

"You thank?"

He bent to take a tawny nipple between his lips. "It's just a hunch," he mumbled, his mouth full of her.

"Dang it! Saxon—"

"All right." Lying back, he pulled her with him. "I don't know anything for sure yet, but my detectives have located . . . several B. Winslows in New York."

She sat up and stared at the wall in front of her, her body stiff. The revenge she'd wanted for so long seemed close at hand now. But where was the thrill she'd expected? In its stead was a strange foreboding.

Saxon mistook her mood for one of impatience. "Keely," he said, his voice reaching out to caress her, "give me more time. I swore I'd help you get your revenge and I will, little one." *I will*, he told himself firmly, but that oath was becoming more and more tempting to break.

She gave him a kiss that sweetly lingered and hinted at what would soon follow. Her sleek hands, her slender fingers hungered for the feel of him, her own body sliding closer to his, warming him, setting him afire and making him yearn for the indescribable magic that was Chickadee's alone.

"Promise me somethin', Saxon." She sighed.

"Anything."

"Don't never brang no kind o' seriousness inter this here bed agin," she pleaded, loath to hear any more about the bargain she'd begun to regret making. "It ain't no place fer a-jawin' about problems and miseries. The onliest sorter talkin' that should go on betwixt these sheets is what our hearts say ter one another."

Saxon's fingers dropped from the silky tangle of her hair. She'd been doing a lot of that kind of sweet-talking recently, her words always accompanied by that look of devotion in her eyes. He still didn't know what to make of it, he only knew her tenderness made him want more of it and none of it at the same time.

Chickadee placed her hand on his chest. "Heart voices don't got no kind of sound, but iffen you try, you can still hear what they say. And you got eyes in thar too. All's you got ter do is open 'em up and see."

Saxon grabbed her hand when her fingers began to ripple across his chest. "Keely, what are you saying?"

She smiled knowingly at his question. "Shhh. Just listen, Saxon," she said, yanking her hand out of his grasp and slipping it beneath the covers to slide it down his thigh. "Let yore heart tell you what all I'm a-sayin'."

The roaring flood of desire was the only thing Saxon could hear. The sorcery of Chickadee, her mysterious essence poured over him, into him, and through him, sending him spiraling into the nest of passion she'd made ready for him.

"I hear nothing but my need for you, Keely. Like a beggar, it cries out for sustenance, reaches out—and will not cease until appeased."

Her nails scored his back, but his hiss of discomfort never reached her ears, so quickly, so violently did she respond to him. His plunging hardness brought her within a hair's breadth of pain yet snatched her back to pleasure. He slowed his frenzied pace and then quickened it again, guiding her, abandoning her, offering, refusing, alternating his rhythm of lovemaking until she no longer knew where she was, no longer cared, could no longer think, could only melt within the blaze of fulfillment that finally consumed her. She throbbed wildly around him, the shudder of her release bringing Saxon's own, her sigh of pleasure intensifying his.

And then the air, still cool in the room, drifted past him, drying his moist skin. The chill he felt brought him back to the reality passion had erased from his mind. Winslow, Chickadee's return to the Appalachia . . . the whole damn bargain came back to him then.

With a heavy sigh he slid to the bed and gathered her into his arms, hugging her tightly until weariness loosened his hold on her. "Bargain," he whispered into her hair before sleep overtook him.

Chickadee waited until his breathing was slow and even, got out of bed, dressed quietly, picked up her rifle, and left the room, Khan following her. More familiar with the house now, she made her way downstairs with no mishaps and was outside in a few more moments.

It wasn't the first time she'd walked alone at night. The mansion was stuffy and hot, and the fact that Saxon didn't like the windows open had led her outside nearly every night since they'd arrived in Boston. He knew nothing of her nightly escapades since he was always asleep when she left him, and Chickadee was certain he'd try and put an end to them if he ever found out.

Only when she reached the thick woods did she slow her pace. She breathed deeply of the brisk night air, savoring the fresh smell of the plants and earth. After propping her rifle against a large tree, she sat down on the forest floor and crushed a handful of brittle leaves.

"I'm all tore up inside, Khan. Jist a short spell ago, when Saxon mentioned that dang bargain? Well, it near about kilt me ter hear him say it. And it plumb confounded me when I didn't go inter some sorter franzy when he said he mighta found ole Barton. I didn't feel nothin' but a real empty feelin'."

Khan lay down and closed his eyes.

"Khan Snow McBride! Open yore eyes, you ornery thang. When thur bolted shut, it's like I'm a-talkin' ter mysef, and only crazy folks does that."

He opened one eye.

"I cain't figger out how it happened, boy. I

thought I could love Saxon jist a smidgeon, but 'pears I was the worstest kind o' wrong. And I never had no idee jist how much I love him till he talked about a-findin' Barton Winslow. I got ter go home when the man's done tuk his fall, y'know. Dang that God-burn bargain ter hell and back!"

She found a small twig and rubbed Khan's snout with it. "Still . . . I cain't be withouten my mountains ferever, Khan. But I cain't leave Saxon neither. Not even a-countin' the way I feel about him, he needs me. You seed fer yoresef how these Boston folks is, and they jist ain't good fer him."

Khan rolled onto his back, his hind leg shaking when she began to scratch his belly.

"But I'm jist one girl. I cain't change nothin' about this here city. Cain't make it right fer Saxon no matter what I do. And it ain't only that neither. Saxon thanks he *likes* this kind o' life, boy. He thanks thur ain't no better kind ter have."

She tossed away the stick and rested her chin in her hands. "I knowed in my heart I shouldn't orter love him, but I went and done it anyway. I always knowed love was somethin' powerful, Khan, but I didn't never know jist how unbeatable it is. You cain't control it, boy. Cain't love jist a little bit like I reckoned. Thur ain't no measurement when it comes ter love. Either you love or you don't. It's the curiousest thang I ever come acrost."

She closed her eyes. Saxon and the Appalachia. In her mind she saw them both—Saxon on one side, her beloved mountains on the other. She remembered her blue Carolina heavens and then recalled Saxon's sky-blue eyes. She heard the song of the hills in the mountain breeze, and then Saxon's laughter, his whisper, his sweet, sweet words. She felt the Blue Ridge sunshine pouring down on her, but weren't Saxon's arms as warm and comforting?

"Look at me, Khan. I'm a-settin' here a-feelin' some kind o' powerful sorry fer mysef. You'd thank I don't got no more guts'n a butterfly."

Her giggle chimed through the cool woods. "I been so dumb. Why, I reckon iffen brains was leather, I wouldn't have enough ter saddle a flea! I got ter tell him, Khan. Got ter tell him I love him! And I got ter keep on a-tellin' him. It's gwine take a lavish o' time ter git through ter him, but I'll do it. I'll do it on account o' I'm gwine be as persistent as a starvin' bedbug!"

She jumped to her feet and grabbed her rifle. "Come on, boy. I'm gwine go wake up Saxon and tell him the truth about how I feel." She fairly flew through the forest, smiling broadly at the song her heart was singing within her. Everything was going to be fine now. She'd make Saxon believe she loved him, and then, somehow, she'd make him love her back.

That thought brought her to an abrupt halt. "Saxon ain't like Barton, Khan. And I ain't like mama. Mama was a kind soul, but she was lonely and a mite ripe when ole Barton come a-wanderin' up ter her holler. She tuk one look at him and falled plumb ter pieces. Warn't her fault, but she didn't never see Barton was sech a blackguard."

She knelt and took Khan's snout in her hands. "But I've knowed Saxon fer nigh on seven months now, and that's time enough ter know somebody good. He ain't gwine do me like Barton did mama. I mean ter git ter that little boy in him, and once I do that? Well, that young-uns gwine mix with the man, and Saxon's gwine be whole. A whole man ready ter give and git love. And o' course, I'll be right thar a-givin' it ter him. And after he's shed of all them ghosts, we'll thank on what ter do, whar ter live, and all them other thangs. Ever'thang's gwine be jist fine."

Straightening, she continued toward the edge of the woods, only to stop short when a squirrel scampered in front of her. Her fingers trembled as she tightened her grip on her rifle.

"You see that, Khan?" she whispered, her skin

rippling into goose flesh. "It was a omen, boy. Both me and you know withouten nary a doubt that when a squirrel runs acrost yore path at night? Well, thur's the worstest kind o' luck a-comin' yore way. Dang, dang, dang it! Jist when I got ever'thang straight-ened out real good, this has ter happen!"

Her steps much slower now, she reached the clearing, her skin still moist, her heart still pound-ing. She couldn't be certain what ill fortune would befall her, nor did she know when it would come, but nevertheless, her eyes darted around her sur-roundings.

And then the fine hairs at the back of her neck rose.

She cocked her rifle and raised the stock to her shoulder before she even knew what it was she would shoot. Khan too sensed peril, the fur on his back standing erect in his apprehension.

Before she had the chance to squeeze the trigger, Khan went flying toward a man who'd stepped out of the thick darkness and, as Chickadee tried to bring the scene into proper focus, someone from behind her reached around and pulled the gun from her grasp. A rank-smelling hand went around her mouth, and within seconds her assailant had gagged her. She fought both the man and her fear, but when she heard Khan's piercing whine her dread turned to terror.

She saw his prone form, bloody and still, his at-tacker standing over him, dagger in hand.

Chickadee struggled valiantly, her horror increas-ing her strength, but the men soon joined forces and she had little chance of escape. Still, though they outnumbered her, they were hard-pressed to pull a large bag over her head, so wildly she fought them. When they finally accomplished the task, they quickly tied the opening. That done, one of the men picked her up, slung her over his shoulder, and be-gan to run. His companion took one last look at Khan's unmoving, crimson form and followed. They soon reached the wagon they'd hidden on the other side of the woods and tossed Chickadee into the back.

For what seemed like hours, the horses raced as if the devil himself was after them. Chickadee was powerless to keep herself from being thrown around in the bed of the wooden cart. With each lurch of the vehicle, she was banged against its hard planks.

She felt no pain, she could only think of Khan, wounded or perhaps dead. But the time for sorrow would come later. For now, there was only time to hate the men who had kidnapped her; only time to ready herself for what she would do to them once she had the chance.

That opportunity never came. The wagon hit another rut in the road, this one deeper than the ones before. Chickadee was flung toward the back of the cart, her weight and the momentum of her slide forcing the flimsy gate open. She crashed to the cold, litter-strewn ground of the North End.

The wagon, its drivers oblivious to their loss, was soon far away, and Chickadee, helpless, afraid, and jarred, was left to the mercy of the North End.

Chapter 15

❦❦"**F**aith, and what have we here, I'm askin' ye laddies?" Shane said as they reached the rolling bag.

"'Tis a live thing." Gallagher backed away. "What with the kickin' and fightin' it's doin', 'tis an animal. A wild one at that. Leave it be, I'm warnin' ye."

"'Tis a coward ye are, Gallagher," Shane said. "Afraid before ye even know what yer afraid of!"

"Freein' it is what we'll be doin', Gallagher," Killian said as he bent to loosen the bag's ties. "Run if 'tis what yer guts tell ye to do, man, but have a care in case it comes after ye!"

When the sack was open, homemade leather shoes, the feet in them still flailing wildly, were the first things the men saw.

"Sweet Mary above, 'tis a person!" Gallagher shouted, his deep voice echoing down the alley and sending rats scurrying hither and yon.

"Ye were scared fer naught, Gallagher!" Killian responded. "Because if ye care to have a look, ye'll see these legs have nae a hair on them! Smooth and soft as the silk of corn. 'Tis a lass, to be sure it is."

"'Tis takin' the bag off her we need to be doin'," Gallagher said, joining Killian on the ground.

"Ho! Ho!" Shane exclaimed merrily. "Afraid he was, Killian, but now that he knows 'tis only a lass, 'tis wantin' to be the first at her he's doin'!"

"Ye'll have yer chance, Gallagher," Killian said, pushing his friend away. "But 'twill be meself who—"

"Yerself?" Shane roared. " 'Twas *I* who found the bag, Killian! Ye dinna see it first, so—"

"And who was it who opened it, might I be askin'?" Killian demanded. " 'Tis only fair that I—"

"Ye've been divilin' me the whole night, Killian," Shane warned. "Ye said ye'd buy the drinks, but 'twas nothin' but lint ye had in yer pockets when the time came to pay! And now ye've got a fine nerve to be wantin' first turn at the lass! Nae, Killian. The Lord help ye, the only thing ye've got comin' to ye is me fist!"

Gallagher watched his two friends fight, until a muffled scream erupted from the bag behind him. " 'Twould serve them both right if 'twas pockmarked and painful to the eye ye turned out to be, lass," he told the struggling female as he dragged the sack off. But his hopes were dashed as he gazed down at Chickadee. Never had he seen such a lovely woman—nor a more indignant one.

"Shane! Killian! 'Tis disbelievin' ye'll be when ye see the little colleen!"

At his shout, the men ceased their ruckus and stumbled to where Chickadee lay. "Bonny she is, or I'm nae an Irishman," Shane remarked and wiped at his cut lip. " 'Twas worth fightin' fer her."

"Aye, 'twas at that," Killian agreed, rubbing his bleeding knuckles before he bent to touch a red curl.

Chickadee responded to his actions by throwing him to the other side of her. One down, she stood quickly and motioned for Shane and Gallagher to try and come for her. When neither man moved, she ripped the smelly gag off.

"Don't reckon I can lick all o' you-uns, but I'm fer God-burn shore gwine bang you up afore I'll let you lay a hand on me! Saxon tole me you Irish folks is a mite fighty-fied, but so is mountain folks. Come on, you dang-blasted furriners!"

Shane and Gallagher, their eyes never leaving the furious slip of a girl, went to help Killian to his feet. Now standing side by side, the three amazed men watched as Chickadee dared them with her balled fists. She danced before them, her feet never slowing, her body in constant motion as she moved in a small circle while waiting for one of them to come toward her.

" 'Tis mad she is," Shane said softly. "Doin' a jig like that. Lost her wits, she has."

"She tossed me to the cursed ground!" Killian growled. "Caught me by surprise, and she'll nae get away with outwittin' Killian Rafferty!"

"No?" Chickadee challenged. "Come on then, Killy, or whatever the hell yore blasted name is! I'll give you a knock-fight the likes of which you ain't never had!"

Killian smiled at her bravado. " 'Tisn't a fight I had in mind, lassie," he said, walking slowly toward her. "Nae, 'tis pleasurin' meself with ye I've a mind to do. We'll be gentle with ye, colleen, to be sure we will."

"We mean ye nae harm," Shane said. "We'll let ye go when we're finished. A lass with yer bonny looks has had a man before, so ye've nae need to worry about the pain."

"Leave her be," Gallagher said. "Faith, she's so young, laddies. Less than twenty years, if me eyes don't deceive me. Surely ye'll nae have another peaceful night's sleep if ye do this to her. She's a wee lass—"

"I don't need no defendin' from you!" Chickadee yelled. "You was jist as hot ter git at me as they was! I'm as miseried as I can be over how poverty-poor you-uns is here in Boston, but poverty ain't no reason ter turn on folks who ain't done nothin' a'tall to you! I'm jist as agger-pervoked with this dang city as you-uns is, and—"

"Does she nae make sense?" Gallagher pleaded. "What has she done to us to deserve—"

"What more is it yer thinkin' ye know about us, lass?" Shane asked Chickadee and ignored Gallagher. "And where are ye from? 'Tis plain yer nae from here."

"Yeah? Well neither are you, so I reckon we're even."

"A point well taken," he replied. "But ye dinna answer me question."

"I ain't gwine answer nothin' but yore sneakin' grin! Answer it by a-knockin' ever' dang one o' them teeth you got outen yore head! You-uns got some kind o' powerful gall ter thank you can rape me, and me let you do it! What do you thank I am? Some sorter feather-legged, sissified pansy?"

Unable to control himself, Shane burst into laughter, and Gallagher and Killian soon joined in his mirth. "All right, lassie," Shane said. "Ye win. We won't touch ye. 'Twould seem Gallagher was right in bein' afraid o' ye, aye, that he was. Shane Flannagan's me name, and this lad is Gallagher O'Neill. Eh, *Killy* here, ye've met."

Chickadee lowered her fists. "You-uns talk real strange."

"And 'tis the Queen's English yer speakin', I suppose?" Killian teased her. "From where do ye come, colleen?"

"My name ain't Colleen. It's Chickadee. Chickadee McBride Blackwell."

"McBride, is it?" Gallagher asked, walking up to her. "Are ye Scotch? Irish?"

With the aid of the flickering streetlamp, Chickadee noticed his eyes were as green as hers. And so were Shane's and Killian's. They looked to be about the same age as Saxon, maybe a bit younger, and were powerfully built. Shane and Gallagher had black hair, but Killian's hair was almost orange. All in all, they didn't seem to be bad men. Just a mite snockered.

"I reckon I got a smidgeon o' Scotch or Irish blood in me," she finally answered. "Maybe both. My people come acrost the ocean-sea jist like you-uns done. Heared tell they was Irish, but warn't nothin' writ down in my family, so it's a mite hard ter tell. All's I can tell you is I'm from the North Caroliner mountains. I live here now though.''

"And what were ye doin' in that bag, lass?" Shane asked. "Were ye stolen from yer home?"

"Yep, and I got ter git back right now. Khan coulda been kilt, and I cain't waste no time a-gittin' back.''

"Is Khan yer mate, Chickadee?" Gallagher asked.

"He's my wolf, and them bushwhackers knifed him afore they tuk me away," she explained hurriedly, her fear for Khan increasing steadily. "Only I don't got no way ter git back. Left my dang weddin' rang on the dresser, so I cain't trade that, ain't got no money with me, and the Blackwell estate is—''

"Estate?" Killian repeated. "Are ye a maid there?"

"No, I'm Saxon Blackwell's wife."

Shane and Killian laughed, but not Gallagher. "Pay them nae a bit o' mind, Chickadee. If ye say yer the mistress o' the estate, I'll believe ye. Come, 'tis gettin' money fer yer cab fare we need to be doin'.''

She let him take her hand. "You got any?"

"If I had but one cent to me name, I'd give it to ye, colleen, to be sure I would," he said, squeezing her hand reassuringly. "But 'tis a rare occasion when I have money to lend. I make little on the docks, and—''

" 'Tis spendin' his wages on whiskey he does," Shane broke in. "Nae, lassie, ye'll get naught from him.''

Chickadee looked over her shoulder at the street behind her. She had no idea how to get back to the estate, she only knew it was far from here. And with no money . . . She'd just have to walk. If she asked for directions and met with no mishaps along the way, she'd make it by morning.

"I admired a-meetin' all you-uns. But I cain't stay. I'm worried somethin' awful about Khan." She turned to leave the alley.

"Surely 'tisn't walkin' yer plannin' on doin'?" Killian called after her. "Come back, lass. We'll get the money fer ye. Won't we laddies?"

"Aye, we will at that," Shane and Gallagher promised.

She turned. "Right honorable o' you-uns, but I cain't ask you ter steal."

" 'Tisn't stealin' but *sellin'* we'll do to get ye the money," Shane informed her, winking at his comrades. "Now, will ye be trustin' us, or would ye rather walk alone at night on some deserted road?"

She wrinkled her nose. "What you got ter sell?"

"Come with us, lass, and we'll show ye," Gallagher requested. " 'Tisn't too far from here."

"And ye'll be with us," Killian added. "We'll nae let any harm come to ye."

Sensing their eagerness to help her and realizing money would get her to Khan's side faster than her legs ever could, she nodded and joined the "dangerous" Irishmen who had become her friends.

"Well, iffen that don't beat all," Chickadee murmured when she saw the rows of little pots on the ground, each containing homemade rye whiskey. "Irish likker."

"Have a taste, lass." Shane handed her a dipper.

She sipped a bit but promptly spit it out. "Lord o' mercy! That's the worstest stuff I ever did try and swallor! Thur ain't no way you-uns is gwine sell this."

Gallagher kicked the bushes that hid the whiskey pots. " 'Twas only a few weeks ago we started makin' it. We're nae knowin' how to do it properly yet."

" 'Tis Keefe Delaney who makes a fine whiskey,

but he willna' show us how," Killian grouched. "Us, his kinsmen, tryin' to make a livin' just as he!"

"Aye," Shane agreed. "The curse o' the divil be on his black soul fer turnin' on his own brothers. But we've nae given up, colleen. We'll keep tryin' till we find the right recipe. 'Tis only a matter o' trial and error."

Tentatively, Chickadee sampled another sip of the whiskey and shuddered. "I allus thought this was what pizen would taste like iffen I ever did git pizened by somebody."

"Poison?" Killian repeated. "Now that's a fine compliment if I ever heard one."

"I don't tell no lies, Killian. The stuff's bad, ain't nobody gwine buy it, and I ain't gwine git the money I need ter git back to Khan. I orter a-walked. I done wasted nigh on a hour a-comin' here with you-uns, and now—"

"Oh we'll sell it, to be sure," Gallagher told her, picking up a few containers of the whiskey. "We know a painter. But he's nae a painter o' art. Roy paints houses. We'll go awaken him now and make the sale fer ye."

"Y'mean this Roy feller actually *likes* this mess?"

"He's never tasted it," Killian said sheepishly. "But he says 'tis the best paint thinner he's ever used!"

Though dawn had barely broken, a small lamp lit the room sufficiently for Chickadee to see. At the sight before her, she staggered for the bedpost.

Candice hurried to her. "Chickadee! Oh thank the dear Lord! Mr. Blackwell has been looking for hours—"

"Is . . . is he dead, Candy?" Chickadee whispered.

Khan, lying on a blanket on the floor, was motionless. There was barely a spot of white on him, his thick fur was so matted with dark blood.

"No," Candice said softly, leading her to the wolf.

Chickadee sank to the floor and reached out to touch Khan. The blood was hard, and scary, and horrible.

"I did everything I could for him," Candice squeaked. "Mr. Blackwell said he would bring a doctor back and—"

"We ain't got time ter wait. Git a pot o' water a-bilin', brang whiskey, scissors, a needle and thread . . . and fetch me my yarbs."

When Candice left, Chickadee cradled Khan's snout in her hands, her heart stopping when she noticed the bloody saliva oozing from his mouth. Something in him, one of his innards was wounded! Bleeding from the inside . . . *Lord o' mercy!* She didn't know how to repair him *inside!*

"Khan," she murmured down to him, her fear coagulating in her throat. "We been through too much fer you ter leave me now, you ornery thang. Y'know I cain't abide this Boston place withouten you by my side. I know yore right at the hinge creak o' death, but you got ter fight, boy. Please don't die on me, Khan."

As her hands caressed him, his hind leg twitched once. His body shuddered violently.

And then his chest ceased to rise.

"Khan? Khan?" She snatched her hands away from him and tried to take a breath. But there seemed to be no air in the room. The only thing around her was death. Before her, beside her, everywhere, death. She felt light-headed with grief. Finally, she was able to inhale raggedly. "Khan!" she wailed. "Khan, oh Khan!"

"Keely!" Saxon crossed the room in three strides, his black cape whipping behind him. He jerked her into his embrace. "Keely, what—"

"Saxon, Khan died!" She buried her face in his shoulder, her knees trembling and then buckling.

He caught her as she fell and carried her to the bed. "What happened to you? Keely, who—"

"He's gone," she whispered, her eyes dazed. "He left me, Saxon. I tole him not ter go, but he—"

"I'll need privacy if I'm to work, Saxon," an elderly man with a black bag said from the doorway. "I've already spoken to the maid, and she'll be here shortly with what I need. I'll call you and your wife when I'm finished."

Saxon went to him and urged him back out into the hall. "Dr. Larson, it appears we have no need of your services. The wolf has died. I'll have my driver take you home."

"Step aside, Saxon," Dr. Larson instructed, already going back into the bedroom. He went directly to Khan and crouched over him. "Knife wounds sometimes cause a condition I like to call false death." He opened his bag and removed his stethoscope. "The medical term is coma, but that sounds too scary to most people."

"What's he a-doin?" Chickadee asked, and sat up in the bed.

"He's listening for a heartbeat. But Keely, what hap-"

"A coma is a state of profound unconsciousness, Mrs. Blackwell," Dr. Larson said. "If you're not familiar with it, you can indeed mistake it for real death."

Hope climbed like rising steam. "You mean he ain't dead?"

"Precisely." Dr. Larson studied the room. "Clear off that table over there and lay a clean sheet on it. Saxon, you help me with the wolf. And you," he said to Candice when she arrived with a length of white cloth, "tear that into strips."

After everyone had done as ordered, Chickadee watched the doctor place several shiny instruments on the surgery table. "Tell me what ter do ter hep, Mr. Doctor Man."

"Keely, we'll disturb him if we stay," Saxon said, taking her arm. "Surely you don't want to disrupt his concentration?"

Dr. Larson stared at Chickadee. "She doesn't appear to be distraught, Saxon. It's her pet, and I may be able to use her assistance. Do you have a strong stomach, young lady? Because if you faint, I'll leave you on the floor and continue with the operation."

"She can't stay, doctor," Saxon barked. "I've yet to find out what happened, and—"

"Saxon, you try a-takin' me outen this room, and I'll lay you so low, you'll be able ter wear a top hat and walk under a snake's belly!"

Dr. Larson chuckled. "Better leave before she makes good her threat, Saxon. I cannot possibly do two surgeries at once."

With a tremendous sigh, Saxon left the room, knowing full well no power on earth could induce Chickadee to leave Khan.

When he was gone, Dr. Larson picked up a scalpel. "Talk to your pet," he instructed Chickadee. "Tell him you're here. Tell him the things you always tell him. Remind him of life."

Chickadee nodded and bent close to Khan's ear, speaking so softly, only Khan and God could hear her.

Saxon threw another heap of soiled straw into the wheelbarrow. The barn was the only place he could think of to go while waiting for Khan's surgery to end. The house's walls had seemed to be closing in on him.

"Mr. Blackwell, sir," Josh, the stableboy, said. "I've just come from putting the horses out to pasture and was going to—well, it's my job to muck the stalls."

"Take the day off, Josh!" The boy hurried away, and Saxon leaned against the handle of the pitchfork.

Ain't nothin' like hard work ter cure a ailment in the mind, outlander, he remembered Chickadee telling him once. *It's a knowed fact that when you sweat? Well, that sweat wrenches you dry of the uneases.*

He went back to work and cleaned each of the thirty stalls. Two by two, he brought the horses back to their fresh compartments, fed and watered them, and then took up the pitchfork again.

"It didn't work, Keely!" he raged, breaking the wooden handle of the tool over his knee. "Dammit, what happened to you? Who took you?"

Still muttering to himself, he walked out of the barn and looked up at the mansion. His eyes zeroed in on the window of his bedroom where Chickadee still remained, and there he kept them for many moments before he went to relieve another Blackwell employee of his job. Heedless of the cold wind that bit at his moist skin, he ripped off his shirt. Over and over he swung the ax. He split log after log, sending splinters flying every which way, his muscles straining with both exertion and anger.

It might have been you instead of Khan, Keely, he seethed inwardly. *You with the wounds . . . the blood.* The picture he painted in his mind was so vivid, he gritted his teeth and flung the ax far away. Taking in great gulps of air, he sorted through his tortured emotions and tried to understand why he was so terribly, deeply disturbed.

Chickadee was fine. She'd shown no signs of injury whatsoever. So why couldn't he relax? "Because you could have been killed, Keely!" he screamed, spinning on his heel to stare at the bedroom window again.

She'd been up there for hours, dammit, and that was long enough! Khan or no Khan, she was going to leave that room and tell him what had happened. He'd been out of his mind with worry when he'd discovered her missing, and when he'd found Khan, no dread he'd ever felt had been worse. He'd notified the police immediately and then set out to scour Boston on his own. For hours on end, he'd ridden through the streets, calling her name. There was no way in hell he was going to wait another minute to find out what had happened to her.

He stormed toward the house, his emotions so frenzied that when he entered the mansion, servants scurried out of his path. A knock at the front door stopped him from going up the staircase. Realizing it could be the police with news of Chickadee's abductors, he rushed to answer it.

Cynthia Hamilton stood on the doorstep, her pink lips curling when she saw Saxon's bare chest.

"What do you want, Cynthia?"

She swept past him, her heavy perfume making him wince. "Saxon, do be civil," she chided, and handed him her fur cape. "I've come to congratulate you on your marriage."

He threw her wrap toward the coat stand and missed. "Thank you. Now, if you will excuse me, I was just on my way upstairs." He started for the steps.

"Oh my!" Cynthia exclaimed, her hand on her forehead, her body swaying. "Saxon, I do fear I'm . . . I'm going to faint!" Artistically, she began to crumple.

Saxon was at her side immediately. "Dammit to hell, Cynthia," he said and lifted her into his arms. "What's the matter with you?"

She embraced him. "Take me to the parlor sofa."

He looked at the staircase, every fiber in him longing to race up it and take Chickadee into his arms. But he couldn't very well leave Cynthia lying in the foyer. Aggravated beyond belief, he stalked toward the parlor.

At the top of the stairs, Chickadee looked on in anguish as he carried the blond beauty into the privacy of the drawing room.

Chapter 16

"I'll send Thatcher in with some cool tea," Saxon said and tossed Cynthia to the sofa. "Your fur probably made you overly warm."

Her fingers toyed with the front of her gown. "I am warm, Saxon. So very, very warm." Her large breasts sprang free from within their pink silk prison.

Saxon stared at the white globes. Revulsion rose within him. "Cover yourself, Cynthia. You look disgusting."

Her ivory complexion reddened. "You used to—"

"Perhaps. But no longer. However, if you simply must have a man right now, Thatcher—"

"How dare you!"

"Cynthia, fix your wig. It's askew." With that, he left her to cope with her impotent rage alone. As he stepped into the foyer he met Dr. Larson. "Doctor, how's—"

"If infection doesn't set in, the wolf will be fine. But your wife is rather out of sorts."

Saxon paled visibly. "You mean she's been hurt?"

"No, but she seems sad. Strangest thing, really. She was fine during the operation, and when we finished she was ecstatic. Went flying out of the room to tell you all the news but returned shortly."

Dr. Larson rubbed his chin and shook his head. "She was disturbed when she got back and said she couldn't find you. Maybe that's all it is. You know how women are when they have thrilling news. I'm sure it's nothing to worry about. But she *is* overly tired from her ordeal. My advice to you is to let her rest before you start interrogating her. Now, I really must be leaving.''

''Thank you for coming, Dr. Larson. You've no idea how much your kindness means to us.''

Dr. Larson laughed. ''You'll be getting my bill, but I'm not really sure if I deserve to be paid. I don't know who did more for the wolf, me or your wife. During the entire surgery, she dribbled some sort of concoction into his mouth. Said it would help stop his bleeding, and I'll be damned if it didn't. I'm a good surgeon, but I couldn't have stopped the bleeding that fast. That strange brew she fed the wolf worked. Never did understand what she said it was, but I remember the smell. I'm off to sniff every herb I can find in this city.''

After seeing the doctor out, Saxon raced up the stairs and into the bedroom. Chickadee sat by the fire, Khan's head in her lap. ''Keely?''

When she didn't answer, he went and took her hand, dismayed when her fingers didn't curl around his. ''Keely, what's the matter?'' he asked and knelt beside her. ''Are you still worried about Khan? Dr. Larson said—''

''Khan's gwine be fine.'' She turned away and gazed into the fire, her chin held high, her shoulders thrown back so far it seemed to Saxon they would soon meet in the middle. Why was she sitting like that: so unyielding to him?

Maybe last night's events were finally hitting her, he reasoned. What with her worry for Khan, the surgery, she'd had no time to dwell on last night until now.

Surely she could give him a few brief details. He realized her weariness was great, but his impatience was greater. ''Will you tell me about last night? I'm anxious to know, but I'll understand if you're too tired—''

"Khan got knifed, two men throwed a bag over me, carried me to a wagon, and tuk me to the city. The wagon gate opened, I falled out, them men went on, and then three other men come. They let me outen the bag, give me cab money, and I come home. Here I am, none the worser."

He deliberated. He expected to hear a frightening tale, but the way she told it, the story seemed more of an adventure than anything terrifying. "Did the men say anything at all that might help me find out—"

"Never heared 'em say a word about nothin'. They jist drived to the North End—"

"The North End?" Horror choked him.

"Cain't be shore iffen that's whar they was a-takin' me or not. The North End's whar I falled out, and I'm gwine back as soon as Khan gits a mite better."

Somehow, he was able to keep from protesting. There was something in the way she was looking at him that told him not to object right now. "So the three men who helped you get home were Irishmen?"

"Nicest men I ever knowed. And I owe all three of 'em."

"I'll see to it they're well rewarded."

"Somebody a-givin' 'em money ain't what they need. They'll jist spend it and be broke agin."

Her sharp tone jarred him. "Fine. We won't give them any money. But why are you so irritated with me? Keely, do you know how worried I—"

"You a-carryin' on behind my back, Saxon?"

"What? Carrying . . ." His mind reeled at the accusation. "What the hell would make you think . . ."

Cynthia.

Chickadee must have seen him with the conniving bitch! That explained the odd, rapid mood change Dr. Larson had described. His heart jumped at the thought of having inadvertently hurt her. "Keely, you don't understand. Cynthia—"

"Cynthia! You a-warmin' over old soup?" She rose.

"I am not carry—"

"Call it whatever suits yore fancy, you dang—"

"Keely!" Saxon jerked to his feet. "You—"

"Yore a dang-blasted, God-burn tomcat! As hot as a billy goat in a pepper patch! As—"

"*I am not seeing Cynthia Hamilton!*" He grabbed her shoulders and saw blazing fury in her eyes, and understood then she was showing every green symptom of jealousy.

His first impulse was to soothe her and lay to rest her doubts about his fidelity. But when he realized how desperately he sought just the right words to convince her, anger overcame him. What right did *she* have to be so possessive, and what the hell had gotten into *him* for worrying that he'd hurt her! When and how had this happened?

When had the bargain ceased being a bargain, and what was going on between them now?

His own confusion and the boiling emerald seas in Chickadee's eyes catapulted him from mere anger to rage. "I am not involved with Cynthia, but even if I were it would be none of your concern. Our marriage is a bargain and nothing more! I owe you no fidelity whatsoever. Remember that!"

He spun on his heel and left before Chickadee had a chance to retort. She had no idea what *fidelity* was. All she knew was that their marriage was nothing but a cold agreement to Saxon. One she suspected he would now try to dissolve as soon as possible.

She'd be going home soon.

Falling to her knees beside Khan, she allowed herself to do the one thing she hadn't let herself do in years.

She wept.

As heartbroken as she was, Chickadee agreed to talk to the police and several hired detectives who came to interrogate her and everyone else on the estate. But she had little to tell, and try as they did, neither the authorities nor the detectives could find any leads. Eventually they concluded that she'd been kidnapped for ransom money, and because no evidence could be found the case was soon closed and dropped.

But Saxon's anger was not so easily dismissed. The jealousy Chickadee had displayed continued to irritate him. What was her problem anyway? Their relationship was only a temporary one. She had no right to expect loyalty from him. He cared nothing for Cynthia, but he didn't love Chickadee either. He owned her nothing.

But another part of him, the part deep inside that made his stomach sink when he thought of how she was hurting . . . Ah, to hell with *that* part of him— that soft, sentimental part that he'd never known until meeting her! He hadn't needed it before, and he didn't need it now!

Convinced he was doing the right thing and weary of battling the strange emotions her sad eyes evoked, he packed his bags and left for New York without saying a word.

Just as she had every day since he'd gone, Chickadee was at the window looking for Saxon's barouche to come rumbling up the drive. Desdemona stood beside her, and Chickadee held her hand, knowing her sister-in-law was as lonesome for Saxon as she was.

"I know the two of you miss him, but he'll be back," Bunny said, reaching for a fourth biscuit from Chickadee's breakfast tray. "Besides that, he's only been gone for five days, and you're both acting as if he's been gone for years."

Chickadee noticed Bunny had put an inch of butter on the biscuit. "A-havin' a little biscuit with your butter?" She went to Khan and bade him lap up her herb potion. Desdemona followed and rubbed the wolf's ears.

"Are you sure you're all right?" Bunny queried, eyeing a sausage. "My goodness! You might have disappeared from the face of the earth had you not fallen from that wagon!"

Vanish was exactly what she had yearned to do when she'd seen Saxon and Cynthia together.

But there was Khan to look after.

And there was Saxon.

She wanted desperately to hate him. But her heart was so full of love and the desire to somehow make him love her back, that love moved over and let forgiveness in. Maybe it even created it, for all she knew.

Either way, sometime while he'd been gone, she'd forgiven him for the hurtful things he'd said to her. It wasn't as if theirs was a love match, and according to that stupid deal they'd made, she was supposed to be leaving as soon as Barton was destroyed. So as Saxon said, he really had no obligation to be true to her.

It hurt terribly. But she knew from experience that nothing came easy in this world. You had to struggle for every little thing you received, and it seemed the greater the thing you wanted, the harder you had to work for it.

And Saxon's love was the greatest thing she'd ever wished to have. In mere weeks that one wish had erased years worth of anxiety over Barton Winslow, and she found herself praying Saxon would never find the man whose destruction would mean her own.

"My invitation to the grand ball arrived three days ago," Bunny said, and swallowed the last of the sausage. "I ordered a yellow satin gown yesterday. I'm so excited!"

"What's so dang excitin' about that party?"

Bunny's plump cheeks pinkened. "Well, I don't believe you've met him yet, but Saxon's best friend here is Max Jennings. Max has been traveling for the past few months, but he's back now and he'll be attending the ball. He's the most adorable man ever to walk the earth! Sandy blond hair, big brown eyes, a crooked smile, muscles . . . oh my, he's got so many! I fell in love with him the minute I met him. You *have* to go to the ball, Chickadee. I'm dying for you to see him. You and Saxon did receive an invitation, didn't you?''

Chickadee escorted Desdemona to the dressing table and began to brush the girl's long, ebony hair before she answered. ''We got one. I had Candy read it fer me.''

''You had Candy— Chickadee, you can't read?''

''No, but I'm gwine larn one o' these here days,'' Chickadee replied, not at all embarrassed. She twined a lavender ribbon around the long braid she'd made of Desdemona's hair.

''You must ask Saxon to hire a tutor who— Oh Chickadee!'' Bunny exclaimed. ''Why can't I teach you? You can always hire a real teacher later. We could begin today! When Saxon gets home, he'll be so proud of you.''

''He'll be so proud o' me,'' Chickadee murmured to herself, her thoughts dancing.

She memorized the entire alphabet that day. Bunny returned every morning, continuing with lessons on phonics and handwriting. Each evening Chickadee sat with Desdemona and taught the silent girl everything she herself had learned that day. They sat by the fire in Desdemona's room, Chickadee writing and saying the alphabet and Desdemona working on the quilt Chickadee had started at the sewing circle. Afternoons found them outside near the barn. There, Chickadee worked on the sled they were building, all the while going over the alphabet sounds with Desdemona.

''You're doing splendidly,'' Bunny proclaimed one day when Chickadee began reading simple words. ''It wouldn't surprise me in the slightest if you were reading quite well by Christmas. The way you practice, your overwhelming desire to learn—

why, there's no telling what you can do when you really set your mind to it, is there?"

Chickadee pushed her chair away from Saxon's desk. "Thur's no tellin' what *anybody* can do when they set thur mind ter it, Bunny Hamilton—and that includes you."

At that moment, Candice wheeled in a cart laden with refreshments. Bunny's eyes widened with pleasure. "Take it away, Candy," Chickadee instructed.

Bunny heaved herself out of her chair. "But it's customary to have tea—"

"It ain't gwine be customary no more, Bunny. And afore you commence a-yarnin', thur's a few thangs I want ter know. Has that Max feller been a-carryin' you around?"

"Carrying me around?"

"A-jularkin'. A-courtin' you!"

"No, but I'm sure it's only a matter of us getting to know each other better." Her chin dropped to her chest.

"Bunny, don't you never hang your head!"

"Are you mad at me?" Bunny asked, her eyes watering.

"I couldn't never be mad at a good friend like you. Yore like the sister I didn't never git. You and Desi both. Now, does that Max feller got him a sweetheart?"

Bunny flinched. "He . . . he used to act interested in Cynthia. But she only had eyes for Sax—for . . ."

"It's all right, Bunny. I know about her and Saxon."

"Saxon never loved her though. Oh, he escorted her to various socials, but I could tell he didn't care a thing for her. And Cynthia would come home from those affairs and have fits in her room. I imagine she knew the truth, too. But she continued to throw herself at him, and when we heard that Saxon had married, Cynthia nearly destroyed the house. Dr. Larson had to come and give her a sedative!"

The elation Chickadee felt at that information nearly tore her asunder, but with tremendous will-power, she contained her thrill in the face of Bunny's problem. "Uh, you say Max never tuk you nowhars?"

"No, but as I said, we don't know each other well."

"Yore gingham-purty, Bunny. Smart and nice ter be with. Thur ain't no reason why Max shouldn't orter want ter keep comp'ny with you. No reason 'cept one, and I thank y'know what that is. This speech ain't gwine be sugar-mouthed on account o' I know you'd ain't holt together with flour paste. I want you ter take this with yore daubers up, hear?"

Bunny's bottom lip began to twitch.

"Bunny, yore as heavy as a ton o' lard in a bucket o' molasses. You—"

"I'm leaving. I don't have to stand here and lis-ten—"

"No, you ain't got ter stand," Chickadee pushed Bunny into a chair. "You can set. You can stand or set. Don't differ nary a jag to me, but you ain't gwine light outen here jist on account o' you don't like what all I'm a-sayin'."

"Why are you saying such mean things to me?"

"You want Max fer yore man or don't you?"

"More than anything, but—"

"No buts. Iffen you want him, you can git him, and the first thang we're gwine do is git rid o' them warts you got on yore hand. I see you allus a-tryin' ter hide 'em, but I know a way ter git shed of 'em. Wait here." She left the room but returned shortly, a silk scarf in her hand.

"What's this for?" Bunny asked when Chickadee handed her the scarf.

"Betty Jane tole me about this omen? Well, she swears iffen you rub a piece o' clothes that belongs to somebody else over yore warts, they'll git offen you and go to the other person. That thar scarf's Ar-aminty's, so iffen this works she'll git yore warts!"

Absently, Bunny smoothed the scarf over her hand and then crushed the cloth into a tight wad. "Oh, what's the use? Warts or no warts, Max will never notice me. And why should he? What man would want to be with . . . a girl who looks like me?" She began to sob.

"Bunny, iffen thur warn't nothin' we could do about this, I'd cry right along with you. But the war ain't even commenced yet, and you've done give up. You got ter fight. Got ter shed that fat and—"

"I can't! I've tried before."

"Yeah? Well, yore gwine try agin. And this time yore gwine do it on account o' Chickadee McBride don't never give up and she don't let her friends give up neither!"

Settling back in his plush seat aboard the New Haven, Saxon muttered a strong oath. Normally, he would have thoroughly enjoyed the train trip, but he was too deep in thought to notice any of the luxuries in his Pullman car. He drained his glass of Madeira, signaled for more, and cursed again.

He'd taken the trip to forget her, arriving in New York with a definite plan. It should have been so easy to do.

He'd begun Barton Winslow's ruination two weeks ago, and the man had fallen for his scheme more quickly than Saxon believed possible.

He'd struck up a swift friendship with Barton, using all the charm he possessed to gain Barton's trust. It wasn't all that hard; Barton didn't have too many friends and was eager to be acquainted with Saxon Blackwell, a man well-known on Wall Street.

And then he had lit the fuse to the bomb that would eventually blow Barton's fortune right out of his hands. He recalled the scene clearly.

"Barton, I don't normally share my inside information with anyone. But it's rare to find a real friend on Wall Street, you know. Keep this to yourself."

Barton had agreed, flattered he'd called him a

friend and eager to learn the privileged information. Saxon had gone on to say a certain company was in bad trouble. Barton, who owned a hundred thousand shares of the company's stock, nearly had heart failure upon hearing the news.

"Not to worry, Barton," Saxon had continued smoothly. "There's still time to save yourself. Remember, not many people know about it yet."

And now it was only a matter of time, Saxon thought to himself as he sipped his wine. Barton was going to sell the stock. And in his rush to be rid of it, he would also short it—selling stock he didn't own, but had control of, and would have to buy back in the future. And he'd have no trouble at all selling it, although it wouldn't be until the very end that he would discover who was buying from him.

His unnamed buyer would be Saxon.

Because Saxon knew when stock was bought heavily, the price usually went up. And with each point it rose, Barton would lose money. Lots of it. Soon Barton would try and buy it back. And Saxon would accommodate him.

But of course he'd sell it for much more than Barton paid for it in the first place. Barton would never even be able to break even. He'd eventually run out of money with which to buy, with which to save himself. With which to live.

Chickadee would have her revenge.

And then she'd go home.

At least that had been the plan when he first arrived in New York. His only goal was to fulfill his part of their bargain as quickly as possible. He'd planned on convincing her that her father was ruined, giving her a small fortune, and then sending her on her way, forgetting ever having known her. Because, dammit, she had no right to believe he belonged to her! No right to be so damn possessive!

No right to lay claim to emotions, to touch the vulnerable core he was only just beginning to realize he possessed.

He'd had no desire whatsoever to continue with his mockery of a marriage. But now, as the screeching and hissing train began to slow near the Boston depot, the only thing Saxon could think of was seeing her again. Kissing her, holding her, apologizing to her, telling her . . .

Telling her what? How much she meant to him? What *did* she mean to him?

And dear God, what did *he* mean to *her*?

It was late afternoon when Saxon arrived home from the depot. As he entered the house he called for Chickadee.

"She's out, sir," Thatcher informed him. "She's been in the North End all day."

"And you let her go?" Saxon thundered.

"Sir, am I to understand you are instructing me to keep her here against her will?"

Saxon threw Thatcher a murderous look and headed back outside, fully intending to go to the North End and find his wayward wife. But no sooner had he reached his barouche when another Blackwell coach sped up the drive. The door burst open and out jumped Chickadee. He drank in the sight of her, like a man dying of thirst.

"Saxon!" she shouted, flinging herself into his arms. "Lord o' mercy, I missed you, outlander! I didn't thank you'd ever git home!"

He buried his face in her hair and then snapped his head back up when he sniffed the strong scent emanating from her. Forcing her away from him, he took her hand and marched her inside the mansion, past Thatcher, up the stairs, down the hall, and into the bedroom. There he let go of her hand and slammed the door behind him.

Chickadee flexed her numbed fingers. " 'Pears yore as ready fer me as I am fer you," she said mischievously.

"You were drinking with those damned Irishmen?"

"Damned Irishmen? Don't you dare slur—"

"Answer my question!"

She turned up her nose and went to Khan. "I can do whatever I dang well please. You ain't got no right ter—"

"You will never go to the North End again! I appreciate what those Irishmen did for you, but never, and I mean *never* will you go there again! Is that understood?"

"I will so go! I got ter finish what I started thar, and thur ain't nothin' you can do ter stop me!"

He mentally counted to ten and succeeded in restraining himself from wringing her neck. "Keely," he said softly, "fighting is not what I had in mind for this afternoon. Now, shall we solve this problem calmly?"

"I got me three new friends. They live in the North End, I go ter visit 'em. Thur ain't no problem as fur as I can see." She gave him a flippant grin.

His eyes narrowed. "*That* is the problem! You see no farther than you *choose* to see!"

How very blue his eyes became when he was angry, she thought. And that funny little cleft in his chin kind of closed up when his facial muscles tensed. She could even see his heart pounding by watching his neck vein pulse. And she wondered if he knew his ears moved when he shouted.

Saxon knew clearly he'd been defeated. An air of saucy defiance floated around her. And how her stubborn eyes gleamed, like fresh, wet grass. Even her hair, copper fire, seemed to shine more intensely, framing her face with an avalanche of red-orange-gold that gave her cheeks a furious glow. He wondered if she knew how the skin covering her collarbones stretched with each breath she took, highlighting the delicate arches of those bones to perfection, making her seem like some exquisite sculpture wrought by the hand of a true master.

He swallowed, feeling humbled before such rare beauty and rather guilty over his show of temper.

The thought of her in the North End still angered him, but surely they could come to some sort of agreement about it.

What a fool he'd been, making his silly plans. Send her home? Forget her?

No man could forget a woman as beautiful as she. No man would ever want to let her go. He swallowed again. "I—I missed you."

She cocked her head sideways.

She reminded him of a pretty puppy when she did that. "Of course, I probably missed you only because I'm so used to being with you," he added lamely.

Chickadee realized it was her turn to speak, but she stood there silently, some ten feet separating them. She knew instinctively Saxon was leading up to something, and she decided to let him do it on his own. Besides, it tickled her to see him so ruffled.

He was bewildered. He expected her to tell him she had missed him too. Yes, she'd already told him she had, but for some reason he wanted to hear her say it again. "I'm sorry I stayed away for so—"

What the hell was he apologizing for? he asked himself. He'd left on account of her possessiveness in the first place, and now here he was playing the contrite husband as if he really were guilty of something! Damn her to hell and back for bending him as she always did!

"You've no right to be angry with me, Keely! If I choose to go somewhere for a few weeks, there's not a damn thing you can do about it!"

It looked to Saxon as if she bit back a smile.

"I don't plan to make a habit of it, but if I have to travel—" Again, Saxon broke off. He felt he was digging deeper and deeper but couldn't quite figure out what it was he was digging himself into. Just why had he begun this conversation, and where did he intend to take it?

"And as far as Cynthia Hamilton goes," he continued, words flowing from his lips as if by magic, "she's only a girl I used to know. Whatever it was you thought you saw that day was nothing. You must realize however," he said, attempting a look of sternness and failing, "that if I *was* involved with her, it should make no difference to you. I may take a hundred mistresses if I wish. Just as you may take lovers."

Her eyebrow raised at that.

Saxon stiffened at the impish ascent of her brow. "You . . . that is to say, you haven't taken any, have you? I mean, not that it matters to me . . . There's probably no one here you'd like anyway . . . but if you ever found anyone . . . as long as you're discreet . . . Of course, I'd find out eventually . . . not that it'd matter . . . wouldn't matter."

He shuffled on the carpet and noticed the startling contrast his black boots made with the gold rug. A change of subject was definitely in order before he reached the bottom of whatever it was he was digging himself into.

"So," he said, thrusting his hands deep into his pockets, "what did you do during my absence?"

She smiled; her head was still cocked to the side, her cheek almost touching her shoulder. "Spend time with Desdemona?" Saxon prompted, her smile unnerving him. Dammit, she was looking at him as if he were a total fool!

He was mortified then. What possessed him to confess he'd missed her? Sure, he was taken with her, but it was only her beauty and lovemaking he'd missed!

"I can see you've taken good care of Khan," he rambled on. "Keely, if it's not asking you too much, would you mind opening your mouth to talk to me?"

Her head went up, and she, too, dipped her hands into her pockets. But she remained quiet.

Saxon sighed heavily. "On my way back home, I wondered about something. It's nothing of earth-shattering importance, but—"

How do you feel about me, mountain girl? he asked in silence, completely unable to get the question to his lips.

His trepidation reminded him once again how indecisive he'd become because of her. Who the hell cared what she felt for him anyway?

"Forget it," he muttered. "It doesn't really matter."

She began to rock back and forth from toes to heels, as if she were moving to the beat of some secret inner music. And when she finally spoke, her voice was like a song.

"I love you, Saxon Blackwell."

Chapter 17

Saxon watched the chandelier in Max Jennings's gaming room shimmering above him, its prisms shooting rainbow spears all over. Chickadee's words pounded in his mind.

You cain't keep on a-runnin' from what's never gwine let up a-follerin' you. Cain't git away from it any more'n you can escape yer shadder. Love's like shadders, the way I see it. And I love you, Saxon.

But Saxon *had* escaped. He'd left the estate immediately, her speech about love and shadows following him all the way to Max's house.

He glanced at his hand of cards. She had to be lying. No, she did many things, but lying was rarely one of them. Dammit! He'd wanted the answer to how she felt about him, and now that he had it he didn't know what to do with it!

Love. How did one recognize it? Did it have a certain face? Sound? If it existed, what the hell was it?

Maybe she just *thought* she loved him, he argued, throwing his losing hand of cards at Max. After all, he was the only man she'd ever known well. And he'd given her clothes, jewels—everything he could think of to give her. And he'd seen to Khan too. She'd been very grateful for that.

Max laid his arms on the table and dragged all the money toward himself, making a high pile of it in front of his chest. "These impromptu games always seem to end in my favor. That shouldn't trouble you, though. Hear you've married. Doesn't that mean you've won 'the fortune'?''

Saxon nodded, the deep-seated thrill he usually got from discussing "the fortune" curiously weak tonight. "But not until Grandmother is dead," he stated flatly.

Max grinned. "She says she has a bad heart."

Saxon smiled, too. *Creakin' doors hang the longest.* That's what Chickadee'd once said when he'd mentioned Araminta's heart. "Doors that creak—" Rubbing his hand over the stubble on his face, he closed his eyes and saw Chickadee. Saw her standing there when she'd told him she'd loved him. His stomach leaped as it always did when he thought of her.

"What's that about doors, Sax?" Max asked, wondering why Saxon was talking like a drunk man. "Doors?"

Max soon realized Saxon was daydreaming. "What's Chickadee like? Odd name. When I first heard it, I laughed."

Saxon picked up stray coin and flicked it across the room. "She's named for a bird."

"Does she look like one too?" Max chuckled before he lifted his bourbon to his lips.

"Would I marry a woman who looked like a bird?" Saxon tried to look sarcastic, but unable to help himself, he grinned. "Actually, she *does* resemble a swan." He remembered her graceful collarbones and dragged his fingers through his hair.

Max laughed. "I was sure you'd think of something to thwart Araminta's plans for you. Good God! You're *married*, Sax! Till death do you part . . . married!"

Saxon's vision glazed over. *Till death do us part, Keely?* he asked her ever-present image. The question seemed to smother him.

When he arrived home, he saw the bed was still made. Three o'clock in the morning, and the bed was still made! Saxon's eyes flew to the corner where she kept her rifle. It was gone.

She'd left him! His fingers dug into the palm of his hand . . . and unfurled when he heard the thump of Khan's tail. She wouldn't leave Khan. Dammit, she was out walking! And after he'd forbidden her to do it again!

He raced downstairs. What was in that mind of hers, going out at night after what had happened to her? Did nothing frighten that little twit?

"By all that's holy, I'm going to strangle you when I find you, Keely," he muttered as he strode across the courtyard. Without realizing it, he quickened his pace and called her name aloud.

He never saw the dip in the ground ahead until he was face down in the dirt, the wind jolted from his lungs. As he struggled for breath, his fury mounted.

"Nice night fer a stroll," she taunted him from above. "Reckon it's a nice night fer a-layin' on the ground, too."

Without looking up from the dirt clod that touched his nose, he demanded, "Just where the hell have you been?"

" 'Pears to me I been outside. From the looks o' what I see around me, reckon I'm still out here."

Air filled his lungs again. He leaped to his feet. "Get back to the house."

"No."

"Now!"

"No."

One, two, three . . . he counted mentally. "Ah, to hell with that!" He slung her over his shoulder, her rifle bouncing on his behind as he trekked back to the mansion. Then he stopped. "Well, aren't you going to fight me? Toss me to the ground? This docile obedience is completely out of character for you."

"Tell you what, outlander. I'll let you tote me around iffen you'll head fer the barn. Thur's lots o' hay in it."

"You're in serious trouble," he said, sliding his hands down her thighs. "I'm madder than—"

"A wet settin' hen?"

"I was going to say *fire*."

"A wet settin' hen's a sight worser. You ever seed a wet settin' hen?"

He placed her back on the ground. "I told you not to walk at night anymore. What if those men come back for you? What if they're here lurking in the shadows? What if—"

"What if you jist hesh up and kiss the breath plumb outen me? What if—"

His mouth swallowed the rest of her words. His arms crushed her to him, his fingers dug into the small of her back. Her scent of cool night woods permeated his nostrils and seeped into his brain, making him shudder with sensation. She seemed so tiny in his embrace, as if, with one strong squeeze, he could break her into bits.

But she proved she was made of stronger stuff, in the way she was accepting his savage kiss. More than accepting it, actually. Liking it, loving it, yearning for more.

"The barn," she managed to tell him.

And then they were there. Thirty horses peered out of the stalls in the thick darkness.

But Saxon knew that barn and went directly to the tall wooden ladder that led to the hayloft. Again he threw Chickadee over his shoulder, climbed up, and tossed her to the soft, soft hay.

From a window in the loft, pale silver streams of moonlight lazily drifted in, dust from the hay filtering through the light. In the far corner they heard a small noise—probably a mouse. And though it was cold, they provided their own special heat.

"Disobey me, will you, mountain girl?" Saxon charged. "Venture out where danger awaits?"

He watched her fingers slither over the buttons of her shirt, the fabric falling away as if by magic. She had beautiful breasts. Full, ripe, and his for the touching, the tasting.

"The breeches too," he ordered when her hands fell to the hay. "Everything."

Her palms met the waistband, rolling the garment slowly, so very slowly, down over her hips.

Saxon stared at the silken nest of hair that was soon revealed to him. Beneath it, he knew, blazed a fire: a deep, smoldering fire he would soon fan to flaming heights and then quench.

Her firmly muscled legs, smooth as polished marble, squirmed out of the breeches. A goddess. She was a goddess from the hills. His own clothing seemed to drop from his body of its own volition. He never remembered removing it. But there it lay at his feet, with hers.

Kneeling, he began at her ankles and kissed the satiny expanse of her skin all the way up to her mouth. His tongue wet her lips, and he saw how they glistened in the moonlight. He saw her skin, as pure as fresh cream, and then watched how even her freckles began to gleam beneath the moisture that suddenly bedewed her face. Her eyes glittered as if with fever.

Wanting to see as much of her as possible while he made love to her, he sat, pulled her into his lap, and watched her eyes widen when he slid into her. Saw how her head fell back as he plunged and filled her.

This place, this deep, soft place inside her was the only part of her that was ever empty. The rest of her was filled to capacity with that special something which made her so wonderful.

"Who are you, Keely?" he moaned as he guided her hips. "What is it you have that no other girl I've ever known has had?" His eyes traveled from her face to her breasts, and down to her belly. Her legs were around him. How good they felt, he thought.

And the feelings he was experiencing this time were more than physical. Yes, he felt the familiar pleasure, but he felt as if he was using a part of himself he'd never used before.

How it drove him to please her. He held her close, all the while moving her, circling his hips next to hers so she could feel more of him. He gave her more than his body, but he had no idea what it was he gave. His arms closed around her, felt her tense, and supported her as she shuddered with her release.

She slid from his lap and reached for him, smiling at the confusion in his azure eyes. Lying back, she pulled him down, wanting to feel both his familiar weight upon her and the bite of the hay on her back. And though he'd only just slipped from inside her, she gasped when he entered her again.

Tightly, as if he might move off her, she squeezed the skin of his back. She thought she heard a moan, but dismissed the sound promptly, her mind turning to the tender feelings she'd perceived in him only moments ago.

She wondered if he knew she'd sensed them.

His own release came violently. His groans and soft yells were so like music, she mused while holding his still-quaking form.

How she loved this man.

"Keely," he began, slipping from her, "I've told you before you're special to me. I haven't changed my mind about that. But Keely," he said, his voice wavering slightly, "you are to take my feelings for you for exactly what they are. Do you understand?"

A tiny needle of anxiety pricked her. "What are they?" She nestled against his chest.

Knowing she could hear how wildly his heart was thrashing, he willed the organ to slow. "Even before we left the Appalachia, I told you I enjoy being with you. I'm *used* to you, Keely."

She smiled. Saxon was going to resist until the very end. "You beat all. You wanted ter know how I feel about you, and then you got all franzied over my answer. I love you, Saxon. I mighta started lovin' you the minute I first seed you. Don't matter no how. I love you now, and—"

"Keely, you're only *grateful* to me."

"Grateful? What fer am I grateful ter you?"

"I've given you many things. I'm taking care of your neighbors back in North Carolina, I saw to Khan—"

"Saxon, I'm jist one fraction from a-workin' mysef into a snit. Afore that happens, git it inter yore fool head I'd love you iffen you was as poverty-poor as all git out. Yore money don't mean nothin' ter me. I like all them clothes and jewries, and I *am* obliged ter you fer a-gittin' that doctor man fer Khan. But them thangs ain't why I love you. I love you on account o' what's inside you. Shore, yore the fancy Saxon Blackwell on the outside, but *inside?* Well, I love that little young-un in thar. I love—"

"Stop saying that!" Saxon jumped to his feet. "I don't want to hear you say that ever again!"

"Then why'd you want ter know about my feelin's?"

"How do you know that I did?"

"Jist knowed. So why'd you want ter know?"

"Because . . . because . . . How the hell should I know? It was just one of those stupid things people do sometimes. But the fact of the matter remains that you don't love me, and that's that!"

Chickadee pulled a piece of hay from her hair and casually tickled her nose with it. "I do love you, and that's that."

"No you don't!"

"Yes I do."

"I don't want to hear it anymore!"

"Too bad. I love, love, love, love—"

"Dammit, Keely!"

"Dang it, Saxon."

"You're mistaken! You only *think* you love . . . There's no such thing as . . . I don't believe in . . . You're breaking the agreement!"

"It warn't writ in blood, was it?"

''The bargain . . . You—I . . . You're supposed to leave here when I destroy your father!'' He walked across the floor of the loft and stared out the window.

Chickadee joined him. ''New York. You . . . you found him, didn't you, Saxon?''

His gaze swept over her face, searching in vain for whatever it was that made his heart shrivel at the thought of her leaving him.

No, he couldn't let her go. Not until he was tired of her. That would soon happen. It always did. Dammit, it *would* happen!

''Keely, I'm sorry. I haven't found him.''

Chickadee kept telling Saxon how much she loved him. Every day she found new ways to say it and to show him how. Her supply of the tender emotion seemed bottomless to him, and, despite his efforts to the contrary, she soon occupied every waking and sleeping moment of his life.

His mind strayed from his work to her. His dreams were never of anything but her. There was nothing beautiful in the world that didn't, in some way, remind him of her.

And he began to wonder if he really did have a heart after all. For didn't you have to possess a heart to be so dangerously close to losing it?

His feelings were so foreign to him, and his inability to understand them tortured him. He spoke to no one, not even Max, about them, for to discuss them would be to admit them. And he was too careful a man to trust something—most especially emotions—he didn't comprehend fully.

To gain the distance and time he needed to sort through his confusion, he threw himself back into the life he'd led before ever meeting the girl who'd caused the total uproar of his senses.

He accepted every invitation that came his way and saw his old friends so frequently that Chickadee found she had no time to show him the devotion from which she knew he was running.

Frustration plagued her as she looked for a sure-fire way to make him understand how deep her love for him was. When she could find no solution to her dilemma, her frustration became fear. For the first time in her life, she was at a complete loss about what to do.

Araminta, however, was delightfully aware that something wasn't right between them. She had high hopes the mountain girl would soon leave, but when Saxon began to insist she escort Chickadee to various assemblies, her hopes plunged. She adamantly refused his demands until his demands suddenly gave birth to a new scheme.

She resolved to put her strategy into action immediately. "You haven't been anywhere at all since the sewing circle," she told Chickadee one afternoon when they met on the staircase. "I was just coming up to invite you to a tea that will be held at the Quinten estate in one hour. Ashley Quinten is about your age, and I thought you might like to meet her."

Chickadee immediately became wary. This was the first time Spider Woman had deigned to speak to her since the sewing meeting. And now Araminta was actually *inviting* her to a tea! "Yore a-bein' mighty nice terday, Araminty. Yore usually about as refined as a cabbage." Her brow arched.

"You needn't look at me that way," Araminta snapped. "I am not inviting you because I enjoy your company, of *that* you may be sure. I am only offering to take you because Saxon insists I assist you back into society. He has become increasingly irritating about it lately, and I am inviting you to go with me to stop his badgering."

She looked away lest Chickadee see through her lies. She had every reason to believe her scheme would work wonderfully. The mountain girl would undoubtedly cause an uproar at each assembly she attended, the gossip would be horrendous, and Saxon would eventually be humiliated over his wife's neverending, ill-mannered antics. He'd ignored gossip before, but if it were to go on and on, becoming worse and worse . . . well, not even Saxon could bear that. He would send the girl back to where he'd found her. It made perfect sense. After all, Chickadee hadn't really had the opportunity to cause the kind of chaos that would mortify him. It was up to Araminta to see that she had as many of those opportunities as possible.

Yes, her own good name would also be sullied, she realized, but only for a short while. And after the yokel was gone, things would return to normal quickly. Araminta was sure of it.

"Well?" she prompted Chickadee. "Do you wish to come, or not? It seems to me you would be anxious to do the things Saxon wants you to do. You did say you loved him. Doesn't that make you want to please him?"

Chickadee's narrowed eyes suddenly widened. Araminta, witch though she was, had a valid point, she realized. If she were to throw herself into the social whirl, heart and soul, wouldn't that prove to Saxon how much she loved him? He was well aware of her loathing for society. Surely if he saw how hard she was trying to adapt to his way of life, he would understand how much he meant to her! After all, he was the only one in the world for whom she would do something so disagreeable.

And the Quinten tea was indeed disagreeable. It started out well, but when Chickadee saw two beautiful, exotic birds imprisoned in a gilded cage, the trouble began. She'd had no idea Ashley Quinten's father had paid a small fortune to have them shipped from South America as a birthday gift for Ashley. Her only thought as she released them was that birds as pretty as those should be free.

And at Jacqueline Richard's luncheon—well, how was she to know Jacqueline was an accomplished

wax sculptress? The bowl of fruit looked real enough
to her. The apple she took a huge bite out of was
the prettiest apple she'd ever seen, and it was only
when it stuck to her teeth and Jacqueline began the
most God-awful shrieking known to man that she
realized she'd done something wrong. Well, whoever heard of wax fruit anyway? And if Jacqueline
didn't want her art eaten, she never should have
placed it in the middle of the dining room table.

And that huge guard dog she met at Dee Gentry's
didn't make any sense either. All of Boston was fascinated by the vicious beast. Chickadee heard Mr.
Gentry say the dog was surely the meanest in the
land. But why would anyone be so proud of such a
terrible animal? True, Khan was dangerous too, but
only when he was forced to defend his loved ones.
But that Gentry monster wouldn't even let the *Gentrys* near him! They kept him in a pen and had to
throw his food to him from a distance! And all they
fed him were raw cow livers. Anyone would have a
vile temper with a diet like that, she thought. And
what if the thing got loose and killed the Gentrys?
Having such a bloodthirsty animal around was definitely not a good idea, and she set about correcting
the matter when the Gentrys and the guests had
tired of taunting the beast and returned to the mansion. It didn't take long to do. She discovered all the
dog needed to calm down were some softly spoken
words and a hambone she filched from the kitchen.
Now he was as gentle as a kitten. It was beyond her
comprehension why the Gentrys had gotten riled
instead of thanking her for taming him.

Her confusion with these Bostonians mounted
when Araminta took her to an English fox hunt.
She'd never seen anything so cruel in her whole life.
All those howling hounds, that loud bugle, that
cracking whip, those galloping horses . . . all that
fancified fuss for the slaughter of one poor, defenseless fox. There was no way on earth she could have
sat there and remained a spectator to it all. Relying

on her hunter's instincts, she'd trailed the fox and found him trapped in a dense thicket. Cooing to him, she'd caught him, tucked him inside her coat, and then beat off the hounds when they arrived. No one could induce her to free the shivering animal, and the hunt ended on a very sour note.

Now she was the talk of Boston, the subject of every gossip session. Her name and the descriptions of her antics were bandied about from one end of the city to the other.

The outlandish tales finally reached Saxon through Max. "She fed him a hambone?" he demanded, tears of laughter streaming down his face.

"You're not worried?" Max asked and smiled.

"What about? Keely seems to be enjoying her time with society. She doesn't complain about it anymore as she once did. And Grandmother is taking her everywhere. You know how Grandmother is, Max. She's fanatical about her reputation and would never risk her own name if it were really all true. Besides that, even if the gossip *is* based on truth, it'll die away. It always does."

Max agreed. "Yes, we've both been the victims of outrageous chatter. You're right, Sax. It'll die away."

They laughed together awhile longer, and later that night, while Chickadee lay sleeping in his arms, Saxon chuckled again when he remembered Max's words. "Outrageous chatter," he whispered too softly for her to hear. He pulled the sheet over her bare shoulder and smiled in the darkness when he thought of Jacqueline Richard's wax apple.

"Seems to me she should have taken your mistake as a compliment. I'd have been flattered you thought the fruit was real. And as for the birds . . . Mr. Quinten caught them, so what harm was done? The Gentry dog has turned out to be a nice playmate for the neighborhood children, and the fox . . ." He paused a moment to laugh quietly. "Keely, I'd have

given anything to see you beat off those hounds."
Smiling, he pulled her closer and held her for a long
while as he thought about how much he'd missed
being with her lately. He'd enjoyed none of the out-
ings he'd attended.

"My life is boring without you in it, little one.
Perhaps it's time we go to something together. As
soon as this latest gossip is forgotten, you can make
a new start. I'll be with you, and then I can see for
myself what chaos you cause." He snickered again
at all the wild tales he'd heard and was still grinning
when he fell asleep and allowed her to invade his
dreams.

Dreams were on Araminta's mind too. Dreams of
yet another scheme to be rid of that creature Saxon
called a wife. She sat at her desk downstairs, scrib-
bling furiously, and dwelling on her disappointment
at Saxon's total disregard for all the gossip.

"But then I should have realized mere hearsay
wouldn't affect you," she said aloud. "You must
witness that girl's humiliating behavior with your
own eyes. You must experience firsthand the bitter
shame she is capable of causing you. You've no idea
what it's like since you've never had to endure
them!"

She caressed her brooch and sneered. "But Saxon,
my boy, if you experience first-hand the mortifica-
tion that mountain creature can and will bring you,
you'll have no choice but to divorce her. Surely you
won't relish spending the rest of your life wallowing
in shame! Once she's gone, you'll have to remarry
for your inheritance, and this time around, I'll make
certain you court only the most refined ladies in Boston!"

She looked down at the paper on her desk and
scanned what she'd written. It was time to hold the
annual Blackwell sled race, and she knew society's
opinion of Chickadee Blackwell would make no difference in the size of the crowd. Hadn't she herself

joined undesirable gatherings for the express purpose of harvesting gossip?

The time was ripe: it was a case of adding fat to the fire. This had to be done before Chickadee's recent behavior was forgotten, while society was still in an uproar over it all. People would come in droves to witness further scandal. After all, if the disaster didn't occur in their own homes, they'd have nothing to fear and everything to gain. Araminta had no idea what the girl would do to embarrass Saxon, but she knew the creature wouldn't let her down.

"Heathen," she hissed. "You escaped the death I planned for you by falling from the wagon that night. You escaped Saxon's wrath over the gossip. I did not rid myself of you with those two plans, but I will surely succeed with this one."

That thought dancing in her mind, she addressed the last invitation to the sled race and placed it on the stack.

Chickadee was more and more thrilled with each passing day. Saxon was no longer socializing and was at her side almost constantly. He even missed work several times to spend the day with her and Desdemona; Saxon concentrating on work he'd brought home from the office, and she and Desdemona quietly sewing on the quilt.

"I like these lazy Saturdays with you, outlander," Chickadee purred after an hours-long session of lovemaking. "But it ain't jist Saturdays. It's all these days lately. It's nice a-havin' you here." She drew tiny circles over his nipples before she leaned over and kissed them. "I love you, Saxon."

He sighed. But whether it was with pleasure or disquiet, he didn't know. All he knew was that he'd fought a losing battle in his attempt to understand what it was he felt for her. He'd decided to let his emotions flow freely and see what happened. He was confident his confusion wouldn't last forever.

Sooner or later he'd find a name for the feelings he had for the beautiful girl he'd married.

Chickadee smiled at the bewilderment she saw in his sky-blue eyes and started to kiss him again. But a noise coming from outside stopped her in mid-action. She slipped out of bed and went to the window. "Lord o' mercy, Saxon. Git over here and take a look at all them people down thar!"

He joined her and saw the large congregation in the courtyard. "What the hell?" He yanked his robe on and threw Chickadee's to her before he rang for Thatcher.

The butler came without delay. "I will see to your bath immediately, Mr. Blackwell. No doubt you are anxious to join your guests."

"*My* guests?"

"They are here for the sled race, sir."

"Sled race? What sled race?"

Thatcher sniffed. "The annual Blackwell sled race. Mrs. Blackwell is holding it in honor of you and your wife this year, sir. I understand she is planning on formally introducing your new bride to society. She—"

"That will be all, Thatcher," Araminta said as she arrived at the door. She waited for the butler to leave and then swept into the room.

"Law, Saxon, Wesley Melville's down thar!" Chickadee shouted from her vantage point at the window. "Dang that buzzard. He's right nervy a-showin' his face around here after the way he acted when we met up with him at that eatin' place. But don't you worry none, outlander. This time I'll have my shootin'-arn with me. Cain't take Khan down thar on account o' he's still on the mend, but—"

"You are not taking your rifle anywhere!" Saxon asserted. "Keely, you—"

"Why aren't the two of you dressed?" Araminta asked and tapped her brooch. "You were expected downstairs over an hour ago."

"Why wasn't I informed of this little get-together?" Saxon demanded.

"It is by no means *little*. And I thought I'd mentioned it. So sorry. It must have slipped my mind."

The shriveled hag was up to something, he realized. He knew it by watching that Cyclops's eye at her throat glitter. Then he noted the undisguised pleasure in her eyes as Chickadee marched to the corner and picked up her rifle.

His eyebrow rose high. Why would the rifle and Chickadee's obvious determination to use it please Araminta? he wondered. Surely she was aware of the chaos Chickadee could cause with a gun. Didn't it upset her that Chickadee might actually be goaded into *shooting* someone? Why, that telltale, spiteful gleam in her eyes made it plain she was actually *counting* on trouble!

But why? "Grandmother, why have you waited until now to introduce Keely to society? We've been in Boston for months already, and—"

"Because I thought she would have met most everyone by now. But she has attended very few affairs, and many people have not had the . . . *pleasure* of meeting her. And it *is* customary to formally introduce a bride, is it not? I realize I should have done it months ago, but it never occured to me to do it until now."

And why did it occur to you now? Saxon asked her silently, keeping a close eye on her brooch. Why now, when all of Boston was gossiping about Chickadee? When she stood the least chance of being welcomed? When—

The vein in his neck pumped rhythmically as he began to understand. It was *because* of all the gossip that she was doing this! *Because* society was sure to spurn her now! Damn the shrewd crone to hell and back!

He would not allow her to even begin her scheme. He'd fully planned on escorting Chickadee into society himself but, dammit, not until people had had time to forget her recent mistakes! "It's a real misfortune you neglected to advise me of your plans, Grandmother. I'm leaving for my office, and I'm taking Keely with me."

"But Saxon!" Chickadee cried, excited by the idea of a sled race. "Today's Saturday!"

"Work can wait until Monday," Araminta said. "Our guests are waiting *now*, and you've *never* missed our sled races. In fact you've won them year after year. And what about the new sled you had custom-made last year? If I remember correctly, you paid a small fortune for it. I would think you'd be anxious to use it again."

Chickadee flung her rifle to the bed and rushed to him. "Oh, Saxon, please! We'll have a larripin' good time, and maybe Desi'll come too!"

He looked down, saw the happiness in her eyes, and realized she was absolutely thrilled with the chance to go to the race. His mind spun with possible reasons that they couldn't attend, but none were feasible. And if he told her the real reason— that society already looked down on her and this day might possibly cause her to be banished forever—it would devastate her. She'd been trying so hard to fit in. But dammit, the time just wasn't right! "Keely—"

"Please, Saxon," she begged and squeezed his hands. "I want ter go so bad. Please let's go."

There was very little he'd ever been able to deny her when she looked at him that way, and he felt his determination waver now, too. Perhaps he was worrying for no reason. After all, he'd be with her all afternoon. Surely he could see to it she behaved herself. "All right," he said softly. "Grandmother, inform the guests we'll be down shortly."

He was soon bathed and dressed, and Chickadee was still rummaging through her closet for something to wear. He realized there was only so much he could do about what she might say or do, but he could damn well make sure she looked beautiful when she was introduced. He joined her in searching through her many clothes, soon selecting a gorgeous gown of dark green velvet and soft kid boots.

"I'll meet you in the courtyard, little one," he said as she dressed. "I'm trusting you to leave your rifle here. Do something nice with your hair, and wear your best fur."

He'd help her as much as he could, he thought when he reached the staircase. He'd do everything within his power to keep a close eye and a firm grip on her. He could interrupt her if it appeared she might say something unacceptable. It wouldn't be easy, but what else could he do? And as far as what *she* might do, without her rifle or her wolf, the worst would be throwing someone over her shoulder. Even that he could probably prevent.

But still, he was uneasy. He muttered *damn* with each step downward, reaching a grand total of forty-eight *damns* by the time he stepped off the last one. Well, at least he wouldn't have to worry about her appearance, he reminded himself. He'd selected her outfit himself and she'd look lovely. With that thought in mind, he headed for the courtyard.

Chickadee, still in her bedroom but now dressed, quickly ran a brush through her tangled hair and left it to fall free about her shoulders. Saxon would like that, she thought as she went back to her closet.

"Let's see. He said ter wear my best fur."

Eyes twinkling, she found the one she wanted. Carrying it out of the closet, her hands fondled it as she held it tightly to her breast.

"Bahr fur," she whispered. "Best dang fur thur is!"

Chapter 18

"So where is she, Sax?" Max asked, his breath frosting in the cold air. "You talk of no one but her, yet I haven't laid eyes on her. It's about damn time I got to meet her."

"Yeah, Sax," Nate said. "We're all anxious to meet the girl about whom we've heard so many . . . anecdotes."

"Heard she's rather, uh . . . unusual," Oliver added.

"Unique might be a better word," Kyle ventured.

Charles smirked. "It would appear Saxon has little to say, fellows. After all, what can he add to tales that are already so outrageous?"

Vaguely, Saxon heard them talk, but his mind was on Chickadee. What was she going to do today? he wondered. What sort of havoc would she manage to wreak despite his every precaution?

Trying to rationalize the situation, he reminded himself it was only a simple sled race, but he groaned at that thought. Nothing was ever simple when Chickadee was involved. She'd find a way to ruin a padded cell, which was exactly where he belonged for ever agreeing to attend this race. It just wasn't the right time for her to mingle with society again, he repeated to himself. He knew well from experience that it was always best to wait for gossip to die down before venturing out into the fashionable world again.

"Hey, Sax," Oliver said. "Didn't I hear your wife has flaming red hair?"

"Not flaming, really," Saxon replied. "It's sort of—"

"Red is red, Sax," Max said, "and the pretty girl skipping this way definitely has red hair."

"What's that thing she's wearing?" Charles asked. "Did you buy that for her, Sax?"

"Most unusual wrap I've ever seen," Kyle observed, squinting to see Chickadee better.

But Saxon's eyes widened. Good God! She was wearing a bearskin rug! When the hell had she made a *coat* out of it? *Dammit, Keely,* he moaned to himself. *I spend a fortune on the finest, most expensive furs for you, and you wear a damn rug!*

"Saxon!" she greeted him gaily. "I hurried as fast as I could. Near about ripped up them fancy underwear thangs a-tryin' ter git 'em on. Finally left 'em off on account o' thur so dang scratchy anyhow. But here I am, all ready fer the race!"

Saxon's friends and some others who had just joined the circle gaped at her. Their wide eyes went from the top of her bare head to her boots, already soiled with mud.

"What are all you-uns a-starin' at me fer? Got some sorter menfolk secret betwixt you?"

Max's slight grin broadened to a warm, friendly smile. "Mrs. Blackwell, you've no idea how long I've been waiting to meet you." None too gently, he nudged Saxon.

Jolted back to reality, Saxon quickly made all the introductions. As he introduced Chickadee to the men, he felt a strange irritation when a few of them began to snicker.

"Well," Chickadee said, bending to pick up a handful of snow, "when's the race gwine commence? I'm ready ter try and win it. 'Course, it ain't gwine be easy a-settin' on a sled with these dang skirts. I'll have ter hike 'em up—"

"The race is for men only, Keely," Saxon interrupted. "The ladies merely watch it."

"Watch it? What fun is that? Saxon, why cain't I—"

"Because you just can't," he broke in, smiling as if he and Chickadee were only teasing one another.

Chickadee angrily molded her snow into a ball. It wasn't fair. Why couldn't she race? She had a sled . . .

"Uh, unusual fur," Oliver remarked. "What is it?"

"Bahr," she replied, her eyes still boring into Saxon. "Warmest fur thur is. I kilt this here bahr about two years ago. Used ter be a rug on Betty Jane and George Franklin's floor. Thur my neighbor-people back home in North Caroliner. But me and Desi made it inter a coat. Desi done most of it. She sews good, huh?"

The men nodded obediently, many of them still snickering. Saxon found it difficult to stifle his annoyance.

"Saxon!" Wesley Melville reined his sleek stallion to a halt. "Care to make a wager on the race?"

The smell of alcohol on his breath was strong. No doubt it was the whiskey that gave him the courage to come face to face with Chickadee again, Saxon mused. That, and the fact that he was mounted and could make a quick getaway. "Wesley, you came in last, last year. What makes you think you'll win today?"

"I've got a new sled," Wesley answered smugly. "It's made of the finest steel available, wrought by Europe's finest craftsmen."

"Take the lay, Saxon," Chickadee pressed. "Take it and then beat the dang hell outen him in the race."

All the men save Max gasped at her words, and then began to laugh harder. Saxon's irritation with them grew close to anger. "Keely, why don't you go see if you can find Bunny? And there's Desdemona too, little one. Didn't you say she might join us?"

"Done backed and forthed with Bunny and tole her ter wait up thar fer me. Desi ain't gwine come. She's a-sangin' to Khan. Don't no sound come outen her yet, but she lips them words ter her songs real good. Now, you gwine make the lay with this weasel or not, outlander?"

"Afraid, Saxon?" Wesley taunted.

Chickadee's snowball hit Wesley square in the forehead. "Slur Saxon's name agin, and it'll be my fist you feel on that ugly mug o' yore's next, you dang—"

"Keely!" Saxon took her elbow and tried to lead her away.

"How nice having a wife to protect you, Saxon," Wesley taunted, wiping the snow off his cheeks. "Is that why you married her?"

Chickadee whirled. "Why you—Saxon, let me go, dang it! I'm gwine bang him plumb inter next week!"

Wesley laughed, feeling quite safe on his fleet stallion. "A real lady you've got there, Saxon. Isn't she something, friends?" he asked the men who were watching the scene with open mouths. "She is female beneath those skirts of hers, isn't she, Saxon?"

Saxon's face contorted with fury. He clenched his fists.

"He's offering a bet on the race, Sax," Max hinted. "Bet him his horse."

"Robespierre?" Wesley asked. "Fine. Robespierre and Hagen. Or are you afraid you might lose, Saxon? Tell you what, old pal, why don't we make the bet even steeper? Say . . . if you agree to it and then back out at the last minute, I still win Hagen. And the same goes for me."

"He ain't gwine back outen nothin', you lowdown, triflin'er'n pig slop, contrary, half-witted—"

"Keely, please!" Saxon tried to cut her off.

"—no 'count, bedevilin'est, ill-mouthed—"

"Keely—"

"—shiftlessest, God-burn varmint, you!" Chickadee continued without pause. "You got about as much guts as a skeleton, Wesley Melville! A-settin' up thar on that ridin' critter whilst you flang them slurs ever' which way. Git down offen that ani-mule!"

"Haven't seen much of you lately, Sax," Wesley said, blatantly ignoring Chickadee. "But with a wife like yours, who needs men friends?"

Max saw Saxon's jaw clench and quickly intervened. "Sax, a fight will spoil the day," he whispered. "The race will serve the same purpose. You know it'll pain Wesley sorely to lose Robespierre, and victory in a sport is an honorable way to achieve satisfaction." He winked at Chickadee and then put his arm around her shoulders. "You've never seen your husband race. No one's ever been able to beat him."

She gave Max a brilliant smile. "Make the lay, Saxon," she pressed him again.

"You've got a bet, Wesley," he growled, his jaw finally unclenching. "I'll see you at the starting line."

"Dammit!" Saxon crashed his fist into the side of the shed wall. "It's been destroyed!"

Chickadee looked at the steel sled runners. They were bent and mangled as if someone had taken an iron mallet to them. "Wesley done it," she hissed. "That's why fer he was so dang-blasted anxious ter make the lay with you. The man's as crooked as a dog's hind leg."

"And if I can't race, it'll be the same as losing. I'll have to give Hagen to that cheating bastard!"

"You ain't got ter give up nothin', outlander. You're gwine race, and you're gwine win."

"What would you have me do, Keely? Slide down the hill on my belly?"

She threw back her head and laughed. "No, I reckon that'd be a mite painful."

"There's no other sled available. All the men are racing the ones they brought, and there's no time to go and buy another one. The race starts in ten minutes. Dammit, I was a fool not to suspect Wesley was up to no good!"

"I got a sled fer you. It's up in the woods covered with brush. Me and Desi finished it last week. Ain't had the chance ter take it fer a ride yet, but—"

"Keely, you heard what Wesley said. He's got a sled imported from Europe. The finest steel, the best—"

"Confidence in me, Saxon. I swear to you his fancified sled ain't no better'n the one I made."

But her oath seemed ridiculous when Saxon saw her sled. Wood. Not a sliver of steel on it. Sure, she'd done a nice job on it, but race it? Win with it?

He was going to miss Hagen.

Chickadee ignored his look of dismay and began to pull the homemade sled toward the hill where everyone was waiting for the race to start.

"Keely, I can't race that thing!"

She ran until she reached the top of the hill. It was a few moments before anyone noticed her arrival, since everyone was gathered around Wesley's impressive European sled. But when they saw her, they left Wesley and went to meet her.

Surrounded, Chickadee introduced herself and smiled at all the curious guests. A few murmured forced greetings, but no one said much, everyone trying to decide what to look at—the bearskin-rug coat, the ridiculous-looking sled, or the flame-haired rustic who owned both things.

"This what you're going to race, Sax?" Oliver asked.

"It would seem my own sled has seen better days," Saxon replied, glaring at Wesley.

Wesley returned the look with a smug nod.

Muttering, Saxon snatched the sled ropes from

Chickadee and pulled it into the line of other sleds. Settling himself into his favorite position aboard the sled seat, he ignored the laughter and infuriating remarks that rippled through the air. He ignored the smirk on Araminta's face as she watched him from the sidelines.

He ignored everything but the pride in Chickadee's grin. He saw her excitement, her surefire confidence in her sled. He saw her unabashed faith in *him* too. How brightly it shone!

And then she was gone, following the crowd as it left to congregate at the finish line.

"Positions!" the starter shouted and pointed a pistol at the sky. "Ready . . ."

The gun exploded, and the race began. Vaguely, Saxon heard the yelling and cheering coming from the crowd below, but he concentrated on handling Chickadee's sled. He leaned forward, trying to get the feel of the homemade vehicle, anticipating grave problems as it gained momentum.

But the ride was smooth. The sleek runners, painstakingly carved by Chickadee's talented hands, slid through the snow like the fin of a shark slicing through water. The sled took each bump, each curve as if it had a mind of its own. It passed Max and Kyle. It sprayed snow in Oliver, Charles, and Nathan's faces. Faster it went, so fast that everything Saxon passed was blurred, and still its speed increased, until he was side by side with Wesley.

The two raced neck in neck, their eyes narrowed into mere slits, their backs as flat as they could make them as they leaned over their sleds. Snow and ice whirred around them, the wind bit brutally, the speed with which they traveled making the race a dangerous one now.

And then Wesley made it even more treacherous. With one vicious jerk to the side, he rammed his sled into Saxon's. Fine steel runners sliced into wooden ones, sending splinters flying.

"Damn you, Wesley!" Saxon shouted as he tried

to regain control of the careening sled. He heard Wesley laugh, but again he fixed his concentration on the race. Only a hundred feet or so to go before the finish line, he guessed. But could he win with a damaged runner?

And then he watched Wesley speed ahead. In only moments the bastard would win the race and Hagen too! Saxon fumed.

Then he saw how sloppy Wesley's form was becoming. The man was sitting upright, the force of the wind slowing his ride considerably. "Damn sure of yourself, aren't you, Wesley?" Saxon muttered, more determined than ever to catch up. "I'll—"

A loud crack cut short his threat. Chickadee's sled began to wobble and falter, the ruined runner cracking and finally snapping away from the seat.

In a fraction of a second, Saxon's mind took him back some twenty years, back to when he was a boy, and he and Max sled-raced down this very hill. How many hours on end had they practiced tipping their sleds to the side, trying to race with a single runner? They'd never been able to do it, their immature muscles simply not strong enough to hold the sleds in a sideways position. They'd always lost control and crashed.

But Saxon was not ten years old anymore.

He threw himself to the good side of the sled, forcing the bad side off the ground. His shoulder was nearly level with the snow as he sought to somehow equalize his weight on the one runner.

Balance, he told himself, every muscle in his body straining. *Easy, easy does it.*

Only twenty feet to go, he estimated. The sled shook alarmingly, and the wood groaned, but the remaining runner withstood the demands he made on it.

A loud cheer went up as he passed a very surprised Wesley, rising to deafening heights when Saxon sped across the finish line to win the race.

* * *

"Great race, Sax!" Max exclaimed as he, Saxon, Chickadee, and Bunny went to the dining room, where the other guests were waiting for the hot meal that would end the day. "When I saw you tip over the way we tried to do when we were boys . . . damn good thinking!"

"You raced superbly, Saxon," Bunny added.

"I can't take any credit." Saxon took Chickadee's hand and smiled warmly into her eyes. "I've never raced such a fine sled, little one."

His gesture did not escape Max. It reminded him of his own current interest. "Bunny, I saw Cynthia earlier. She's still here, isn't she?"

The glow in Bunny's eyes glazed over with hurt. Her entire body ached from all the running, walking, wood-chopping, and dieting Chickadee had made her do. Wood-chopping, of all things! And it was all for nothing! Max didn't even notice her weight loss. Quickly, she yanked her sleeve over her warts and willed the tears not to come.

Chickadee's heart went out to her friend. "Cynthia's done left, Max. Heared her a-sayin' she had ter see her dressmaker." Chickadee elbowed Saxon in the ribs, her eyes pleading with him. "Ain't Bunny purty today?"

"What?" he mouthed. "Oh. Uh . . . My you're looking pretty today, Bunny," he stammered, comprehension slowly dawning. "Your dress—beautiful shade of pink, don't you think, Max?" He glanced at Bunny. Strange. There really was something different about the girl.

"Pink looks nice with your hair," Max said politely, then took a closer look. He couldn't quite put his finger on it, but there was something about her he'd never noticed before. She really had lovely features, he decided. Beautiful eyes.

"I . . . uh, thank you." Bunny smiled, suddenly welcoming the ache in her muscles.

As they entered the dining room, Saxon frowned when he saw he and Chickadee had been placed directly in front of Wesley. The smirk on Araminta's face proved she'd arranged the seating cards in this manner with a very definite purpose in mind. She was still counting on Chickadee to cause trouble, Saxon realized angrily. Ignoring her and everyone else who was staring at him, he helped Chickadee into her chair.

"Pay Wesley no attention," he whispered down to her, his words more a plea than a command.

She did not respond but began blowing on the hot soup in front of her. But her hostility grew, and before she knew it she'd blown her soup onto the tablecloth.

"It's obvious you don't know how to eat soup out of a bowl," Wesley jeered, too angry over the loss of Robespierre to worry about Chickadee's retaliation. Besides, he was on the other side of the table and there were lots of people around to help him should she become violent. "How do you eat it in the mountains? At the stove, out of the pot?"

"Wesley," Saxon began, struggling with his ire.

"Soup's hot," Chickadee interrupted, also fighting her fury.

Wesley picked up his spoon and pointed it at her. "It's acceptable to blow on hot soup, but not to spray it out of the bowl."

"Well excuse me fer a-bein' so dang dumb," she responded, her voice deceptively sweet. "I reckon I'm so dumb, I couldn't pour piss from a boot withouten directions. But I don't keer fer this soup no how."

Despite his dismay at her colorful language, Saxon smiled into his napkin. No one in the world could match Chickadee's eloquent way with words. But still, he couldn't let things get *too* out of hand. He remained ready to intervene.

"It would be a breach of manners not to at least eat a portion of it," Wesley informed Chickadee insolently.

She stood, her rage visible. Saxon took her arm,

part of him wishing he could let her do whatever it was she planned for Wesley, and the other part of him knowing it would do her more harm than Wesley.

She yanked her arm from his grasp. "I don't like this soup, Wesley Weasel, but since it 'pears yore so God-burn worried that it ain't gwine git et, eat it fer me!"

Saxon reached for her bowl, Wesley ducked, but neither of them was fast enough. The bowl glanced off Wesley's forehead, spilling soup, thick and hot, down his face and onto his immaculate cambric shirt. He'd barely wiped the liquid from his eyes when a roll, generously buttered, came flying through the air and bounced off the end of his nose.

"You wanted ter know how mountain folks eat soup, Wesley? Well, they eat it same as you-uns lessen they insist on agger-pervokin' somebody whilst thur a-eatin'. Iffen they do that? Well, then they don't eat the soup—they *wear* it!"

She stepped away from the table and saw Saxon staring at her. She sent him a silent apology before she whirled and left the room, her gait proud and regal.

Saxon watched her until she'd disappeared and then turned back to the group of people in the dining room.

Wesley stood. "I demand an apology for—"

"Shut up, Wesley."

"Yeah, shut up, Wesley," Max repeated, grinning broadly. He suspected what Saxon was about to do and he would not stop his friend this time. Wesley had gone much too far, and Max understood Saxon's need to defend Chickadee's honor.

Araminta rose and pointed her cane at Saxon. "Saxon—"

"I suggest you and everyone else continue with the meal, Grandmother. Wesley and I need to . . . *discuss* a few things in private. Wesley, please give me the honor of your company in the library."

Wesley blanched. "I will give you no such honor. You—"

"What's the matter, Wesley?" Max asked. "Are you afraid to go have a . . . little talk with Sax?"

Wesley looked around. Everyone was staring at him. "Well . . . no. I'm not afraid. But I refuse to—"

"Now, Wesley!" Saxon slammed his hand on the table, rattling the silverware and upsetting glasses.

Wesley had no choice but to follow Saxon out of the dining room. As he trailed behind, noting Saxon's angry stride and balled fists, he tried to rationalize the situation. Surely Saxon wouldn't go through with this. They were all civilized people! The elite of the city! The privileged class didn't resort to fistfights. It was all a bluff!

By the time they reached the library, his hypothesis had bolstered him, and his courage had trickled back. It returned full force when he saw Charles, Oliver, Nate, and Kyle enter the room and come to stand behind him. "Well now, Sax," he taunted anew. "Can you handle yourself without your bodyguard? Perhaps she *larnt* you some of her mountain moves?"

Saxon grabbed him by the collar.

"Think he'll do it, fellows?" Wesley asked confidently, still sure Saxon would not demean himself by brawling like a common dockman.

Saxon's fist ached with the need to punch Wesley's nose. But Wesley, though tall, was not a well-built man. He was no match for Saxon, and Saxon had never fought a man who stood no chance of winning. Slowly, reluctantly, he uncurled his fist. "I'm going to give you one chance to apologize for bullying Keely, Wesley. You will apologize to me, and then you will ask forgiveness from her."

"Listen to him, friends." Wesley jeered. "Without his mountain whore defending him, he doesn't know what to do!"

Molten fury erupted inside Saxon, burning from

his mind every thought of restraint, every consideration he'd had for Wesley's physical inadequacies. The only thing he could think of was his uncontrollable, savage desire to champion the girl whose name had been so viciously slandered.

The power in his fist was backed by every shred of his hatred for Wesley, every fiber of his strength, every splinter of his anger, and every wondrous wave of love that crashed through him at the thought of his redheaded mountain girl.

The sickening crack that followed told all that Wesley's jaw was broken.

"My God, Saxon!" Nate shouted, helping Wesley to his feet. "You broke his—"

"I don't give a damn what I broke! Get him out of my house before I break every bone—"

"Now see here, Sax!" Oliver took Saxon's arm. "Wesley needs medical attention!"

Saxon yanked his arm away from the man he'd once considered a friend. "Wesley, you bastard, keep her name out of your mouth. Because if you dare to sully it again, it won't be medical attention you need, it'll be a coffin! If I ever hear *any* of you talk about her—if you so much as *think* about her in the wrong way, I'll make sure it's the last thought any of you ever have!"

Saxon stalked out then, but his warning, like a black cloud, hung heavily over the room.

Chapter 19

Shane took great care to keep his huge form hidden behind the bushes. "Smooth," he whispered as he sipped at the liquor. "Aye, 'tis just right, Chickadee." He handed her the flask and grinned, his teeth gleaming in the moonlight that lit the North End.

Chickadee took a sip. "It ain't as good as George Franklin's but it dranks all right, I reckon. 'Pears ter me you boys can start a-sellin' now."

Gallagher's eyes caressed the contraption Chickadee had constructed several weeks ago. It had taken him, Shane, and Killian a while to find all the parts she'd described to them: copper cooker, cap, slop arm, plug stick, rags, copper worm, barrel, and water pipe. But they'd found them and watched as she built the rig. Relying on memory, she made a replica of the stills she'd seen George Franklin make many a time.

And then she set about remembering the recipe for his whiskey. "We're gwine use whole grain white corn, put it in this here barrel, and cover it with warm water," she'd explained to the three amazed Irishmen. "We'll leave it set fer a day and a night. Then we'll put it in that thar sproutin' tub on account o' it's got a sieve in the bottom fer a-drainin'. We'll keep on a-pourin' warm water inter it, and put a hot cloth over it till all the water's done drained out. In about three days, them corn kernels

273

is gwine be sprouted. We'll dry 'em with heat and grind 'em inter corn grits. Then we'll put them grits inter a barrel with hot water and let the whole mess git real ripe afore we thin out the mash with more warm water and add rye malt and sugar ter it. After a few days, we'll stir the mash real good and let it work fer two or three days more. Then we'll run through the still."

The Irishmen's astonishment grew when she did exactly what she'd explained she would. The first runoff, what Chickadee called singlings, had been a dingy, poisonous fluid. So she made a second run of doublings, this one at a lower temperature, and had produced a clear, two-hundred-proof liquid.

Now, as the foursome sat and sipped the home-made liquor, they all knew the whiskey would bring a good price.

"I'm nae knowin' how to thank ye, Chickadee," Killian said. "Ye've given us a trade, lass, aye, that ye have. We'll be keepin' our jobs on the docks, but 'tis thanks to ye we'll be able to make money on the side now."

Gallager nodded. "I've spoken to several people, and 'twas anxious they were to buy from us. 'Tisn't a whiskey sold in the bars that can outdo this ye've made fer us."

"How can we ever repay yer kindness?" Shane asked.

Chickadee gazed warmly at the three men. "You-uns heped me git back ter Khan that night. We're even now."

The four friends sat in the splash of moonlight for a while longer, the Irishmen quietly reminiscing about the green homeland they'd left behind and Chickadee remembering the scene with Wesley. After she'd left the dining room she'd taken a coach and sought sanctuary here.

But the look Saxon had given her before she'd left, had followed her here. It hadn't been a furious expression, but neither had it been gentle. He masked his emotions well, but she presumed she'd broken one of those Boston rules he once tried to explain to her. Throwing soup was probably against the law here.

She just couldn't do things right no matter how hard she tried. Nothing she did was working. As if she'd ever had him, she was losing Saxon, and there wasn't a thing she could do about it. Boston, with all its fancy rules—Saxon himself, with all his ghosts—there were so many things that stood in love's way. Oh how she missed those happy times they'd shared in the Blue Ridge.

She smiled sadly at her friends. They were all kindred spirits. Each of them lost and trying to adjust to Boston; each of them knowing Boston would never be, could never come close to the wild, unspoiled beauty of their homelands.

Saxon was just leaving as she entered the bedroom.

"Whar you gwine at this time o' night?"

"Where am I . . . Where have *you* been? I searched the grounds everywhere, and when Josh finally told me you'd taken a coach and—"

"The North End," she said wearily, dreading an argument but knowing one was brewing.

"I told you never to go there again!" He forced her into a chair and then caught her scent. "Dammit to hell, Keely! You've been drinking again!"

"Saxon—"

"How often have you gone there?"

"Not ever' day."

He glared at the top of her head. "That's not an answer."

"Well, it's the onliest one yore a-gittin'!" She pushed him away and stood. "I love you more'n more ever' dang minute of ever' dang day, Saxon. But I ain't gwine do ever'thang you tell me ter do. My friends needed hep bad. I tole you I was gwine keep on a-seein' 'em."

"Why didn't you just tell me you wanted to go? If it was that important to you, I'd have taken you there myself! I just don't want you there alone, Keely. Those bars are—"

"Ain't never been to nary a bar. I don't go thar ter drank."

His eyebrow rose. "Then why do you reek of alcohol?"

She raised her nose and straightened her shoulders. "I only been *a-samplin'* likker. I ain't been a-drankin' it fer real. You got ter taste it iffen you want ter know iffen it's right."

His eyes widened. "You're *making* it? You and those Irishmen have been out all night—"

"I ain't been out all night! Saxon, they need money. Thur so dang poverty-poor, my heart hurts fer 'em. I larnt 'em how ter make George Franklin's likker on account o' it was the onliest way I knowed how ter hep 'em."

Saxon slammed his fist into the palm of his other hand. "Of all the harebrained— I've a good mind to have those three Irishmen arrested for moonshining!"

"Then I'll go ter jail too."

He exhaled raggedly, attempting to calm himself, because arguing with Chickadee and winning when she was in one of her famous hardheaded moods was an impossible feat.

"Saxon, I didn't do nothin' all that bad, and nobody seed us thar," she explained convincingly. "I didn't mean ter stay gone fer so long, but the night's so purty and the moon's so bright. And what with the still right thar, the heat o' George Franklin's likker a-warmin' me . . . well, it sorter memoried me of my holler. I reckon I tuk sick fer home tonight."

Her poignant smile and the faraway look in her sad eyes explained clearly what words could not. He turned and went to the window. How she loved those hills! Those blue-green mountains were as much a part of her as the golden freckles on her face and, in all probability, the Appalachia was calling her back to its soothing bosom.

He thought about the affairs she'd attended with Araminta and realized what an effort she'd made to make him see how much she cared for him. He knew now that she'd been scorned and insulted at each of the assemblies, and yet she'd led him to believe she was enjoying herself. She'd wanted him to be glad she was doing as he wished her to do. Dear God, he thought to himself. Her love for him had enabled her to bear all that suffering.

"What a truly remarkable emotion love is," he whispered, his breath fogging the window. Only love, the very thing he'd once believed to be pure myth, could have made him feel the way he had today at the race. He'd been irritated by the way people laughed at her, angered by the condescending way everyone looked and sneered at her. The whispered insults he'd heard had infuriated him, and Wesley's slander had finally hurled him into a rage.

The savage need to defend her was the most uncontrollable emotion he'd ever experienced. And only one thing could have possibly caused such a violent need.

Love. Love was real.

And how eager he was to tell her he'd discovered that sweet truth, to fervently profess his love for her. He wanted to tell her to stay with him forever.

But he couldn't do that now. Not when he was just understanding what his wish would mean. She was nature in all its untamed glory, and this was Boston in all its refined elegance. The two, very simply, did not mix.

"I realized that from the start," he whispered again. "Knew it but hoped . . ." He ran his hand through his hair.

And he couldn't return to North Carolina with her either, he fumed. That would mean leaving Desdemona, for he could never take her with him. To hell with the fact that Araminta still retained custody over Desdemona, but the girl, though she'd improved mentally, remained frail and weak physically. She'd not last a week enduring the rough life Chickadee yearned to have back again.

There was only one course to take. Pain gripped him as he thought of it. As much as he longed to give Chickadee all his love, the love that had been there from the beginning, he would have to conceal it from her. He could never even let her suspect its existence.

Because if she knew, she would never leave Boston. She'd stay here and endure her homesickness with her indomitable fortitude. She'd be brave for him, keeping her yearning for the Appalachia carefully hidden.

But he'd see it each time he looked into her eyes—those sparkling orbs that were as green as her mountain forests. He'd feel it every time his fingers played through her copper hair, those tresses that were the same red-orange-gold of the mountain leaves in autumn. He'd hear it each time she laughed, that sweet, happy song that rivaled even the lovely melody of the Blue Ridge breezes.

Staying in Boston would be a sacrifice too great to expect of the girl he loved. And so, when the Winslow business was over—something he knew would occur shortly—he would have to send her home.

"Why, dammit?" Why had it happened this way? Why had Fate allowed him to discover love and then forced him to send it away? It was the cruelest injustice he'd ever known. He pressed his forehead against the cold pane of the window and shut his eyes against the pain he knew would never go away.

"Why what, Saxon?" she said softly and joined him.

God, he would miss that voice, he thought as he turned to enfold her in his embrace. "Keely," he whispered and wondered what would fill the void in his arms when she was gone.

He swept her from the floor, and because she was a rare treasure it would be agony to relinquish, he held her closely and tenderly while he still had the time to do so. He carried her to the bed and slowly undressed her, savoring each revealed part of her before uncovering the next.

He shed his own clothing quickly, and when he lay down beside her, he kissed her with all the adoration he wished he could put to words. And when he began to caress her, it was with more passion than he'd ever shown her before. He made love to her languidly, thoroughly, as if each passing minute was his last with her.

And when at last he had finished and Chickadee dried his sweat-drenched face with her soft hair, she had no way of knowing that one of the droplets was a tear.

The Christmas season brought with it a fresh snowfall and Khan's complete recovery. Chickadee spent a lot of time outside, Saxon, Desdemona, and Khan never far from her side. The Blackwell grounds were soon covered with snowmen, most of them sprayed yellow by the very territorial wolf.

Saxon, as a surprise for Chickadee, went out and bought holiday decorations for the house—all of them arranged with galax leaves. He thought it would please her to see how galax was used, but when she fingered the heart-shaped leaves and wondered aloud if she was the one who'd picked them, he was reminded anew of how much she missed the Appalachia.

Chickadee had no idea her homesickness was the reason for Saxon's depression. She only knew he'd changed and didn't smile much anymore. More than anything, she wished there was a way to bring back his sweet, mocking grin.

Her wish was granted on Christmas Eve. Saxon, denied real Christmases as a child, ignored the bitterness the holiday always brought to him, and in the privacy of their bedroom he played Santa Claus and presented Chickadee with the gift he'd had made for her.

It was the most beautiful rifle she'd ever seen; sleek, gleaming, and perfect in her hands. But more than that, its stock was the one she thought had burned so long ago.

"I found it on the floor of your cabin that day," Saxon explained. "I had a gunsmith here use it to make a replica of what the original rifle must have looked like."

She was speechless with gratitude and disbelief, and many moments passed before she could find her voice and present him the gift on which she'd been working so hard. Sliding her hand beneath her pillow, she brought forth a small book and held it out for him to see.

He was confused. The book of poetry already belonged to him. "For me?"

In answer, she only smiled and flipped through the pages until she found the one she wanted. " 'When the br-bright sunset fills,' " she began to read slowly, " 'the sli-silver woods with . . .' " She paused then, her nose wrinkled as she tried to read the next word.

"Light," Saxon whispered in amazement.

" 'Light,' " she continued, nodding, " 'the green slop . . . slope throws its shadders in the hollers of the hills, and wide the up-upland glows.' "

Her eyes afire with pride, she closed the book, caressed it, and then looked up at Saxon. "I larnt ter read, Saxon. It's my Christmas gift ter you."

His eyes went from her book to her face, and what he saw there made his heart skip a beat. She was beaming with happiness over her accomplishment. "Who taught you?"

"Bunny. First we read, and then I make Bunny go out and work off that lard she's a-totin' around. She don't like it much, but she's bound and compelt ter have Max as her man and knows she's got ter git shed o' all that fat. Anyhow, she larnt me ter read, so I figgered I'd hep her back. And I been a-larnin' Desi ter read too.''

"Longfellow," he said softly. "You read Longfellow. A passage from 'An April Day.' ''

His eyes and voice caressed her. She melted in the heat of his tenderness. "I liked it. It made me thank o' the Blue Ridge. You reckon that Longfeller ever went to the Blue Ridge? This here poem he writ sorter makes you see them mountains in yore mind, don't it?''

"Yes it does, Keely," Saxon agreed sadly. "It's a beautiful poem, and it does indeed describe your hills.''

She watched as that strange melancholy filled his eyes again. "Saxon, ain't you proud o' me? Didn't it make you happy ter hear me a-readin' the way I done?''

There were no words he knew to describe the intensity of his feelings at that moment. Almost everything she ever attempted, ever succeeded in doing, she did for him. Dear God, how he longed to tell her how much she meant to him. "Keely," he whispered, taking her into his arms and holding her for a very long time before he spoke again. "You will never know how much your gift means to me. It's the most meaningful present anyone has ever given me.''

"I'd do anythang fer you, Saxon. And it was fun a-larnin' ter read. It's fun a-larnin' new thangs. I don't reckon thur's nothin' I wouldn't try at least once.''

She sat back and ran her fingers over the spine of the poetry book. "Like the grand-ball party that Miz Preston woman's a-havin' at her place soon. I ain't never been ter nothin' like that. I warn't much fer them other git-togethers I been ter, but this ball thang differs. Bunny tole me this story? Well, it was about this girl called Cindereller. She had the worstest kind o' time with her stepmama and stepsisters,

but in the end this fairy come and heped her git ter
the ball at the castle. Cindereller even weared glass
shoes. Wonder why they didn't break and cut her
feet up, Saxon?''

He squelched his amusement. ''They were made
of magic glass.''

''Magic glass,'' she repeated, wishing she could
believe in that sort of thing but knowing full well it
was only fantasy. ''Yeah, well, Bunny said this
grand ball you-uns have ever' year is jist as fancy as
Prince Charmin's ball.''

''Do you wish to attend the ball, little one?'' Their
invitation hadn't been withdrawn, he mused. If
Chickadee wanted to attend Boston's most elegant
affair of the season, he'd take her. He'd do anything
at all to make her happy before he had to send her
away. And if Boston didn't like it, it could go to hell.

''Well, I do sorter want ter go. But, Saxon . . . I
don't know how ter dance real fancy-like.''

''I could teach you to waltz in one afternoon,
Keely. The steps are easy to learn, and you are nat-
urally graceful.''

She threw her arms around him. ''Oh Saxon,
thanky!'' Flying from the bed, she began to twirl
around the room, already practicing that thing that
Saxon called a waltz.

He watched her and thought of how much like
Cinderella she really was. A rare beauty with a heart
of pure gold, mistreated by society, much as Cinderella had been abused by the stepmother and
stepsisters. And he, he thought with a pang of longing, might have been her Prince Charming. The only
thing missing in the story-come-to-life was the fairy
godmother.

The thought jerked him to his feet. He stood staring at Chickadee, his only movement the slow smile
of newborn hope spreading across his face.

''Saxon?''

His grin broadened, his gaze still riveted on her.

Why couldn't *he* be her fairy godmother . . . er, god-father?

"I might need me some spectacles," Chickadee said, "but I could swear that's a smile a-turnin' up yore lips. Didn't never thank I'd see it agin. What brung it on?"

"If I could transform her . . . like the fairy did with Cinder—" he mumbled quietly to himself. "Make Boston see her in a different light . . ."

"What's that about light, Saxon?"

He began to pace, his hands firmly clasped behind his back. "If people began to accept her, stopped ridiculing her . . ." He stopped in front of a wall, stared at it for a second, and then turned for another walk around the room.

Chickadee couldn't understand his incoherent words. "Saxon, what—"

"She herself said learning new things was fun," he went on, his speech still slurred. "If society ceased its scorn, would she begin to . . . Maybe if she were given a warm welcome wherever she went . . . it's quite possible . . . really quite possible that she might . . ."

Chickadee took a quick sniff of him as he passed her on his journey across the room but smelled nothing but his bay rum soap. So why he was acting so snockered?

"She might begin to *like* it here," he muttered. "If she did, she might want to stay. It would be her *own* choice to stay. Wouldn't be a *sacrifice* if it was something she truly, deep down wanted to do!"

"Dang it, Saxon, what are you a-carryin' on about?"

"How do you feel when people say mean things to or about you, Keely?" he queried loudly.

"What? Well, that's the stupidest question any-body ever—How the hell you thank I feel? Don't nobody feel real good when other folks is—"

"Would you like to put a stop to it?"

"Cain't nothin' stop them snakes from bad-

mouthin' but a death chill. You a-sayin' I should kill
'em the next time they—''

"I don't think we'll have to resort to murder," he
said with a chuckle that turned into full-fledged
laughter as he swept her into his arms and swirled
her around.

"Saxon, what's got you in sech a franzy?"

"Listen to me, mountain girl," he said excitely
and put her down. "You've defended me at every
turn since your arrival to Boston. It's my turn now.
No one is ever going to have reason to snub you
again. Do you understand, Keely?"

"But how are you gwine—"

"Cinderella!" he yelled and planted a kiss on her
forehead. "You're going to be Cinderella at that
ball."

"Cinder—Saxon, what—"

"Just picture it, Keely." He pointed dramatically
toward the wall. "Here you come, sweeping down
the staircase and into the ballroom. Every pair of
eyes in the room watches you. Everyone wonders
who you could be. There's something about you that
looks familiar—but they don't know any real prin-
cesses, and that's certainly what you appear to be.
Your beauty, charm, grace . . . surely only a princess could possess such an abundance of those en-
viable qualities."

He spread his upraised hand wide. "And now,
Keely, listen to the whispers that ripple all around
you. 'Who is that lovely girl?' 'Where does she come
from?' 'Why haven't we met her before?' 'We must
acquaint ourselves with her.' "

"And what am I a-wearin', Saxon?"

He smiled when he saw how hard she was staring
at the wall. "Your gown? Gorgeous! Gold satin, isn't
it? And your emeralds, the ones I bought to match
your eyes. See how they glitter in your hair, at your
ears, throat, and wrists? And what's this I see? Who
are all those men lining up to dance with you? And
what are you saying to them? What? That you'll only

dance with me? And there we go, Keely. Look how we're waltzing. Hear how loudly everyone is applauding!''

"What fer are they a-doin' that?'' Her eyes were mere slits, she was concentrating so hard on the imagined scene.

"Because you're so elegant and delightful. You've captured the interest of everyone, and look! The ball has ended, and everyone has crowded around you asking you to visit them. Inviting you to their homes and—''

"Hold on, Saxon!'' she exclaimed, the dream dissipating instantly. "Them folks cain't stand me. They ain't never gwine—''

"Oh, but they will. Because you see, Keely, they'll have no reason whatsoever not to. We'll work hard to—''

"Work? But—''

"You said there wasn't anything you wouldn't try.''

"Well, yeah, but—''

"Mountain girl turned to princess!''

"Saxon, I ain't never gwine be no prin—''

"Please, Chickadee.'' He could see no other solution to the dilemma that was causing him such agony; his plan was a desperate attempt to hold on to the one person who had given his life meaning, the woman he loved with all his being. "Trust me, little one.'' His eyes echoed his plea.

Chickadee, with the eyes in her heart, saw his sincere hope that she'd agree. And his hope gave her back her own.

Maybe he'd begun to care for her.

Saxon drilled Chickadee day and night; Desdemona was their quiet audience. Unless they were practicing table manners, they rarely even took time out to eat. He showed Chickadee how to sit like a lady, rise like a lady, curtsy like a lady. He demonstrated how a lady holds her glass and even extended his pinky finger in a very feminine manner. To show her what a lady should look like when dancing, he wrapped a large tablecloth around his waist, picked up a bit of it in his fingers, and waltzed around the room, careful to hold the fabric in such a way that it flowed and swirled around his legs. He showed her the way a lady fans herself, and even peeked over the fan and batted his eyelashes at her. He was a lady in every sense of the word while giving her lessons, and on more than one occasion, Chickadee laughed herself into fits. Even Desdemona giggled silently.

Saxon joined them in their mirth. He was well aware of how ridiculous he looked pretending to be a lady and realized he could have had Bunny come to demonstrate all the ladylike gestures and ways, but he'd never had as much fun in all his life. He felt like a little boy again and surprised even himself at his silliness. He was "climbin' fool's hill", as Chickadee put it, and she was his willing partner in the climb.

He only hoped his plan would make it possible for them to scale it together forever.

The long-awaited night had finally arrived, Saxon mused as the coach rumbled toward Eugenia Preston's estate. His eyes rested lovingly on his Appalachian Cinderella. In a matter of minutes she would attend her first ball. She would meet an English duke. She would face her enemies. She would remember everything he'd taught her, or she would forget it all. But whatever happened, *he* was her Prince Charming tonight.

She was a vision, a flame-haired angel swathed in a cloud of gold satin. The emeralds he'd bought her glittered from a tiara in her hair, her ears, her throat, her arms, and her hands. How he loved those emeralds on her.

As he continued to observe her she snapped open her fan with perfect execution, but how strange it looked in her hand, he thought. She'd had no need for fans in her hills. The cool mountain wind had been her fan. And then she slipped her hands into her gloves. Hands that had already done more hard work than most Boston ladies did in a lifetime.

He watched as she peered out the window. He knew she was seeing mansions, well-kept gardens, and clean lanes, lit by the streetlamps. Her nights in the Blue Ridge had been lit only by the sheen of the moon. Her mansion had been a small cabin, her garden the most beautiful nature had to offer, her avenues rocky paths lined with dense tangles of laurel.

And though she was dressed as elegantly as he'd ever seen her, her rich clothing and sumptuous jewels could not disguise her earthy looks. Yes, she could be a princess sitting there in all her gleaming finery, but encased in that costly gown was an Appalachian mountain girl. An unaffected rustic who would either succeed gloriously or fail miserably.

Whatever the outcome of this night, he knew it would decide both their futures.

Chapter 20

Eugenia poked her head into the doorway of the huge Preston kitchen and watched the three French chefs at work. Eugenia rolled her eyes.

They were Sarah Bancroft's chefs. For weeks before the ball, Sarah had begged Eugenia to allow them to create their culinary masterpieces for the duke, proclaiming the chefs were famous throughout Europe. She'd badgered her so incessantly that Eugenia had acquiesced just to silence Sarah's hysterical pleas.

But the Frenchmen *did* seem to know exactly what they were doing, Eugenia admitted as she watched them. No doubt the meal they created would be excellent indeed. Satisfied, she left the kitchen to inspect the sparkling ballroom.

Accepting a glass of champagne from a passing waiter, she thought of the many years she'd played the part of Boston's grande dame, its matron of society. Ah, the things money and an honored family name could do. How she'd enjoyed her status among the elite!

But the diversion had quickly worn off.

She'd grown tired of the strict rules, the stifling decorum. Alas, no one else in Boston could uphold the standards of society as she could, and Boston trusted her judgment implicitly.

Tonight, though, she would betray that trust, and love doing it. Sipping her champagne, she pondered her reasons for anticipating this night with such excitement.

No one had ever dared defy her. No rule had ever been broken, no gathering had ever been disrupted in any untoward manner. For years Boston had been caressed by the breeze of elegant propriety.

Until a refreshing Appalachian wind had blown into it.

During the months since the sewing circle meeting, Eugenia had listened to all the horrendous gossip concerning that mountain tornado and had not laughed so hard or so long in years. Even now, it made her smile and chuckle. Yes, society had had a good, strong dose of some wonderful medicine, and just as she'd suspected would happen, Boston was completely cured of that malady called boredom.

She suspected society would not forgive her for inviting the girl it shunned to tonight's festivities. But she cared not one whit about stepping down from the throne that had become too hard and cold for her liking, about relinquishing society's scepter.

"I don't envy the next queen in the least," she told a young maid who was scurrying into the ballroom with an arrangement of flowers.

The maid stopped, a poinsettia petal poking her nose. "Ma'am?"

"That little mountain marvel," Eugenia said more to herself than the maid, "has opened my eyes. I almost wish I were more like her."

She waved the maid away and surveyed the luxurious ballroom once again. It was gorgeous. But it was a chilly room—despite the hundreds of candles and the blazing fires, it lacked warmth. And though the music the orchestra played was beautiful, there was still something missing. The very atmosphere was wanting. True, the room was opulent, but it was so conventionally elegant, it was boring.

But not for long, she reminded herself. Soon this room would change. It would echo with laughter

and be heated with a special feeling that was hard
to describe.

Because soon, very soon, Chickadee Blackwell
would be arriving.

Gilford Cavendish, duke of Amherst, stifled a
yawn and looked at the silly women chattering beside him. They were talking among themselves as if
he were invisible. Why did people do that? Why did
they seem almost *afraid* of him? Did they think he'd
bite them? Order their heads to be chopped off?

What a disappointment his tour of Boston had
been, thus far. He'd heard these Americans were
different than the English. That they were less stuffy
and more open and unconventional. He'd looked
forward to being with them and learning about their
different way of life.

But from the second he'd set foot in Boston, the
red carpet was rolled out for him, and everyone he
met bent over backward for him. If he didn't know
better, he'd think he was still in his own country.
These Bostonians were exact replicas of the people
who made up the ton in England. Wealthy, sophisticated snobs—the same sort of people he took great
pains to avoid. He had no patience with their incessant gossiping and lofty airs. Was there no place in
the world where things were simple and unaffected?
He sighed and looked at his watch. He'd only been
here a half hour. It seemed like hours already.

"Oh dear God," Sarah, the woman beside him,
whispered loudly. "*She's* here!"

Millicent's mouth popped open. "What utter gall
she has coming here uninvited!"

"But Millicent, Saxon is with her!" Evelyn pointed
out. "Granted, he's shown an extreme lack of good
judgment since wedding that girl, but *no one* would
attend the grand ball uninvited. Not even Saxon!"

"Oh heavens, this is just terrible," Sarah whispered. "I can't imagine why Eugenia invited her!
What on earth shall we do now?"

Hester frowned. "Well, what *can* we do? As Evelyn said, she *must* have an invitation. Obviously Eugenia wants her here!"

"Surely there must be some mistake," Thelma argued and twisted her ruby ring. "And if there's not—oh my! I suggest we go find Araminta immediately. Perhaps she knows more about this."

Gilford ran his finger over his gray moustache and watched with detached interest as the group of women scurried away. Briefly, he tried to find the woman about whom they were speaking but soon decided he didn't care who it was. The lady in question was more than likely someone of whom the catty women were jealous. Women were like that. They worked themselves into fits over the most trivial of things, some of them even fainting to the floor! How predictable the female sex was.

He looked at his watch again.

From across the room a voice announced the names of the arriving couple. The crowd parted as the handsome man led his beautiful lady down the steps. She seemed to float on them, like a swan on quiet waters.

"Who . . . That isn't Saxon's wife, is it?" someone asked.

"That couldn't be her."

"No. Couldn't possibly be. He must be slipping out on her. That must be is new mistress!"

"You're wrong. It's her all right. Look at that hair!"

"But—why, she's positively *graceful!*"

As they descended the last step, Saxon took his lady's hand, squeezed it reassuringly, and dazzled her with his sweet, mocking grin. "Welcome to your first ball, Cinderella."

She realized with a rush of happiness that her situation was, indeed, akin to that in the fairy tale. And the man she loved had made it all come true for her. She looked up at him, the emeralds in her eyes lost in the diamonds of her tears.

He had never seen such unmitigated joy on anyone's face. He prayed he would be able to give her a whole lifetime more of it.

"Good evenin', sir," Chickadee said when a man stopped to stare at her. Gracefully, she gave him her hand and waited for him to kiss it. When he hesitated, her eyebrow rose. "Sir, ain't you gwine kiss my hand? It's what yore s'posed ter do, y'know."

The man snapped out of his daze. "Of course," he said and pressed his lips to the top of her hand. "How rude of me to forget. But your loveliness disarmed me. I assume this beautiful girl is your wife, Saxon? The famous Chickadee?"

Saxon's smile was afire with pride. "She is indeed, Professor Wells. Keely, Professor Wells was my mathematics teacher long ago. Uh, he taught me how to work with numbers," he added in case she didn't understand.

"Numbers, huh? T. J. Howe larnt me numbers. He don't know a lot about figgerin', but he knows enough. I larnt real good too. When I go ter sell galax and sang back home, them buyers is allus a-tryin' ter cheat me. But I don't never let'em."

Professor Wells had no idea what sang was. He chuckled. "I'm sure you don't. I'm surprised your buyers would even have the nerve to try!"

Chickadee smiled, batted her lashes a few times, and then raised her silk fan so that it covered her chin. "Yore very kind, kind sir."

"And you are kind too, kind lady," the professor said and winked at Saxon.

They chatted for a short while, and when the professor left them, Saxon kissed Chickadee's nose. "You're doing splendidly, little one. Professor Wells was quite impressed."

Encouraged by his compliment, Chickadee was anxious to meet more people. She was congenial with each person she met and pleased when her friendliness was returned. Saxon saw no need to inform her that the people he was introducing to her lived too far out of Boston to have heard the gossip about her, and only hoped their acceptance of her would lead the rest of society to do likewise.

"Saxon!" Eugenia gushed as she hurried toward them.

Saxon bent and kissed her cheek. "You're looking well, Mrs. Preston. You've met my wife, Keely, have you not?"

"It's a pleasure to see you again, my dear," she said to Chickadee. "I was unable to come to your sled race. As for the other assemblies you attended . . . why, you popped in and out of them so quickly, I could never quite catch up with you! You've no idea how I've been looking forward to this night and the chance to know you better."

Chickadee's eyes widened. *This* was Eugenia Preston? Why, this was the woman she'd threatened at the sewing get-together! The same woman Saxon said ran everything in Boston. Well, maybe it wasn't too late to mend things.

"Mighty obliged fer the invite, Miz Preston. Real thoughty o' you ter thank of us. I ain't never been ter no party like this one, and I'm sartin, withouten nary a doubt I'm gwine have a larripin' good time."

"We all will," Eugenia replied, her gray eyes glowing with excitement. "Now, if you will excuse me, I must see to the receiving line. The duke of Amherst is here, as I'm sure you know. Saxon, Chickadee must meet him. The line will be over there." She gestured toward a long marble wall and scurried away, her step light and happy.

Saxon watched as the throng of guests rushed to get in line, everyone anxious to be formally introduced to the duke. "Keely, the line of people waiting to meet Lord Cavendish is very long, and it'll be a while before it's our turn. Why don't you sit down for a few minutes, and I'll bring you your first taste of champagne?"

She glanced at the line and saw Bunny in it. How beautiful Bunny was tonight! It was quite obvious she'd lost weight. And there was Max too, grinning crookedly and looking as handsome as ever. But . . . but he was with Cynthia, of all people! Chickadee seethed but managed to control herself. The evening was young yet, she remembered mischievously. There was still plenty of time to set things right for Bunny.

She allowed Saxon to escort her to a chair. As he walked away in search of that drink he said she'd like, she watched how easy and elegant his stride was. The thought of his tender concern warmed her all over. Oh, what a wonderful feeling it was to know he cared about her feelings and that it infuriated him when people scorned her. He'd done everything possible to keep that from happening to her tonight, and she would not let him down. She would remember everything he taught her.

Smiling, she bent to sniff the huge flower arrangement beside her, but as she savored its perfume, she became aware of another odor. Her nostrils quivered. It wasn't an unpleasant scent, but what on earth was it?

Smoke. *Law, is the house on fire?* She stood quickly and followed her nose. When she was out of the ballroom, she closed the doors to it to keep the odor from disturbing the other guests. After walking down a long corridor, she turned a corner and came to another hallway. She continued down it until the smell became stronger and led her to another door. She flung it open, and her eyes widened at the sight before her.

It was the kitchen, and it was filled with smoke. Something was burning to a crisp, and no one was doing the slightest thing about it. Chickadee raced inside. "What are you-uns a-doin'?" she shouted at the three men who were sitting at a table in the far corner. All she got in reply was a wave and two silly grins.

Her eyes watering, Chickadee tore around the kitchen until she found the source of all the smoke—

an oven. She grabbed a thick cloth and tried to remove the sizzling pot, but it was too hot to handle even with the cloth. Not knowing what else to do, she picked up a large bucket of water and tossed it into the blazing oven.

After fanning the air, she bent and saw a huge, black piece of meat as well as several other hunks of charred food. Then she saw that the other pots and kettles in the kitchen were smoking also. *Lord o' mercy, the whole meal is burning!* She splashed water everywhere, and when she had no more to throw, she began to beat frantically at the ever-growing flames that came from all four hearths.

When the blaze burned no longer, Chickadee stormed toward the three men who still sat there, smiling happily. "What the hell's the matter with you-uns a-lettin' me put out them fars withouten nary a bit o' hep?"

They seemed not to hear her, but only lifted their cups and downed the contents with great slurping sounds.

Snockered! They were as drunk as boiled owls, she realized. So dang pickled, they would have let the whole house burn down around their ears! She gasped. There was only one kind of whiskey in the world that could make a man *that* senseless.

George Franklin's.

She snatched a cup from one of the men. "Mademoiselle!" he shrieked at her, standing and swaying.

"Don't you be a-callin' me no names!" she blasted and pushed him back into the chair. Shakily, she took a sip of the fiery brew and knew it was none other than mountain corn liquor. But how had these men gotten hold of it?

"Sweet Mary above, what has happened in me kitchen!" a woman yelled from the doorway as she scanned the horrible mess in her once immaculate workplace.

"Who are you?" Chickadee asked, unconsciously wiping her greasy hands on the front of her gown.

The woman began to cry. "I'm Mrs. Preston's cook. She gave me the night off, that she did, sayin' those chefs were to prepare the dinner. And look what's happened, lass! Ach, dearest mother o' God, me kitchen! 'Tis destroyed!"

Chickadee tried to soothe the distraught woman. "Whar'd them men git that likker?"

"Liquor?" The woman looked baffled.

But Chickadee's confusion was dissipating rapidly. "Yore Irish, ain't you?"

"Aye. Bridget Rafferty's me name."

"Rafferty? You kin ter Killian?"

"He's me brother. Do ye know him?"

Chickadee nodded and looked at the three chefs again. "And I got me a feelin' them men over thar do too."

Bridget glanced at the Frenchmen and saw the jug they were still passing around. She blanched. "Faith, 'tis Killian's whiskey, to be sure! A fine nerve he has to be bringin' it here!"

"He didn't bring it," said a voice from the doorway. Chickadee turned to see a young lad whose coloring proclaimed his Irish heritage. " 'Twas meself who brought it. I've seen Mrs. Preston sippin' wine, Bridget, and ye said yerself Killian's whiskey is the finest ye've tasted. I only thought to gift the good Mrs. Preston with it."

Bridget's pale face turned red. "Gift her with homemade whiskey, Nevin? Saints preserve us! Do ye have any idea what yer *gift* has done tonight?"

"He yore brother too?" Chickadee smiled at the boy.

"Aye. Mrs. Preston hired him on as a stableboy a few weeks ago. Nevin, do ye have any idea what ye've done, lad?" Bridget repeated and began to weep again.

Nevin too started to cry. Chickadee watched for a few moments and then laughed. "You-uns is somethin' else," she said merrily, pushing up her satin sleeves as far as they would go. "A-cryin' over somethin' as silly as this."

Bridget looked at her with wide, red eyes. "But 'tis furious Mrs. Preston will be! The people out there, they'll be wantin' their dinner, and we've naught to give them!"

"Miz Preston ain't gwine be riled at you, Bridget. You didn't have nothin' ter do with this. And a-seein' as how Nevin over thar's jist a young-un, she cain't fault him none neither. It's them furriners who's ter blame. They didn't have ter drank whilst they was a-cookin'. But they did, and now thur so dang wet that iffen you was ter go over thar and blow on'em, they'd ripple."

"But the dinner—'tis ruined, miss . . ."

"Chickadee Blackwell. Now, 'pears to me that you and me orter quit a-geein' and a-hawin' and commence a-cookin'!"

"But there's nae enough time! Nae plannin' has been—"

"You aimin' ter let Miz Preston down? You want her ter be embarrassed over all this?"

"No, but—"

"Then let's git ter work. We can still git supper iffen we commence a-makin' it right now. Now, show me what other kinds o' vittles you got around here."

"Linguistics," Lord Cavendish said. "When my wife died, I was already an old man, Mr. Blackwell. Too old to become accustomed to another woman. And so I took the passion I had left and gave it to linguistics, the study of speech."

"Linguistics?" Saxon repeated and looked over his shoulder again. Where the hell had Chickadee run off to? She'd been missing for an eternity! "Uh, will you excuse me, Lord—"

"Languages, dialects . . . I've been studying them for years," the duke informed him, so engrossed in his own conversation he never heard Saxon's plea for release. "My favorite is Elizabethan English. Extraordinarily interesting. I find it so pure, so picturesque."

"What? English, you say?" Saxon asked, his gaze sweeping every inch of the ballroom for his wayward spitfire.

"Dinner is served," a stone-faced butler announced loudly and gestured toward the dining room doors.

"Saxon," Eugenia said as she joined him and the duke, "where is Chickadee? She's not gone, is she?"

"I'm sure she'll be along any moment, Mrs. Preston," he tried to reassure his hostess and himself. "She's probably off in some far corner mingling with the guests." Yes, that's it, he told himself firmly. She's a grand success, and her time is being monopolized by all the people she's impressed.

But if that were true, why was he so worried?

Eugenia glanced around the room. "Well, I suppose that could be so. Or perhaps she's already in the dining room. Shall we go see?" She took the duke's proffered arm and Saxon followed.

But much to his dismay, Chickadee was not in the dining room. "Mrs. Preston, will you excuse me for a few minutes? It could be that Keely is exploring your gardens. I realize it's cold outside, but she has this need for air, you see."

"By all means go and look for her, Saxon," Eugenia agreed. "Without her, Lord Cavendish will be denied a very entertaining dinner partner: she's to sit next to him."

Gilford wondered just how boring this Mrs. Blackwell would be. He stifled the urge to look at his watch again.

"Git yore hands offen me!"

Hester refused to relinquish her hold on Chickadee's arm. "Shhh! Keep your voice down! You're a fright, and the duke is over there! You simply cannot—"

"I can do anythang iffen it dang well pleasures me ter do it! And iffen you don't git yore hands offen me, I'm gwine give you a pain so deep, you ain't even gwine be able ter figger out whar it is, lady!"

One sight of Chickadee was all Saxon needed to know his plan had gone awry.

Her hair was one hopeless copper tangle. Her emerald tiara hung from one side of her head. From bodice to hem, her gold satin gown was blotched with black smudges, and one of her sleeves seemed to be scorched. There was some kind of white powder all over her face.

A painful lump leaped into his throat, but he did his best to swallow it down. If there was any way to do it, he had to try to save the situation. To accept defeat now would mean sending her home. Surely she had a good reason for being so disheveled, he rationalized desperately. People simply did not get into that kind of mess without cause.

Of course, Chickadee was not just any person. He grimaced at that thought and started for her, his mind reeling with possible ways to smooth things over.

Lord Cavendish caught his arm. "Who is that girl, Mr. Blackwell?"

Saxon smiled a bittersweet smile. "That's my wife. The most beautiful, unpredictable girl God ever created."

"Saxon, this heifer says I cain't be here no more!" Chickadee exclaimed when he'd reached her. "She don't got no right ter tell me that, huh? I mean, it ain't her ball, it's Miz Preston's."

"It's *your* ball, little one," he said quietly and gave Hester such a glare that she shrank back. "And you've every right to be here. But what have you been doing? Rolling in the dirt?"

"What?"

"You're a tad filthy. Come, I'll take you upstairs where you can clean up." Ignoring the staring guests, he started to lead her away, determined to find out what she'd been doing so he could think of a way to mend things.

"Dang it, Saxon, wait! I ain't met the duke yet!"

"Go and calm her down, Saxon," Hester commanded.

"I don't need no calmin' down, Hester. Yore the one who's so dang fitified."

Hester lifted her chin. "I only sought to—"

"Oh hesh up, lady. I ain't gwine argufy with you about it. You was a-takin' on like all git out. A-shakin' yore head like some dog a-killin' snakes when I tried ter—"

"Merciful heavens, what is this?" Sarah Bancroft twittered, panic-stricken as she saw the many platters the servants were uncovering. "Where is the stuffed trout? The chilled oysters! The roast—"

"Burnt up," Chickadee announced. "Well, them orsters warn't burnt, but me and Bridget tuk'em and made soup outen'em. And them furrin cooks had some sorter bread a-bakin', but it warn't fittin' ter eat. So we made biscuit-breads. Bridget was a-wantin' ter use butter in 'em, but I tole her thur ain't nothin' like pure hog lard fer the God-burnin'est best biscuits thur is."

Sarah clutched at her bosom. "Hog? My chefs—"

"And me and Bridget cut offen the burnt part o' the meat and used the middle part of it," Chickadee continued. "Made a stew outen it. That fish was a mite done too, but we saved it by a-makin' fish cakes outen it. They ain't real fancy, but they eat good. And thur's tater pie too. We made duck and dumplin's outen the roast ducks. I ain't never et duck with dumplin's, but the way I see it, it prob'ly don't differ too much from chicken. Fried up a mess o' apple rangs too."

Sarah's eyes were so wide it seemed they would fly out of her head any moment. "What have you done to my chefs!"

Eugenia rushed to Sarah and put her arm around

the hysterical woman's shoulder. "Sarah, you are shouting, my dear. Creating a scene. Please take your seat, and we will proceed with dinner."

"But . . . but what has happened to my chefs?"

"They been a-drankin'," Chickadee answered.

Sarah gasped and swayed. "They're intoxicated?"

"Lady, thur so snockered that iffen mosquiters was ter bite'em the mosquiters'd need a chaser."

Before anyone was able to rise from their chairs, Sarah had fainted dead away, her form a silken lump on the floor. At Eugenia's request, a few of the men carried her to a bedroom upstairs.

Saxon looked at Chickadee, unsure whether he should thank her or upbraid her; whether he should enfold her in his arms or strangle her. He understood clearly she'd only been trying to help, but he was also aware that despite her good intentions, she'd lost points with the unyielding members of society. Her success tonight was now hanging by a thread.

At his obvious dismay, Eugenia cleared her throat loudly. "Everything looks and smells simply delicious. We all owe you a tremendous debt of gratitude, Chickadee. It's obvious you and Bridget worked very hard preparing this meal for us. Come now, my dear. I've placed you and Saxon over here with Lord Cavendish."

Chickadee allowed Eugenia to take her hand but stopped when she saw Max at a nearby table. He was sitting next to Cynthia, and Bunny was at another table, seated between two old grandsires. "Miz Preston, I know this is yer ball-party and all, but would it ill you iffen I was ter change this here settin' arrangement?"

"But don't you want to sit by Lord Cavendish?"

"Oh shore. I'll set by him," Chickadee returned, wondering which of the many men staring at her was the Englishman. "That ain't the change I want ter make."

"It's not your place to change anything," Hester flared. "Eugenia has already—"

"Nonsense," Eugenia cut her off. "I owe Chickadee thanks for saving the dinner. The very least I can do is allow her to make whatever changes she wishes."

Having been given permission, Chickadee smiled smugly at Hester and then went to Max's table. "Git up, Cynthia."

Cynthia withered in her chair. "But . . . but I don't want to change seats with anyone." She smiled up at Max, her eyes begging him to assist her.

But Max was grinning at Chickadee and wondering what she was up to. He'd been glad to have been seated by the lovely Cynthia, but the green twinkle in Chickadee's eyes made her plans for him seem much more amusing.

"You ain't a-settin' by Max, Cynthia. Yore cousin Bunny's gwine set here with him." She looked up and caught her friend's surprised gaze. "Bunny, come on over here."

Bunny blushed deeply, but realizing it would do little good to argue with Chickadee, she went to Max's table.

"Now git up, Cynthia," Chickadee repeated. "Git up or I'll—"

"I'll see you after dinner, Max," Cynthia blurted, her ivory complexion splotched with fiery red as she went to the chair Bunny had vacated.

Once Bunny was seated beside Max, Chickadee proceeded to her own chair. "You the duke?" she asked the man who was standing by Saxon. "The feller all this frolickin's gwine on fer?" When he nodded, she picked up his hand, pumping it vigorously. And then, remembering Saxon's instructions to be extra polite to Lord Cavendish, she reached out and slapped the duke's back as good friends often do.

A loud, horrified gasp rose from the crowd, many

people shaking their heads, others covering their faces with their napkins. Some even slithered from their chairs as if they wanted nothing more than to hide beneath the table, embarrassed no end that the duke was being treated in such a fashion.

"I heared yore a lord, but you ain't *my* Lord," Chickadee continued. "I'll be nice ter you and all that, but I ain't s'posed ter bow ter you or nothin', am I? Cain't do that, y'know, Mr. Duke. Cain't do it on account o' I don't bow ter nobody but God, and you ain't Him."

Lord Cavendish frowned fiercely. The ripple of whispers in the room gave way to an ominous hush as Time itself seemed suspended.

Then, his deep brown eyes closing, his lips twitching, the duke of Amherst threw back his head and laughed out loud.

Chapter 21

After a dessert of warm oatmeal cookies, the guests returned to the ballroom. Araminta, however, lingered in the dining room, Thelma, Hester, Eleanor, and Millicent circled around her. The four matrons were still chilly toward her, but as Araminta unfolded her seemingly infallible plan, they all listened avidly.

"Queen Eugenia has lost her crown tonight, ladies," she said. "Society cannot, *must not* ever forgive her for condoning that mountain twit's behavior."

Thelma fiddled with her ruby ring. "But the duke—"

"His grace's exquisite manners are the sole reason for his congeniality to that girl," Araminta injected smoothly. "He cannot very well show his real feelings if he believes that hill person is accepted here."

"True," Hester whispered thoughtfully.

Araminta slid her cane through her fingers. "And even if he *were* drawn to her for some ridiculous reason, Lord Cavendish does not live here. He will be departing for England soon."

"We, unfortunately, must stay and endure her," Millicent hissed. "For though she seems to have changed in some subtle ways, she remains as uncivilized as she was the day she arrived. When she slapped the duke's back . . . well, I almost died! And Saxon doesn't appear to be the least ruffled over—"

"Saxon," Araminta broke in, "believes he has made a lady of her. He has spent hours trying to educate her. He sees this night as her debut or some such nonsense, and hopes it will mean her acceptance into society. I'm sure none of you want that to happen."

"But how can we prevent it?" Thelma asked.

"There really are people besides Eugenia who seem to be warming toward her," Eleanor whined. "I heard several guests talking about her beauty and grace. And many people enjoyed that crude meal she made."

"We will bring about her failure ourselves and prove to everyone she is unworthy of their approval," Araminta announced. "And we will use Saxon to do it."

The women frowned in confusion.

"What is the one thing that girl has expressly forbidden us to do?" Araminta slyly asked.

The matrons frowned again.

"Hasn't she threatened to . . . *meller* each of us if we dare blacken Saxon's name?" Araminta reminded them and smiled when the women nodded. "Then we shall goad her into it. We shall—"

"You mean let her hit us?" Eleanor asked, shocked.

"I doubt it will come to that," Araminta said and tapped her brooch. "I believe all she will do is abuse us verbally. And we will push her into losing her temper by slandering Saxon. Oh, I realize it will take some time to do since he has drilled all those manners into her, but I cannot believe he has changed her through and through. She became aggravated with you at dinner, didn't she, Hester?"

Hester raised her chin. "That little heathen—"

"Exactly my point," Araminta said. "Beneath her elegant exterior, there still lies a heathen. Her natural tendencies will overpower her newly learned social graces, and once people witness the fit she'll throw, they'll realize she is unworthy of—"

"But Araminta," Millicent interrupted, "if people hear us trying to annoy her, they won't blame her for her reaction. Why, they may defend her right to be angry!"

"Not if our insults are for her ears only," Araminta explained. "You see, we must whisper them to her in passing. We can catch her when she's alone for a moment, or when she's walking by. Any time will do as long as there is no one else around to hear. And once we've planted the seeds of wrath in her mind, we'll rush away before she has time to retaliate. If we can keep her simmering throughout the evening, I am certain she will explode before the night is over. No one will understand her sudden rage, and all will condemn her violent behavior!"

"And if she accuses us of provoking her," Thelma ventured, "we will act as innocent as newborn babies. No one will believe her. Society has known *us* longer that it has known *her.*"

"Besides that," Eleanor said, "most everyone has heard the gossip about her anyway. And as for those who have not, we can make sure they hear it tonight. Everyone will think about her past behavior, add it to what she does this evening, and that will be the end of her!"

The matrons smiled at Araminta and gathered close to perfect the plan that would bring about the downfall of the Appalachian princess.

Saxon, blithely unaware of the vicious scheming taking place mere yards from where he stood, was again searching for Chickadee. She'd mumbled something about a surprise for him, and before he'd understood what she meant, she'd disappeared into the crowd. He strode across the marble room, his anticipation and apprehension rising steadily.

But when he finally found her, saw the new arrival she was escorting into the ballroom, his anxiety was replaced with astonishment. His legs might as well have turned to stone, for he could not move them. The other guests were still also, every pair of eyes in the room directed at Chickadee and the young woman she was embracing.

The girl was beautiful, her loveliness rivaling that of any woman in the room. She wore a dazzling gown of violet silk that matched her eyes perfectly. Her ebony hair was arranged in tiny ringlets, some swept up to the top of her head to form a soft bed for her crown of flowers, the rest cascading to her alabaster shoulders.

Desdemona.

As his sister floated toward him, Saxon tried to swallow but discovered his throat was as paralyzed as his legs. Why had he never noticed Desdemona's elegance or her arresting features? Was this vision really the painfully shy and reclusive Desdemona?

"Well, Saxon," Chickadee said, "what do you thank about this purty little surprise I had Candy brang fer you?"

"I . . . Desdemona, I can't believe it's really you," Saxon stammered, his eyes widening when he saw his sister blush. Blushing, of all things! This girl who never spoke, who rarely showed emotion, was actually blushing!

"Now go on, Desi," Chickadee prompted.

Desdemona found the encouragement she sought in the mountain girl's sparkling eyes. Her own eyes fluttered closed briefly before she reached for Saxon's hand, squeezed it gently, and gave him a tremendous smile.

Chickadee laughed at Saxon's disbelief. "Lord o' mercy, outlander, yore shet up tighter'n a mornin' glory! Ain't you gwine say nothin'?"

"Does . . . does she talk too?"

"We ain't got that fur yet, but we're a-workin' on it, ain't that right, Desi?"

To Saxon's utter amazement, Desdemona nodded. "Keely, how did you do this? What have you been doing? How—"

"Been a-spendin' ever' bit o' time I can with her, outlander. I talk and talk and talk ter her. We near about finished that quilt we been a-makin', and I sang to her whilst we're a-sewin' on it. It don't really matter what all you do with her as long as you do it. She likes ever'thang.'' She patted Desdemona's cheek. ''All right now, Desi, what'd I tell you ter do next?''

Desdemona turned to look at the dance floor and trembled slightly before she walked toward it, pulling Saxon behind her. Then she looked back at Chickadee and grinned at what her sister-in-law was doing.

Chickadee, in an effort to remind Desdemona of what she was supposed to do, was holding out her arms as if there were a man enfolded between them. She waltzed alone, oblivious to the snickers around her, and was intent on urging Desdemona to copy her actions.

And Desdemona took the cue, slipping her arms around Saxon and moving her feet to the rhythm of the music. Her concentration was evident in her stiff body and in the way she bent her head to watch what her feet were doing.

When he realized how hard she was trying, Saxon snapped out of his silent awe and lifted her chin. ''Let me see your face, sweetheart. Just look at me and let me do all the work.'' His heart did a flip-flop when she nodded and, ever so slowly, slid her hand up his neck to rest it on his cheek.

Immediately, he stopped dancing. ''You remember,'' he whispered. ''Your hand . . . on my cheek. You loved to put it there when you were a child.''

She smiled, her eyes bright with emotion.

''Oh, Desdemona,'' was all he could manage to say. Holding her close, he swept her across the marble floor, his mind swirling with joy at this wonderful change in her.

Chickadee watched them with the same joy. But her pleasure faded when Hester sidled up to her.

''He looks ridiculous out there,'' the woman said too softly for anyone but Chickadee to hear. ''A waltz should be danced slowly. Saxon looks like he's dancing a jig. Ridiculous. Simply ridiculous." With that, Hester scurried away.

Chickadee started after her but thought better of it. Saxon had warned her about keeping her temper, and that was exactly what she would try to do. Still, it was only with extreme effort that she managed to subdue her anger.

"You've wrought a miracle in Desdemona," Bunny said as she joined Chickadee. "I never believed I'd see what I'm seeing now."

"Desi don't differ from nobody else, Bunny," Chickadee said, still glaring at Hester's retreating back. "She jist needed love and a jag o' pushin' in the right direction."

Bunny's eyes embraced her friend. "I don't imagine Desdemona will ever forget this night, nor will I. I admit I was flustered when you made Cynthia change seats with me, but thanks to you, Max and I got to know one another. We've much in common. We like the same writers, plays, and performers, and we both enjoy composing our own poetry!"

Chickadee nodded in satisfaction. "He say anythang about a-wantin' ter see you agin?"

"Well, he complimented me on my weight loss and asked me how I'd done it. I told him about all the long, brisk walks you and I have been taking, and we plan to take one together tomorrow in the Common! All thanks to you."

"Bunny, you done it all yoresef. You wanted ter shed that lard, so you jist got ter work and shed it."

As the song ended, Bunny went in search of Max, and Chickadee clapped wildly for Desdemona and Saxon.

"You should pat your hands together lightly when applauding," Millicent said quietly over Chickadee's shoulder. "Didn't that imbecile you married teach you anything?"

Chickadee gasped but bit back her hot retort as she watched Millicent melt into the crowd. When she turned around again, she saw Saxon and Desdemona coming toward her.

"Did you see Desdemona out there, Keely? Oh, little one," Saxon whispered, bursting with the need to tell her of his love, "you've no idea how much I—"

"Lord o' mercy, Desi!" Chickadee shouted, reaching out to steady the girl who'd become as white as the alabaster pillar beside her. "You this weared out after jist one dance? Hep me git her ter a char, Saxon."

As he led his trembling sister to the row of chairs, Saxon was reminded once again how very frail she was. She would undoubtedly take sick from all the excitement of tonight and have to swallow gallons of her medicines to be well again. Dammit, every time he wanted to tell Chickadee how he felt about her, something happened to stop him!

Still, the night wasn't over yet, and she was behaving quite nicely, he reminded himself as he watched her fuss over Desdemona. His plan could still end in victory.

"Desi's gwine be jist fine, Saxon. But she don't need ter dance no more. You jist set right here and watch me and yore big brother, Desi, hear?" She patted Desdemona's shoulder and then grabbed Saxon's hand.

She began to waltz before they'd reached the dance floor, and Saxon was hard-pressed to keep from jostling people as Chickadee swirled him into the midst of the other dancers. "Keely, you're supposed to let me lead."

"Why do menfolks allus git ter do ever'thang and women jist got ter set by and let 'em? I can lead jist as good as you can."

"But the man is the one—" Saxon laughed down at her and then pulled her closer. She wore no perfume, he noticed, but her scent was sweeter than any in the room.

"Mr. Duke! Mr. Duke!" Chickadee yelled, her

voice so loud it overwhelmed the music. "I ain't danced with the duke yet, Saxon." She left his arms and rushed toward Lord Cavendish.

Heads turned to stare at her. Saxon felt that lump in his throat again as he followed and promptly lost her.

"Your gown is gorgeous, Chickadee," Eleanor said when Chickadee was near her.

Chickadee stopped and looked at the woman.

"Or it least it *was*," Eleanor added softly. "Now it's nothing more than a rag, soiled and scorched. Saxon was stupid not to take you home. I cannot imagine why he is allowing you to remain at the ball looking as you do. It is apparent to me he has lost what little wits he used to have before marrying you."

Chickadee panted with outrage, then shuddered with her attempt to subdue it.

"Did I hear you calling me, Mrs. Blackwell?" Lord Cavendish asked as the crowd parted to make way for him.

Anger boiling inside her, Chickadee watched Eleanor escape. With a sigh, she turned her attention to Lord Cavendish. "Mr. Duke, you and me ain't danced yet. Saxon larnt me with a tablecloth, and I don't hardly never step on toes. Ain't that right, Saxon?" she asked her husband, who had finally caught up with her.

Lord Cavendish chuckled. "Mr. Blackwell, will you do me the honor of allowing me to dance with your wife?"

"I will indeed, your grace. There is no greater honor I could do you." After giving Chickadee a silent look of warning, he bowed and left the floor.

"Yore a right common man, Mr. Duke," Chickadee told Lord Cavendish as he whirled her away. "I know yore somebody important back thar acrost the ocean-sea whar you come from, but you shore don't put on the dog about nothin'."

"Put on the dog," the duke repeated thoughtfully

and then winced when she stepped on his foot. "Am I correct in assuming that expression means I don't put on airs?"

"Call it whatever strikes yore fancy, but yore a real nice man, and I'm God-proud ter know you."

"As I am to know you. You are exactly what I thought all Americans were like, and you've brought zest to an affair I would otherwise have found boring and tedious."

"You don't like these ball-parties?"

"I detest them."

"It's this slow music, ain't it? Don't got much of a beat ter it like the fiddle music my neighbor George Franklin plays at home in the Blue Ridge. You ever hear good fiddle music, Mr. Duke? Do you-uns play it over thar in Angland?"

He smiled at the way she pronounced the name of his country. "I've heard violin music like what these musicians here are playing, but I seriously doubt it's anything like what your George Franklin plays. It's a real shame he's not here to play for us. I would have enjoyed that immensely."

Chickadee looked at the musicians, for the first time noticing their violins did indeed resemble George Franklin's fiddles. But could they be made to sound like fiddles too?

There was only way she knew of to find out.

"You want ter hear fiddle music, I'll make shore you hear it, Mr. Duke. Them *violins* them musicianers is a-playin' ain't nothin' but fancified fiddles, the way I see it. Go grab yoresef a woman and git set ter hear the toe-tappin'est music you ever did hear!" With that, she left the duke and walked quickly toward the orchestra.

"Yes, I agree with you, Thelma," Millicent said when Chickadee was within hearing distance. Swiftly, she moved away from the other guests, closer to Chickadee. "Saxon was quite the fool to believe he could make that hill person into a lady."

"Well, he was *always* a fool, Millicent," Thelma

agreed quietly. "That yokel he married simply made him *more* of one!"

Wrath rumbled through Chickadee. She turned toward the two women behind her, only to discover they'd vanished. Her gaze swept the ballroom in search of them, but it found Lord Cavendish instead. The sight of him reminded her of what she'd told him she'd do, and she waved her arms in front of the musicians, gesturing for them to cease playing.

Lord Cavendish went to Eugenia Preston and whispered into her ear. She laughed into her hands. "Ladies and gentlemen," she called loudly. "Chickadee Blackwell is going to entertain us with the music she enjoys in her mountains. Please select a dance partner!"

Many guests shook their heads at Eugenia's unseemly behavior. Nevertheless, there was soon a large crowd of couples on the dance floor. It would never do to disobey their hostess, even if it appeared she *had* tossed her wits to the wind.

Araminta and her cronies were delighted their scheme had begun so smoothly and that Chickadee herself was unknowingly helping them with it. Imagine a guest taking over the orchestra! they exclaimed to each other. Surely this was but the start of the mountain girl's ill-mannered antics!

Saxon, as he watched Chickadee take a violin from one of the musicians, pulled at his suddenly strangling collar. "During all the long hours I tutored her," he murmured to Desdemona, "I . . . well, I never thought to tell her not to rob the orchestra of its job!"

Eugenia came up behind him in time to hear his words. "I think it's perfectly delightful, Saxon."

He clasped her hand warmly. "Would you care to dance, Mrs. Preston?"

"Why, I would adore it! But I will have to wait for the next song, my dear. I hate to miss a single note of Chickadee's music, but one of my maids just informed me that poor Sarah Bancroft is completely beside herself. I'm on my way upstairs to bring her a whiskey. She *does* drink whiskey, you know. On the sly, of course.''

Saxon laughed as she hurried away, but his grin became a scowl when Araminta joined him. "You married a moron, Saxon. Look at her up there with the musicians!''

He forced himself to face her malevolent glare, the one that had always frightened him as a boy, that still brought back the horrible memory of those years. "Grandmother,'' he seethed, his hands aching to choke her withered neck, "one more word, and—''

"Saxon!'' Cynthia exclaimed, slipping her arm around his waist when she arrived at his side.

Saxon's eyes widened at the strong odor coming from her. It wasn't champagne, he knew. It was bourbon. She smelled as if she'd bathed in the stuff.

"You haven't danced with me at all, you devil!'' she admonished him. "Come, let's join the others. This dance, I imagine, will be most interesting.'' She pulled him toward the dance floor. Saxon did not object, knowing if he didn't leave Araminta, he would soon be arrested for murder.

From the platform, Chickadee observed the way Cynthia was pressing herself against Saxon, but his obvious irritation told her he wasn't enjoying Cynthia hanging all over him. She smiled at her audience, brought the bow to the violin, tapped her foot three times, and began to play.

She closed her eyes and let her music fill her. She remembered George Franklin instructing her to *feel* the music, to let her emotions and instincts play rather than her fingers. The violin seemed to come alive in her hands, the Scotch-Irish melody she played twisting and changing in rhythm. It sang slowly, sweetly, and hauntingly, and then switched to a sound so happy, so overwhelmingly joyful, Max and Bunny began to clap their hands.

Cynthia's hands, however, were otherwise occupied. When Chickadee opened her eyes again, the first thing she saw was Cynthia's cloud-white fingers curling into Saxon's black hair. Instantly, she stopped playing. The guests looked at her, baffled by her angry expression, then followed her line of vision to Cynthia.

Cynthia shrank back as Chickadee bolted from the platform and stormed toward her. "Saxon, for God's sake, don't let her touch me! Look at her! She's going to—"

"I been a-watchin' you ternight, Cynthia," Chickadee hissed, all memory of proper etiquette disappearing beneath the weight of her tremendous fury. "You commenced with Max, and when you couldn't git him, you went ter ever' other man here. You been on more laps than a napkin, and now yore a-tryin' ter git Saxon! You better git them twitchy breeches of yores away—"

"Keely," Saxon intervened gently. "Please—"

"I ain't afeared of you, Cynthia. You touch Saxon one more time, and I'll meller you so bad, you'll look like you been a-chawin' bakker and a-spittin' in the wind!"

Cynthia angrily looked to Araminta and the other influential matrons for support but saw only slow-spreading smiles on their powdered faces. Why, the bitches were actually *enjoying* her embarrassing predicament! No longer able to control her hatred and jealousy of Chickadee, and bolstered by the strong liquor still flowing through her, she lunged toward her rival.

But the mountain girl, who could have easily subdued Cynthia, merely stepped aside, grabbing the top of Cynthia's elaborate hairdo. To Cynthia's utter horror, her hairpiece came off in Chickadee's hand. Cynthia covered the sparse, mousy-brown strings of hair that straggled around her scarlet face as best she could and raced from the room, stumbling over her own feet in her haste to disappear.

When she was gone, Chickadee looked at the wig in her hand and then glanced up at Saxon. "I swear I didn't mean ter snatch her bald, outlander."

"I know, Keely," he said quietly.

The sadness in his voice almost killed her. She'd made a terrible mistake. She shouldn't have gotten so riled at Cynthia. It was just that when it came to anything concerning Saxon, she could barely control her temper.

The duke, who had been resisting the urge to laugh, clapped to break the tense silence. "An unfortunate occurrence, but what's done is done, is it not? Please, Mrs. Blackwell, let us continue with the dancing, shall we?" He took the wig from her and deposited it in the hands of a passing waiter.

She regarded him with grateful eyes. "Why don't you commence a-callin' me Chickadee?"

"I'd be honored."

"And what's yore first name?"

The duke entertained an expression of surprise. No one other than old acquaintances had ever presumed they could call him by his first name. "My name is Gilford."

Chickadee's lips twitched merrily. "Gilford? Gilly fits you better. Is Gilly all right with you?"

Araminta smiled when she heard the gasp that rose from the multitude of guests. She watched the men shuffle uneasily, the women fan themselves frantically. She saw Saxon loosen his neckcloth, and knew everyone, most especially her grandson, was dreading the duke's reaction.

"Gilly?" his grace asked and hid his grin while rubbing his chin. "Gilly. Well . . ." His voice trailed off as he repeated the name to himself.

Araminta quickly turned to her four friends. "We've made sure every person here has heard about what that girl has done since her arrival to Boston," she whispered hurriedly. "While we were spreading that gossip round, she took over the orchestra. Then there was the little scene with Cynthia, the wig and Chickadee's hot-tempered threats. I suspect it is no longer necessary for our plan to continue in secret. Everyone in this room has heard about and witnessed her crude behavior. Now, in defense of Lord Cavendish, our guest of honor, don't you think someone should . . . *explain* to the girl that nicknaming a duke is simply not done?''

Millicent smiled spitefully and rushed forward. ''Forgive her, your grace,'' she said to Lord Cavendish. ''As I'm sure you already know, she is not from here and is unfamiliar with our way of life.'' Turning to Chickadee, she said, ''You will call him my lord, your grace, or Lord Cavendish.''

Saxon raised an ebony eyebrow at the malice in Millicent's eyes. ''Mrs. Ashbury, Keely is quite fond of nicknames and means no insult. On the contrary, it has been my observation she only shortens the names of those for whom she feels affection,'' he said to Millicent, hoping the duke would understand.

Millicent's eyebrow rose higher than his. Lord Cavendish, sensing an argument was brewing, started to intervene, but stopped when Chickadee held up her hand to him. ''Millicent—''

''It's *Mrs. Ashbury* to you,'' Millicent said stiffly.

''I think you'd ruther hear me call you Millicent than what I'd *really* like ter call you.''

Millicent gasped and looked at the shocked crowd. ''Did you hear what she said to me?'' she asked the guests, gratified that many of them looked sympathetic.

''Keely,'' Saxon whispered directly into her ear. ''Please calm down.''

Before Chickadee had time to reply, Thelma, nudged onward by Araminta, stepped forward. ''*I* heard what she said, Millicent! Surely she deserves a piece of your mind!''

''Thelma, she cain't spare it,'' Chickadee retorted and swallowed the rest of what she wanted to say.

Eleanor decided to take her turn and went straight to Saxon. ''Saxon, why—''

"Eleanor," Chickadee broke in quickly. "I'm a-warnin'—"

"Keely," Saxon began, "please—"

"Saxon!" Eleanor repeated. "How can you just stand there and let her say these things to us?"

Chickadee had had enough. Her anger raged like a swollen river inside her, and she could no longer keep the flood behind the dam. "Eleanor, I can take whatever sass you flang at me, but you say one ill word ter Saxon, and I'll lay you so low yore socks is gwine blindfold you! You and them other snooty sows been a-starin' at me and Saxon all night. I been a-turnin' a blind eye to it so fur, but—"

Saxon took her arm. "Keely," he whispered. "Remember yourself."

She took a deep breath and held it, hoping it would smother her fury.

"We have not been *staring* at you," Hester chimed in. "We've merely been *observing* you. We all had high hopes when we heard that Saxon was trying to teach you social graces. But after what we have all witnessed tonight, it is apparent that he has—"

The duke cleared his throat loudly. "If I may—"

"Hesh up, Gilly," Chickadee flared, her eyes still fixed on Hester's face, oblivious to the horrified gasps from Eugenia's guests.

"Saxon," Millicent said calmly and confidently, bolstered by the crowd's response. "Your wife's conduct is deplorable, her appearance slovenly, her manner of speech utterly disgusting. You have failed miserably in your efforts with her, and she has succeeded in turning this ball into a circus. Please take her home."

He drew himself up to his full height, his blue eyes flashing. "Mrs. Ashbury—"

"Millicent, yore tongue's so long and sharp you could cut yore own throat with it!" Chickadee shouted. "And you done gone too fur with it now, lady. Either you take back that slur on Saxon, or yer gwine git embrangled with my fists!"

"You wouldn't dare!" Millicent exclaimed, but backed away as Chickadee advanced.

Again, Saxon caught her arm. "All right, Saxon," she said to him sweetly. "I won't bang her up none. Her face already looks like somebody's done hit her with a bagful of pennies, and I ain't a-lookin' ter make her any uglier'n she already is!"

Eleanor shook her finger at Saxon. "This disastrous evening, what is left of it, is on your head. Look at that person you married! Listen to her! How could you bring such a woman to our peaceful city? How—"

"And as fer you, Eleanor," Chickadee said, the green volcanoes in her eyes erupting at this latest slander of Saxon, "you ain't much better lookin' than Millicent! Yore face is so creased, 'pears to me somebody plowed it! The onliest thang on yore face that ain't wrankled is yore mouth, on accounta it's allus stretched open so wide it don't never get no chance ter git no creases. Now, use it ter say yore sorry to Saxon, or I'll find a way to make shore you cain't never open it again!"

Thelma rushed to defend Eleanor. "Now see here—"

"And here we have Thelma," Chickadee interjected smoothly, yanking her arm from Saxon's grasp. "I reckon you thank I ain't fine-haired enough ter be around you Boston folks neither. You-uns is allus a-makin' more noise'n a mule in a tin barn about ever'body's looks and a-doin's. You say Bunny's fat, you say another lady's got on the wrong color, you say so-and-so's a-showin' off with her jewries, and you say Saxon's mizzled fer a-marryin' me! But you don't never take no looks at yoresefs, huh?"

She walked closer to Thelma, so close they were eye to eye. "Thelma, yore eyes is so cross-eyed, I reckon when you cry, yore tears run down yore back! But it don't differ nary a jag that thur messed up, huh, Thelma? Crossed or not, you still see ever' dang-blasted gwine-on you *want* ter see. Why, I reckon ever'body's doin's tickle you more'n they do anybody else on accounta you git ter see 'em *double!*''

Saxon, as dejected as he was at seeing Chickadee's debut end this way, couldn't help but smile. His plan had failed, and there was nothing he could do about it now. These *snooty sows* were getting exactly what they so richly deserved, and though this night would mean Chickadee's return to the Appalachia, he was sadly comforted by the fact that she would be leaving a city that, try as it might, had never beaten her.

Hester noticed his smile and took full advantage of it. ''Saxon, are you as idiotic as this wife of yours, allowing her to insult us like this? Good heavens! Has being with her for so long made you as savage as she?''

Whatever answer he might have given her was lost as Chickadee whirled on Hester. Hester melted into the crowd when she saw Chickadee stalking her.

''Afeared, Hester?'' Chickadee taunted. ''Well you ben a-askin' fer the rope I'm a-fixin' ter hang you with all evenin'. Yore nasty enough to vomit a buzzard, lady. A God-burn stampede cain't run down as many people as you do. And even though yore a-actin' skeered o' this back-cussin' I'm a-givin' you, you ain't really got no reason a'tall ter worry. After all, the onliest thang that gits the last word when yore around is yore echo!''

Exhausted, she panted with fury at all the people who had maligned Saxon's name, who had forced her to forget all the things Saxon had tried to teach her, who continued to hate her despite his best efforts to change their opinions. She was never going to be accepted by these people no matter what Saxon did. All his efforts had been for naught.

And the glimmer of melancholy she saw in his azure eyes echoed that sentiment. She'd let him down. He'd had such high hopes for this night, and those hopes had disappeared like stars falling from the sky. Biting back her tears, she lifted her skirts and left the room with the regal stride of a true princess.

Saxon turned to the silent crowd. "I thought I could make her one of us. I now thank God I failed in such a ridiculous undertaking. My wife is already perfection. I will not apologize for a thing she said or did. In fact, I think I will applaud her," he said and clapped, the noise bouncing off the marble walls for several moments before he went to Desdemona and helped her up. "With or without your leave, I bid you all farewell."

"Saxon, where are you going?" Eugenia queried loudly as she entered the ballroom and saw him leaving. "Where is Chickadee? My goodness, what has happened here?"

He gestured toward the crowd. "Ask them. I'm sure they'll relate every word of the tale as soon as I am gone. Goodbye, and thank you for a lovely— thank you for the invitation."

"Mr. Blackwell, please wait," Lord Cavendish called. "I would like to say a few things I believe you will enjoy hearing." He clasped his hands behind his back and walked among the guests, soon stopping in front of Millicent.

"Mrs. Ashbury," he said in his most imperial tone, "you believe Chickadee's manner of speech to be utterly disgusting? That *is* what you said, is it not?"

His blank expression told her nothing. Was he agreeing with her? "Her grammar is not correct, your grace," she said shakily. "I realize I am not a linguist as you are, but I am educated enough to know—"

"And you, Mrs. Rush." The duke cut off Millicent and went to Thelma. "Do you agree with Mrs. Ashbury?"

Thelma twisted her ruby ring. "I do. The girl has

no idea what proper grammar is. She uses double, triple, *quadruple* negatives in one sentence, and—''

''Yes, she is rather fond of negatives isn't she?'' Lord Cavendish walked to Hester, his mahogany eyes searing into her. ''Mrs. Eliot, what have you to say about Chickadee's speech? Do you feel the same as your friends?''

''Oh, most assuredly, your lordship! The way she speaks—why, it hurts my ears! Her habit of adding *a* in front of some words—like *a-dancing, a-walking*—it is most regrettable you were forced to—''

''My dear lady, I do not allow anyone, save royalty, to *force* me to do anything,'' the duke snapped.

Saxon watched Hester's face fall, and observed that Araminta, Millicent, Eleanor, and Thelma looked disturbed also. In fact, the whole assemblage seemed to be apprehensive. He felt the lash of hope whip through him. The duke was going to defend Chickadee, he realized, but would his defense sway society's opinion? Would it mend the damage done?

Lord Cavendish accepted a glass of champagne from a servant, went to a chair, and sat down. '' 'Thou hast spoken no word all this while, nor understood none neither.' '' He sipped at his champagne, giving his words time to sink in.

His audience was baffled. Why was his lordship speaking in such a fashion? some people whispered to one another.

''A line written by Shakespeare,'' the duke announced. ''A line containing no less than four negatives, if my counting is correct. Our dear Chickadee would say the same line like this—'You ain't said nothin' in a right long spell, and you ain't understood nothin' neither.' ''

No one in the crowd spoke. Saxon knew everyone was waiting for the duke to finish his point, but he himself had already realized what it would be. He smiled broadly.

Araminta looked on with apprehension. Lord Cavendish was standing up for the mountain chit!

Already many guests were gathering around him with great interest, and if the duke succeeded in swaying society's opinion . . . Damn the heathen to hell and back!

" 'Now might I do it pat, now he is a-praying,' " the duke continued. "That was a line from *Hamlet*. Shakespeare, it would seem, spoke much like Chickadee. Is it right for us to condemn speech so closely related to Shakespeare's? Speech, my learned listeners, that is the closest to Elizabethan English I have come across in all my years of studying dialect?"

Max, thoroughly intrigued, stepped forward. "And what of her trouble with diphthongs, your lordship? She cannot seem to say *going* but always says *gwine*."

"Ah, yes," the duke said, nodding his head and smiling. "Let me see if I can think of an example to give you of that." He closed his eyes for a moment and then opened them, their gleam rivaling the lights in the room. "Alexander Pope. I'm sure many of you have read his works. For those of you who have not, let me assure you his poetry is fine indeed.

"One couplet in particular comes to mind," he continued. "It is from 'Essay on Man,' written by Mr. Pope in 1732. It goes: 'In praise so just let every man be joined and fill the general chorus of mankind.' "

He set his glass on the floor and leaned forward. "When I recited that, it didn't rhyme, did it?"

Max shook his head.

The duke smiled. "But Mr. Pope *meant* for it to rhyme, Mr. Jennings. Thus, we must think about the diphthong in *joined*, wouldn't you agree?"

Max nodded.

Again, the duke grinned. "Therefore, we must say *jined* in order for the couplet to rhyme. *Jined* rhymes with *mankind*, and that is how Mr. Pope meant for the words to be pronounced. So you see? Again, we can compare Chickadee's speech patterns to another great writer."

He scanned the doubtful faces in the crowd and saw that many of the guests were still unwilling to give credit where credit was due. But he wasn't through yet. Before he left Boston, he would do all he could for the marvelous mountain girl who had been ridiculed so unjustly.

"I heard Chickadee say the word *argufy*," he pressed on firmly. "That word is archaic. And the word *afeared* dates back to Middle English—the English of about seven hundred years ago. Chickadee's habit of using compound descriptive words such as *biscuit-bread*, *ball-party* and *ocean-sea* is characteristic of Anglo-Saxon English. Chaucer himself used these self-explanatory words. Indeed, in his narrative poem *Beowulf*, you will find the word *un-living* for dead and *bone-box* for body. Do those words not sound like those Chickadee might use?

"And what of her *you-uns*?" he went on relentlessly. "Wouldn't you all agree that *you-uns* sounds suspiciously like the *ye ones* of Chaucer's time? It is apparent to me, as it should be to all of you, that Chickadee's English is purer than that of anyone here, myself included."

He stood and looked at all the faces around him. "I am the duke of Amherst, as you all know. You have all treated me royally, going out of your way to show me the respect you deem I deserve. I am grateful to you all for such. However, though it may be quite rude of me to say this, when I return to my estate in England, it is not this glittering ballroom I will remember. The sophisticated chitchat as well as the elegant music the orchestra performed tonight will all be forgotten."

He smiled. "Instead, I will recall toe-tappin' fiddle songs. And when I remember them, they will bring to mind the beautiful music of mountain speech. A melodic dialect so picturesque, I will carry its sound with me forever. I will always cherish my memories of this night, and never will I forget the Appalachian girl who created them for me."

Chapter 22

As Chickadee left the Preston mansion, she turned, fully expecting to see Saxon behind her. But he was nowhere to be seen. Was he trying to put together the broken pieces of the fairy tale? The question stung her eyes with tears she refused to let fall.

"Chickadee!" Gallagher hurried toward her and kissed her cheek. " 'Twas hoping we'd see ye tonight, we were! And ye look like a princess, aye that ye do, lass!"

"We came to take Bridget and Nevin home, but they're nae ready to leave yet," Killian said, bending to embrace her. "Bridget told us about all ye did with the meal. 'Twould seem yer quick thinkin' saved the night."

Brusquely, she wiped at her eyes. "Killian, I tole you ter be keerful with that low bush lightnin'. I know you didn't know nothin' about Nevin a-takin' it, but—"

"What's this I see, colleen?" Shane asked and brushed a tear from the tip of her nose. "Are ye weepin'?"

The vision she had of him blurred as more tears came to her. "Iffen you-uns got a wagon, will you ride me around fer a while?"

The three men glanced at the mansion, each of them wondering what had gone on inside it to make their dear friend cry. They gathered around her, sur-

325

rounding her within a wall of brawny Irish muscle should she be threatened anew. Together they murmured their assurances they would, indeed, take her anywhere she wished to go.

And when Saxon finally appeared, Desdemona in tow, there was nothing left of her but the gold slipper she'd lost in her haste to be gone.

Desdemona clung to Saxon with every pitiful ounce of strength she possessed during the ride home. She shivered and wept so hard on his shoulder, his heart broke for her. "Desdemona, you'll see Keely soon," he said as tenderly as he knew how. "It could be that she's already home waiting for us. Don't cry anymore, sweetheart."

But when they arrived home and Candice informed them that Chickadee wasn't there, Desdemona's tears increased. She refused to walk and hung on to Saxon as he carried her up the staircase to her room. Her cold hand remained pressed tightly against his cheek, and though Saxon was anxious to go out and search for Chickadee, he remained with his sister until sleep finally relaxed her hold on him. The clock was striking three when he finally raced to his own room, tore off his elegant apparel, and dressed for riding.

Candice met him as he prepared to leave the house. "Mr. Blackwell, you'll search in vain. She's hurting, and you must give her time to do whatever it is she has to do with herself. She's different from us and sorts things out in her own way. Let her come home of her own free will."

He gave her a furious look, but she refused to relent. "I speak to you not as your employee, Mr. Blackwell, but as someone who cares for her as much as you do. And it would never do if she returned needing you and you weren't here for her. Let her be, sir."

His shoulders slumped. Candice was right, and he knew it. Besides that, if Chickadee didn't want to be found, a pack of bloodhounds wouldn't find her. He nodded to the maid and went directly to the parlor, Khan trotting along behind him. There he grabbed a bottle, sat down, and sought some answers in the burning liquid.

But the brandy gave him no solutions. The only hope, the sole prayer he had was the effect Lord Cavendish's speech might have had on Boston's elite. He could do nothing but wait.

When Araminta, upon her return, entered the parlor and poured herself a sherry, wolf and man were still waiting in that dark corner for the missing girl they loved.

"Didn't you get enough champagne at the ball, Grandmother?"

Her glass fell to the floor and rolled beneath a chair. "What are you doing in here?"

He lifted his bottle of brandy in response.

Araminta cackled. "Ah, yes. No doubt drunkenness is the only condition that enables you to bear that hill hellion you married."

"Watch your tongue if you value that scrawny hide of yours. I've company here with me." Saxon snapped his fingers, and Khan slinked into view. "Khan, I'd invite you to eat her, but I'm sure she'd give you a stomachache. I know she's giving me one."

Araminta eyed the wolf warily and then looked back at Saxon. "Quite a show your little wife put on tonight."

"Lord Cavendish—"

"Does not live here," Araminta sneered, her smile like a thin stick glued to her face. "His stand was an influential one, I grant you that. But he will depart for England soon, and I dare say his defense will quickly be forgotten by society. It is my guess your wife's name, as well as yours, will remain sullied."

Saxon slumped further into his chair. "And what

of your own place among the aristocrats, Grandmother? Your name too is Blackwell."

She fingered her brooch. "I can return to England, where I retain both my reputation and many old friends." But she had no intention or need to return to her homeland. Despite the duke's lecture, she was intent on continuing with the infallible scheme she had devised at the ball. They would persevere until Chickadee was goaded into threatening every Bostonian alive. In gratitude and admiration for her ingenious strategy, the matrons had accepted Araminta among them once more.

But there was no need for Saxon to know that. "I've no desperate desire to leave Boston, but I am in no way bound to it either," she said. "But you— you must stay here and wallow in your misery. You've nowhere else to—"

"I can go anywhere I—"

"Then go. Go and forever worry about your sister's welfare. And should I return to England . . . Do you think the cold, wet English fog will agree with Desdemona? No doubt she would soon lie in the family cemetery. Now that's something to consider. I wonder why I never thought of it before. I guess my brilliance comes at exactly the times I need it most!"

The bottle of brandy flew only inches past her face, but Araminta never moved. "Where is your yokel— the cause of your violent fits of late? Has she left you?"

"She'd never do that. She loves me."

"Ha! What is there about you for anyone to love?"

He winced at the question with which she'd tortured him daily years ago. Unbidden, childhood horrors slithered into his memory. It took every shred of his willpower to crush them down again. "What do *you* know about love, Grandmother? You've never loved anyone in your whole life."

Pain flashed through her, but she masked it instantly. "Your plan for tonight failed dismally, didn't it, Saxon? Mine, however, succeeded gloriously.''

He bolted from the chair, a cobalt storm brewing in his eyes. ''What did you do to ruin—''

''Always look for the weaknesses of your enemies, my boy. Find them, and you win the battle. One of the many flaws I find in your wife is her overwhelming determination to defend you in all ways, shapes, and forms. It took but a few insulting comments about you to push her into losing that famous temper of hers. A lady is allowed to become slightly irritated, but never may she lash out as viciously as your . . . uh, *lady* did this evening.''

''Why you old—I'll—''

''You can do nothing! I hold you within my palm and can crush you without warning. Without my money, you can never have custody of Desdemona. Try and make your own fortune as you once did foolishly, and I will take her to England and its cold fog immediately. Steal the pitiful, delicate thing away, and she will most likely die within a week if I don't find her first. And I do assure you, I will scour every inch of this earth.''

Saxon searched desperately for an argument that would defend him against her malevolence. But there was none. Her hatred was her deadliest weapon, and it seemed to make her ominipotent. He fell back into the chair.

''It is true, Saxon, that you followed the stipulations of my will to the letter, but your method of following them will bring more misery to you than you ever dreamed possible, because I will never stop forcing both you and that female barbarian to see she does not belong here. Get rid of her! She's an outcast and will never be anything else. No doubt she is in the thick of more trouble even as we speak.'' Gathering her gloomy skirts, she swept from the room.

* * *

The next morning, Saxon raced up the sun-washed steps of the city jail, snatched open the door, and whisked inside, failing to see the velvet cording that partitioned the room he'd entered. He tripped over it, landed on his stomach, and slid several feet on the slick, polished floor. When he stopped, one gold slipper was pointed at his face.

"Saxon, I knowed it warn't gwine take you but a whipstitch ter git here, but I warn't a-lookin' fer you ter come a-skimmin' along on yore belly."

He looked up at her, his eyes nearly popping out of their sockets when he saw she was wearing only the bodice of her gown and her pantaloons. "What happened to your dress?"

"I couldn't do nothin' with all them dang-blasted skirts a-hangin' all over my legs, so I ripped them and my petticoats off. Had ter be real quiet-like when we snuck inter Ruford Sinclair's house. Y'know how he allus has that room whar he keeps his paintin's lit up? Well, last night them winders was dark. I knowed somethin' was wrong so I—"

"Keely—" Saxon jumped to his feet, jerked off his coat, and threw it around her. After a glance around the room, he saw the chief of police sitting at a desk.

"Captain, I'm Saxon Blackwell, and one of your officers came to me this morning to inform me my wife was jailed for theft," he said, never pausing to wonder why Chickadee was not in a cell. "Whatever the amount of her bail, I'll—"

"The charges were dropped fifteen minutes ago," the captain said. "Mr. Sinclair dropped them when we caught the real thieves. Caught them red-handed about an hour ago with several of Mr. Sinclair's paintings."

Chickadee smiled at the officer. "Much obliged fer the breakfast, Mr. Policeman."

"And many thanks to you, Mrs. Blackwell, for bringing the weaknesses of our cell locks to our attention. She broke out twice," the officer informed Saxon. "We finally had to tie her up."

"You ready ter go on home now, outlander? Shane, Killian, and Gallagher left afore you come. Thur a mite sore from all the fightin' so I tole 'em ter go and—"

"Fighting? What the hell are you doing here, Keely? What happened last night? Why were you at Mr. Sin—"

"Well, I was on my way home, but when we passed ole Ruford Sinclair's place I seed them winders upstairs was dark. I ain't never seed 'em dark, so I knowed fer shore and sartin he was in trouble. But when we got inside? Well, it was so dang dark that Killian knocked Gallagher over the head, Shane mellered Killian, and then it was jist me and Shane agin' the robbers. But when we looked fer 'em? Well, they'd up and left already. Mr. Sinclair was fainted on the floor, but when he come ter he thought we was the thieves, and about that time his manservant come along with about fifteen policemen.

"Did y'know Mr. Sinclair only has one servant, Saxon?" she interrupted her own story. "He prob'ly don't want ter pay no more'n that. He's stingy, jist like you said he was. I give him what fer about that too. Tole him it was plumb selfish fer him ter keep all them paintin's ter hissef. But he was too fitified ter listen good. Anyhow, when the policemen come, they tuk me and my friends here. Nobody believed our story till the real thieves was—"

"Fine, fine, little one," Saxon cut her off when he noticed several men looking at her scantily clad legs. "We'll talk more in the coach."

But the drive home was a silent one. Exhausted from the night's activities, Chickadee promptly fell asleep, and Saxon was left to imagine why and how she'd gotten herself into such a fix.

Oh, how the gossip mongers would love this. It wouldn't make a bit of difference to them that she was innocent, he thought wearily. They'd harp on the fact that she, Mrs. Saxon Blackwell, had spent the night in jail, and Lord Cavendish's compelling tribute to her would be dismissed and forgotten as speedily as Araminta had said it would be. Nor was there anything he could do about the situation. With a resolute sigh, he forced himself to accept the painful truth.

Chickadee would never be his. This latest escapade of hers was the icing on a cake that already had so many layers, it nearly reached the sky. The girl asleep on his shoulder belonged to another world, one in which he could never join her. Nothing he'd done, could ever do, would change her. She was wild, wonderfully wild, and would stay that way forever.

He reached for his satchel. Her bail money was not the only thing in it. He pulled out an envelope, opened it, and reread the letter that had come from his associate in New York two days ago.

Barton Winslow had fallen. The plan had worked perfectly. The man was penniless.

After replacing the letter, Saxon drew his mountain girl closer to him. "I was a fool to try and change you into Keely Blackwell, for you will never be anyone but Chickadee McBride," he told her quietly and with a sad smile. "And what's wild has to stay wild, little one. You said that yourself when you set free that bear cub so long ago. Now you and I must live by your own words."

He knew she'd fight his decision. But he'd stand firm because, as heaven was his witness, he was doing it out of a love so deep, he had no other choice.

He would send her back to where God always meant for her to be.

"It's worser'n the North End," Chickadee said, her voice edged with uneasiness. "He don't live too good, huh?"

Saxon put his arm around her. The train trip was over, and they now stood in front of a dilapidated old building in the worst section of New York. Somewhere within was Barton Winslow. Saxon's detectives had kept a close watch on the man, informing Saxon that this slum, this putrid place, was where Barton had been forced to take up residence.

The wood-planked floors groaned as they entered the dingy dwelling. Mice scurried about, and several times Saxon was forced to swipe at huge cobwebs and step on the falling spiders. A mangy dog crept out of one corner, growled, and then slunk away. The smell was nauseating.

"Which one o' them rooms is Barton's?" Chickadee whispered.

Dusk had begun to fall, making it too dark to see the numbers on the doors. Saxon lit a match and held it out before him. "The one on the end," he replied, leading the way. He knocked loudly at the door.

There was no answer.

"He ain't home," Chickadee said and turned to leave.

Saxon threw down the match and caught her arm. "Keely, wait! I thought you were anxious to come face to face with him? Didn't you once say you wanted to fill his ass with buckshot?"

She bit at her bottom lip. "I ain't got my shootin'-arn."

"Well, you can still give him a piece of your mind, can't you?"

"I . . . Saxon, I don't know what ter say ter him," she squeaked and rubbed her arms briskly. "I mean, I used ter dream about this day, but now that it's here . . ."

Saxon pounded on the door again, anxious to get her out of such squalor. There was still no answer, so he reached for the knob and turned it.

"Saxon, wait. Let me thank on what I'm gwine say."

"You've had eighteen years to think about it. We're going to get this over with right now. I don't like seeing you in this filth. Disease might jump out and get you." He attempted to smile but failed. Instead, he pushed the door open and lit another match. The weak light slithered into the small, fetid room.

Inside, a man lay on the floor in his own vomit. Beside him were dozens of empty whiskey bottles. He was dressed in a suit that must have cost a lot of money, but was now torn and filthy. His thinning hair was stark white and crawling with lice, his frame horribly thin, his skin so transparent his veins seemed painted on it.

Chickadee's breath caught in her throat when she saw him. She reached for the door frame for support.

"I'd say you've got your revenge, little one," Saxon ventured. "A man can't get any lower than this." He took her arm and led her closer to Barton.

"I . . . I changed my mind," she stammered, her eyes stricken with horror. "I cain't do it, Saxon."

His face creased with confusion. "What do you mean you can't do it? Look at him, Keely. There he is, at your feet, just like you wanted him to be. Remember your mother's heartache. Her death. You've avenged it now."

She had to force herself to look at the man on the floor. Whatever sins he'd committed, this pitiful old man was her father. Her mind reeled. "I . . . Saxon, I was wrong," she said, so softly Saxon almost couldn't hear it.

"You were wrong?"

She covered her mouth tightly to keep from being sick, staggered from the room and out into the dark, littered street. When Saxon caught up with her, she reached for him and threw herself into his arms. "Saxon, you got ter hep him! Git him a doctor man afore he dies in thar!"

He thrust her from him. "You had me destroy him, and now you want me to save him?"

Chickadee looked back at the horrid building that was her father's home. "I was so wrong. I didn't have nary a right ter do this ter him. What he did ter Mama—Saxon, it warn't my place ter punish him. I didn't understand that. I didn't figger on a-feelin' this way till I seed him in thar all drunk and sick. Afore terday, I allus seed Barton in my mind as jist some rich blackguard. I never had a face ter put with what I had him figgered out ter be!''

"But he *was* a rich blackguard!''

"Saxon, we jist cain't let him die in thar! He's already a-gittin' cold from the feet up, and iffen—''

"Keely—''

"Saxon, please do this fer me!'' She grabbed his hands and brought them to her mouth, kissing them many times before she spoke again. "I ain't never begged fer nothin' in my whole life, but I'm a-beggin' now. Please don't let him die!''

Barton Winslow did not regain consciousness to see his daughter, but the doctors were confident he would recover. Upon his release from the hospital, a man representing Blackwell Enterprises would see to his well-being, providing him with a job and a clean place to live.

Saxon, without another word of argument, had done everything Chickadee had begged him to do for Barton. She knew he was baffled over her change of heart, but her love for him had taught her many things, and forgiveness was at the top of the list. The way she saw it, her father had been punished enough for what he'd done to her mother. He'd lost everything he had, and though he was assured of a job, he would never be able to amass another fortune. He'd paid sufficiently for his misdeeds.

Now she could forget Barton Winslow and concentrate on the most important person in her life.

But Saxon gave her little chance to do that in their hotel room that night. He wasn't cold toward her, but neither was he warm. And though he slept beside her, she felt she slept alone. The worry that had begun the moment he'd told her he'd found her father grew steadily within her.

It blossomed to full-fledged foreboding during the trip home the next day. Saxon remained aloof. She felt a tremendous urge to ask him what he was thinking, planning, but her fear of his answer kept her from inquiring. The entire trip passed in silence.

As the train screeched to a halt at the Boston depot, Chickadee could bear the silence no longer. "I love you, Saxon."

He only stared out the window.

"I love you," she said again as the Blackwell coach carried them home.

He carefully avoided meeting her eyes.

"I love you," she repeated as he helped her from the barouche. "I love you," she said one last, desperate time when they entered their bedroom.

Saxon shut the door behind them. He couldn't face her, couldn't allow her to see the echo of her words in his own eyes. "Keely, you hardly said a word during our trip to New York. You were unusually pensive both in the hotel room last night and during our trip home. Therefore, I've reason to believe you realize what our journey to New York signifies, do you not?"

Dread enveloped her. "I . . . I love—"

"So you've said. But it's over now. Everything we set out to do has been done. You're going home."

Chapter 23

"**N**o! Please no!"

Saxon turned to look at her, saw her panic, and escaped to the window. "I've already made the arrangements for your return. The *Sea Siren* is ready, my bankers are seeing to the money you'll need for the trip, and—"

"Saxon, don't make me go!"

He still couldn't face her distress, for to see it would be to see his own.

Her cold palms began to perspire. She wiped them on the front of her gown but could not seem to dry them. "I ain't gwine go, Saxon. I love—"

"Stop!" He whirled on one foot, the heel of his shoe digging into the thick carpet. "You *are* going, Keely! The agreement we made has come to an end."

Her mind exploded with the fervent hope that this wasn't happening. "You . . . Saxon—the day you come up with that bargain, you said you needed me and I needed you!"

Dear God, if only he could tell her how true that still was! "I'm well aware of what I said, and it was very true at the time. But it is true no longer. I began divorce proceedings several days before we left for New York."

"Divorce!" The word was like poison in her mouth.

His eyes stung as he continued. "Keely, as I made

337

the arrangements for your departure, I belatedly realized that staying married to you would mean con-
demning you to a life of loneliness. I humbly
apologize for not thinking of that when we first
made our bargain. Wed, you wouldn't be free to find
another husband. Divorce is the only answer.''

"But thur ain't nobody I want but you, Saxon!''

"We are not compatible. We never will be. I want
you to find someone who will love you. You need a
man who—''

"I need you!'' She ran and threw herself into his
arms. "Saxon, don't do this ter us!''

"There is no *us*, Keely,'' he said, trying to pry her
from him. "There never was. We've completed everything we set out to do, and it's over.''

"But Araminty's will says you got ter be married
ter—''

"I'm aware of that!'' he snapped, his guts twisting at the prospect of having any other wife but the
girl clinging to him. "I will remarry, as will you.''

The thought of him married to another woman, lying in someone else's arms, having a child with . . .
"No! Lord o' mercy, Saxon, please—''

"I'm not the man for you!'' This time he succeeded in thrusting her from him. He glared down
at her, hoping she saw only the feigned indifference
in his eyes and not the love he could barely conceal.
"I'm cold. You're warm. I'm held fast to my money,
and you want no part of it. I crave all things elegant;
you're the epitome of simplicity. I'm a bitter, suspicious man. You're innocent, trusting. We are as
opposite as a raging fire and a glacier.''

Fire and ice. She saw them both in her mind. If
the flames were hot enough, big enough, wouldn't
they melt the wall of ice? The question reverberated
through her brain. "You ain't got ter be so bitter, so
cold. You—''

"I've been like that for almost thirty years,'' he
choked. "If you stayed in Boston, you would become as poisoned as I.'' It was true, he realized then.

Boston. There was no freedom here. Yet he was tied to the city forever. He would not allow it to be Chickadee's prison too. He left the window and stalked to the bed.

"But you was a-comin' around! Saxon, you was a-warmin' up ter all the love I been a-givin' you. You—"

"I had a good time with you, and that is the extent of it, Keely. You were different. A nice change from normality. What has that to do with love? People can enjoy something without loving it, can they not?" *Dear God, how many more lies will I be forced to tell you, my love?*

She hurried to him, desperate to get a hold on this situation before it was too late. "Saxon—"

He took her by her shoulders. "Keely, I am not who you think I am. You see only who you want to see. You want me to be warm and loving and full of only happiness. Therefore you believe me to be that way. But I am nothing at all like the man you want me to be!"

Releasing her, he began to pace. "There are bitter things inside me. I can't explain. You would never understand. There's nothing either you or I could ever do. You," he said and stopped to look at her, "would never understand." *At least that is no lie,* he fumed, and crushed down the age-old pain.

Her eyes widened when she heard the chilling truth in his voice. She understood a lot more than he thought she did, and one thing she comprehended fully at that moment was that she'd underestimated the power of his demons. Before now, she hadn't realized just how profound were the wounds Araminta's hatred had inflicted upon the boy she'd glimpsed that night in the library so long ago. She'd mistakenly thought *she* could reach that frightened child inside him. But she realized now that only Saxon himself could do it. Only by remembering, defying, and conquering his ghosts would he ever be truly rid of them. Love had surely weakened them but had not overcome them. Not yet.

The final, bitter battle between love and hatred would be waged here and now, she decided. Her love against all the hatred tucked away within him. Tonight would determine which of the two fierce emotions was the stronger. And then . . . maybe then . . .

But how would she make Saxon fight? He'd been running from his childhood memories for years. She had no doubt he'd do the same now.

He saw the contemplative gleam in her eyes. "If you're trying to come up with a way to change my mind, Keely, don't. My decision is final." He snatched off his neckcloth, crushed it in his fist, and then unwadded it.

She watched him lace it between his fingers and knew he was trying to avoid looking at her. She walked to where he stood, reached for his hand, and closed her own around it.

The contact jolted Saxon, spiraled through him, filling him with an urgent yearning to take her into his arms and tell her he loved her now, would love her tomorrow, would love her for all eternity.

But that same love gave him the strength to yank his hand out of hers. He went back to the bed, tore off his shirt, and flung it at the door. "Do we understand each other now, Keely?"

She joined him and ran her hands down his chest. "Make love ter me, Saxon." Lightly, she traced his collarbone with the tip of her tongue. "Make love ter me." Her arms went around him, her fingers slipping into his hair as she brought his face down to hers. "Make love ter me," she whispered in the breath of the second before their lips met.

He crushed her to him, kissing her deeply, thoroughly. Dammit, he would have all of her before the night was over! Have her and live on it for the rest of his miserable life. "Leave," he mumbled into her mouth. "You will leave, Keely."

She pulled away from him, reached for the fastening at his trousers, and made quick work of undressing him. Saxon, caught fast in the magic web of desire, was helpless as he watched her hands slither sensuously over his hard body.

"Sorceress," he hissed and then moaned when her mouth began the journey her hands had taken. "But your spells, too, must come to an end." He reached for her, pulled her to her feet, his stormy gaze aimed into her smoldering one. "End, mountain girl. Tonight is our last."

Her auburn brow rose before she went to a table and poured two brandies. She handed him one and toasted him. Neatly, she drank hers and then smiled slowly, meaningfully. "Then let's make the mostest of it."

It never entered his mind to question her sudden acceptance of his decision. His burning need for her consumed every thought in his mind except his passion for her.

With an air of mystery about her, as if she were unveiling a secret treasure, she reached for the silken ties of her bodice and pulled at them with agonizing slowness. The heavy satin rustled to the floor, drowning her feet in a turquoise sea. Her creamy undergarments followed, creating white-capped waves upon the vivid blue. She stood before him then with only her earrings on. The exquisite diamonds glittered, the reflection of the firelight dancing within their facets. She reached for them and, one by one, slid them off her ears; in cupped hands, she held the shining ice for one brief moment before she let it splash into the satin pool at her feet.

"Whatever sorter woman I am, I'm still a woman," she whispered huskily. "And whatever kind o' man you are, yore still a man. Make . . . love . . . ter . . . me . . . now."

He took a step forward. The brandy he still held sloshed onto his hand. He watched it drip to the rug. Looking back up at Chickadee, he pointed to the floor.

A question in her eyes, she sank to her knees. He shook his head. She sat. His blue gaze told her *no*. She met it with one that said *anything* and stretched out on the luxurious carpet. He knelt beside her, inserted his finger into his snifter, and painted her lips with brandy. "Drunk. I am drunk with lust for you, mountain girl. Tonight I will drink my fill."

Drop by drop, he wet her body with the brandy. From toes to forehead, she was thoroughly moistened with the potent fluid. "I have no idea," he said and bent to lick at the brandy pooled in the hollow of her throat, "which is the more intoxicating, you or the brandy. But after tonight I will know the answer."

His mouth drank the amber droplets from her ivory skin. At her toes he began; to her calves, knees, and thighs he went. Upward, onward, his tongue, his lips, his teeth traveled, biting, licking, sucking alternately at her flat belly, the gentle curve of her rib cage, the swell of her breasts, the velvet slope of her neck, and finally the peach softness of her mouth. Her scent, the perfume he'd never been able to describe, permeated his mind and soul. He gulped at the taste of her, and still his thirst for her could not be quenched. Her skin rippled beneath his hungry mouth, her moans filled his being, lifting him to greater heights of desire.

"Saxon." His name was her plea. He needed no other urging and gave her that for which she begged. She accepted him with all the love she had for him and indulged herself with one brief moment of the pleasure mounting within her before she mentally tore herself away from it. Steeling herself from the anger she knew was just on the horizon, she used every bit of willpower to rise above the desire that continued to lance through her.

"Remember," she panted into his ear and never

slowed the rhythmic circling of her hips. "You was about four, five years old."

He became still.

"Make love ter me, Saxon."

Had he imagined what he'd heard her say? Unsure, he resumed his lovemaking. The pleasure was intensified with each of the wild movements she made beneath him.

"You wanted lovin' hands, but she only had pizened fangs. She was a spider a-layin' in wait fer you."

His stomach wound into a hard knot. "What?"

"Love me, love me," she purred, her tongue flicking in and out of his ear. She tightened herself around him and continued to stroke him within.

"Keely," he began but was again lost in the bliss her body offered him.

She let him savor it for a while longer before speaking again. "You couldn't run away then, and you cain't run now neither. She hurt you, and that hurt never went away. Let it out, Saxon. Git shed of it ferever."

He realized he was hearing correctly. "Stop—" His every muscle strained as he tried to control the explosion of memories Chickadee's whispered reminders loosened within, but even as they escaped from their chains, his unbridled passion for her continued to grow. His entire body was welded to hers in one way or another. He shook his head in an effort to clear it of his past, wanting to concentrate on nothing but Chickadee. But the memories still remained.

Chickadee knew it by his body's sudden stiffening. He was remembering.

"Let me see . . . from the time you was old enough ter understand thangs, Araminty set a-plantin' it in yore head thur was somethin' so dang wrong with you that it jist warn't possible fer her ter love you. But that warn't enough. She tole you nobody else was ever gwine love you neither. Ain't that what she said?"

His only response was to try and lift himself from her, but his efforts were futile. She clung to him, body and soul, giving him no quarter.

"Stop this at once," he growled, then moaned when she shifted beneath him and he slid deeper into her.

"Iffen I close my eyes, I can near about see you as a young-un. You prob'ly got inter all sorter mischief jist like all young-uns do. And ole Spider Woman was allus thar with that cane, a-mellerin' you ever' time you—"

"Dammit, Keely!" he shouted, his mind ravaged with pain. "Don't—"

"Yore little heart was a-breakin' fer her ter love you, and yore little body was a-achin' fer her ter hold you. But she didn't never do them thangs. She only kept on—"

"I'm warn—"

"And finally that cane o' hers broke more'n yore body. It broke yore spirit. Beatin' after beatin', and her allus a-tellin' you that nobody warn't never gwine love you. Allus a-sayin' that you didn't know how ter love nobody neither. Over and over agin, ever' minute of ever' day and night. She didn't never let up. She—"

"Enough!" But it was too late. Like red-hot lava, the memories spewed forth from the volcano he'd kept dormant for too many years. Destructive and uncontrollable, they covered him with burning rage.

He crushed her face between his hands. His gaze, like a blue bolt of lightning, sizzled into her. "Go on and slap me, Saxon. Y'know dang well you want ter hit somebody."

He dug his fingers into the back of her neck.

"Still cain't do it? Well, let me hep you. Thank on all them thangs Araminty done ter you. Remember that cane, how it felt on yore bare skin. How you cried and begged her ter stop. And how she didn't never stop!"

Her sweet face seemed to melt into Araminta's

heinous one. He shook his head, searching for Chickadee again, but he couldn't find her. "Keely?"

"What did she do? Have Thatcher hold you down? Did she tie you up with ropes?"

The need to release his violence overwhelmed him. With tremendous determination, he tried to expel Araminta's horrible visage from his mind, but she remained, sneering, cackling, her black brooch glowing.

"Yore afeared." Chickadee goaded him on and arched her hips against his. Her efforts were rewarded by Saxon's involuntary moan. "Yore skeert o' them feelin's you got pushed down so deep. Y'know iffen you let 'em go and brang 'em ter mind, thur gwine make you hurt agin—jist like they hurt when you was little."

"So you're saying if I talk about them, they'll go away?" He let out a horrible laugh. "Things like that don't go away, Keely! Not ever!"

"Yeah? What makes you so dang shore? You thank you know ever'thang, but you—"

"Stop!" He raised his open hand and brought it toward her face so rapidly his action was a blur. But when his hand was but a fraction of an inch from her cheek, he balled it, squeezed it tightly, and hammered it down to the floor.

"Saxon—"

"Quiet!"

She kept him within her, and while her body tormented him sensuously, her lips tortured him verbally. "It's a sour tit, but you got ter suck it. Ain't nothin' else in the world but mem'ry, and that'll mend what Spider Woman done ter you. Yer gwine have ter reach down and get holt o' that little boy who's still inside thar. He's been covered with pain, fear, and hatred fer too many years. Even when his body turned inter a man's body, his little mind, heart, innocent needs . . . No, thur ain't two ways about it. Yer gwine have ter git mad enough ter bite a nail in two and then let it all out afore—"

"Why are you doing this?"

"I love you! And that's why fer I'm a-doin' this ter you, you dang fool! So git mad, Saxon!"

Tremendous fury thundered through him. "If it's rage you want, Keely, I grant you your wish!" Brutally, he drove into her.

Instinctively, she had known she was the only instrument he could use to overcome the pain. "Go on," she urged him. "Here I am, ready ter take ever' bit o' hatred you got ter give. All the frustration, wrath, and sorrers. Give it all ter me, Saxon. I'm gwine take it and turn it inter love!"

He rammed into her, his devils driving him unmercifully. Everything came back to him full force, all the horrible memories. He couldn't separate himself from them any longer. They tore through him, and with them rose a loathing for the woman who'd caused them.

And Chickadee knew then the fight between hatred and love had begun.

She could feel nothing but misery surging through him. His lovemaking was barbaric. He plunged into her with a strength akin to madness. "You want ter be crazy, Saxon? Have at it then!"

Her hips circled faster and her movements, frenzied now, caught up with the pace of his and matched them, soon outdoing them. She pushed at his buttocks, demanding he seek even more deeply inside her.

Though he was now thrusting into her with incredible power and urgency, she took all of him, her love forming a warm cushion against the pain. "Saxon, by all them angels in heaven, I love you. With ever' bit o' what and who I am, I love you."

Her hands swept up his back to grab at his hair. She pulled his head away from her neck and then caught his lips with her own. There was no gentleness in her kiss as she plundered the inside of his mouth. She bit at him until she tasted his blood, and still she continued to kiss him, allowing him no chance to escape her.

"The trunk," he gasped down at her, the memory flooding him with remembered terror. The trunk. The years fell away. He was only five. "She locked me in it!"

Chickadee's eyes fluttered closed in horror. "I'm in thar with you, Saxon!"

He felt her warmth seep into him. "Once," he choked into her hair, "she locked me in it for two whole days. No food, no water, and in my own stench. When she let me out . . ."

"Feel me with you, Saxon," Chickadee encouraged him, and rained kisses down the length of his neck.

"When she let me out, she—"

"Beat you?" Chickadee guessed and knew she'd hit on the truth when his face tightened with the effort to control the memory that was too horrible to bear any longer. "That dang cane again?"

"Cane." He drove into her again, his mental image of Araminta still driving him violently onward. "It was a black serpent in her white claws! It bit, and its bite was deadly time and time again!"

"Feel my hands, Saxon," Chickadee said as she swept them down his sides. "I ain't got no cane. Thur ain't nothin' in my palms but the itch ter hold you."

Another memory seared into his mind, branding him with more anguish. "One time . . . I wanted to put flowers on my parents' graves," he whispered raggedly. "I took my pony one morning and went to the field where I knew they were buried. I didn't know exactly where they were though, so I scattered wildflowers all over and prayed some would land where their bodies lay."

She hugged him fiercely. "You ain't in that field alone, Saxon. I'm right thar with you."

"I wasn't alone then either. Thatcher followed me. He caught me and returned me to Grandmother. She made me watch as she had my pony slaughtered. My pony, Keely!''

His misery became her own. Her tears slid freely down her face and into her hair. ''Yore poor, poor pony.''

His frenzied lovemaking slowed a bit as he felt her tears wet his face. It seemed so strange to know someone else was sharing his pain. It had been his and his alone for so long. The memories—

He tensed again as more erupted. ''I'm still here, Saxon,'' she reminded him.

He told her all of it, holding nothing back. She fought nausea as she listened. That a small, defenseless child should have had to endure such atrocities, that Araminta had threatened separate orphanages for him and Desdemona should he try to escape or tell anyone . . . It was almost too much for Chickadee's compassionate heart to bear. But bear it she did for Saxon. He'd lived with it for years all by himself. He would never be alone with it again.

And he would soon be rid of it all. ''Saxon,'' she whispered when he became still atop her, his fight with his past steadily draining him. ''You mem'ried all them thangs. Now you got ter thank on 'em in yore mind and in yore heart. See 'em fer what they are. Let 'em do what they will. Let 'em do thur worstest, and when they cain't do no more, they'll disappear.''

The battle within him quickly rose to a climax. His pent-up hatred for Araminta, his ever-growing love for Chickadee, the war between the two, coursed violently through his body, heart, and soul. They weakened him again, and he wondered if he could continue. Yet when he was at the point of collapsing, he felt Chickadee's strength rush into him, filling him with yet more power, more need for her. His muscles, his entire body seemed to execute his actions not with *his* stamina, but hers.

And how it lifted him. Like a whirling, furious tornado, Chickadee coiled around him, elevating him and taking him into her world. And there, Saxon was besieged by emotions so heated, so profound, he shuddered from the force of them. They writhed through him, seeking, finding, burning, and finally melting the old glacier within him.

"Keely!" he called out to her, vaguely hearing her answer him in kind.

Together, they continued the frenzied spin through the cyclone of Chickadee's love. It wrapped around them both, clutching and demanding until both were yearning for release. And finally, when their bodies could stand no more, when their souls met and meshed, the whirlwind that held them captive exploded and sent them hurling into the pounding, fiery bosom of ecstasy.

There they stayed for an eternity, their pleasure never seeming to diminish, their bodies still trembling and longing for the last shreds of fulfillment.

And when at last it was over, Saxon, his chest heaving, slid from Chickadee, and searched through the battleground inside him. He found writhing memories scattered everywhere, bloody and wounded, but still alive. His first instinct was to turn from them, but a force stronger than he had ever known kept him watching them. His eyes closed, his heart and mind opened to it all, and he saw his childhood horrors, one by one, die and disappear forever. And in their place was peace, a tranquillity that could only be called heartease.

"Love . . ." Chickadee began hesitantly, longingly, ". . . won. Ain't that right, Saxon?"

The irony of it all, he thought, his eyes still closed. Chickadee—the love of his life, the one person who had given his existence meaning, the enchantress whose magic had overcome the spell of hatred, the most beautiful and extraordinary girl in the entire world—lay quietly beside him, her love still wrapped firmly about him . . . and he still had to make her go. The miracle she'd wrought tonight didn't, couldn't change that.

A cold dread settled over him. He shivered, sat up, and then stood. "The ghosts are gone," he stated flatly.

She stared up at him apprehensively. "And—and now?"

She was begging for his love, he knew. She'd worked so hard for it. She already had all of it, but she deserved the happiness he had no way of giving her here. She'd taught him the real meaning of love, shown him that love was generous in all respects and never egotistic. Love gave; it did not take. True love was honorable and selfless.

He turned from her, guilt consuming him. He'd been such a self-seeking beast with her. From the very beginning, he'd thought only of himself, his own needs, his own goals. Her love for him had allowed her to bear it all.

And his love for her would take that burden away forever.

He turned to her again and forced himself to narrow his eyes. Willed more coldness into his voice. "And now . . ."

She waited in vain for him to continue, wondering what to do, what to say and, in the taut silence, she felt foreboding replace hope.

"Keely, what happened tonight," he started and swallowed. "It changes nothing between us." At the look of protest on her face, he knelt beside her and took her hand. "You aren't happy here. You never will be. You must return to the only place where you can find joy and peace. Boston can never be that place for you."

"But—"

"No arguments."

She yanked her hand from him, fury exploding within her. "Yore so dumb, you'd hold a fish under water ter drown it! When you got love, Saxon, thur ain't nothin' in this here world that can lick it. Whatever problems you thank thur are, we can mend 'em!"

She wasn't going to bend, he realized, wasn't going to accept his decision. They could argue until Judgment Day, and she'd still be fighting it.

Anguish pierced him. He would have to hurt her deeply to make her leave. She was like that bear cub of so long ago. She'd had to throw sticks and small rocks at it to make it find its freedom. She'd made it hate her for its own good. It had run away, and it had never returned.

He stood and choked down his horror at what he was about to do. "You've given me no other choice but to tell you the truth, Keely. I tried to be gentle, tried to make you leave without resorting to this, but you wouldn't listen. The problem, *mountain* girl, cannot be mended. The problem, *mountain* girl, is you."

A hint of hurt swam into her eyes. "Me?" she whispered.

"You. You want me to love you, but I never will. We are of two separate breeds. I've enjoyed your company, but love you? No. Not ever. You don't fit into my life."

Slowly, she rose and reached for him, tears filling her eyes when he stepped away. "Tell me . . . tell me yore a-lyin'."

He clenched his jaw before he could go on. "I cannot love someone like you. That's why I tried so hard to make a lady of you. When I failed to do that, I realized you would never be the lady I need by my side. Do you understand that? *You will never be a lady!*"

She stared at him, tears dripping from her face to her breasts.

He made himself stare back, his gaze hard and cold as ice, his heart withering at the lies he had to invent, at the thought of making her loathe him. "Because of you, society is banishing me," he pressed on relentlessly. "During the past months my name has been dragged down with yours in every gossip session held in this city. You are an embarrassment to me. My reputation is in shreds, and only when you are gone will I be able to put it back together. I can no longer stand the scorn, the unending ridicule. Only with your departure will it cease." He tensed, waiting for the attack that would surely follow.

But she only began to tremble, a slight quiver that became a violent shaking that nearly sent her to the floor. Then, just as quickly as it had begun, it stopped. She raised her chin and threw her shoulders back. In her eyes was a look of pride and courage.

Saxon knew any other woman would have broken down completely at hearing such hurtful things from the man she loved. But not Chickadee McBride. She would not degrade herself by shouting out the hatred he knew she felt for him now. He should have realized that. By God, there had never been and never would be another woman like her. She was a lady in the true sense of the word.

Chickadee went to the dresser, slipped into her homemade clothes, and quickly packed the rest of her meager belongings from home. She then reached for her sterling silver brush but snapped back her hand in an instant and ran her fingers through her hair instead. Her emerald wedding band snagged on a curl. She removed it from her finger, turned toward Saxon, and tossed it to him.

"Where are you going?" he asked when she headed for the door.

"Downstairs," she answered, her hand on the doorknob. "I ain't gwine leave the house, so you ain't got ter worry about that. Jist let me be, Saxon."

"Keely—"

"You done what you had ter do, said what you had ter say. I ain't gwine have no hollerin' match with you over it. What good would that do? I tole you once that folks should larn the difference betwixt thangs they can do somethin' about and thangs they ain't got no control over. I larnt that a long time ago. Cain't unlarn it now jist on account o' I don't like it. Come mornin' you can come down fer me, and I'll be ready."

She left Saxon then; yet she remained with him. He saw her everywhere he looked.

He knew it would always be so.

Daybreak found him standing by the window, where he'd stood the entire night. In his hand was a raccoon tail. He'd held it for hours while he'd prayed for this morning never to come. But the sun was up, its light pouring over him. The day would start with Chickadee by his side, where she'd been for months now. Before night came, she'd be gone. Forever and always.

He bathed slowly. He cleaned and polished his boots until they gleamed, and he saw his own sad reflection in them. He dressed with the same purposeful leisure. He even tidied up the room—something he'd never done before. When it was as orderly as he could make it, when he could find no other reason to delay, he left and headed downstairs.

He found her in the library, sitting by the dying fire. It looked as if she was stitching something. Upon approaching her, he saw she was sewing furiously. "What are you making?" He could think of nothing else to say.

She slid her needle through the quilt again. "Started this here quilt with Desi long, long ago. Been a-sewin' on it all night."

"You're trying to finish it?"

She didn't answer. Instead, she rethreaded her needle and continued to sew for a while longer. Saxon, not knowing what else to do, sat across from her and waited.

"You was right," she said abruptly, startling him from his melancholy contemplation. "I got ter go. Back ter the only place on God's green earth whar thur's any chance of a-bein' happy. Thur ain't nothin' here in this dang-blasted city but misery of the grandest kind.''

His heart lurched. She was really and truly leaving, and by her own lips he heard she was eager to do so. And why shouldn't she be anxious to leave him? She hated him for the things he'd told her last night. This calm, unruffled behavior was merely her way of saving her pride. It was so typical of her. ''Uh, of course you're right. You must leave. The boat is ready.''

''Miseries and heartache. That's all that's here. But home? Well, the Appalachia . . . I'm a-honin' fer it somethin' fierce. A-pinin' away fer its smell, its green, green purtiness, its freedom. It's whar my heartease is a-waitin' on me.''

Her heartease, he mused. She'd find it again. He felt glad for her, miserable for himself.

Quickly, deftly, she put the finishing touches on the picture she'd embroidered on the back of the quilt. She folded it neatly, placed it on the floor, reached for her bag of belongings, and stood. ''I'm ready ter go now.''

Saxon rose also. ''You've said goodbye to Desdemona?''

She nodded.

''She's going to be all right? She accepted this situation?''

''That all depends on you.''

He nodded.

They left for the wharf.

The *Sea Siren* sounded its shrill whistle; the white-capped waves of the harbor pounded in answer. Cold, cold was the morning air. It wrapped around Chickadee and Saxon like a cloak of pure ice.

''Saxon, don't fergit ter give them goodbye letters I writ to Bunny, Killian, Shane, and Gallagher. They ain't writ good, but—''

''I'll deliver them all personally.''

"And tell Bunny ter keep on a-rubbin' that scarf over her hand. She'll know what you mean."

Saxon tightened his wool muffler around his neck. But it was abysmal emptiness that strangled his voice. "I will." Viciously, he kicked at a stray piece of rope and watched it fall into the harbor to bob along on the waves. "If there's anything I can ever do for you . . ."

"Saxon, I did jist fine afore you come along, didn't I? But thur's somethin' I can give ter you. It ain't nothin' you can put in yore pocket, it ain't nothin' you can see, but it'll come to you when yore a-needin' it most."

She withdrew her hand from her bearskin coat and touched Saxon's cold-pinkened cheek. "It's jist a piece of advice. Sorter a tale. The onliest thang I have ter give you. The onliest thang I can thank of that'll keep this here city from a-mellerin' the life plumb outen you."

Did her goodness have no bounds? he wondered. He'd hurt her deeply, yet despite the loathing he knew she felt for him, her tremendous compassion demanded she continue to worry about him. Her unique mettle enabled her to accept all the pain he'd been forced to give her. Thank God she possessed that strength—it would see her through anything. "A tale? A story?" he asked.

"Saxon, life ain't really nothin' but a strang. You can yank on it, allus a-tryin' ter find whar it leads. But you ain't never gwine know lessen you jist up and foller it. And I cain't tell you no more'n that on account o' yore gwine have ter figger it out all by yore lonesome. But Saxon, the day you quit a-tuggin' on it, that strang's gwine take you to whar you was allus meant ter be."

His brow rippled into a frown in a desperate attempt to understand her parting words. "String? What—"

"Like I done tole you time and time agin, some thangs are better larnt by yoresef. Jist keep them eyes in yore heart open wide, and you'll see all you need ter see jist when you need ter see it.''

She kissed his forehead and smiled at him wistfully. Their gazes locked for a moment that was over all too soon for Saxon. ''Goodbye,'' she said softly, but her whisper thundered through him. Snapping her fingers for Khan, she began to ascend the ramp that led to the steamboat.

Saxon watched her every move. He returned her wave until she disappeared from his sight and then felt the frigid dampness of the day settle into the marrow of his bones. The swirl of her copper hair was the last he saw of her.

''Sort of red, sort of orange, sort of gold. Goodbye, mountain girl.''

In moments the *Sea Siren* was slicing through the water. With only memory for a companion, Saxon stood on the dock and watched until he could no longer hear Khan's mournful howl, until the vessel was eaten up by the hungry mist of the harbor. The brisk wind blasted past him, blowing away the tears he never realized he'd shed.

Chapter 24

"**Y**our grandson has returned," Thatcher announced from the hallway outside of Araminta's bedroom.

"And you are absolutely sure the girl is gone?"

"As you instructed, I followed them. They went to the docks, she got on the boat, and I watched it leave."

Araminta scratched her chin, went to her dressing table, and dabbed some powder on her pallid face. "Have my coach brought around. Boston must be informed that the heathen is gone. Though there were some who actually *liked* her . . . Well, never mind *those* stupid fools. Those who matter will be relieved to know society is again safe. And the sooner that information is spread, the sooner Saxon will be accepted again."

Thatcher turned to do as she bade him.

"Oh, and Thatcher?"

"Yes, madame?"

"Throw away this powder," she said, scratching the reddened area beneath her mouth again. "It's making my chin itch."

Days turned into weeks, weeks turned into months, and Saxon buried himself in his work. Invitations to dozens of social gatherings arrived daily, but he crushed them all into tight wads, without even bothering to send his regrets. He left for his office at daybreak, rarely returning home before midnight. Many nights he failed to come home at all, finding the sofa in his office preferable to his big, empty bed.

His obsession with work, his ruthless business dealings, soon brought in an astonishing profit. Like rain pouring into an already swollen ocean, money streamed into the Blackwell accounts. But though Araminta was overjoyed that he was increasing the family fortune, she worried. She realized his fixation with Blackwell Enterprises was an effort to forget Chickadee. The business was the only thing in his life that did not remind him of her, the one thing Chickadee had not shared with him.

Araminta also knew his mania with work would soon wane, and then he would begin to dwell on the rustic once more. Something had to be done before that happened.

She soon decided to put an end to his mourning. "I would have a word with you before you leave for your office," she commanded when he entered the foyer.

Saxon ignored her and reached for his hat. "It'll have to wait. I've pressing business to—"

"May I remind you Blackwell Enterprises belongs to me? I can fire you if I wish."

He could almost feel her scrawny neck between his hands. With extreme effort he managed not to change the thought to reality.

"In the drawing room," Araminta said, leading the way. "I'll get right to the point, Saxon. The sole affair you've attended in months was Max and Bunny's wedding, and heaven only knows why you wished to see those two imbeciles marry. You have been avoiding that which you can no longer avoid. You must return to society, this time with a respectable woman."

"My divorce from Keely is not yet final." *Keely.* He caressed her memory mentally, as he did daily.

"The divorce will surely be final within the next

few weeks," Araminta snapped. "That is how long you have to find a new bride. Why, the day your divorce comes through could be your wedding day!"

He watched a smile slide over her face, like a pale snake slithering over white sand. "Courting takes time."

Araminta cackled. "If I allowed you to have your way in this matter, I imagine your courting would never begin. No, my boy. It begins today. I've arranged an outing for you. You are to escort Myrtle Windsor to an art exhibition at two-thirty this afternoon. Ruford Sinclair surprised all of Boston by putting his collection of masterpieces on display at the Athenaeum."

Liquid wrath replaced his blood. "How dare you—"

"How dare I? Why, it's simple. I dare, I do."

She was glaring at him with the malevolent stare that used to terrify him. But now . . . He stared back at her, feeling none of the fear of his boyhood, for there was no frightened child inside him any longer. That youngster's tears had been dried by the soothing kisses of a mountain girl.

But though his remembered horrors had vanished, the woman who'd caused them remained. Araminta retained control over his future. He would fight her no longer. What would be the use anyway? He'd lost Chickadee, and without her, he cared not a whit about the years to come.

He walked to a small table and picked up the vase it held. "Wedgwood." He rolled the vase around in his hands.

"Put that down, Saxon. It is costly."

He tossed her the taunting smile he knew she detested. "You hated Keely, didn't you?"

"I made no secret of it."

He threw her vase into the air, catching it just before it would have crashed back to the table.

"Saxon, put that down!"

His smile mocked her again. "If you hated her,

then you probably hate everything associated with her. Therefore, everything that comes from her mountains would be as repulsive as she. Correct?"

"I doubt anything her mountains hold would be of interest to me."

"Do you think this Wedgwood vase is beautiful?" Saxon pressed.

Her eyes narrowed with bewilderment. "It is magnificent. Now put it down!"

He ignored her command. "Josiah Wedgwood. An extraordinarily talented potter." Again, he tossed the vase toward the ceiling and caught it.

"Saxon, I am warning—"

"It's made of nice clay, wouldn't you say? So smooth to the touch, so pleasing to the eye."

"Give it to me!"

"Of course. Anything you say." He threw it to her.

She failed to catch it and it fell to the marble table beside her, shattering. "Oh, look what you've done!" she shrieked and gathered up the jagged pieces of her treasure.

Saxon folded his arms across his chest and leaned against the wall. "So sorry. I guess my aim was off. But really, Grandmother, you shouldn't allow yourself to become so upset. After all, you said yourself you didn't want anything from those Blue Ridge mountains."

Araminta glared at him, fury and confusion in her gaze.

"Once, an Englishman visited those *worthless* Appalachian Mountains," Saxon explained. "He found clay in them. Beautiful clay. As he held it, he thought of his friend, Josiah Wedgwood. After haggling with the Cherokee Indians who lived in those mountains, he was able to take a sample of the clay back to England with him. He showed it to Josiah, and the proof of what Mr. Wedgwood thought about it is now in your hands, Grandmother. Josiah was so delighted with the wonderful clay, he made a trip to the Blue Ridge himself. He took tons of it back to England, and—''

''That is enough!'' Araminta stood and shook a piece of the vase at him. ''I do not care if the clay came from those Carolina hills or the pits of hell! The fact remains you have destroyed something of great—''

''And suddenly I am filled with the need to ruin more!'' It took him a mere second to cross the room and yank the ebony cane from her hand. He stared down at the hateful object for one moment before he tightened his hold on it and took a great, rapid swing at the crystal chandelier above. Araminta pulled at his elbow, but he brushed her away as if she were nothing but a bothersome insect.

''You're insane!'' she charged, her fingers quivering around her brooch.

Saxon continued to bash the fixture, ignoring her until there was nothing left of the chandelier but its sterling silver arms. It somehow reminded him of his destructive spree with Chickadee so long ago, and it gave him a curious pleasure to see the crystal scattered everywhere. Spying an unbroken prism, he picked it up and handed it to Araminta. ''This crystal is like ice,'' he growled, his features twisted with disdain. ''Cold and hard. Just like your heart.''

Araminta raised her hand, the prism locked between her bony fingers, and started to throw it at him. Saxon caught her wrist and squeezed hard. ''Spider Woman,'' he spat, and saw that her stare held the tiniest fragment of fear. ''Where is your poison now?''

''Release me!'' she screeched.

Saxon laughed before he let go of her arm. Araminta shivered with apprehension, like an animal that senses its own defeat. Saxon's gaze held not a glimmer of the fear she'd worked so hard to instill. Yes, he'd stood up to her several times in the past, but always with a thinly veiled anxiety. Now it was completely gone. When had this happened, and how? "What are you going to do?" she screamed when he started for the foyer.

He stopped under the arch of the doorway and leaned against it. "Why Grandmother! Have you lost your confidence? Are you so unsure of yourself now that you believe I will *disobey* you?"

She could read nothing behind the contempt in his eyes.

"I go," he began, then made her wait while he lit a cheroot, "to propose to Myrtle Windsor."

Araminta's eyes widened. "But—you will *propose* to her? You barely *know* her!"

He blew a smoke ring and waited until it vanished before he spoke again. "I've seen her once or twice. I think I may even have danced with her on occasion. I don't know. All Boston maidens look and act the same to me."

Araminta was thoroughly baffled. "But surely you do not believe Myrtle will agree to marry you without becoming well-acquainted with you! Why, she is but one of the long list of maidens I have chosen for you to—"

"I choose her."

Araminta looked fixedly at him, trying in vain to understand if he had some scheme that would ruin her plans.

"And as far as her acceptance of my proposal," Saxon ventured, "what maiden in Boston wouldn't consent to become my wife? Do you think me stupid, Grandmother? I've received over a hundred invitations to various affairs since Keely left. Invitations from every damn matchmaking mother in the city. For what mother wouldn't jump at the chance to see her precious little girl wed to the man who will soon inherit the famed Blackwell fortune? Myrtle will marry me. I will return this afternoon a betrothed man. You may plan the wedding, just as you have planned my entire life."

Araminta was convinced. Everything about Saxon—his voice, his stance, his choice of words . . .

He would do exactly what he said he would. "Myrtle will make you an excellent wife."

"All I want from her is the heir you have badgered me about for years. After I get a son on her, she will cease to exist for me. And hopefully you too will cease to exist. After you see me married and lay eyes on your great-grandson, you may die as you've been promising you will soon do. The Blackwell fortune will pass to me, and you may lie in your grave satisfied all has happened according to your commands."

He left the house. As the coach carried him toward the Windsor estate, he thought of Myrtle. He knew her better than Araminta believed. He'd lain between her milky thighs once, long ago. And the memory of that night was what induced him to choose her for his bride.

She was a cold bitch with not an ounce of passion in her perfect body. She was made of ice and was nothing at all like the warm, loving mountain girl whose spirit accompanied him wherever he went. No, Myrtle would never remind him of Chickadee, and that was exactly why she would be his bride.

The barouche stopped. Saxon stepped out and stared at the magnificent Windsor mansion. Within waited his future wife. He walked mechanically up the alabaster steps and pounded on the door.

The day had arrived. Saxon read the letter from Mr. Devonshire, the Blackwell attorney, a dozen times before he finally tore it into shreds and flicked the pieces off the desk in his bedroom.

The divorce would be final today. He had but to sign the necessary papers. Had but to sign his heart and soul away on the dotted line.

Anguish crushed him, as it had ever since she'd left. "Keely, my own true heart," he whispered to her, willing his words to somehow find their way to her. "God, how I miss you, love you."

The rustle of silk caught his attention. He looked

up and saw Araminta. "Have you gone to see Mr. Devonshire?" she demanded.

"Maybe I have, maybe I haven't."

She knew he hadn't gone. "I have just returned from seeing Myrtle and her parents. The wedding will take place this very evening at the Windsor estate, in a matter of hours! You must go see Mr. Devonshire now. When you return you will barely have enough time to dress for the ceremony."

"So you arranged it after all. My divorce and wedding the same day. My, how busy you've been."

"It will be a quiet affair with only family present. I saw no need for a grand ceremony—a ceremony that cannot take place until you go sign the final draft of the divorce! Go sign the papers, Saxon! You—"

"I'll go later and not a second sooner. Calm yourself. Remember your heart. Or would you like to add your own funeral to the divorce and wedding you have already arranged? I'll stop and see Mr. Devonshire on my way to Myrtle's. What does it matter if the papers are signed hours before the wedding or mere minutes? Either way, I'll be divorced when I marry Myrtle."

Araminta shuddered with impatience and the urgent need to see him married before something prevented it from happening. "Oh, very well! Get dressed now. Be quick about it! I will wait for you downstairs and accompany you to both Mr. Devonshire's office and the Windsor estate. I will see you properly wed this day, Saxon. Nothing, no one, will thwart the marriage!"

She hobbled out of the room, leaving Saxon to dress for his wedding. He chose a black suit to reflect his black mood and not the pearl-gray outfit Myrtle had requested he wear. As he dressed, he was somehow able to remove a part of himself from his body, and as odd as it was, he felt as though he were watching another man prepare for his wedding. For he was already married. Divorce or no divorce, Chickadee would remain the wife of his heart.

Ready, he went to the door, paused, and looked back into the bedroom. It would be the last time he ever saw it. He and Myrtle would share a different room, one that held no reminders of the girl who'd once slept with him here. Gently, so he wouldn't disturb a single memory, he shut the door.

He reached the staircase, but the sound of someone weeping stopped him. He listened again and realized it came from the room Candice was fond of calling the sun room. She often took Desdemona there.

Desdemona. Weeks had passed since he'd seen her. She'd refused to see him. She'd even thrown a pitcher at him the last time he'd tried to visit her. After that he'd given up. She was angry with him, and he knew it was because Chickadee was gone. She blamed him for it, and rightly so, but how could he make her understand why he'd done what he'd done when she wouldn't even let him in the same room with her?

He looked at his watch. The wedding was an hour and a half away. Time enough for him to try and explain things to Desdemona. He'd force her to listen if he had to sit on top of her to do it!

The bright, sunny room down the hall was a cold, sad room in Saxon's eyes as his gaze rested on Desdemona's sobbing form. She sat in the far corner, Chickadee's quilt in her lap.

"Desdemona." He reached for her, pulled her to her feet, and withdrew his handkerchief to dry her tears.

She pushed him away. Saxon caught her face and forced her to hold still. The taut feel of her skin and the sharp definition of her bones beneath his fingers made him gasp. His trembling hands traveled over her shoulders, her rib cage, even her ankles. Her frail form horrified him.

"Desdemona! You're nothing but flesh-covered bones!"

His shout frightened her. Fleeing to the side, she tried to escape, but Saxon held her firmly to him. She fought him like a wild thing, scratching and kicking out at him. From her clenched teeth came a hissing sound before she bit her lip, drawing blood. The sight of the red droplets against the gardenia cream of her skin sent a surge of panic tearing through Saxon.

"All right!" he screamed and released her. "Let it all out! Show me how mad you really are!"

She heaved with exhaustion and hostility. Then, flinging herself against him, she beat at his chest. Saxon stood still and allowed her to vent her rage, knowing this was the explosion of many, many years of pent-up, seething emotion. She'd suffered every bit as much as he. She'd suffered then, she was suffering now.

Each time one of her tiny hands struck him, he cringed not from *his* pain, but from *hers*. He remembered her as a child. A sweet but silent little girl. He saw her as a lovely but distant young woman. The years had tumbled by, and as they had, he'd paid her very little mind.

"But I did try, Desdemona," he mumbled down to her and then winced when her nails raked his cheek. "Remember? I told you your eyes would make the best marbles if only we could get them out of your head. But you didn't answer me! You *never* answered me! You were a fragile doll who sat where you were placed, dressed in what someone chose for you, and slept where you were lain!"

He caught her pummeling hands. "I was little too! I didn't know how to play with dolls. And when I grew, I had even less time and patience to learn. You have to understand, Desdemona! I didn't know what to do with you! Dammit to hell, I *still* don't know what to do with you!"

Swirling from the deep recesses of his mind came

the image of someone who *had* known. Chickadee McBride. It had taken the touch of a whimsical, uneducated mountain girl to bring the doll to life.

Saxon's eyes narrowed as he stared hard at Desdemona. "You're going to die, aren't you? You're *willing* yourself to die! Without her . . . without Keely . . ."

Roughly, he pushed her back into her chair. "Listen carefully, Desdemona. She's gone, and she's never coming back. I sent her away because she wouldn't have been happy here. I couldn't let her stay, can't you understand that? You love her as I love her! Because of that we have to let her be where she needs to be!"

Desdemona looked up at him, profound sorrow spilling from her huge violet eyes.

"Her departure didn't mean she didn't care about you, Desdemona. One of the last things she told me was to take care of you. You've given me little chance to do that, but I won't let you die, do you hear me? All those things you miss doing with her—making snowmen, building a sled, picking flowers, singing—I can do all those things with you. Hell, I'll go shoot a bear and we'll sew it into a coat if that'll make you start living again! We're going to have a new life together, you and I. We'll do whatever you want, I'll give you whatever you desire. Desdemona, ask me for the world, and I'll see that you get it. Once we inherit our fortune—"

She flew from the chair, her hand slamming across his mouth, her fingers pinching his cheeks. Quickly, she slipped her other hand into his coat and withdrew his wallet. Snatching all the money from it, she shredded it into tiny pieces, flung them into the air, and threw herself on the quilt lying on the floor. There she sobbed anew.

Saxon shook torn money from the top of his boot. Desdemona obviously wanted no part of money. Dammit, she was going to continue to wither away!

Without Chickadee, she was going to be dead before—

His head snapped up. He stared at air, at nothing. Without Chickadee, Desdemona had no will to live. But Chickadee wasn't coming back. She would never set foot in Boston again. His shoulders slumped. What the hell was he going to do now?

"You'd die in the mountains, Desdemona! Life there is too primitive. I can't see you there. You're so delicate. How could you survive the life you'd have in those hills? There are no comforts there whatsoever. There aren't even any doctors for miles around! Betty Jane—she only has herbs. You'd have to bathe in streams, eat bear meat and greens that are so potent you can barely swallow them!"

Iffen I changed the cookin' water of these here greens, the pot likker wouldn't be no good. Pot likker richens the blood, y'know.

"Richens the blood," Saxon whispered Chickadee's words. "Desdemona . . ." *Pot likker richens the blood.*

Desdemona's sobs slowly ceased. For one long moment she gazed up at Saxon, a plea in her amethyst eyes.

"You'd survive there, wouldn't you?" he asked incredulously. "If Keely were with you, you'd survive in hell! You'd not only survive, you'd *thrive!*"

Desdemona knifed to her feet and threw herself into his arms, her head bobbing on his chest.

"No!" he bellowed down at her and snatched her from him. Misery smothered him. Anger at the injustice of it all. "Desdemona, I can't take you to her! I had to make her *hate* me! There was this bear cub . . . she was like that animal. Wild, Desdemona, *wild!* I could think of no other way! Sticks, rocks—I had to throw them at her! I had to hurt her!"

He stormed toward the window and viciously kicked at a potted plant in his way. "I told her things she won't ever forgive me for! I made her loathe me! If I went to her, tried to explain they were only lies . . . she'd never believe me! I tried to make a lady out of her. She'll remember that and see it as proof that I wanted her to be someone other than who she was! I made her bleed . . . The wounds . . . they'll never heal. They're too deep, too severe!''

Desdemona rushed to him. She took his hands and placed them over her heart, then she put her hands on his.

''Hearts,'' Saxon bit out. ''Love? No, Desdemona. She doesn't love me anymore. I destroyed her love for me on purpose. That was months ago. By now— dammit, by now she's probably already seeing someone else! And why shouldn't she? She thinks she's repulsive to me and that I'm humiliated by her! *I made her believe that!*''

He left Desdemona and stalked to the other side of the room, stopping in front of the chair. He stared blankly at it before sinking into it. ''In less than an hour I'm to be married, Desdemona. Wed to a woman I can't stand the sight of! And here I sit, and there you are. Neither of us wants to be here, yet it's here we must stay. You will die, and I? I already have, Desdemona. I died the day she left.

''Look all around us, sister. This world—this diamondlike world with its brilliant facets has destroyed us both. You were caught in its coldness, shivering through year after year. And I . . . I immersed myself in it and was soon frozen within its frigid walls. And then came the sun, the warmth, Chickadee McBride. The only person either of us has ever known who had the ability to melt this glacier we live in, and what did I do? I sent her away! Dear God, Desdemona, what did I do to all of us?''

He welcomed the horrible ache inside him. But no matter how much it hurt, he knew the pain he'd given Chickadee had been far worse. That she'd suffered at his hands, cried her rare tears for him . . . Her hatred was no more than he deserved for not having enough faith in their love. For not believing in its powers to overcome all obstacles as she'd begged him to.

His chin fell to his chest. He saw her quilt lying at his feet. Bending, he picked it up and ran his hands over its colorful design, for the first time noticing one side of it was patchwork, and the other side was intricately embroidered. "She was working on this the day she left," he mumbled. "She seemed desperate to finish it."

The need to see her threaded picture suddenly seized him. He spread the quilt out on the floor and felt his body grow alternately cold and warm as he deciphered Chickadee's beautiful embroidered message.

There were four separate scenes stitched on the covering. The first, at the top left-hand corner, portrayed buildings, gray and ugly. Boston? Saxon wondered. His brows knit in determination as he tried to understand, and then he noticed a shiny gold thread woven through the city scene. Curious, his eyes followed it. It left the city and ran through a large section of blue he took to be the ocean and entered the next scene.

Chickadee's Appalachia. Hills, some green, others turquoise, were the background for a tiny brown cabin. Patches of green Saxon knew to be mountain laurel surrounded the cabin, and there was even a black bear peeking out from behind the lush vegetation.

The golden string twined through the hill scene, swam through another piece of ocean-blue, and led up to the top of the quilt again, where there were more stitched buildings. Yes, this was Boston. Saxon smiled sadly at Chickadee's ugly interpretation of the city.

The thread then traveled through more sea-blue and down to the right side of the quilt, where there was another Appalachian scene. It curled through sapphire streams, twisted through emerald treetops, and wreathed around verdant shoulders of more mountains. The string seemed almost alive as it danced and glimmered through all the soft hues of the Blue Ridge.

And there it ended.

Saxon's breath caught in his throat. He felt light-headed from the lack of oxygen. But understanding was far more important than air. His fingers clutched at the quilt while his eyes retraced the golden string's journey.

Life ain't really nothin' but a strang. You can yank on it, allus a-tryin' ter find whar it leads. But you ain't never gwine know lessen you jist up and foller it. And I cain't tell you no more'n that on account o' yore gwine have ter figger it out all by yore lonesome. But Saxon, the day you quit a-tuggin' on it, that strang's gwine take you to whar you was allus meant ter be.

"My life—this string," he mumbled to his sister, his eyes never leaving the quilt. "She told me this story . . . The string—it starts in Boston. But see where Keely ended its journey, Desdemona—in her Appalachia."

He stood and looked at his sister, but it was many moments before he could speak. "She gave me what she said was the only thing she could give me," he said quietly, understanding slowly coming to him. "Said she hoped it was going to come to me when I needed it the most."

He looked down at the quilt again, smiling so broadly that his grin took over his face. "She knew—Desdemona, she knows I love her! She knew it when she left, she knows it now! I thought it was her pride that kept her from telling me she hated me! But it wasn't pride, Desdemona, it was love! She saw right through that act I put on for her. She left me this message—she wants me to follow her! Desdemona, don't you see? She *knew* I was lying to her! Somehow, probably those heart eyes of hers, she figured it all out after she left the bedroom that night! At this very moment, she's waiting—she knows I'm coming! With her, in the Appalachia! It's where I was always meant to be!"

He ran to his sister, picked her up, and whirled her in circles, his laughter bouncing off the walls.

"What a touching scene," Araminta's voice dripped from the doorway. "Simply touching."

Saxon looked at his grandmother and crossed to her, his expression, his stride, his very aura frightening her. She reached up, her scrawny hand shivering over her brooch.

Saxon stared at the pin and smiled. "Whatever power that thing had is lost, for I feel none of the fear it used to make me feel, Grandmother."

Araminta shrieked when he reached for the brooch and tore it from her gown. With horrified eyes, she watched him fling it at the window. It sailed right through the glass, flew into the courtyard, and finally landed in a small pond, where it floated for a second before it sank, leaving only ripples as evidence that it had ever existed.

"For years that thing scared me," Saxon admitted. "When I was a little boy, I was sure you'd stolen it from a Cyclops and that the monster would come to this house for revenge. Even after I was a man, it made me nervous. Just as you did."

He stalked her. Araminta backed away until she met the wall behind her. "Get away from me! Thatcher!"

Saxon loomed above her, then bent his head closer to hers. His eyes were drawn to the area beneath her mouth. "Warts?" he asked, staring at the three growths on her chin. "They must be new. I've never seen them on you before. But how well they suit you, Grandmother. A witch is not a witch without warts!"

As his gaze stabbed into her, Araminta knew without a doubt that whatever mastery she'd hoped to retain over him had vanished. This was a new Saxon before her: one she'd seen slowly evolving as of late; one she'd done everything within her power to keep from surfacing. This was not Saxon, her grandson.

This was Grayson Blackwell's son.

She would stand up to him just as she had stood up to Grayson! she decided, her snowy brow lifting. "Unless you cease this disrespectful display immediately, I will be forced to destroy you, Saxon. I have shouldered as much as I am able to, giving you chance after chance to redeem yourself and be the man deserving of the Blackwell fortune. But you insist on taunting me just as Grayson did. And not even marriage to Myrtle will save you this time. Unless you show the respect due me, I shall change my will for the final time and cast you out into the streets this very afternoon! Just as I did with your father, I will disinherit you, and this time there will be no hope for you!"

Saxon laughed. "No hope? My dear lady, where there is love, there is always hope. I was a fool not to believe that before now!"

"You . . . you—"

"I am a man in *love*. Not with money, not with society or my estimable station in life. I am in love with the mountain angel who saw a part of me that miraculously escaped your venom, and if I live to be a thousand years old, it won't be enough time to thank her for nurturing what little good there was about me. I love Keely, Grandmother. I leave this very afternoon to find her, and I'm taking Desdemona with me!"

Araminta reached for her brooch before she remembered it wasn't there. "Penniless! You'll go penniless!"

"Wallow in your gold, Grandmother! I want none of it! My pockets are empty, and I'll go from here with nothing but the clothes on my back, for doesn't everything I own really belong to you?"

"Most assuredly it does! Everything—"

"Except my heart. Except the one thing you never managed to get control of. But how you tried to make me love money. And I did, I suppose. But it never loved me back, Grandmother. I'm not leaving as the poverty-stricken man you believe me to be. I leave here with a treasure so boundless there is no way I can ever get my fill of it! Love!''

Desperately, Araminta searched for another weapon. ''Yes,'' she hissed when she remembered what that weapon was. ''Desdemona . . . I still retain custody—''

''You'll never find her. With Keely's help, Desdemona and I will elude you and any detectives you send after us. And if you dare try to stop us before we leave, I assure you I will lock you in that trunk you used to lock *me* in!''

''Thatcher—''

''If Thatcher stands in my way, I will personally knock his sniffing beak right off his face! Nothing, no one, will keep Desdemona and me from leaving. Do your worst, Grandmother. But no matter what you do, you will never hold me within your power again!''

Araminta recoiled from the hatred she saw in his eyes.

''Desdemona,'' Saxon called to her, ''when our father died, he bequeathed us everything he had. Until now, I believed he'd left us nothing. But his estate was the courage he had to follow his heart. His devotion to our mother allowed him to give up his fortune, and now I understand how much richer he was because of it. He had love, and there is no prize on earth more valuable.''

Desdemona's eyes widened, her lips trembled, and for one brief moment Saxon thought his sister was trying to speak to him. But his hope shattered when she turned from him and fled the room.

Seeing Saxon's concern for his sister, Araminta began anew her litany about how Desdemona would suffer in the poverty she'd be forced to endure. He allowed her to rage on, and decided that instead of returning fire, he would laugh at her. The sound of her screeching and his laughter rang and echoed in his ears until a small, almost inaudible voice sliced through it.

"S-Saxon?"

He turned toward the unfamiliar voice, one he'd never heard in his life. And there, in the doorway, stood Desdemona.

"Saxon?" she repeated. "I . . . this . . . I s-saved this." She drew up her arm, indicating a yellowed piece of paper pinched between her slender fingers.

Araminta gasped with horror as she recognized the document Desdemona held.

Chapter 25

S he lunged toward her granddaughter. "Give me that!"

"S-Saxon!" Desdemona flew to her openmouthed brother.

Saxon had been struck dumb at the sound of Desdemona's voice, but her terrified plea for aid swiftly dispelled his shock. He flung her behind him, his body shielding her from Araminta's advance. "Touch her, and I'll show you the full meaning of the word *wrath*, Grandmother!"

His perilous gaze stopped her so quickly, she almost lost her balance. Saxon reached around and pulled Desdemona to face him. "You spoke," he whispered and hugged her fiercely.

"She has what is mine, and I demand it be returned to me!" Araminta again started toward Desdemona.

Totally perplexed, Saxon urged his sister behind him. He'd never seen his grandmother so hysterical. He could barely believe this was his haughty, regal grandmother. "What is it you've got there, Desdemona?"

From behind him, her hand shaking, Desdemona slid the yellowed paper through the crook of his elbow. As Saxon reached for it, so did Araminta, but Saxon grabbed it first and held it high over his head while he stared in bewilderment at the panic-stricken woman who was still grappling for it.

"Grandmother, step away before I *force* you to do so!"

"The police! I'll have you arrested for keeping what is mine!" She attempted to jump up to Saxon's raised hand, but could not manage to leap more than a few inches off the floor.

"If indeed this paper is yours, I'll return it to you."

"It *is* mine! I swear to you it's mine!"

"Then you've nothing to fear, do you?" With more gentleness than he really wished to use, he took hold of her bony shoulder, forcing her to keep still while he read the paper.

But as his eyes scanned it, his grip tightened, his fingers dug more deeply into her skin until finally she screamed at the pressure.

Ignoring her shriek, Saxon turned to Desdemona in disbelief. "Desdemona, our grandfather's name was Courtland Blackwell. This is his will," he said, the softness of his voice a contrast to the fury building inside him. "Where did you get it?"

Desdemona gulped convulsively. "She . . . Grandmother p-put it in her d-desk drawer."

"She lies!" Araminta yelled. "Though she has spoken today, she is feebleminded, Saxon! Surely you will not believe what she says!"

Saxon snatched off his neckcloth. "Another word out of you and I'll gag you!" He turned back to his sister. "Desdemona, remember how many hours Keely spent trying to get you to say something to her? Think of her courage, little sister, and tell me what you know about this document."

Desdemona's eyes brightened at the memory of her loving sister-in-law. "I . . . was only s-six, but I c-could read easy words. I . . . A m-maid . . . t-tried to t-teach me to read when Gra-Grandmother wasn't look-looking. When I stole that p-paper, I read s-some of the words on it. I c-could read the word *will*."

"Go on," Saxon said as gently as he could in light of his impatience to know the story behind the document in his hand. "You've no need to be afraid, Desdemona. I won't let Grandmother hurt you."

"It was n-night, and I was th-th-thirsty. I came downstairs, and just as I r-reached the foyer, I heard v-voices coming from Gra-Grandmother's sitting room. I . . . was scared, b-but I wanted to s-see who was in there w-with her. I went and p-peeked in the d-door crack. There were three m-men in there."

Her delicate fingers shivered inside Saxon's strong ones. "I . . . I heard everyth-thing they said, but I was t-too afraid to t-tell anyone. I thought the p-police would come and t-take Grandmother away if I t-told! And . . . and if she went t-to jail, you and I w-would have b-been . . . *separated!* We w-would have gone to d-different orphanages! Sh-she always t-told us she would s-send us t-to different orphanages! R-remember, Sax-Saxon?"

"Yes, yes, I remember that, Desdemona. But why did you think the police would have come for Grandmother?"

Araminta hissed. "Don't listen to her! She's a liar! She's making all this up because she hates me!"

"I doubt she needs to make anything up," Saxon speculated harshly. "If she hates you, her hatred undoubtedly stems from *true* things about you."

"Gra-Grandmother had someone k-killed for that p-paper. I heard it all. There was a m-man. His name was Geoffrey B-Babcock. Grandmother p-paid the three men to k-kill him!"

"Lies!" Araminta cried, her face as white as her hair.

"Silence!" Saxon thundered as he looked at his grandfather's will again. *Phillip Babcock*, *Attorney at Law* was written at the top of the page. "Geoffrey Babcock," he muttered, his mind a sea of confusion. Father and son? Brothers?

Desdemona saw his look of puzzlement and struggled to erase it. "The . . . the men t-told Grandmother Geoffrey Babcock was d-dead and . . . and they gave her that p-paper. I saw her g-give them a lot of m-money before they left through the b-back door. Grandmother st-started to leave the room too, but as she did, a s-servant girl arrived and inquired if . . . if there was anything a-amiss. Grandmother was very st-startled, and she sh-shoved the p-paper into her desk d-drawer. Sh-she was anxious to g-get rid of the girl. She took the m-maid out into the hall and t-told her to br-bring some t-tea. When . . . when they were out of the r-room, I ran to the d-desk and st-stole that paper. I t-took it to my room and hid it inside the fr-frame of my small p-painting of M-Mother and Father. I only t-took it b-because I wanted to up-upset her . . . I *hated* her!''

Sobbing, Desdemona threw herself into Saxon's arms, her torrent of tears drenching his shirt. ''I . . . f-forgot about it, S-Saxon! Please don't b-be mad at me! I never r-remembered it was there until . . . until today w-when you and Grandmother b-began to argue about the w-will! *Will!* I r-remembered reading that w-word on the p-paper! When I heard you and Grandmother arguing about it, that n-night so . . . so long ago came rushing b-back to me as if it were yes-yesterday! Saxon, I'm s-so sorry! It's all my . . . f-fault!''

Saxon realized there was no way she could have understood the enormity of Araminta's actions that long ago night. Though she'd recognized the word *will* on the paper, she'd had no idea how important a document it was. At six, she'd already slipped well away from reality, and the only thing she'd truly understood that night was that it would grieve Araminta sorely to lose a paper she'd had someone killed to possess. Her grandmother's dismay had been all that had mattered to her. And what with Araminta's constant threat of the orphanages . . . As time had passed, Desdemona had withdrawn even further into her distant world, and until this day the will had been totally forgotten.

Her self-recrimination tore at him. ''Desdemona, you are in no way responsible for any of this!'' His arms tightened around her as his mind struggled to make sense of the story she'd told him. "Grandmother, if what Desdemona says is the truth—and I believe it is—you are going to spend the rest of your life in jail. You—"

Her demented howl cut him short. "Courtland had no right to do what he did! He had left everything to *me*, Saxon! And then . . . then he changed his will and left everything to Grayson! How dare he do that to me—his loving wife!"

Wisely, Saxon remained quiet.

"I didn't know he had changed his will until the day after he died," Araminta raged, spittle frothing at the corners of her pinched mouth. "His attorney, Phillip Babcock, came to me and showed me the new will. I . . . I was *stunned!* But Phillip had an idea. He said if I would reward him for his efforts, he would destroy the new will and give the old will to the courts—the one that left everything to me!"

Her eyes took on a crazed sheen. "I paid him great sums of money every month for his cooperation. I never dreamed he hadn't destroyed the new will. Oh, may his black soul roast in hell for what he did! I was only trying to correct the great wrong done to me! Phillip had no right to abuse my trust in him, the devil take him!"

Saxon frowned in bewilderment at what she began to do then. Her arms held out before her, as if embracing an invisible partner, she was swaying and even bobbing her head in time to the silent music she was hearing. "Courtland never took me dancing," she squeaked. "How I love music."

She'd gone insane, he realized suddenly. Gone forever was the indomitable Mrs. Blackwell, and in her place was a withered hag who had no more wits about her than a cat has feathers. "Grandmother," he said quietly, "how did you find out Phillip Babcock never destroyed Grandfather's new will?"

Araminta stopped her musical fantasy and cackled gleefully, her crazed laughter leaving no doubt in

Saxon's mind she was truly mad. "His son," she spat. "Geoffrey Babcock. I was already here with you and Desdemona when Phillip died. His son, Geoffrey, was also an attorney and took over the practice. When he discovered copies of both Courtland's new will and his old one and then found a ledger containing the record of my monthly payments to Phillip, he came to Boston to correct his father's crime."

"And he came directly here and told you what he planned to do," he guessed.

"He had to die," Araminta announced imperiously. "There was no other way. You were too much like your father, Saxon. I could not let you leave me as he did! Only with money—and the fact that without it you would lose Desdemona—could I hold on to you. Grayson never cared a whit for wealth. Somehow, I had to make sure you would not be as foolish as he. So you see, Geoffrey Babcock had to die, my boy. There was no other way."

She started to hum a tune Saxon vaguely remembered his father once singing.

Grayson Blackwell. He had left everything he had to his two children. He'd died believing all he'd bequeathed them was the old, rickety furniture they'd used in their humble home.

But what he'd really left them was the magnificent Blackwell fortune. The tremendous wealth had never been Araminta's at all. It had *always* belonged to Saxon and Desdemona. The will Desdemona had kept hidden for so many years was the proof.

At that realization, Saxon's first emotion was fury: that his grandmother had ruled his life, played him in her hands as if he'd been a mindless puppet, twisting, demanding, blackmailing him into doing her bidding. And poor Desdemona! She'd lived in constant terror and had eventually withdrawn into a world so remote, it was a miracle she'd found her way back from it. It was too much to bear. It was unforgivable. Araminta had to be punished!

"You must listen to me, Saxon," she said, her crackly voice breaking into his stormy thoughts. "Love is a dangerous thing. I loved your grandfather. Yes, I did. But look what he did to me. He would have left me with nothing had I not made the bargain with Phillip. Ah, Courtland. He was so handsome. But he was cold. Our marriage was an arranged one, and he never cared for me. He only wanted an heir."

She shivered at her memories, and it was many moments before she spoke again. "Once, I thought your father, Grayson, loved me. But he left me for that common woman, Sadie. When they died, and I came to be with you, I saw the light of rebellion in your eyes—just as I had always seen it in Grayson's—and I knew you were not going to love me either. But I needed *something* from someone, Saxon! Money and fear! They were the only means I had to make you respect me as a good grandson should respect his grandmother.

"Beware of love, my boy," she continued. "It will only bring you heartache. Do not love, and you will be protected from hurt. You must heed my advice." She sighed heavily and then raised her arms and curled them about Saxon's neck, her feet shuffling on the floor.

He yanked her hands down. "Grandmother, you have committed countless atrocities, and I intend to see that you—that you—" Abruptly, he was silenced by an inner voice so dear, it made him tremble to hear it. Chickadee's words, when she'd spoken of her father, came rushing back to him.

I was so wrong. I didn't have nary a right ter do this ter him. What he did ter mama—Saxon, it warn't my place ter punish him.

Chickadee. In the end, she'd forgiven her father and seen to it that Barton received aid. She'd set an inspiring example.

Saxon looked deep into Araminta's eyes and saw nothing in them but a lunatic sheen. She was insane, perhaps she always had been. No prison cell would be worse punishment than that. Immediately, his anger was swept away by a cleansing rain of compassion.

"Grandmother," he said gently, "I'm sending you back to England. I'll make arrangements for the estate there to be made ready, and a full staff of servants will await your arrival. Thatcher will accompany you, and you may take anything from this house you wish to take. From now on, you may depend on me to take care of you."

"You have never once, in all our years together, asked me to dance, Saxon! You will do so now, or you will suffer the consequences of your lack of respect. The trunk. I'll lock you in the trunk! Maybe being in the dark will teach you not to disobey me! Maybe—"

"There is no need for the trunk," Saxon assured her and put his arms around her.

There was no music other than Araminta's off-key humming. But Saxon danced as if they waltzed to the music of a superb symphony. As he twirled his grandmother around the small room, he found it in his heart to forgive her. And when he did, he marveled again at the wonderful thing called love and lamented the fact Araminta had never known it. Had she experienced it, her life would have been happy instead of bitter and selfish.

Again, pity for her welled up within him. "Grandmother," he whispered into her tiny ear, "there is no doubt in my mind Father loved you. What boy doesn't love his mother? For that matter, what grandson doesn't—"

Could he say what he felt he should without the words becoming lodged in his throat? Did it matter if he didn't really mean them? Would a lie be so terrible if it might mean the whole world to the insane old woman in his arms? His embrace tightened around her. If he let this chance to tell her what no one had ever told her before pass by, she'd die before hearing it, for he was certain no one but himself would ever say it to her. Bending, he pressed a tender kiss to her wrinkled forehead.

"I love you, Grandmother."

Chapter 26

Saxon didn't wait for the coach to stop before he jumped out of it and raced up the pine-straw–littered path that led to the Mansfield home. The trip to North Carolina, though it had been as speedy as he could make it, had seemed an eternity to him. And there had been so much to do before ever setting foot on the boat! Stopping the divorce proceedings, sending Araminta off, explaining things to Myrtle . . . Damn! Her screeches still echoed in his ears.

He reached the sturdy wooden door and pounded on it. That action not enough to assuage his impatience, he began to kick at it also. "Dammit, Heath, where are you?"

"Just a second!" came a voice before the door opened. "Who—Saxon!" Heath grabbed his friend and embraced him.

Saxon tried to end the hug, for he had not a minute to lose. "Heath, I need to leave my sister with you. Dammit, Heath, let me go!"

Heath complied. "Your sister? Where is she?"

"Here! Right here!" Saxon turned around, but Desdemona wasn't there. He swore again and spun on his heel to race toward the waiting coach. After assisting Desdemona and Candice out, he commanded the coach driver to saddle Hagen and get Desdemona's baggage.

Heath was immediately captivated by the shy,

lovely girl who was hanging on to Saxon's arm.
"Heath Mansfield," he introduced himself and
bowed gallantly.

If he wasn't in such a hell-bent panic to get to the
Blue Ridge, Saxon would have taken the time to
tease Heath over his obvious attraction to Desdemona. But as it was, he could think of nothing but
Chickadee.

"Heath, I've a tremendous favor to ask of you,"
he started, and then turned to snap at the coach
driver who was taking too long to saddle Hagen.
"I'm leaving this very minute to find Keely. I don't
have time to explain, but my sister, Desdemona, will
tell you everything you want to know. Heath, can
she and her maid, Candice, stay here with you until
I get back? I know I'm asking a lot, and it's all very
sudden, and I should ask your parents, and—"

"Nonsense," Heath cut him off and held out his
arm for Desdemona. "Never havin' had a daughter
of their own, Ma and Pa'll be tickled to have your
beautiful sister stay with us. And as for myself . . .
Miss Blackwell," he addressed Desdemona, "have
you ever walked through a pine forest at dawn when
the dew is still glistenin' on the needles and the air
is fresh with—"

"Uh, Heath, could you begin your courting after
I'm gone?" Saxon queried, finally grinning despite
his rush. He handed his friend a satchel. "This con-
tains some important papers. If anything should
happen to me, those papers are Desdemona's inheritance documents. I know you'll safeguard both
them and her."

Heath tucked the satchel under his other arm. "I'll
protect them both with my life," he said, winking
at Desdemona and grinning when she blushed.

"Money," Saxon said, his brow wrinkled in dismay. "Dammit to hell, what did I do with the
money?" He turned back to the coach, jumped inside, and began to throw the cushions to the ground

in his haste to find the funds he intended to leave for Desdemona's support.

"Sax-Saxon?" his sister called and smiled. "I have the m-money." She held out another bag.

"Right," Saxon answered and leaped out of the coach. "I'll be back soon, Desdemona. I'll be back, or I'll send for you. Either way, we'll begin all the plans we discussed on the way here. We'll—"

"Go," she told him, her smile broadening. "Go and f-find her!"

"Yes, hurry, Mr. Blackwell!" Candice echoed.

He needed no more urging. He flew onto Hagen's back and headed his faithful steed west.

West, where blue-green hills sheltered his emerald-eyed, freckle-faced, redheaded mountain girl.

Saxon's first sight of the Appalachian Mountains sent a thrill whipping through him. Their verdant peaks punctured the azure satin of the Carolina sky, and he wondered why he'd ever thought he preferred the bustle of Boston to the tranquil beauty he beheld now.

His only stop before he sped toward Chickadee's cove was in the town of Lenior. There he conducted a certain item of business with all the cunning and skill he'd acquired while running Blackwell Enterprises. His brilliant smile rivaled the shine of the sun as he left the small town.

Finally, a few days later, he reached Chickadee's mountain. "Let me remember how the hell to get to her cabin," he prayed. "Dammit, why do all these trees have to look the same? Every rock, bush, and stream—Hagen, do you know where you're going?"

The horse snorted and shook a fly off his ear. "I take it that means no," Saxon said and felt no embarrassment at talking to an animal. After all, Boston was far away. This was the Blue Ridge! Here, he could talk to a damn stick if he wanted to. There was no one here who would criticize or shun him.

It was a few more hours before he began to recognize things. And when he saw the stream he'd once bathed in when he and Chickadee had finished skinning the bear he'd killed, his impatient happiness was of such magnitude, he could no longer contain it.

"Keely!" he thundered, his shout echoed many, many times before it faded away. "Keely, little one!"

He tried not to worry when she didn't answer. She was probably deep in the woods looking for *yarbs* or battling *bahrs*.

"We'll find her, boy," he assured Hagen, patting the horse's mane. "You know how she is. Could be she's watching us at this very minute, planning on jumping out of the laurel and scaring us."

Though he might have reassured the horse, his confident words did nothing at all to relieve his own anxiety. A slowly unwinding dread twisted through him when he reached the clearing where her cabin had once stood. He'd been sure George Franklin would have rebuilt it, yet there was nothing but charred remains as evidence a cabin had ever even existed there.

"Well, of course he'd choose a different spot," Saxon told Hagen nervously, his eyes darting all around. "Here, Keely would be reminded of those wanderers who attacked her."

But his distress rose. Something wasn't right. Even if Chickadee's new cabin *was* in another spot, she'd still know he was here. She knew everything that went on in these mountains. And if she didn't discover it herself, Khan made her aware of it. She was as one with these hills, and nothing escaped her notice.

"Keely, I love you!" he bellowed to the sky. "Dammit, Keely, I love you!"

The only answer he received was the screech of a disturbed bird. His jaw twitching, his eyes narrowed, Saxon turned Hagen toward the Beasley cabin, leaning way over the horse's neck as Hagen tore down the moss-strewn path. Low-hanging branches slapped and bit at his face, but the pain didn't stop him. In fact, he welcomed it. Anything was better than the ominous foreboding that sluiced through him.

His dread heightened further when he reached the Beasley place. The yard was overgrown with weeds, and inside, Saxon discovered, dwelt nothing but spiders and frightened squirrels. There was more than an inch of dust on the floor and not a splinter of furniture to be seen.

Dammit! Without the Beasleys' aid, he'd never be able to get word to Chickadee. Had the two elderly people died? Saxon searched the grounds for burial places, knowing they'd want to be laid by their cabin, but he found no graves.

"I'm going to find you, Keely Blackwell!" he shouted at the hills. "And when I do, I'm going to wring your neck for hiding from me! Do you hear me, you stubborn twit?"

Resolve as hard as the mountains themselves filled him as he raced Hagen toward Chickadee's special place. The spot where she and Khan liked to be. It was the last place he could think of where he might find her.

And he didn't even want to think of what he would do if she wasn't there.

Her beloved paradise was just as he remembered it. As beautiful and as natural as the girl who loved it. Saxon slid to the ground, his boots disappearing into a thick bed of colorful wildflowers.

"Keely!" he called, his voice shrill with anxiety. He hunted everywhere for signs of her, all the while continuing to call her name. The mountains, as if scornful of him for trying to hurt their mistress, threw his shouts back at him.

Finally, after over two hours of screaming and searching, Saxon, his throat raw, his heart bleeding with grief, sat down on the ridge and stared out at the hills. Their beauty escaped him now. The world and everything in it was loathsome and ugly without Chickadee by his side.

Something had happened to her, he knew. These mountains were full of perils and one of them had finally caught her off-guard. It was the sole explanation as to why he couldn't find her. Only death would have kept her from coming to him. Memories of her cascaded through him. The pain that lanced into him was so deep, he was certain it would soon kill him and he would join Chickadee wherever death had taken her. He closed his eyes and waited for it to happen.

His eyes flew open at the sound he heard behind him, and he knew that if indeed death had come for him, it had not come in the form of heartache. The grim reaper, he realized, was a roaring bear.

He felt fear burn through the marrow in his bones as the ground around him began to shake with the bear's tremendous weight. In mere seconds it would reach him and kill him.

And he would do nothing to stop it. Desdemona was now wealthy in her own right, and he was sure Heath would see to her well-being. That one and only worry resolved, Saxon sat still, waiting for the bear's claws to end a life that wasn't worth living without Chickadee.

Chickadee. Her face, form, voice, and personality flooded through him. She was so real to him at that moment, he felt he could reach out and touch her.

His head snapped up. Dammit, what the hell was he doing? If she were here, she'd be cursing him up and down for not defending himself. She wouldn't want him to die! Even now she was probably looking down from heaven, screaming for him to get up and save himself!

He vaulted to his feet. Her image lending strength to his body, his love for her like a shield in his hand, he whirled and faced the bear, damning Hagen for running away with his guns.

Running away with his guns. Just as the skittish

steed had done once before . . . The memory of that day came crashing back to Saxon, so clear in his mind he could have sworn he saw a flash of red in the rhododendron thicket beside him—just as he had that day. Just as he—

He had no time to finish reliving the memory. The bear was suddenly upon him, its horrible teeth shining with spittle, its black eyes glowing with rage, its bone-chilling roar echoing in his ears. In one swift motion, it wrapped its enormous arms around Saxon and squeezed.

Saxon's scream was echoed by the explosion of gunfire. The bear toppled over, carrying its prey with it. Saxon landed flat on his back with a sickening thud. He closed his eyes to the blinding rays of the sun, and when he did, a shadow fell over him.

He didn't have to open his eyes to know whose shadow it was. In his mind, he saw her standing above him. Her eyes, as green as the emerald mountain forests and set in a sweet freckled face, were surely peering down at him. And then Saxon smiled when he envisioned her hair.

Wildly flowing tresses that were sort of red, sort of orange, and sort of gold.

"Saxon, iffen you had any more sense'n what you got, you *still* wouldn't be a half-wit! Are you plumb bereft, a-settin' thar and a-waitin' fer that bahr—"

"Keely." Her name left an ambrosial flavor in his mouth as it slipped through his lips. Slowly, savoring the moment, he opened his eyes and saw her. He'd known seeing her again would be wonderful, but he was unprepared for the full impact her loveliness had on him. He could not find his breath.

"I ain't a-tellin' no lie when I say I was as staggered as a stuck hog when you warn't a-doin' nary a thang ter protect yoresef from—"

"Keely," he repeated, tasting her name a second time, smiling when, again, it filled his mouth with sweetness. And then he laughed. This wasn't how he had imagined their reunion! He'd pictured her running through the cool forest, calling his name, her arms outstretched for him. And then he would have caught her when she'd flown into his embrace, held her tightly and twirled her around and around while she rained kisses all over his face, their laughter ringing through the hills.

But this? Lying flat on his back, a dead bear beside him, and Chickadee standing above him giving him what for? He gave a great guffaw. When Chickadee was involved, nothing in the world turned out the way it was supposed to.

"You ain't never gwine be nothin' but a outlander, Saxon Blackwell," she charged, and snapped her fingers at Khan, who was licking the dirt from Saxon's face. "Iffen I spend ever' second o' the rest o' my life a-tryin' ter larn you how ter take keer o' yoresef, it still ain't gwine be enough time."

It was a while before Saxon could speak, for he was mesmerized by the mysterious magic that was hers alone. "I couldn't find you. The Beasleys are gone. I came here but still couldn't find you. I was certain you were . . . dead. I didn't want to go on without you, so when the bear . . . I was going to let him . . . but at the last second, I realized you'd want me to live. I couldn't deny you what I knew you would want."

She regarded him as if she couldn't decide what to do with him. "The Beasleys moved inter the cabin George Franklin builded fer me. I figgered you and me could build us a cabin of our own, so I let 'em have the new one. Thurs was older'n dirt, y'know. And me? Well, I been a-stayin' at ole Misery's place. Misery, God rest his contrary soul, set his bucket down whilst I was up thar in Boston."

How he'd missed her lilting voice, her beautiful mountain dialect, Saxon thought as he listened. "Keely, didn't you know I was here?"

"I knowed it the second that dumb ridin' critter o' yores set hoof on this mountain."

"Then why did you let me look for you for so long?"

"I warn't gwine to, but when I heared you say you was gwine wrang my neck, I decided ter let you suffer fer a while. I don't take too kindly to neck-wrangin' y'know."

His arms ached for her to fill them. But he restrained himself. He had much to apologize for. "I followed my string," he told her sheepishly. "I brought Desdemona too. Keely, I was a fool. I—"

"Was born ignorant and been a-losin' ground ever since? Saxon, it's a dang good thang you come back to me. Yore jist as helpless as you allus was. You cain't mem'ry ter keep yore gun with you, you let bahrs sneak up on you, and you cain't lie worth a God-burn dang."

She knelt beside him and slid her cool palm against his warm cheek. "I was mighty pained that night when you tole me all them mean thangs. Went downstairs and cried nigh on a hour afore it come ter me you was a-lyin'. I don't know how I knowed really, but I suspicion . . . *suspect* it was love that made me see the truth. I knowed then that the onliest way ter make you see that life ain't worth a dang withouten love was to take love away from you. Y'knowed what love was, but you didn't have enough faith in it, Saxon. You trusted yore brain more'n yore heart, and you shouldn't never do that."

"But how could you have been so certain I would follow? That I would see and understand the message on the quilt?"

"Thur warn't no way I could be shore and sartin. I had my worries, and some days come when I had ter force mysef ter keep on a-hopin'. I tuk the biggest lay o' my life a-leavin' you ter foller me, but I reckon I won it. I was a-playin' the game with love, and when you got love? Well, you allus win no matter the odds. I knowed Desi was gwine be in low cotton over thangs the way they was, and I knowed you'd try ter hep her afore the pearly gates swang wide fer her. I figgered you'd see the quilt then, on account o' she don't never go nowhars withouten it. And once you seed it? Well, I knowed love was gwine hep you understand that I was here a-waitin' on you.

"I coulda tried ter explain it all ter you, Saxon," she continued softly. "I knowed Desi was gwine keep up with them weary dismals o' hers in Boston. Knowed you was too. But you had to see them thangs with yore own eyes. I done tole you time and time agin that some thangs are better larnt by yoresef."

Saxon's whole body cried for the girl who lived by that wonderful advice. He took her into his arms and kissed her. Her lips, pliant and warm beneath his, opened for him, offering that for which he had hungered for months. His kiss deepened as he drank in her sweetness and felt again her magic.

"Grandmother . . . Desdemona . . . There's so much I have to tell you, little one," he whispered. "After you left—"

"Saxon? I know yore a-settin' in ter tell me the whole knock-me-back story. It ain't that I don't want ter hear it, but I'm gwine bust my gizzard strang iffen I cain't tell you my news first. Can I?"

He laughed at her request for permission. "Since when do you have to have my approval before you do something?"

"I'm a-settin' on a nest."

At first, her statement didn't register. "What? You mean . . ."

She smiled in answer, reached for his hand, and laid it across her slightly rounded belly. "We made a baby that night you got shed o' all them bad mem'ries, outlander. I tole you ter give me all the hatred inside you and that I was gwine take it and turn it inter love. Reckon that's exactly what I done."

A million questions erupted inside Saxon, yet his

muddled mind could not put a single one into proper word sequence. "I . . . you . . . we . . ."

Her peal of laughter rang through the hills. But abruptly, she became serious. "Tell you what, Saxon. You and me can gee and haw clear inter the night, but not here. Ole Lareny Lester—remember I tole you about him a-ownin' this here land? Well, he's liable to come up here and commence a-shootin'. He's already run me and Khan off more'n a dozen times this month. Ornery ole varmint."

"A baby. A baby," Saxon mumbled, the shock of pending fatherhood robbing him of the rest of his vocabulary. "Well I'll be damned . . . a real baby."

"Saxon? You hear what I said about Lareny Lester?"

"Lareny Lester?"

"The feller who—"

"Lareny Lester!" Frantically, Saxon dug into his coat pocket and withdrew an official-looking document. He picked up Chickadee's hand and placed the paper in her palm. "Keely, no one is ever going to run you off this ridge again."

Chickadee didn't know what to look at—the devotion she saw pouring from Saxon's eyes or the document he'd just given her. Finally, she scanned the paper.

It was a land deed, and her name was on it.

"Y'mean . . . ?"

"I do. Your special place is really yours now, Keely. I stopped in Lenoir, found Lareny Lester, and bought it for you. I want to make every dream you've ever had come true, little one. We'll build the God-burnin'est-best cabin you ever laid eyes on right smack in the middle of the place you love most in the world!"

Her fingers quivered, the deed shaking in her hand. "Saxon . . . you jist cain't know how much this means to me." Impatiently, she swiped at her moist eyes before she buried herself in the soothing shelter of his arms.

Saxon held her close and felt his heart burst with the words he'd never told her and would never hold back from her again. "I love you, little one."

Her tears ran freely as the sentiment she'd waited so long to hear filled her with unspeakable joy.

Saxon bent and captured her lips in a kiss that seemed to have no end. His, now and forevermore, was a girl who would never fail to enchant and amaze him. The thought made him grin and turn his eyes toward heaven.

"Yes, may God always see fit to help me, I love you, Chickadee McBride."